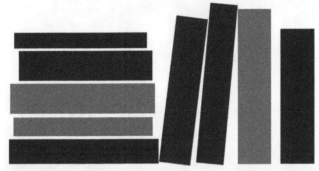

SHADOWS IN THE STACKS
A HORROR ANTHOLOGY

EDITED BY

VINCENT V. CAVA
JAMES SABATA
JARED SAGE

SHORTWAVE
PUBLISHING

Cover design and interior formatting by Alan Lastufka.

First Edition published May 2024.

10 9 8 7 6 5 4 3 2 1

978-1-959565-40-6 (Paperback)
978-1-959565-41-3 (eBook)

CONTENTS

INTRODUCTION
LAUREL HIGHTOWER

Knowledge is power.

A universal truth, so cliché we repeat it ad nauseam, drilled into our cultural lexicon and memory. A talisman against ill fortune—if we can only manage to wrest control of information away from those who hoard it, settled high on their treasure of currency in the form of understanding. Then we'll be safe. We'll prevent the tragic outcomes we read about in fairy tales, urban legends, and our phone screens as horrific events unfold around the world. It seems in keeping with the current trend that we would, as a society, lose sight of some of our simplest truths. That we are all equal. That we are all one. That each person has a right to bodily autonomy and safety. Freedom from genocide. Is anyone surprised that at a time when information is more accessible than ever before, those hoarders of wealth are in favor of book bans?

We're told all the time that nobody reads anymore. Depressing statistics showing declining interest in books. Strange though, because if no one is reading, then why do we need to ban books at all? Won't they just die off, dry up and eliminate the risk?

True, books are not the only source of powerful information. We are barraged daily with sources of digital media—click-bait articles about "ungrateful immigrants" (don't call them refugees; that might imply they're humans in need of help) designed to separate us further. Both-sidesing articles splashed across the pages of what used to be respected journals. Social media rants and blogs and videos elbowing each other for our attention, our clicks, our thirsty minds. Yet the narrative is so often controlled by faceless machinators with an agenda we can only guess at. The Library of Alexandria, it's not. Instead of providing light in the darkness, it's an uncontrolled and dangerous blaze. Yet that knowledge is there, readily accessible to the human race, so why would anyone concentrate on books as the source of the problem?

I think I know why. Because books give us a broadened opportunity to understand. It's not simply the enlarged format that allows a more comprehensive transfer of knowledge, although that helps. It's the ability to reach one another on a grander and more immersive scale. I like to say we know each other best through our stories—when we choose to gift one another without words and our time, it's the most precious kind of knowledge exchange. It's true for any genre you can name—romance, sci-fi, crime. Literary, spiritual, and certainly poetry. But I'm a horror hound, and this is a horror anthology. Call me biased if you will, but I've long believed horror gives us the greatest opportunity to open our hearts to one another. Every story we read has an effect on us, whether we enjoy it or not. We are a tapestry of the tales that have touched our hearts.

Folks outside the genre often express surprise that horror fans are so friendly, warm, and supportive. (There are exceptions to this, as in any sweeping generalization, but I choose to believe there is hope for everyone to find a path back.) It has a lot to do with the humanization of horror. Opening the door to someone else's darkened closet, their eerie cellar, or the attic where *something* won't stop scratching—that little peek tells us so much about one another. Someone we've always seen as outgoing and friendly may reveal a deep-seated fear of loneliness. The most loving and gentle parent you know might live in terror of restarting a cycle of abuse or be suffering in silence with post-partum depression. Someone who's always seemed aloof may be struggling daily with the wounds of a toxic upbringing. Seeing those fears, understanding them, and acknowledging the impact they have on what makes that person who they are and act the way they do, brings them out of the abstract.

That only scratches the surface—when you make an effort to read diversely, you unlock the breathtaking gift of expanding your understanding. Folklore from other cultures reveals all-new legends and cryptids to take flight through your mind. Reading a trans woman's story about the insidious fear of choosing a public bathroom splashes you with metaphorical cold water, opening your eyes to the knowledge that what you take in stride might be someone else's greatest challenge. Communication via books is one long love letter to the human species, so naturally those invested in making us afraid of one another must insert themselves into the equation. Arbitrarily deciding what knowledge is safe and acceptable for the masses, attempting to sway public opinion about all the corrupt, dirty nastiness in books that bare our hearts and souls. They don't *want* us to know each other better. To understand intrinsically, when we look across the ocean at a person unlike ourselves, that they carry the same stardust inside as we do. Better to make us feel shame before we open pages and see ourselves on them, and know that we are not alone, that there are people just like us with all our quirks and kinks and oddities. Because it's always an attempt at purity culture, isn't it? Perfection as defined by a very narrow segment of the population, designed to make anyone who doesn't fit that mold feel further isolated. Anything that doesn't fall into ever-changing parameters is burned before our eyes, and the threat is clear. Just look at any one of a hundred urban legends showing the danger of curiosity, making a Bluebeard's chamber out of the entire world. Tsk, tsk, shouldn't have gone looking. That's what you get. Never mind the clear risk associated with what's been redacted and the way hidden knowledge veritably screams at us to discover it.

Which paves the way for an anthology of the horrible ways information currency can go wrong. The way we hide truths about ourselves to mitigate the perceived damage others could do to the tender parts of us. The way we hide it from others, those we might recognize as kindred spirits if only we were brave enough to let someone see our flaws. Entire communities hidden away in a desperate attempt to keep the inhabitants free of the taint of the outside world. Misconceptions about who holds the power—sometimes it is the very knowing that undoes us, casts a fate of suffering. Love and hatred both hidden, and perhaps most disturbing of all, the blatant choice to reject information and understanding. The dead-eyed stare of someone who should know better, firing shot after vicious shot into our soft middle, refusing to believe in our pain no matter how loudly we scream. And the last great mystery—the hidden view behind the veil. What awaits us when our spirits are stripped bare, nowhere left to hide.

The anthology you hold in your hands *is* that love letter to the human race. An offering from each of the talented authors who bled on the page for the stories you're about to read. A dream of what could be, a nightmare of what is. A light in the darkness of a ban on books, hands joined to protect one another and our precious gifts of knowledge. Join them—join *us*. Hold tight and know the hands that hold yours, be they never so rotted or clawed or slippery with gore, belong to hearts formed of the same swirling nebulae of stardust. No matter how dire things look, be that flame in the dark.

After all, if books didn't give us superpowers, then why the hell are they so afraid?

SHADOWS IN THE STACKS

NATHAN BALLINGRUD'S HAUNTING HORROR RECS

CLAY MCLEOD CHAPMAN

Holy shit, we're driving down to North Carolina to get Nathan Ballingrud's horror recs. Once the thought locked in our collective heads, there really wasn't any getting rid of it. Wasn't like Asheville was all that far away, anyhow. We're talking seven—maybe eight hours, tops. Straight shot down I-240. Who wouldn't make a pilgrimage to meet The Man? The Legend?

Nathan Fucking Ballingrud.

The idea came about on our couch, about four tokes after my friend Benji mentioned Ballingrud worked in a bookstore.

"Yeah, right," I said. "That's some cockamamie, fanboy bullshit if I've ever heard some."

"Hand to God, man. . . I read it somewhere. Reddit, I think." He repeated himself, just under his breath, a record skipping: "*Readitonredditreaditonredditreaditonreddit. . .*"

"Dude's a horror icon," I said. "What the fuck does Ballingrud need a day job for?"

"Keeps him real," Benji said.

"He's got a book coming out from a top five publisher—"

"*Allegedly.*"

"That's some six-figure shit right there. The hell's he doing working at a bookshop?"

"Maybe he just likes books." Then Benji did this thing with his fingers, wriggling them in my face like they're a bunch of haunted hot dogs or something. "*Scaaaary boooooks.*"

"Knock it off."

"You think he just sits behind the counter all day," Benji wonders out loud, "then when some customer comes up and asks for a recommendation, he like, recs his own stuff? I would."

Here, I imagine Ballingrud saying, *Try this book. I think you might like it. . .*

"Dude doesn't need to recommend his own books." I felt like I needed to defend Ballingrud's honor. Not that he needs it. He's got his rep locked down tight. The man doesn't do conventions. Doesn't make public appearances. Doesn't show up for the Stokers or accept whatever award he nabs. The dude doesn't even do interviews. Not anymore. No social media presence whatso-fuckingever. He's got one author shot—the same damn photo for over twenty years now. "People probably just come to him. Bet they bring copies of his books all the time."

"He's classier than that. Bet you he's got, like, a *no autograph* policy when he's working."

"Damn straight."

Benji discovers something tucked between the couch cush-ions. A shard of a potato chip. Still crisp from the crunch of it. "Wouldn't it just blow your fucking mind to walk into that book-shop and spot Nathan Fucking Ballingrud behind the register? Like he's just waiting for you?"

Waiting for me. *You made it,* he'd say, *I thought you'd never come.*

"I'd lose my shit," Benji said, "Dude's a legend."

"An honest-to-God legend," I agreed, "Bet he recs so much

scary stuff. Like, books you've never even heard of before. . . Books that would just shatter your mind into a million pieces."

"No doubt. Nathan *Fucking* Ballingrud."

"Nathan. Fucking. Ballingrud."

"Legend," Benji said.

"God, what I wouldn't give. . ." And there it was, all teed up, the idea formulating from the fog in my mind just as the words abandoned my mouth. "How about we go find him?"

Who the hell is Nathan Ballingrud, you ask?

Dude's a fucking legend. Anybody who's dipped their toe into contemporary horror lit knows about *North American Lake Monsters*. That short story collection is a fucking classic. Canon, man. They'll be teaching that shit in college lit for centuries. Why Hulu had to change the title of the TV show was a dumb fucking move. Now nobody knows it's based off his book. They're, like, *actively* denying their own core audience demographic. But they've been fucking us fans over from like the get-go, you know? When it comes to Ballingrud, you've learned a little about heart-break. Ever read *Wounds*? His batshit insane novella? Trick ques-tion, asshole. If you were a *real* fucking fan you'd know that it wasn't called *Wounds* until they made the movie. Its original title is *The Visible Filth*, published back in 2015. Don't come at me like you're some Nathan Ballingrud aficionado if you don't know the difference between *Wounds* and *This Visible Filth*. Fucking amateur hour, man. You and Armie Hammer fucking deserve each other.

When word got around that Ballingrud was finally writing a novel, I nearly shat myself. Finally, at long goddamn last, fans were getting a full-blown masterpiece from our main man The Notorious N.F.B.

Not that most folks would have a chance to read it.

The book got pulled five months before its release date. Before that shit even hit shelves, the publisher got all weak-kneed and yanked it. Nobody knows why. Not really. I've heard dozens of reasons—beta-readers losing their shit, bloggers vomiting, Book-stagrammers posting suicide selfies—but I'm calling BS on all of that. His move into the mainstream was always going to cause some ripples. Like Dylan going electric. Whatever the hell it was, you'd have better luck nabbing the Holy Grail than an advanced reader copy of Ballingrud's new novel.

Like I said: *legend*. The man's mythic.

I'd be lying if I didn't admit I've spent a few late nights traipsing through AbeBooks. eBay. Amazon. I even peeked at the pirate sites. Just to see if somebody out there's selling a copy.

Nothing. Not a single goddamn PDF. That shit simply doesn't *exist*.

"Is it Ballin*grood* or Ballin*gruud*?" Benji asked somewhere around Kingsport, Tennessee.

"I hear you pronounce it Ballin*gruhd*."

"I think it's *grood*."

"The hell, man?" I grip the steering wheel, ready to pull this piece of shit around right then and there on Interstate 40. "It's got to be *gruhd*. Who says *grood*? It's *uhd*. *Uuhd*."

The humidity has climbed to neck-sweat proportions by the time we cross into Carolina. The A/C doesn't work so well, spitting out dribs and drabs of cool air, so I roll my window down. There's a shrill hiss in my ear, eclipsing our conversation. We've got to holler at each other now.

"That's how I heard it," I shout over the wind shear. "With one of those l'il umlaut-thingies."

"Dude's not Motley Crüe. It's *grood*. Ballin*grood*."

"Grüd with an umlaut."

"Fuck off with that umlaut-bullshit. . ."

"Five bucks says it's Grüd."

"You're on."

We'd been driving nonstop for about six hours by then. No pitstops, no piss breaks, fueling ourselves up on Mountain Dew and Andy Capp's Hot Fries. We didn't want to lose any momentum. At the rate we were going, we'd reach Asheville with a few hours to spare before closing time. Maybe Ballingrud would want to hang with us after he locks up. Maybe he'd shoot the shit for a bit, tell us what he's working on next. There's just no telling what he'd want to do.

And maybe, just maybe. . . he'd have an advance reading copy of his new novel, *The Weird*, from uncorrected proofs, just tucked under the cash register. *Not intended for resale. Please check any quotes for review against the finished book. Final cover to be revealed.*

Benji really needed to pee. "Bladder's about to burst."

I told him to go in his bottle. No way I'm pulling over. Not when we were this close. I could nearly feel the gravitational pull of Ballingrud, reeling us deeper into the Blue Ridge like the man was some cosmic black hole in the mountains, rupturing the whole horizon. My bleary eyes could nearly see the skyline distorting into blurred bands of pink, purple, and green. An oil spill in space, blotting out the cosmos, all because Ballingrud's fans demanded his new book.

We'd already gone through his stories. Picking which one's Ballingrud's best. "The Monsters of Heaven." Obviously. The dude won a Shirley Jackson award for that shit, so you know it's top shelf. Benji said his favorite was "Skullpocket." Fine. I'm not going to quibble.

"You think he gets people coming in all the time?" he wonders. "Asking for autographs?"

"Maybe, maybe not. . . Maybe we're like, the chosen ones. Like, not everyone's got what it takes to make this quest. Maybe only a few select fans even go on the journey. . . and maybe not everybody makes it. Reach the mountaintop or mecca or whatever the hell Asheville is."

"We're totally Frodoing this shit," Benji shouts.

"Hell yeah, we are!"

"One ring to rule them aaaaall, bitches!"

All we wanted were his horror recs. What book is Nathan Ballingrud going to point to and say, *Hey, yo, this is some scary shit.* If he says it's terrifying, then you know it's true. Fucking Ballingrud seal of approval. Slap that sticker on the cover and see how fast it flies off the shelf.

Or, maybe, just maybe, he's got something else. Something special.

Something just for me.

Why all this fuss over some author? Why Nathan Ballingrud?

Dude. If you even need to ask. . .

You get guys like John Langan. Or Laird Barron. Or, sure, even Paul Tremblay. Kick ass writers. Fucking A-list cosmic shit. But none—and I mean none—of those guys are putting themselves out there like my main man Nathan Ballingrud is. Do you see Tremblay working behind the counter of his local B&N? Nope. I mean, I heard he teaches high school math somewhere. But still. You think Barron is putting himself out there? On the consumerist front lines? Fuck no.

Only Ballingrud. You just got to find him. Make the effort. *Come to me*, he's beckoning.

Who's listening?

We are. Me and Benji over here, sitting shotgun. Damn straight we're answering the call. This all had to be more than just some job for Ballingrud. Dude's got Hulu money. He doesn't need to work at a bookstore. There's got to be a secret reason, some under-the-counter specialty, he's hiding. He's putting out this psychic evite to his fans, and we're RSVPing: WILL ATTEND. Only those who are brave enough, willing to put in the pilgrimage, are going to get his horror recs. His *real* recs. Not a Goodreads list or some algorithmic suggestions from Amazon.

The real fucking deal. The truly scary shit.

Or maybe, just maybe, a little something-something. For my

eyes only. Not even Benji. *I'd really love to hear your thoughts,* I imagine him saying. *You're one of the first to read it. . .*

Me. The first. The chosen.

The Weird.

So, we didn't *actually* know what store he works at. Malaprops was the obvious call. That's the shop everybody knows. But by the time we walked in, they're all like *Ballin-who?* Fucking kid behind the counter's acting like he didn't even know who Nathan Ballingrud was.

"He lives here," I told him. "He's like, your neighbor and all. You don't know who Nathan Ballingrud is?"

"Does he know you're in town? Can't you call him?"

So, it turned out Ballingrud doesn't work at Malaprops. *Fuck.* Where else could he be? How many other bookstores can one Podunk town even have? Two? It's not like it's a big city. It's just some rinky-dink mountain town. Crusty granola hippy-dippy shit. Artsy-fartsy yoga shit.

Where the fuck was Ballingrud?

Turned out there's another bookstore. A used one. Made sense, if you thought about it. Of course Nathan Fucking Ballingrud is going to work at a used bookstore. None of that new shit. He's surrounding himself in dusty editions. Low lighting. Yellowing pages all around. Books stacked so high, reaching the ceiling. Pull the wrong one off and they'll all come toppling down.

Now we just needed to find it.

Nobody seemed to know where this used bookstore was. Or if it really even existed. The fine citizens of Asheville sure didn't seem to take too kindly to us guests and our goddamn quest. It got to the point where it felt like everybody's just fucking with us. Acting like they don't know. *Never heard of it,* they all said. *You sure you're in the right town?* We couldn't even get a name for the place. Like the locals didn't even realize they had a used bookshop to begin with.

"It's an act," Benji whispered. "Bet they're just protecting him."

"Ballingrud?"

"Hell yeah. He's, like, a hometown hero. They want to keep the fans away, you know? Total Salinger-style."

Made sense. They're all in on it. All of Asheville. Somebody was probably calling Ballingrud that very second, wherever he was hiding, tipping him off that we were here.

"We better hurry," I said. It's not like there are many roads to pick from. The town's on a mountain. Go too far in any direction and the switchbacks spit you right out in the valley below.

We'd been driving for an hour before Benji spotted a wooded turnoff. "Stop the car."

"You see something?"

"Turn around," he shouted, leaning his head out the window. "Turn around, turn—"

"Where? There's nowhere to—"

"Just turn the car around!"

I perform a three-point-turn in the middle of a highway, dumb fucking call, but I circle back and turn onto a backroad I didn't even notice before and immediately we're immersed in a new neck of Asheville. Crabgrass chokes the shoulders. Trees on either end. The pavement crumbles the further we go and now we're plopped into a ghost town. Not exactly a ghost town.

There's only one building. That's it. Just one.

Looks like it's been here for centuries. General store-style shop selling sarsaparilla and shit. Gold rush shit. Old fogie in a rocker on the front porch shit. Banjoes and six-shooters shit.

No name on the storefront. But this has to be the place. Where else is there? I can nearly feel it calling to me. Feel *him*. His name's whispered through the mineshafts at our feet.

Ballingruuuud.

In we go.

The front door's got one of those brass bell thingies that rings when you open it. I'm hit with mildew as soon as I step in. Smells like a library that sprung a leak in its roof, drenching all the books below. The air is thick. Fungal. There's some NPR playing over the sound system, but the music's all muffled because the speakers are buried behind stacks of yellowed paperbacks.

There he is.

Standing right behind the front counter. Pricing out some paperback.

Holy mother of God, it's him. Actually *him*.

Nathan Fucking Ballingrud.

He *almost* looks like his author pic. Almost. If I squint, he sort of resembles the dude in the photo—only the man in front of us is way older now. Thinner now. We're talking *gaunt*. He's got that same bald pate from the photo. His beard is a little longer, but the colors are sort of the same. Tawny mustache. White chin whiskers. He looks like a cigarette after someone's taken a long drag, nothing but a slender column of ash now, gray skin barely holding the rest of himself together. One simple blow would send Ballingrud just toppling right over, crumbling into dust.

"Let me know if I can help you with anything," he says, totally nonchalant. No big deal. He doesn't even look at us for long, glancing back at the stack of paperbacks he's pricing.

Nathan Fucking Ballingrud.

"It's you." What else can I say? It's all that makes sense to me in that moment. We've come so far, crossed state lines, ascended the mountaintop. We answered Ballingrud's call.

I want to fall to my knees. I want to weep.

Now Ballingrud takes both me and Benji in. Sizes us up. Weighs our souls on the scale. Determine if we're worthy. "Is there something in particular you're looking for?"

My throat's all dry. I want to say, *yes, yes,* but it comes out like a croak. I cough a bit, clear my throat, but I can't speak. I fantasized about this moment—this exact second—going over what I'd say in my head a million times, but now that I'm here, actually here, in his presence, I've got nothing. I'm all empty. The words are just not in me anymore. Fucking fail.

Benji speaks up for the both of us. "We came for you."

"I'm sorry. . . ?" The dude doesn't get it. Doesn't understand.

It's a test. Got to be.

"We're here for your horror recs," Benji says.

But it's more than that. *Let's be honest with ourselves here*, I want to say. This isn't just about getting Ballingrud's top reads. This is about getting his book. *The* book. The novel I was promised before Penguin pulled it. I didn't come all this way just for a recommendation.

"I want *The Weird*," I blurt out. Whether Benji was ever aware of it or not, I don't know. Don't care. He can pick up as many paperbacks as he pleases, but I've come here for one book and one book only, the forbidden publishing fruit, the fucking book I was promised months ago.

I came so far. I have nowhere else to go. I can't go home without it.

Ballingrud doesn't say anything. Not a fucking word. All sound gets absorbed by the surrounding books, sponging our exhales up. I can't breathe anymore. He must get this question a million times. Does he know who we are? What we've done just to be here? Are we worthy?

Then Ballingrud asks, "Are you sure?"

Who says *yes* first is up for grabs. Maybe me and Benji answer at the same time, but Ballingrud grins. He slips out from behind the counter, nodding his head toward one shoulder.

"Then follow me."

I turn to Benji and attempt to telepathically broadcast: *Can you believe this shit? It's happening! Actually happening!* But something about Benji's expression throws me. My boy looks nervous.

He's not saying anything. Just staring at me. Eyes wide. Like we shouldn't go.

The hell is that all about? There's no turning back now. Not when I'm this close.

Ballingrud leads me down an aisle. There's a turn I hadn't noticed before. It leads to another aisle, which then connects to another aisle. How big is this shop? Definitely didn't seem this expansive from the outside. Maybe it's carved into the mountain or something.

Benji's behind me. We don't say anything. We just follow. We want to be, uh, *deferential*. Respectful, you know? Simply being in Ballingrud's presence makes us hush. We're waiting for him to say something, but the dude picks up his pace, slipping down the aisle and turning again.

The bookshelves tighten. Constrict. The aisle tapers, closing in on itself. Books brush against both shoulders the deeper I go. I have to actually turn, side-stepping now, nearly crab-walk down the aisle, for fear my shoulders might knock these books over and cause a cave in.

Ballingrud is way up ahead. He's moving at such a quick clip; I've really got to hoof it. I almost ask him to slow down, *wait up*, but then Ballingrud turns down yet another fucking aisle.

Where in the hell is he going?

Where's he taking us?

The lighting is dimmer now. I glance up and I see the books reach the ceiling, eclipsing the florescent lighting from the neighboring aisles. It's colder here. Got that subterranean climate vibe, you know? Like when you're in the basement and the temperature just drops?

Only this isn't a basement. This is a bookstore. Or supposed to be. There's a part of me that wonders what would happen if I pulled a book off the shelf. What I'd see. I'm getting the sneaking suspicion that there wouldn't be a shelving unit behind there. . .

but rock. A cave carved into a mountain. I'm following Nathan Fucking Ballingrud into the deepest cavities of Asheville.

Where the hell is Benjamin? He's not behind me anymore. I turn and look and can't find him. We must've gotten lost. Separated somehow. Did he take a turn down a different aisle?

I call out his name—"Benji?"—and it echoes back.

Ballingrud halts. He doesn't turn to face me. He's just frozen. Peering over his shoulder, I realize the aisle just. . . *stops*. Dead end. The bookshelves tilt a bit, the walls no longer straight. They're curving now, arcing overhead, pushing the books out at loose, awkward angles. Almost clinging to the ceiling. Stalactites. Water drips off the paperback's spines in these distant plips.

In faded marker, I see the section is marked HORROR/SCI-FI/MYSTERY.

Ballingrud glances up and down this one particular shelf. He's searching for something. Something special. Not just any book, but The Book. A book just for me. I'm ready to get weird.

Please let it be The Weird, *please let it be* The Weird, *please let it be—*

"Here," he says as he tugs a book off the shelf. He has to really yank, the book giving him some resistance, refusing to release itself easily from the shelf. I hear the slightest *snap* and suddenly I don't believe it's a book, *that's not a book at all*, but a piece of subterranean fruit.

Ballingrud holds the book out to me. It doesn't have a title. Its cover is a faded red, and in my head, I remember something Benji echoed hours ago: *readitonredditreaditonredditreadit*

"Start with this," Ballingrud says. "Let me know what you think."

I take the book out of his hand. It's so light. It squishes a bit between my fingers, like it's more of a sagging bag than book. All the words inside are gelatinous tapioca pellets.

"I think you'll really like this one," Ballingrud says.

"What is it?"

"Something I've been working on," he says. "Maybe it's been working on me."

I can't help myself. I have to ask. "Is it *The Weird*?"

"They're all weird."

"How much?"

"Whatever you're willing to give," he says. Then Ballingrud is off and wandering back down the aisle, leaving me behind. He calls out over his shoulder, "Stay as long as you like. Until you're finished. Don't worry about closing. We keep odd hours."

So I do as he says. What else am I going to do? Nathan Fucking Ballingrud just told me to sit and read, so I'm going to hunker down in the aisle and read.

I start flipping through. The book's got gauzy, almost hazy, pages. Practically transparent. Like onion skin. No—not onion. More like fly's wings. Whatever that stuff is called. *Membranous.* My fingers keep getting stuck every time I flip. The pages are so sticky, tacky, like a spider's web.

I hold onto the book, nestled into my lap, cradling it against my crotch. Just as I'm ready to begin reading, dive in and get this horror show on the road. . . the words start to wriggle, working their way off the page. Not words. Eggs. Spider eggs, hatching, crawling all over me. On my legs. I try brushing them off, but I can't let go of the book. My skin is clinging to the cover. I'm trying to pull my fingers free, but the tips start to tear and now they're bleeding all over the book, blood guttered by the crease. Whatever part of me the book touches, it sticks, like a glue trap for mice. The more I wrestle against the book, the more its pages cling to me.

If I bring my knee up to my chest and get my foot in between me and the book, maybe I can kick it off, but it just kind of folds me in more, wadding my body into a ball. Now the book is sticking to my shins. Its pages are, *shit, shit,* its pages are expanding out, spreading over my legs.

What the hell am I even reading? Or is it reading me?

I glance up and notice the novels oscillating on the shelves. Every last book looks as if it's about to burst, the yellowing paperbacks ripe and ready for plucking off the stacks. Succulent.

The pages are draped over my shoulders. I've wrapped myself in its chapters, cocooned by its cover. I don't want to believe the paper is somehow sealing up around me, but once that thought worms its way into my head, there's not much else I can think of. The open book is only inches away from my face, sliding over my shoulders, squeezing, hugging me, bringing me in.

Ballingrud's horror recs really are spot on. This book is fucking terrifying.

IMMACULATE DECEPTION
LUCY LEITNER

She probably shouldn't go out tonight. But some fanatic with a box cutter could fly a plane into her dorm, and life could be over tomorrow. She shouldn't follow the sophomores from her suite down the hill to this Thursday night kegger where a red Solo cup is free for girls and five dollars for guys, if they're admitted at all. She shouldn't risk oversleeping her nine a.m. recitation again, shouldn't fill her free cup from the Keystone Ice keg in the acrid basement, each sip adding to the flabby paunch muffining over her jeans and threatening the microscopic fetus growing inside it.

So, what did a boring recitation led by a TA matter when she'd be a mother before freshman year was over anyway? Her life was about to become someone else's.

And why not experience it before someone else takes it? Whether it's a terrorist or a son. Yes, it would be a son. Who ever heard of God's daughter?

Sure, they were all children of God. Mary, the three suitemates: Jen, Heather, Ally. The man behind the counter of the fried chicken joint down the hill from upper campus where they waited in line for Ally to buy her Parliament Lights. The two homeboys with glazed red eyes and what Mary recently learned were Phillies Blunts tucked behind their ears, agonizing over which potato-based slop they'd take home. Blonde Jen, effortlessly gorgeous in a university hoodie, who, if she'd ever gained the Freshman fifteen had now experienced the Sophomore negative twenty. Heather shivering, hugging her bare arms over her orange tube top revealing her tiny waist and the Chinese character on her lower back that she thinks means "angel." Even the terrorists who hijacked a plane, the passengers who diverted it into a field, so close to home; they were all God's children.

Just over six weeks now. Six weeks since she'd said okay to a drink. It's not a sin. Even pastor Henry drank. Her parents could smell it on him, didn't approve, but who were they to judge a man of God? And in the grand scheme of good and evil, these sopho-mores weren't close to Beelzebub, were they? It's just what they did. What everyone did but Mary. Until that night. When classes were canceled and all the phone lines were tied up and she couldn't reach her parents for several excruciating hours and the news was filled with fire and smoke and brimstone and counts of the dead and you didn't know if it was over. And nothing to do but watch and wait and hope the skies were clear. And they were. Miles away from explosions, it was a beautiful day on upper campus. And yes, Mary would go to the party now that she finally reached her parents and confirmed no one on the ground was killed.

So she was just as susceptible to temptation, drinking Satan's swill just like them, so why did God choose her? Not someone stronger like any one of those passengers on Flight 93 who actually did what Jesus would do?

Why Mary? Why not Jen or Heather or Ally? She was just like them now anyway. Maybe just a little more pure. She hadn't asked, just assumed. They could all be pregnant by less than divine means.

Surely a foamy, warm beer couldn't harm the literal son of God, the half-divine being no bigger than a pea she carried as, their shins screaming, they walked down the steep hill, past a corner dive, two pizza shops, Chinese takeout, and a dollar store boasting western Pennsylvania's largest selection of real human hair. But tonight she'd be strong, show God he was right for choosing her, of all the billions in the world to deliver the son that would deliver them all from evil.

"I don't think I'm gonna drink tonight."

"Easy to say before you inhale that sweet smell of Keystone Ice as it flows from the serpentine tap to the scarlet vessel."

Laughter.

"Did you smoke a bowl laced with opium again, Heather?"

"You don't think that kind of language is right for my future memoirs?"

More laughter from the sophomores as they round the corner, and everything spins into reverse. Walking forward, the sparse, skeletal shrubbery still, yet pushing against wind, an invisible force, sideways gravity. But there is no wind, no physical resistance. With heavy footsteps, as if trodding through sand, she continues forward as the magnetism tries to pull back, restraining her, telling her she should go no farther. This street doesn't want her. Not anymore.

Mary has seen this street before, this row of old homes on the right, but it should be on the left. The four-story apartment buildings with sad balconies should be on the right. Everything is transposed, a mirror image.

Is she walking backward? No, moving forward, foot passes foot. This isn't right! Something's wrong, like she's turned around.

The main drag soundtrack: tires squealing, engines sputtering, urban white noise fades as the girls walk down the reverse street, the trio of sophomores ahead of her the only thing keeping her from slipping. So disoriented, trying not to look at the wrong houses, the wrong buildings. Laughter. Maybe Heather made another joke.

And they're turning again, this time not into another street but a broken walkway through a grass lawn muddy from the afternoon's rain, and the noise is now the muffled cacophony of drunken students shouting, talking, screaming, a hundred conversations had at once slipping through the cheap windows. All given a rhythm by a bass pulsing through a stereo system, the veins of a house, giving it life.

Busted window, hastily patched with duct tape. Frat boy engineering. Aluminum planks, once blue, now the color of a polluted sky. Not that Mary can see that by the dull, flickering light that barely illuminates the broken cement path leading up to the flimsy-looking door with its cracking white paint. She knows it. The house leaves a permanent eyesore.

Paint bubbles up and peels off, giving the impression of papier-mâché. The whole house could explode like a piñata. It should be in a swamp, not just off a college campus. It should house the Blair Witch, not the Delta Kappa fraternity.

Mary finally looks up at the dark house and she understands why everything was backward. That's how she'd seen it before. She shouldn't have come here.

"I've been here before."

"Yeah, this is where you passed out on the couch last month, right?"

"Passed out on the couch? That's what they call it?"

"I'm so lucky no one drew on my face or anything."

Now she sees it, her dawn escape, still dark when she gathered her purse and someone's jacket and fled, the sun rising as she trudged up the endless hill that was so much easier when the booze hadn't worn off. Flashing her ID at dorm security, rushing into the elevator, a quick shower in the suite, and catching the first bus down to campus an hour early for recitation. Later, her roommate asking where she'd been, explaining the couch. Her face reddening, promising herself not to drink anymore, breaking that promise down on Atwood Street not twelve hours later. Why did God choose someone with so little willpower? So she would so easily do his bidding?

"Good thing you're not drinking tonight. Time to redeem yourself."

"Stay away from the jungle juice," Jen says, pushing open the door. "Wasn't that what got you in trouble last time? Everclear and Lord knows what else."

"How did they even get Everclear?"

"We're only an hour from the great state of West Virginia." Ally exhales a ring of smoke, giving the air the acrid tobacco scent that will eventually settle on the light jackets piled atop the tattered couch, its green and pink stripes losing contrast with the once-white ones.

"You got all cozy under the jackets last time?"

Was this the couch where she'd lay unconscious for hours? She forced a memory of the texture of the canvas. The angle her neck must have been on that rigid arm rest; could she recall a pain on her walk of shame up the hill? She stares at the couch, straining to remember, as blackness envelopes her. She shakes her head, shaking the infinite darkness off, back to the dimness of the room that was likely intended as a living space for a family, presumably one without so many brothers who nailed their Greek letters haphazardly above the crooked mantle.

"It was warmer then."

Jackets and hoodies tossed on the pile, the girls push through what was intended as a dining room, now the place for thirty or so college kids to consume only liquids, vapors, and one another's saliva. Just before the kitchen, the door-free entry leads them to rickety plywood stairs and the basement. On the right, the missing door, in its new incarnation as a beer pong table. On the left, the keg beckons.

She shouldn't have come here. Is this where God wanted his unborn son? In line for a cheap cup of mostly foam in an unfinished basement, vibrating with the bassline of a foul DMX song? Was it what Mary wanted? The college experience before she had no youth left? It wasn't like God asked her permission. She reaches for a red cup, hand dislodged by a headbutt.

A waif of a girl, jeans hanging off her hips like that cheerleader at her high school who disappeared for months to an eating disorder clinic. A skeleton hand reaches out from the baggy long-sleeve tee into a dirt mound in the corner where the muddy sub-floor meets the decaying wall. She turns around, the face of Norman Bates' mother with a beaming, rotting-tooth grin. She stands at the end of the missing door—propped up on cinder blocks to form a table—next to her beer pong partner. Also skeletal, yet somehow distended in the belly. The cheap red V-neck hanging off the shoulders and chest, pulling taut around the gut that spills over the sides of the flare jeans looking more like JNCOs on her bony legs. The identical outfit as Mary's.

The orange hairs on the corpse's head sprout in fuzzy tufts through patches of graying skin, giving the appearance of ground cover in the desert. A brown eye dangles from its optic nerve, just out of the socket as the torn skin closes over the other, aiming the perfect shot. The thing dressed like Mary cocks its bony fingers, flesh sloughing to the door table and settling like the ashes from one of Ally's Parliaments, and releases the detritus-speckled ball. As it lands in the opposing Solo cup, the corpse with the Fred Durst cap removes it and swigs the beer, flotsam and jetsam coursing through the viscera skin should have covered.

God doesn't want her here. She understands that now. This is a warning.

She pushes away from the keg, from her friends, from

Heather's voice, "Where are you going? There's sober people in Europe!", from a man's arm around her shoulder, "Hey, it's Low Five," into the dark mass of students, moving almost in unison to the sound of what she recently learned is "Pony" by Ginuwine.

Blood oozes from the lesions in their charred skin, blackened, the texture of greasy pumice. Beneath the cratered flesh, a red glow, as if they're burning from the inside. Is this what the passengers looked like when their planes exploded against the towers? Smoldering flesh, still alive, still moving while their organs immolate, bursting bile from an interior more mutilated than the ruined skin. The news didn't show photos of this carnage. She must have imagined it. She must be imagining this!

They can't be real! But how to explain the globs of sticky, viscous blood smeared on her arm as she shoves through the mass of bodies, so many bodies, too many bodies in what seemed like such a small space from the stairs? The stairs. Where are the stairs? Ashes fall from the smoldering arms that raise up on Petey Pablo's command, cascading down in a flurry of dandruff. Shirts stay on, not overhead like helicopters, so Mary doesn't brush against slimy entrails as they encircle her in the center of their mosh pit, sucking her down, down. No! She's not sinking, just feeling like it as the shedding corpses enclose, swaying to the beat, their burning organs emitting a suffocating heat.

With a wave of burnt hair, old beer, and something acrid she can't identify flowing into her lungs, she presses through a tiny gap between bodies, surging toward the wood plank stairs. Grasping the splintered handrail, she pulls herself up, shouldering past the skeletal creatures in low-rise denim descending to the dungeon.

Back in the dining room turned waiting room, that in-between space no one stays in long since it lacks a keg or a bar, the bodies have their flesh intact. Maybe it was all a hallucination, some brutal honesty of what a party really looks like when she attends sober. Sober. What was she thinking? You don't go to a party without pregaming. That was a rookie mistake. But she is still a rookie. Maybe it was a manifestation of the trauma of so many rapid changes. Leaving home. Planes crashing in fields and skyscrapers and geometric government centers right when she's meeting all these girls who take birth control and recreational Vicodin. Maybe it was loss of innocence, the world revealing its ugly true face.

She needs something to calm down. A drink would be ideal, but she can't face the basement again without it, a catch-twenty-two, a paradox. A boy, turned three quarters away from her, blows smoke up to the yellowed ceiling, avoiding the two girls he's made giggle. A gentleman, he looks vaguely familiar, maybe he appears in one of the photos with "random guys" that keep falling off from where Jen taped them to the dorm room cinderblock wall, has a gut feeling his name is a nickname.

Mary taps him on the shoulder. The face that meets hers is what's left of a face when it covers a black hole. Skin so taught it's about to crack in black, veiny fissures, pulling into every empty orifice, about to collapse in on itself. The event horizon of a head. She jumps back, once again shoving her way out of a room.

She shouldn't be here. This isn't what college should be, so gritty and like the real world and above all, so fucking short. Four years, it was supposed to be four years. Would she get one before she'd have to drop out? It's not like God would get a job. She'd be raising his son in a trailer park outside of Somerset. And when he turned water into Iron City Light, she'd be praying for his help in getting someone, anyone to believe it.

Believe it. Even if it is a message, it's God telling her something, and she should listen. Maybe some of those passengers taking off from Newark saw melting flight attendants, what they thought were paranoid fantasies actually premonitions of their impending incineration. No one in this world would ever know. Mary wasn't going to find out.

Back at the couch in the darkened living room, she tears through the pile of jackets that's swelled to cover all the exposed stuffing of the sofa, tossing them to the armrest, the floor, wherever they can reveal her imitation black leather from the others like it.

A sensation runs up her spine, a touch so light it could be spectral. She jumps, turns around. Instinct distracts from her task. Curiosity overrides self-preservation. Not a good maternal trait.

"Leaving so soon, Low Five?"

Flounder. That's what they call him. A hazy image. We have the best Flounder, they said. Doesn't he look just like him? Every frat says they have a Flounder, but ours is the best. Everyone laughing, Mary smiling, pretending she was in on the joke like the rest of the room, but just seeing the chubby, dark-haired boy barely taller and older than her. His wasn't a Freshman fifteen gut. He was always the fat kid. Joined this less-than-prestigious fraternity in this dingy house in this sketchy neighborhood on the outskirts of the urban campus to finally fit in, at least at a superficial level. Something in his dark brown eyes, maybe an honesty, a clarity even if clouded by the beer also on his breath, maybe it's just because they were normal living human eyes, half closed, but not black vacuums filled with negative energy or burning orbs seeping ocular fluids told Mary she could trust him.

"I need to go home."

"Oh, come on. You're a high five to me." He gulps down whatever remains in his red cup, tosses it on the floor. Both hands free, he wraps them around Mary's growing waist, pulls her to him. "Pretend I'm Chase."

His tongue plunges into her mouth with the impact of a belly flop from a high dive. Slobber on her cheeks as the tongue explores with all the finesse of the belly flopper dog paddling to the pool edge. It sends a bomb down her tongue, past the uvula, down the esophagus, through the lungs, and into those organs padded by new fat in her abdomen. Burning. She pushes out of his embrace, dislodging his tongue from her mouth, but not putting out the fire raging back from her gut to her throat. What was Flounder's face is now a ball of ash, the end of a cigarette, but darker, blacker, the ashes of his burnt face swarming in a head shape losing density as it blows into her eyes.

Mary shoves past him, covering her mouth to keep the ashes out and the rising explosion in. Not the front door, blocked by a throng of what appears to have recently been students, their faces voids of matter. Up the stairs. Something in her subconscious telling her this is where she needs to go. Or maybe it's God guiding her as she skips steps and pulls herself up the banister. At the landing, doors on either side. A line of girls, some boys, mostly girls, along the railing that is sure not to keep all of them from plummeting one story to life in a chair, reaching another door at the end of the hall. Mary bolts past them, her chunky heeled boots pounding on the worn, discolored carpet. She rips open the door that she intuited wouldn't be, couldn't be, locked. "Hey, bitch, don't you see the line?" as she bursts through the door past the girl on the toilet and her, "Don't you knock?"

She tears open the shower curtain, collapsing on the hard, peeling laminate floor inches from the girl's jeans pooled around her feet, the fire reaching Mary's mouth just in time to expel it into the tub.

"Oh, you have got to be kidding me. It's not even eleven. Jesus, lightweights." The toilet flushes. Stomping footsteps. The shouts, laughter, and cacophony of music from different rooms competing for supremacy. Will Lit triumph over Ludacris? "I would not go in there yet unless you want to puke too."

She wipes the bile and Flounder's saliva from her lips, smearing the Revlon on her chin along with the shiny fluids. No point in prolonging her monopoly of one of the scarce bathrooms, incurring the wrath of the drunken mob on the landing by rinsing the masticated, digestive juice-slicked chunks of dining hall grilled cheese down the drain. From the pink ring and mildew threatening to turn into black mold, the guys living here likely consider soap scum from a semi-daily shower sufficient tub cleaning.

She heaves herself from the floor slick with what she hopes is Keystone Ice, splashes her mouth, chin, and cheeks with water from the sink faucet. The reflection in the mirror is obfuscated by filth, but it's her. Red lipstick now more clown than cover model, smeared foundation revealing the ruddy chin expected from a mousy, plain, small-town redhead, the type God usually passed right over on his way to the specimens you could believe were made in his ineffable image. But at least it was her.

"Ugh go home."

"Puke and rally!"

"We haven't seen a puker that early since pledge week!"

"Wait everyone, let's all low five her!"

"What's that? Oh!"

A boy in a red hoodie with three rings in his left eyebrow, the supposedly safe punk type—cleaner than the other pierced kids with their cardboard signs, "Need money for beer," on the sidewalk by lower campus—a wannabe punk with parents that can pay for his beer, reaches his hand out just below waist level. The students lining the banister follow, like lemmings, as if their tap routine was interrupted to congratulate the opposing team on a game well played. Mary barrels ahead, won't be sucked into their games anymore, won't wait until their smiling faces transform into blackened skulls.

"Oh, c'mon low five; you used to be fun!"

She takes her first step down the stairs, grabs the railing, stops before her feet meet.

At the bottom of the staircase, his hand on the wall as he leans over a smiling Jen, looking into her eyes like there isn't a party going on around them, his curly chin-length hair buried under the fraternity trucker hat. Mary blinks and she's taken Jen's place under his arm. Just for a glance until she's back in the basement, sidling up next to the curly haired boy at the door-cum-table. Near-empty basement, no one dancing, dead or alive. Her friends, the girls she arrived after pregaming with Vladimir vodka and Stackers back in the dorm, nowhere in sight. No other girls either, except the girlfriends of the few frat brothers that had them. The music blaring. Pearl Jam. "Black". It was that time of the night. When she should have gone home with the others. The night should have been over; the party was. But she was still here, determined after who knows how many beers, to experience life, or what she, in her state, thought life entails. Life. Growing up.

Attaching herself to this guy, a senior she thinks, Chase. She likes his name, his hair, his cleft chin, maybe even how he barely notices her. No, she doesn't like that, just has been accustomed to this invisibility in the eyes of the cute guys, the attention coming from the ones they call Flounder. She smiles, touches his hand while he dunks the pong ball into the gray water amid the flecks of basement floor grime, flirting as best she knows from observation. Asks to bum a cigarette. His eyes, blinking to stay open, still blindly focused on the beer pong game, he nods to the pack of Camel Lights and the shiny silver Zippo on the door table.

His hands, they come back to her. Hands pushing up, but not removing her shirt, pulling off her jeans. The upstairs room almost too dark to notice how his eyes avoided hers. The hands roughly turning her around on her knees atop the bed, holding her hips like she was motorcycle handles, not a person. The thrusts, grunts.

The door opening, light flooding in. The eyebrow ring kid

approaching the bed, raising his hand like he's about to pledge allegiance.

"High five, man."

Chase's voice: "This one's more like a low five."

Laughter. The hand lowered like the ones in the hall. A slap, skin on skin, just a little louder than the rhythmic ones she feels. The door closing, the light fading.

The next thing she knows, she's awakened by snoring. The sun glowing through the curtains gives her enough light to find her purse and she's down the stairs and out the door, seeing the sad street in reverse. Powering up the hill, panting, rubbing her arms like Heather, the early morning chilling her in the borrowed tank top. The walk of shame.

Back in the dorm, a quick shower and a bus down the hill to recitation. In the suite later that morning, when the revelers awoke from a long sleep in their own beds and asked what happened after she refused to leave the party, the lie formed in her mouth.

"I passed out on the living room couch."

Humiliating enough to avoid going back. To believe without letting it define her, both to her suitemates and Mary herself. It wouldn't give her a nickname. Low Five, some groupie every frat had, but she was the best representation of the archetype—the pathetic freshman girl. So, like the song that played in the basement before the parties wound down said, the lie became the truth.

From the bottom of the steps, Chase's alert eyes, not struggling against the lids to stay open like they were on that night, glance away from Jen for a moment, meet hers. No nod, no expression, how you acknowledge the janitor emptying the trash in the dining hall. The busboy who clears your plate, the bus driver who just needs to see your student ID to board. But it's long enough for Mary to see them glow as red as an unfortunate look into the flash in one of Ally's disposable camera pictures. Does Jen see it? Of course not, Mary didn't see it that night. She does now, and, like the window into the soul, it reveals the rest of his true face.

As maroon as his hat, his skin stretches taut against the rising cheekbones. The cleft lengthens with the rest of the chin, curves in on itself into a point. The half-asleep smile you give a girl when you want her to believe you enough to disappear for a while curves upward into a sinister grin. Bending up, up, up until the thin, curling lips meet the temples.

His face, moon-shaped as it's become, is clean, unlike the cackling throng crowding what may have once been called a foyer, the grime from the basement floor sprouting from gaping wounds on their occipital bones. Bubbles like beer head from a warm keg foam from their mouths, spilling onto Y necklaces, T-shirts that say, "It's Thursday night; do you know where your girlfriend is?" It's as if they've become part of the house, permanent fixtures in an eternal party. Dirty, gritty, nothing like the Greek life in the brochures overflowing from Mary's parents' mailbox last year. It wasn't supposed to be like this. It shouldn't be like this.

Chase's red eyes now fixated on Jen, Mary creeps down the stairs, toward the kitchen, away from his view. As she crosses the threshold, she explodes off her back foot, two leaping steps propelling her abdomen into the ninety-degree edge of the Formica countertop. The pain is surface level, like it'll leave a huge bruise on her skin the booze of the last two months has depleted of its nutrients. She backs up, launches herself again.

It's too superficial to kill the demon embryo.

"If you wanna puke, stick your finger down your throat. It's way more effective."

Mary nods, refusing to look at the girl who offered this sage upperclassman advice, doesn't want to see flesh peeling back from each orifice, eyes melting down her cheeks like eggs in a pan.

A cursory check of the drawers yields no implements sharp enough to surgically remove a fetus. The mismatched knives are mostly for butter, some the same model as those in the dining halls, probably stolen. The steak knives are too dull to pierce below the epidermis. How would she start to extract it anyway? She's not even pre-med. It would just be self-evisceration. How could she, with a dull, pilfered butter knife, abort Satan's spawn?

Hidden almost behind a wall by the freestanding stove, she peers into the foyer. Chase and Jen are nowhere in sight. Since arriving at school, she's learned how to read body language. Their communication at the bottom of the stairs told her they weren't going to play beer pong in the basement.

Back on the staircase, Mary retraces her steps from that night last month. She walks past the line for the bathroom, the jeers of "back again?", "low five!", "don't let her in!", reaching the narrower steps at the end of the hall. It's quiet up here, the only signs of the party, the throbbing from below. A line of light shines from the bottom of just one of the three doors. She doesn't need the indication. She's been there before, but it was dark. The only thing she could see before eyebrow ring boy opened the door was the glowing red eyes. Right? Yes, she remembers it now. Like traffic lights telling her to stop, to get out, while the grain alcohol said the opposite.

With a creak, the door opens.

"Fuck off, Steve," Chase slurs from the bed, his face buried in Jen's neck, under her blond hair. Finally, he glances up with the same indifference as when he saw her for the first time this evening. "Fuck off, Low Five."

"Be nice, she's a freshman." Jen extracts herself from Chase.

Slowly, with a scowl, he sits up, his back against the nicotine-stained wall.

"Mary, Heather, and Ally are downstairs. Why don't you go find them?"

"He's the devil."

"I may be an asshole, but I'm not the devil." Chase reaches for his cigarette pack on the floor. Mary kicks them away, the Zippo sliding off it and onto the carpet. Chase shrugs and resumes his slouch, turns his head to Jen, a second chin forming beneath the cleft, that recessive trait Mary thought was so sexy six weeks ago.

"You don't think I'm the devil, do you, Jane?"

"Jen. No, but you are an asshole." She smiles, running her fingers over his chest.

"Heed my words, Jen. He shalt destroy you. Punish you forever in hellfire. That's what the devil does. Whether it's burning you alive in a plane in a field or in your mind. For he takes innocence and blows it up." She scans the room with open eyes—the shoddy desk in the corner with its closed laptop covered by CDs with "Party Mix" scrawled in black marker, the cardboard cutout woman clad in a Busch Light bikini, a filthy lawn gnome in the corner. Atop the scratched dresser, above the partially open drawers, sits a fat, glass bottle marked Everclear 190 proof grain alcohol, a bottle more than half full even to a pessimist. Mary picks it up.

"Good idea, Low Five. Drink up, chill. Just do it somewhere else."

"The Lord has filled me with his power to resist temptation, to rebuke Satan and all his schemes."

"Mary, I don't know what you smoked, but get a beer and balance it out. Seriously, I don't think grain alcohol is the answer. Ally will pour it for you so it's not all head."

Mary twists open the cap, tosses it on the brown carpet. Like the Lord rained frogs on Egypt, she raises the bottle above her head and spills the liter of alcohol, soaking the cheap comforter and the denim-covered legs of the two people on the bed.

"Alright, psycho, get the fuck out."

As Chase finally comes to a seated position, starts to push

himself to standing, Mary drops the empty bottle and grabs the Zippo from the floor. Flicking it, she thrusts the flame against Chase's leg. What was a tiny flame spreads up his pants. As he dances in a panic without the rhythm of the burning corpses in the basement, Mary flings the lighter onto the bed. Jen screams and scrambles from the rapidly spreading flame, like the sinners of Gommorah, too late to escape its clutches. The fire spreads, engulfing the two students, the wooden fraternity paddle suspended between nails on the wall, the bed where Satan corrupted the youngest of adults and attempted to doom the next generation to his offspring's vile reign, the busty cardboard Busch Light girl.

Mary leaves the room, closing the door behind her. Maybe the fire alarms will sound. If the frat boys knew to replace the batteries. And if not, someone is bound to smell the difference between house fire smoke and cigarette smoke. Eventually.

She walks down the stairs, past the partying students, their falling eyelids blinding them from the truth of their subservience to the prince of darkness they've elected their fraternity president. Someone is bound to hear Jen's screams over Ol' Dirty Bastard. She slips past the throng to the front door, breathes the pure air not corrupted by cheap beer, cigarettes, grain alcohol, and burning flesh.

With his father gone, nothing more than a smoldering pile of ash with no more virgins waiting for him, why couldn't the child in her belly be God's son?

If the Messiah could turn water into wine, why couldn't his mother turn lies into truth?

SATANIC PANIC: ON ICE!
WILLIAM STERLING

James and Michael were crouched, shimmying from side to side with their arms spread wide in the middle of an asphalt desert. They were surrounded by a fleet of vehicles that shimmered in the afternoon heat, and the sounds of minivan doors being slammed shut filled the dry, hot air around them. At the pair of dads' feet, a trio of crotch goblins ping-ponged about, bubbling with excitement.

"Giggle Squad! Giggle Squad! Giggle Squad!" the children babbled in a sing-song rhythm.

Michael's wife, Jessie, was still at their car, busy trying to hide snacks inside a diaper bag, as the men danced about, shepherding their flock and trying to make sure none of the munchkins charged into the parking lot Gage Creed style.

"Not paying ten dollars for fucking popcorn again," Jessie mumbled as she angled a pack of wipes over a half-eaten bag of veggie straws. She grunted, then jammed a pair of binoculars down, in between everything, to hold the bag's contents steady.

"There. That should work until we find our seats. Michael, you remembered the tickets, right?"

"What kind of event doesn't have digital tickets nowadays?" Michael grumbled, reaching down and catching Baby Tabitha before she tripped on an untied shoelace.

"That's not an answer," Jessie growled, already on edge from their drive to the arena.

"Yes, I have the tickets."

"Giggle Squaaaaaaaad!" The kids danced in a little circle and swung their tiny arms and legs about, imitating the weird dance moves that a trillion Giggle Squad music videos had seared into their brains.

The antics might have been entertaining if Michael hadn't already heard them sing the song an insufferable number of times on the drive up. But as it was, the Giggle Squad's discography had been stamped into his brain, beaten to mash, and left to rot.

He could name all four members of the Giggle Squad, along with their side characters.

He knew exactly how long the pause was between the end of "Beep, Beep Big Blue Car" and "Party Poppers" when Spotify slipped between the tracks.

He could slam his forehead through the steering wheel at the exact moment that those fucking ukeleles strummed to life at the start of "Oh, Brother Where Fart Thou."

He kept telling himself that the songs made the kids happy. And they did. But at what cost?

Before them, All Farm Arena loomed tall and proud. Inside, the Giggle Squad themselves lay in waiting. Those technicolor bastards.

Michael slid the tickets from his pocket to make sure they actually *were* there while also trying to stay blind to the tickets' prices, which were highlighted on the front, loud and proud, just to mock him.

Look how much you paid for this shit, lol.

The day would have been a complete loss—an hour drive,

followed by two and a half hours of mind-numbing children's songs—but something else crinkled in Michael's pocket as he jammed the tickets back down. Something that was bound to make this whole charade borderline tolerable.

He nudged James and revealed his bag of "adult" gummies.

"Oh, thank fuck," James groaned.

The kids froze and stared up at James.

James stared back.

There was a brief, terrifying moment of anticipation before the kids picked up their chanting again.

"Thank fuck! Thank fuck! Thank fuck!" they sang, loud enough that the other families who were walking past reached down to cover their kids' ears as they shot death glares in Michael and James' direction.

"Dammit all. Gimme one of those, quick." James asked, reaching one hand out while he tried to get his daughter, Amber, to stop cursing with the others.

Michael chuckled and fished around in the bag as he half-heartedly reprimanded the children himself.

"That's a grown-up word."

"We really shouldn't say that, kids."

And finally, the ultimate surrender...

"Hey! Why don't we all sing the Giggle Squad song again? They're right inside and I'll bet they'd love to hear you singing 'Goats, Goats, Goats!'"

The kids took the bait, abandoning the vulgarities and dropping to their hands and knees, crawling around on the ground and pretending to eat grass while singing the song and 'baa'ing at one another.

Michael fished out a pair of gummies and passed one to James while the munchkins were distracted.

Jessie rolled her eyes.

"Really? You're getting high? Again?" she chastised.

"Well, you're gonna get drunk!"

"That's different."

"How?"

"It's. . . I dunno. Science or something. Shut up. Those gummies are gonna rot the half a brain that you two share."

Michael shook his head and laughed.

"Jess, our brains rotted a long time ago. But it wasn't because of these."

"What's this crunchy stuff on the outside?" James asked, picking at some powder on the edge of the orange candy that Michael had passed him.

"I dunno, man. I got them from a new guy. Maybe Sour Patch Kids dust or something?"

"Har-dee-har har."

"Guys! Come ON!" Jessie had turned away from the guys and, like a military general, she had somehow whipped the kids into order. Each of the munchkins was standing at attention, their hands placed on the shoulders of the kid in front of them, forming a tottering, chanting line that marched one by one toward the arena at Jessie's command.

"Down the hatch!" Michael called and tossed his gummy in his mouth. James copied. They both made grossed-out, weird faces towards each other.

"Definitely not Sour Patch Kids powder."

"Nope. The fuck was that?" Michael asked.

But he didn't get an answer. Not from James.

"The fuck was that? The fuck was that?" The kids laughed and sang as Jessie turned back at the front of the line to give Michael 'the look.'

"I guess we'll find out soon enough," James shrugged, and he and Michael hustled to take their place at the back of the procession.

Their seats were mid-level, strategically selected to be at the end of a row so that they wouldn't have to climb over other families each time their rotating door of kids needed bathroom breaks. James and Michael sat against the aisle, their three munchkins positioned to their right, with Jessie as the bookend.

They made it right on time.

The gummies were setting in, and Michael felt all his usual anxieties melting away as he folded his seat down and the overhead lights blinked out.

Darkness fell across the arena as ladies and gentlemen, boys and girls of all ages held their collective breaths.

Four spotlights, one purple, one blue, one yellow, and one green, burst to life overhead. They sent their beams of light spiraling around the crowd, and the little munchkins roared with excitement, their tiny fists raised up towards the heavens in jubilation, their cries all melding together in a sudden wave of sound that would have startled the devil himself.

The spotlights spiraled and descended down the rows of the arena as if circling a drain until they landed on the four shadowy figures who had appeared at center ice.

"L-l-l-let's get ready to Giggle!" Blue's voice erupted from the speakers overhead. A familiar, rhythmic, pulsing beat swelled to life. The opening to "It's Giggle Time." Michael had heard this same drum swell ten trillion times while the Giggle Squad opening credits rolled, but today it felt somehow sinister. Ominous. A war drum portending a looming bloodbath.

Holy shit. Seriously. What was in those gummies?

Michael felt like his newfound paranoia must have been how his cousin, Jed, felt about the Giggle Squad every day.

"Sent by the devil," Jed would claim whenever he saw Michael's kids watching Giggle Squad, or Dora, or even fucking

Sesame Street in the other room. "Them's trying to indoctrinate our babies. Make 'em soft, little hippies. When we was growing up we didn't have cushy shows like that. What we had was some sticks, some rocks, and some woods to play in, and we was happy for the rocks, damnit."

The wholesale lack of joy in Jed's life probably explained why the man was going through his third divorce in ten years and why he kept voting for dumbass grifters every other election. But he did have some sort of a point, Michael had to concede. Especially watching the proceedings now, the way these shows, and the Giggle Squad especially, could entrance the children seemed mystical. Hypnotic. Otherworldly, as if they had tapped directly into some well of enchantment that desperate parents could only dream of partaking from.

The figures on the ice broke apart. They raced towards the four corners of the rink as the drum swell broke, and a collection of ukeleles, pianos, and acoustic guitars picked up the beat to give the song some life. The colorful conductors sang into their microphones, probably, but the kids in the arena all burst into song so loud that Michael was hard-pressed to hear the main attraction.

It's giggle time with the Giggle Squad.
Call your moms and call your dads.
Giggle time, come on let's play.
Hop to your feet and shout hooray!

The Giggle Squad pulled up into a set of synchronized upright spins, and the kids in the front rows, seated against the glass, were into it. The overhead lights segregated the audience into mobs of color. Blue lights pulsed in the Blue Squad Member's corner. Green lights shone in Green's corner, and so on.

Michael looked down at his hands. Saw that he was completely green now. He didn't like it. This green tone didn't seem like a trick of some thin colored glass slid in front of a spot-light. Somehow, some way, Michael knew that his skin truly WAS green now. He had been branded. Claimed as a member of this subsect of the proceedings.

It's giggle time with the Giggle Squad.
Kill your moms and off your dads.
Giggle time, come on let's play.
Lop off their feet and scream today!

The cadence of the song was all off and the hitch in the rhythm confused Michael in his inebriated daze. Strange timing. Different inflections. He kept hearing the Giggle Squad singing the lyrics incorrectly.

To Michael, it sounded like the yellow member kept snarling randomly in the middle of their verses, and the purple member looked like she was doing something weird with her hands, her fingers twisting and contorting, knuckles snapping by her sides as she raced across the ice.

Was anybody else seeing this? Hearing this?

Michael looked down the aisle towards Jessie, but she was busy unscrewing the eyepiece of her "binoculars" and tipping the device sideways to take a swig of wine from its hidden compart-ment. She didn't give two shits about what was happening on the ice.

It was weird that *Michael* gave two shits about what was happening down there, he knew, but still. This whole thing felt off. His kids were cheering and clapping and having a great time, but the hairs on Michael's arms were standing on end.

"James, are you seeing this?"

To Michael's left, James was leaning forward in his seat, eyes aghast as big and as white as the ice rink itself, locked on the proceedings below. He nodded without turning away, face pale.

They had reached the part of the theme song where the Giggle Squad introduced themselves. Purple smiled and crouched down before launching herself into the air, kicking her feet out, and yelling, "Famine!"

She landed to rounds of applause.

"What the absolute fuck is happening?"

James had to yell for Michael to hear him.

"Conquest!" Green called through the speakers as he twirled and writhed.

"Plague."

"Death."

"Nope."

Michael stood and tried to muscle his way out, past James, into the aisle. He was sweating bullets and wanted to be anywhere but there. He turned back to try to grab his kids' hands, but they were enthralled. Eyes glued to the show taking place down below. They wouldn't even look at him.

Jessie, on the far side of the munchkins, had her sneaky canteen tipped up and was scrolling on her phone. She didn't see Michael. Couldn't hear him over the crowd, even when he screamed her name.

It felt like a dream. A nightmare. Everything about the situation was so surreal, from the mob mentality of the children to the dark warble of the Giggle Squad's songs. Michael would have thought he was just having a weird nightmare if it hadn't been for the look in James' eyes. He could see all this too, and he pushed Michael to hurry. To get away from all this, and to make room for him to stand in the aisle along with him.

The Giggle Squad's blue member took off again, cutting towards center ice before hockey stopping with his back to the crowd. He pumped his hands to the beat of the song, exposing his palms to the sky as beneath the ice, something began to glow and swim around.

"The kids. We need to grab the kids!" Michael half-heard/half-lip-read James saying. He turned and reached back across the pair of folded-up seats to seize his older child, Greg, by the shoulder.

But Greg turned and gave his father the angriest, coldest glare Michael had ever seen. Death shone behind those eyes. Murder. Though the child was still singing and shimmying along to the sounds of the Giggle Squad, the violence that vibrated within him was undeniable.

This was no longer Michael's child.

What looked back at him now was something else.

Something claimed by the infernal.

Michael slowly withdrew his hand, and his kid turned his attention back to the show on center ice.

"We've lost them," Michael whispered to James, and although James couldn't hear Michael's words over the din, he had seen the same thing. Recognized the look. Their families were gone. Lost to the seductive powers of the Giggle Squad.

James clamped a hand on Michael's shoulder.

"We have to save them!"

"How?"

"We need to kill the Giggle Squad," James lamented.

The song ended. The lights went low.

But if the surrounding crowd heard James' threat, they didn't react.

"How's everybody doing today?" Green called into their mic. "We hope you're having a *Giggly Time*. Now, for this next song, we need everybody on their feet to dance, dance, dance along to. . . 'Party Poppers!'"

The circles of tiny worshippers rose to their feet as instructed, light-up shoes stomping, hands clapping, voices raised in exaltation.

Michael nodded. James was right. It was the only way.

The crowd's rise helped to mask Michael and James' descent

down the rows, past throngs of munchkins shouting "Pop, Pop, Pop the Party" over and over again. There were no other words to the song. It was just that refrain, again, and again, and again, for all of time, until the sweet embrace of death.

Whatever Michael had seen swimming below the ice had grown larger and sprouted appendages as the ceremony progressed.

"Hurry!" James urged.

But there was nowhere to hurry to. The heavy plastic ring that surrounded the ice loomed before them. A barricade separating slap shots from nose jobs, goons from fanatics, gigglers from gigglees.

"How do we get past this?"

"Is there a gate?"

The purple Giggle Squad member sped past on the opposite side of the glass, sliding backwards, eyes making contact with Michael's for the briefest of moments. The eyes were hollow. Devoid of emotion.

"Pop, pop, pop the party," she sang, and smiled, mockingly.

"Zamboni gate?" James offered beside Michael, snapping his attention back to the task at hand.

Michael nodded and they turned, shimmying down endless rows of wild-eyed children. A few parents grunted and cursed at the men as they passed, but none bothered to look up from their phones. They just grumbled about having to lift their legs and then went on ignoring their demon-worshiping hell-spawn.

"Pop the Party" ended as James emerged from the lowest row, right beside the entrance to the rink's tunnel, with Michael right behind him.

The lights dimmed and a new spotlight sprang to life, this one's beam oscillating colors, phasing through the four trademark tones of the harbingers of the apocalypse as it careened towards Michael and James.

Surely, now, the jig was up. They had been noticed. Security was going to descend upon them, and their souls would be sacrificed to that thing that glowed below the ice. Whatever it was.

But the beam of light just missed the pair, aimed instead down the tunnel beside them to illuminate the arrival of a new member of the proceedings.

Happy Horse.

Some sad, sappy sucker in a white unicorn costume came skating out onto the ice, the lights from the arena reflecting red in his massive glass eyes. Over its head, Happy Horse held the Giggle Squad's Storybook high, and, at their reveal, the children in the audience went bananas.

Happy Horse did a pirouette.

James and Michael screamed.

To the ecstatic children, the storybook looked just like it did on television. There was the purple felt front cover, the green felt back cover, the yellow twine stitching holding together the baby blue pages, which the actors would pretend to read their stories from.

But James and Michael saw this iteration for what it truly was: a tome of ancient evil. A spell book from eons before the first human learned to lace their skates. Before the first sing-along entranced its first child victim.

The air seemed to hum with a sinister energy as Happy Horse and the book did a slow loop around the perimeter of the rink, then spiraled inwards to join the Giggle Squad at center ice.

Happy Horse bowed low, holding the book open for a reading from the scripture.

"We can't let them read from that thing!" Michael shouted to James.

They both looked around. The gate that Happy Horse had entered still hung open, revealing two ways forward. One, across the ice towards the Giggle Squad. The other, down into the bowels of the arena.

Michael put a tentative toe on the ice but screamed as the glowing monstrosity below the surface charged towards him.

Michael withdrew his toe, not trusting a thin layer of cold water to protect him from... whatever that thing was.

"Down the tunnel! We'll cut the power to all of this. If the kids can't hear the Giggle Squad, maybe the spell will be broken," James offered.

Michael nodded. It made as much sense as anything else did.

Together, the half-baked heroes raced into the underbelly of All Farm Arena.

The vibrant, neon-drenched hellscape above gave way to a cold, gray, and damp labyrinth of tunnels and leaking pipes. Signs littered the walls, meant to give direction to people who were lost, but their symbols and patterns meant nothing to Michael or James.

'A1120 this way', one sign read, with an arrow. But what the shit A1120 was, or why they should care, was beyond Michael. James was pointing down the opposite hall.

"The control room's gotta be this way."

"How could you possibly know that?"

James took off without answering.

Overhead, the stomping of little feet made it sound like a hurricane was battering the arena's roof. Trails of dust and crumbling infrastructure reigned down in little streams, and Michael tried to remember what year they had built this thing. He wondered when the last safety inspection would have been.

In front of him, James ran up to the first door he saw and threw it open to reveal a janitor's closet. Two mops protruded from a yellow rolling wash bin, and James grabbed them both quickly, tossing one to Michael.

"For defense!"

"How?"

Again, James ignored the question and raced away, like maybe those gummies had been laced with cocaine instead of sugar.

Michael glanced over his shoulder, back up the tunnel. They were being followed. A handful of the Giggle Squad's acolytes must have seen Michael and James slip down this way and were coming to apprehend them. Backlit by the sights and sounds of the Giggle Squad's show, the oncomers moved so slowly, so steadily, and they shrieked their ill intent.

James and Michael would be stopped. The Giggle Squad's performance would not be spoiled.

"They're coming!" Michael called ahead to James, who hastened his search, throwing doors open, casting hurried glances inside, then rushing farther ahead.

"The breaker's gotta be here somewhere!" James insisted, despite the size of the arena and the fact that so far he had checked behind a total of three, now four, doors out of the hundreds that were bound to exist.

Michael chased James down the hall, glancing over his shoulder to see long, thin shadows lurching across the tunnel behind them. Soon, their followers would round the corner, and there would be nowhere for James or Michael to hide.

Desperate, Michael shoved James through door number five and slammed it shut behind them.

Overhead, in the arena, the stomping feet went suddenly, anxiously, silent.

Soft lights blinked in the room around James and Michael. They heard little motors whirring and machines' gears turning. All around them, racks of clothes had been arranged by color.

Stools waited in front of desks and in front of mirrors, all covered with makeup palettes and inspirational messages.

They had entered the Giggle Squad's changing room.

"What? Do they all change together? That seems. . . weird," Michael voiced out loud.

"Doesn't matter!" James insisted. "We can't stop them with a costume change. We've gotta get to the next room!"

James tried to leave, but Michael caught him mid-spin and used his friends' momentum to twirl him all the way around 360 degrees.

"Stop. Look!"

On a fifth desk in the back of the room, two books sat, illuminated by some mysterious light source that Michael couldn't pinpoint. The books looked ancient and weathered. Bound in something like dried, decayed human flesh. The same energy radiated from them that Michael had felt when Happy Horse passed him earlier, carrying the Giggle Squad's storybook.

Michael stared down at the conspicuously empty, book-sized space on the desk between the two remaining books. They were a set together. A trio of occult tomes.

Cousin Jed had been right after all.

Behind Michael and James, doors slammed, and the walls seemed to reverberate with the sounds of somebody screaming. Whatever the pair were going to do, they had to do it fast. They were cornered in here. Only one door led into or out of the changing room, and their pursuers were drawing nearer.

"James, we have to hurry!"

James stepped up to the vile-looking books.

"We have to destroy them!"

"Do you think that'll. . . what? Stop the ritual?"

"There's only one way to find out!"

James raised his arms high above his head and brought them

down with thunderous force, slamming his fists down onto the cover.

But it was a book. So James' punching did nothing.

"You can't punch a book to death, James."

"Gah!"

"So, how do we kill a book?"

"I don't know!"

"Ban it! Like in Florida!"

"Huh? That doesn't make any sense."

"WHAT ARE YOU TWO DOING?" Jessie shouted from behind the pair of idiots. She came storming into the room, a screaming toddler wrangled beneath one arm, another one on her shoulders in a piggyback ride, and a third grasping her ankle, literally being dragged into the room as Jessie walked.

"Greg ate so many Gummy Worms in the car that he threw up, Amber is pitching a fit, and Tabitha's poop just exploded up her back. And when I turn to handle all of this, where are you two assholes? You're high and you're sneaking away from the mess."

"Yes! But there's demons," Michael tried to explain.

"I know! Now take a demon and get out of here," Jessie snapped, and she passed Tabitha to her dad.

Tabitha smiled at Michael and said, "Poop!" like she was so very proud of herself.

"And you take yours back too."

Jessie pried Amber from her leg and handed her to James.

"But we have to destroy the books," James half-protested as he accepted his daughter.

"Guys, cut it out. You're high and you're acting all paranoid."

"Am not!" James said.

"Well. . . we are. But this feels. . . real?" Michael couldn't claim it with any real certainty though.

"We aren't leaving until we figure out how to destroy the

books!" James cried, firmer, as he gripped his daughter tightly and scowled at the presumably cursed texts.

Jessie looked from the kids to the books on the desk and then back to her crazed husband and his absurd friend. She unscrewed the cap to her binoculars and poured what remained of her wine across both books, knocking them to the floor, then used her boot to grind, smash, and wreck the wet, pulpy pages.

"There! Are you happy?" Jessie asked sarcastically as she did a little bow and pulled Greg from her shoulders.

". . . No. . . ?" Michael guessed, unsure if he was supposed to be answering or not.

"Get to the car!"

Michael and James did as they were told. The kids were unhappy about having to leave so soon, but when Greg vomited for a second time on their way through the parking lot, it was solidified. . . or maybe liquidated. . . as the right call. Greg and Tabitha were stripped naked and buckled in; Michael had forgotten to bring a change of clothes for them. Jessie fired up the engine, spinning the van from the parking lot.

The sounds of the Giggle Squad chased them all the way back to the freeway, streaming, like always through their speakers. Jessie turned the songs up loud enough that the kids couldn't hear her scolding their dads for being such a pair of jackasses.

The Giggle Squad stood in their dressing room, all four gazing down at the ruined remains of their unholy texts. Happy Horse stood guard near the door.

Things had been going so well.

The crowd had been big enough.

The songs had been loud enough.

So many voices, drawn in by the hypnotic powers of the

Giggle Squad, all to be ruined at the thirty-minute mark when Famine had returned to the room and discovered the crime scene.

They had finished the performance for the revelers in the above, but down below, their master had pulled away from their ritual, dissatisfied.

What had happened? They had cast so many illusory spells. Shrouded their actions behind so many layers of dark magic. How had anybody managed to see through their charade?

The night was ruined, but the campaign could still be salvaged.

War was already on the phone, coordinating to have the *original* copies of the books flown down. They had another performance in Houston in three days. This was why they had made replicas. They wouldn't be stopped because of one setback. The Giggle Squad had a whole world tour scheduled. And one of these days, one of these shows, all the pieces would come together.

DOOM SCROLL

JAMES SABATA

"Do you ever feel like you just can't get enough caffeine to start your day? Have you ever considered upgrading your typical boring cup of Joe with something more thrilling? Now introducing. . . HYPERSPACE HUMMINGBIRD!"

"Hyperspace what?" a man turned toward the camera, asking. He wore purple snow goggles on his head, centered over his left ear. He crossed his arms, showing off his crop top sleeveless shirt.

"HYPERSPACE HUMMINGBIRD!" the voice repeated. "The first energy drink scientifically engineered to give you the stamina of an intergalactic star cruiser and the hyperactivity of a hummingbird ON AMPHETAMINES! One sip of this exhilarating elixir, and we instantly redesigned the pyramids, decoded the mysteries of quantum physics, and beat a cheetah in a footrace. . . all before breakfast!"

"But does it taste good?" a green space alien pondered.

"Good is for mundane monogamous mortals. This stuff tastes like a meteor shower in a blender. Bright! Fizzy! Unpredictable! And absolutely otherworldly!

"I don't know if that sounds safe," the man from before added.

This time it was a farther-away shot, allowing his cutoffs and high-tops to be seen.

"Safer than licking a cosmic power popsicle!" the voice boomed. "Although, we'd definitely advise against trying that. So just take our word for it. We test our product on only the finest and fiercest lab-grown extraterrestrial amoebas. Ditch your dull, old coffee routine. Leave that boring partner and grab something that'll get your molecules vibrating faster than lightning! It's not just an energy drink. It's HYPERSPACE HUMMINGBIRD! Your ticket to light speed productivity! Feel like the hero in your very own intergalactic adventure!"

Mason Quinn's voice cut in, "Use promo code MASON for free shipping on your first order."

A cork popped. Drinks poured.

"HYPERSPACE HUMMINGBIRD! We don't *DO* boring!"

A man mumbled, "Side effects may include temporary flight, levitation, and an overwhelming desire to outsmart Einstein. Do not consume while operating heavy machinery or performing delicate brain surgery. Alien amoebas were not harmed during testing. Now available at all reputable, and some not-so-reputable, interplanetary retail outlets."

"Yo, what's good, Masonites? Today's gonna be a good day, and I know that for a fact. Strap in, 'cause today, you ain't got no idea what's about to hit you! We were planning to hook you up with some savage talk on some shenanigans in the pro wrestling world, right? But man, this thing that's popped up. . . it's way crazier than that. Like, epic-proportions-type stuff. We've got the chance of a lifetime to dig into the unknown, bruh. And spoiler—it's gonna set up a road trip on an epic journey of adventure!

"Aight guys, before we dive in, it's vital that I hit you up with some past knowledge, otherwise this ain't gonna connect or hit you with the power punch of this crazy revelation.

First things first, it's about time you got schooled on what the Dead Sea Scrolls are. Nah, don't get it twisted, we ain't talking about some weird new snail species or something bizarre like that, bruh. Ain't got nothing to do with a zombie ocean. Ain't got nothing to do with scrolling on your iPhone. So, check this, these scrolls were found near the Dead Sea—that's where the name came from way back, bro, 1947. So, like most of a century ago. Ain't no prank. Ain't no social media stunt. Some shepherd dude stumbled across 'em in a cave. Yep, some real Indiana Jones shit.

"And bruh, these scrolls were old as shit when they found them. Almost two thousand years old, legit! And guess what? Most of them are like, scriptures from the Bible and papers full of mysteries and a whole bunch of stuff that can straight-up rewrite history. Historians were, like, trippin' when they found these 'cause they're so detailed and valuable. I guess most are currently housed in Israel, but pieces of them keep showing up elsewhere, bruh. What?

"So, check it out. This week, there's this guy, Jace Sullivan, right? Dude went ahead and slapped a picture of a Dead Sea Scroll onto Reddit. Something most people never seen before. And you're thinking, 'Yo, Mason, so what, bruh? Reddit's full of all sorts. Anyone can post there.' But here's the kicker, my man. The plot twist, if you will. Despite their kinda lame quality and the fact that they're not super clear, out of the blue, Dr. Oren Abelman, the leading expert on these scrolls, right? The guy who translated a bunch of them. This big brain pops in and goes, 'Hold up, this shit looks legit. Sullivan get in touch with me, bruh.'

"Now you're probably wondering, 'Mason, why do I care, dude? What's this got to do with anything?' Simple. The answer's easy. Today, or whenever it hits your feed, your boy here is going to link up with Jace Sullivan and chat him up myself. And if we've got luck on our side, we'll be the ones to peep at this mystery scroll and you'll be there with us. Buckle up, squad. Let's get it!"

"And... CUT!" Dylan Holmes smiled.

Dylan's brother Trevor turned off the cameras as Mason looked over at the producer. "Was that good enough, Dylan?"

"That was insanely good," Dylan said. Mason watched for a reaction that betrayed these words but found none. "Honestly, I don't think your followers give a fuck about the Dead Sea Scrolls or any of that shit, but I think you'll get some mainstream attention if you're the one that cracks him." He paused. "Well, I mean, you'll get mainstream attention just for going. But no one else can get a word outta the dude. My money's on you. Getting people to talk is like your superpower."

Trevor ignored the two of them as he reached into a cooler and pulled out a Hyperspace Hummingbird. When he realized they were looking at him, he smiled and held out an energy drink. "You want one?"

Mason shook his head. "Fuck no. I don't drink that shit, and you probably shouldn't either."

Dylan smiled. "That's actually good. If your heart explodes, we all lose our jobs."

Mason smiled as he stretched. "How long's the flight?"

Dylan looked at the floor and then back at Mason. "I don't know. Like six hours?"

Trevor threw his hands up. "Fuck. I'm bringing the whole damn cooler. I'm gonna be needing, like, a legit hundo of these bad boys."

Mason's private jet passed some random city, lighting the darkness forty thousand feet below them as Trevor leaned over to Dylan. "Why we even doing this? Looking for some old people writing?"

"Money!" Mason laughed, stretching the word out.

Dylan shrugged, barely looking at his brother. "Sounds right."

"Cars, mansions, and private jets don't just materialize out of nowhere, bruh," Mason added.

"People care about this enough to watch this shit?" His eyes went to the window where the city was already disappearing from view.

Dylan stared at Trevor. "How long have you worked here? You know Mason's fans would tune in if he talked about the texture of dog shit."

"Haha. Put that on the schedule. Let's do that." Pieces of popcorn fell to the floor as he laughed.

Trevor pointed to Mason. "This man wants adventure! To see things no one has ever seen before! He wants to go places people dream of going and tell them about it 'cause they ain't ever going. He wants the selfie."

Mason shook his head. "Yo, you had it on point the first go-round. Let's score those clicks and shares and rack up more sponsors and stack that cash!"

Trevor high-fived him and then sat back down. "Okay, so we're all on the same page. But so, you get this Red Sea skull, and then what?"

Trevor's whole body twitched as Dylan's hand slapped him on the head. Dylan paused, emphasizing each word as he said, "It's a Dead Sea Scroll you fuck."

"Like the fucking shapeshifter lizard people on Avengers?"

Mason adjusted in his seat. "Christ, your brother is dumb AF, bruh. For real, you sure you're blood? Your mom wasn't having a little extra fun with the pool boy or some shit?"

Trevor's middle finger shot up, but Dylan ignored them both. "We only got about ten minutes till we start descending. So, let's concentrate for a minute." Dylan pulled his phone out and scrolled through his notes. "I read the rest of the comments from Dr. Oren Abelman on that Reddit page. From what he can make out in the pic, he's convinced the scroll is called 'Celestial Struggle: Seraph and Shedim.'"

"The fucking what?" Trevor said, but no one paid any attention to him.

Dylan continued, "Abelman is in Michigan right now, so if all else fails, we can go there, but my contacts say this Jace Sullivan guy is still at the church, so that's where we start. We can go tonight. We can go tomorrow. Whatever. Doesn't seem like he's going anywhere."

"Wow, still there, huh? Aight, tonight's perfect. Let's roll and figure out where that scroll at."

Trevor yawned. "Tonight? Fuck. Throw me one of those Hummingbirds."

Mason stared at him. "Those aren't for you. See?" He picked one out of the cooler and pointed to the words, *We don't DO boring.* "I'm just playing, bruh. I need you awake tonight. Hit this." Mason tossed him a Hummingbird.

"Yo, yo, yo, it's nine in the evening, and your boy Mason Quinn's posted up here in Norfolk, VA. I'm hearing that this guy, Jace Sullivan, has locked himself up in this church for a wild four-day stretch, praying nonstop. No breaks. Not even to hit the bathroom. I seriously don't know if my man's had anything to eat. Hasn't opened his mouth to anyone, priests or staff included. Nothing but prayer coming outta this dude. But just watch, I'm gonna switch up that routine. You better believe Jace Sullivan's gonna do more than pray. I'm not leaving till he hands over that scroll, bro."

Mason stood and ran up the steps of the Basilica. "Let's fucking go!" He threw open the oversized red doors as Trevor followed him with the camera.

Ahead, in the third pew from the altar, a man knelt, simultaneously shrouded in shadows and oddly illuminated.

Mason sauntered up the aisle, slightly distracted by the architectural beauty around him. Lavishly decorated pillars stretched toward the vaulted ceiling. Murals and stained glass threw bright, rich colors at the floor. *Might be time to redo the crib. Get a big window like that with me diving off the top rope onto a can of Hummingbird.* He smiled, telling himself to remember that to use on the show sometime.

Mason approached the man and watched him for a second. He turned and raised both eyebrows to Trevor and Dylan. Mason looked directly into Trevor's camera and put his hands together to mock-pray along with Jace Sullivan. The trio tried not to laugh as they neared the man.

Sullivan looked up at Mason momentarily. He bore an almost unholy twinkle in his gaze, resonating wicked delight. It sparkled within the ice-cold indigo irises that stared unblinking at the altar before him.

Damn. I need to get that look down when I'm cutting promos on people. Mason put his hands in his jacket pockets, one playing with the Hyperspace Hummingbird he had stashed in there. The popular vlogger leaned in, "Mr. Sullivan? Would you mind if we speak for a moment?"

No response came. Sullivan neither looked in Mason's direction nor stopped praying, his lips forming whispers of words and letting them disappear into the thick air around him.

Mason rolled his shoulders, winked at the camera, and said, "Yo, Mr. Sullivan, super stoked to meet you, bro. I was hoping we could rap a bit about the scroll. The Celestial Struggled between Sara... Phan... cellophane? Seraph—"

The man's hands unclasped and one smacked Mason's chest with lightning precision. Mason stumbled back one step. Sullivan's hands were back together as though they had not moved.

Mason sighed. "Yo, dude, don't even think about laying another hand on me. That's not the game we're in right now, alright?" Mason opened his phone and scrolled through his pictures. "Moving on... this is the picture you loaded to Reddit."

Sullivan's head slowly turned until his blue eyes were locked on the screen. The quiet ambiance of the church was abruptly shattered as the man let loose a scream of sheer terror. His voice rang out sharply, echoing within the grand cathedral like a gunshot. Birds perched in the rafters burst into chaotic flight. A tinge of panic and genuine fear caused a chill to settle in the air.

Fueled by terrifying adrenaline, Jace Sullivan struck out, his knuckles connecting with Mason's flesh. The telltale sharp crack of Mason's phone against the stone floor was drowned out by Trevor and Dylan yelling in unison. The screams bounced off the stone walls in waves of desperate, unadulterated fright.

Mason grabbed the phone and shoved it into Sullivan's face, his forearm holding the other man's head in place. "I warned you, mother fucker. Now you look at this and you tell me what the fuck I want to know."

Dylan leaned toward Trevor. "Maybe edit that out?"

Jace Sullivan stared into the picture in front of him. A dark room with enough light to see the undecorated stone walls and modest podium on which the Seraph and Shedim Scroll was centered. The rest of the room appeared empty, but it was that emptiness—not the scroll—that held Sullivan's gaze. Tears filled his eyes but did not fall. His mouth fluttered faster than ever with prayer.

Mason released his grip. "I just want to know where it is. Can you tell me that? And stop hitting me."

Sullivan's head nodded, but his mouth never stopped praying. His right hand moved to his pocket.

"Careful, Mason!" Dylan said, but they watched as Sullivan removed a six-inch antique skeleton key.

The iron shank was worn. The two teeth had tiny pocks and slight discoloration from use. The rounded head had some sort of ornate engraving pattern that Mason couldn't make out. Jace held the key in front of his face, his mouth still moving with prayer.

He suddenly stopped and the world held still.

Sullivan turned slowly to Mason and uttered only, "Matthew 18:9."

"What? Bruh, I don't know the—"

Without as much as a flinch, Jace Sullivan drove the key into the soft part of the eyelid crease at the top of his right eye. Laughter bubbled within his chest, clawing its way up his throat and out into the atmosphere around him. Amidst maniacal chuckles, Sullivan pushed the key further into his eye. The clear, colorless membrane turned red as it mixed with blood. Sullivan twisted the key to the right, mutilating himself. His pupil rent, splitting from the top to the bottom as the key ripped downward. A scarlet flood cascaded over his angular face, riddling it with channels of blood.

Undeterred by the wrenching pain, Jace brandished his blood-soaked key and brought it to the untouched eye. He prayed with an intensifying fervor, lips forming and unforming words. He locked his remaining eye on the statue of the crucifix as his fingers found the cross hanging around his own neck. His fist tightened around the cross as he pushed the key in and opened another doorway in his skull.

The man knelt back down, both frightening and pitiful, drenched in blood, sweat, and pain. His chest convulsed as if it could no longer hold the torment inside of him. The echo of his key clattering to the marble flooring was the only sound as the three men recording him held in their screams.

"What the *fuck* was that?" Trevor exclaimed finally. There had been no words even though the three of them were alone outside the church.

"Money, bruh! That was MONEY! Let's get it edited and get it up *now*."

Dylan stood silently, holding on to the side of the church. He shook his head. "You can't post that."

Mason sneered. "I can't *not* post that!"

"A guy just ripped his own eyes out, Mason."

"That's what I'm saying, bruh!"

"Think of the backlash."

Mason feigned crying. "Think of the shares on the apology video." Mason turned from Dylan to Trevor. "You got all that, right? You got that?"

Trevor's hand shook and it wasn't just all the Hummingbirds he'd slammed. "I mean, yeah, but I can't. . ."

Mason placed one hand on each of Trevor's shoulders and looked him in the eye. "Yes. You can. Yes. We will."

Dylan threw his hands up. "It's too far."

"Yes. We came too far for this. This will be huge."

Dylan's body leaned forward. Mason braced himself for splatter if Dylan puked, but that's not what came out. "Mason, we gotta go get the scroll instead. Those are the streams we need. And they'd let us keep our sponsors."

Mason pointed at the church. "Well, old boy in there ain't talking. Now what?"

Dylan nodded his head. "Hang on. Hang on. Trevor found something. I think we do this."

Mason stared at them each, his mouth hanging open, his eyes barely doing the same. "And if this doesn't work, we load that."

"Okay. Fair enough." Dylan turned to Trevor. "Show him."

Trevor pulled out his phone and started to scroll. When he found the picture of the pretty blonde girl with no makeup, he turned his screen so Mason could see it.

"Not really my type, bruh." Mason smirked.

"This is Jace's girlfriend. The Amish girl who broke his heart."

"How's that help us? I'm severely doubting she has a Snapchat we can hit her up at. And if she does, he won't see it."

"Jace checked in at her colony when he followed her home. If he can't tell us where the scroll is, maybe she can."

Mason reached into his jacket pocket and pulled out the Hyperspace Hummingbird. He handed it to Trevor. "God damn, kid. You did good. You win one of these."

"Yo, Masonites! Check it out. We had a bit of a plot twist meeting up with Jace Sullivan, right? We probably don't need to replay that insanity, but don't you freak! My main man, Trevor, stepped up, got the scoop, and thinks he's tracked down Elizabeth Graber. You know, that Amish chick who straight up crushed Sullivan's heart and bailed on him for full-body cover-ups and church services? Well, next stop, we're heading into her world. Tomorrow morning, we're going right into that Amish community she dipped back to post-Rumspringa.

"Quick rewind for anyone not in the know—Rumspringa is this kinda Amish rite of passage when teens get a chance to experience the bright lights and chaos of everyday life in America. They get a taste and then have to choose: keep the buzz of our world or cruise back to the peace and simplicity. Baffles me every time, but lots choose the latter, Elizabeth included.

"Will we bump into her when we get there? No spoilers, guys! All in good time. And no need to stress about them spotting us early—ain't like they're following me on Snapchat or nothing, right? Onwards!"

The SUV traveled to the southern end of the Highland country, the lower edge of the Maple Syrup trail, somewhere in the middle of Virginia. Mason watched picturesque forests cut across his view of the Appalachians. Sugar bushes populated the area and the occasional roadside stand offered vegetables at such low prices Mason was tempted to pack the plane for the ride home.

Trevor popped the top on another Hyperspace Hummingbird.

Mason sighed. "Dude. Stop drinking those. You don't even know what's in them."

Trevor turned the can. "Looks like filtered water, coconut water from concentrate, citric acid, dipotassium phosphate—"

"I don't mean the list on the can. I mean, you don't know what's *actually* in them."

"We're almost there. It should be just ahead," Dylan said.

"I'm surprised the place even shows up on GPS," Mason grumbled.

They parked on the edge of the community and walked toward the small store. Mason recorded everything as he walked. The area was evocatively simple, contrasting vastly from his usual constantly-on-the-go lifestyle of tech, flashy gimmicks, and product placement. This world was pristine, unequivocally traditional, like something out of a movie his grandpa would have watched. The bare, dirt roads unfurled between fields of verdant pastures. Homes constructed with raw timber and brick chimneys whispered of hearthside family gatherings. A few women came out of a large barn near the center of the back of town. The women had a soothing gentleness about them that exuded calm and serenity, each dressed in solid-colored dresses and aprons, head coverings bouncing lightly with each step.

A symphony of clucks, whinnies, and lowing cattle reverberated through the fresh air. Carts laden with produce lent the ambiance a colorful texture, contrasting with the unpainted exteriors of the homes. Mason wanted to livestream right then while the sun perfectly lit the area, but he knew the large man lumbering toward him was going to tell him not to. And, while Mason wanted the hits, he didn't want to publicize their location until he was sure he'd recovered the scroll.

The man adjusted his wide-brimmed hat before running a hand over each strap of his suspenders. "Welcome." The man spoke kindly enough but could not take his eyes off of Mason's disheveled hair and his purple and yellow sneakers. The man smiled, pointing down. "Keep an eye out for horse apples in the road."

"Yeah. Sure. . ."

The man looked at the three of them. "Look about all you wish, soak it all in. Drop by the store and snag some eats if your belly's growling. Don't fuss none if you fancy takin' some photos of yourselves, but do your best to keep me and my neighbors out of 'em, please."

Mason turned to the others and said, "Turn your phones off. It's just easier."

Trevor wanted to argue but did as he was told. As the man walked away, Mason leaned in. "Don't worry. We'll get the goods tonight. There's nothing here worth showcasing right now."

"God damn, they work hard," Trevor muttered.

Dylan nodded. "Way too hard. Why do that to yourself when you could be happy in a hot tub playing Rocket League or jump on the jet to get some Chicago Pizza?" He smiled at the others.

Mason stared at him. "You mean my jet?" Mason resumed

scanning the area for where he thought the scroll might be kept. There was no clear-cut church like he'd expected. He'd been picturing a tall steeple with an old graveyard on the side of it. "You sure it's here?"

Trevor pointed to a nearby building with a hand-painted "Market" sign. "Has to be. That's where Sullivan checked in."

As Mason entered the Amish market, it felt like he'd taken yet another step back in time. A potbellied stove stood in the middle of the small store. In the winter, it would have many people gathered around it, sharing stories and staying warm. The quality of each item astonished Mason, as did the relatively low numbers handwritten on the price labels. A courteous man in a black hat and grey shirt welcomed them and asked if it was their first time in an Amish market. When the boys confirmed, the man proceeded to tell them about everything from quilts to canned goods to handcrafted furniture.

"Yo, get his business card. We gotta order some of this for the crib." Trevor scanned the high-quality, hand-crafted rockers, bookcases, tables, desks, and even bedroom sets. Most pieces featured minimalist designs with natural finishes. "I want it all." Trevor looked the man in the eye. "Y'all take credit cards?"

The boys walked out with maple syrup, trinkets, jams, candy, and pies. "Let's take it back to the car and then we can look around a bit more," Mason said.

Just then, a young woman approached them. She wore her sun-kissed blonde hair in a practical bun hidden underneath a stark, unadorned white Kapp.

Elizabeth Graber looked different than she had in the Facebook post that Jace Sullivan made, but it was her just the same. Before Mason could say anything, Elizabeth glanced around and said, "I know who you are. They don't. You need to leave. Today. Let this go."

The three climbed into the SUV, chowing down on some of the food they'd bought. Between bites, Mason said, "No, I get it, but it's not worth getting into it with her, bruh. We're coming back tonight either way, so why waste the energy?"

Dylan made eye contact with Mason through the rearview. "So, what's the plan?"

"Drive up maybe a mile and hoof it back after dark. Anyone know what time they go to bed? It's gotta be early, right?"

"I'd say if we're back at eleven, they'll be out." Dylan shrugged.

"Eleven?" Trevor repeated. "Shit, I'm gonna need to drink like eight more Hummingbirds."

"Such a fucking pansy," Mason mumbled. "Let's shoot for ten so your idiot brother can stay awake." As they started to pull out, Mason caught Elizabeth watching them from a distance. She was near the biggest barn on the property. "Why do you think that barn is so much bigger?"

"That's not a barn," Dylan said. The words were muffled over the slice of Friendship Bread he chewed. "That's the church. You know, some communities don't have one. They just go house to house each—"

Mason dramatically shook his head. "I'm very proud you learned so much for this. Great work. But holy fucking shit. The church? I was looking for the church. That's the only place it would be, man! That's where we're going tonight." He pulled out his phone and hit record.

"So, we're pretending to duck out, but I ain't stepping off. We've got the scoop, no doubt. Bet it's hiding out in the church.

And yo, shit's about to get real!" He took a bite of his second sugar cookie. "Oh man, their cookies are absolute fire! If you ever find yourself around these parts, make sure to grab a bite. Ain't nobody sponsoring this shout out! They're that damn good. Catch you in a bit. I'm about to grab that scroll. And y'all are in it for the ride!"

The soft glow of the moon provided just enough light for the three men as they quietly crept along the outskirts of the Amish settlement.

It was only now that Mason realized they should've brought darker clothes to blend in more.

"What do we do if we see a guard?" Trevor asked.

Mason glared as he surveyed his friend. "You think the Amish have guards? What, like some fucking dude in a tower ready to shoot you in the back with a bow and arrow? They're all asleep."

Trevor yawned. "Don't say sleep."

"This shit again?"

Dylan waved them toward the former barn that now served as a church. As they reached it, Mason added, "Yo, I'll tell you what we do if we run into anybody. Just pull up some Pornhub and crank the volume. They won't know what hit 'em. They'll just run."

Dylan smiled. "Trevor's probably got eighteen tabs open already. So, he'll be in charge of that."

"Very funny, assholes," Trevor muttered. His frazzled hair reflected his exhaustion, eyes struggling to stay open. "We picking this door or what?"

Mason reached forward and turned the knob. The doors groaned under the strain of opening. "Like they lock shit around here."

Once inside, the trio turned on their phones' flashlights. The room was a study in the sparse arrangement of only what was needed. Hardwood planks stretched underfoot, creaking lightly in spots worn by countless generations. Solid oak benches served as pews, void of decorations or padding, the grain darkened by age. It was nothing like any church the group had seen and the direct opposite of the cathedral they'd been to the day before. There was no stained glass, but the large windows allowed enough moonlight in for the simple lectern to be seen.

"Videos on. We're not messing this up." Each of the three began recording, Mason and Dylan on their phones, Trevor on his usual camera.

Mason ran up to it, expecting to find the scroll just laid out waiting for him. Of course, it was not. The Bible was on display instead, open to 2 Corinthians 4. Mason ignored it and kept looking for the scroll. Dylan began videoing and waved to him.

Mason quietly said, "Yo, we're posted up in this wild Amish church. Or maybe the opposite of wild. We're on a mission to hunt down that scroll. You already know it's gotta be stashed in here somewhere, but ya boy's striking out right now. No sightings yet." Trevor yawned again. "Hey, cut that yawning Trev. Perk up. I'll hook you up with. . ." Mason pulled an energy drink from his sweatshirt pocket. "My last Hummingbird!" He turned it toward the camera, making sure the logo was visible. "It's our official drink because Hyperspace Hummingbird don't *DO* boring!"

Mason cut his feed and handed the drink to Trevor. "Wake the fuck up."

As Trevor cracked the Hummingbird open, Dylan shined his flashlight near the back corner of the room, "Stairs!"

Dylan kept one hand on the stone wall as the group went down the stairs. Musty, earthy aromas rode the dusty air as particles danced in the light cast by their phones. The trio found themselves in a large underground area, but the heavy darkness betrayed where the boundaries of the room were.

Mason's eyes locked on the scroll not ten feet in front of him. Vindication swept over him. He laid a fist over his heart and threw back his head. "You feel that boys? Victory is here!"

They set up around him, trying to get good shots, but the darkness in the room seemed to swallow any light they shone. Nothing lit the way Trevor knew it should.

Mason was busy running his hands over The Celestial Struggle: Seraph and Shedim, tracing the columns of ancient text with his fingers.

"Trying to figure out what it means?" Dylan said.

"Money." Mason smiled. "It means money. Clicks. Shares. Sponsors. Cash." He pushed too hard on one side of the hand-carved mahogany podium, almost knocking it over. "Shit. I'm shaking like I had fifty Hummingbirds like this motherfucker." He shook it off and posed in front of the scroll. "Livestream almost ready?"

"No bars," Dylan said.

Mason checked his own phone. Same issue. "All ready? Everybody film it so we make sure we got it. We'll piece it together and get it online tomorrow morning."

Dylan gave him the signal and Mason's persona came to life. "Check this out! We got the scroll! Legit, dudes! Straight outta the Dead Sea! This piece might just pre-date Jesus himself. Who knows? I'm lost when it comes to decoding it, but maybe one of you savages out there can do it and give us a breakdown. Let me get in closer."

Mason focused the camera on the parchment, but it wasn't coming up well in the minuscule light. "Guys, throw some light over here."

Trevor walked closer, training his phone's flashlight directly on the scroll. He watched the phone's display as he sipped a

Hummingbird with his free hand. Although the scroll shone brighter, the light still didn't seem to illuminate anything past it, as the area ahead of him stayed dark.

And then he saw something. Mere feet from the base of the podium, laid out in brilliant white salt, was an intricate array of swirling symbols and lines, multiple circles overlapping one another, creating a complex cosmogram.

Trevor's jaw clenched. His heartbeat thrashed in his ears. The more he raised his phone, the more clearly the outline of a gigantic spectral figure came into focus.

It moved. Trevor screamed.

The others looked just in time to see the Hyperspace Hummingbird fall from Trevor's hand and hit the floor. Liquid poured from the can in the darkness.

"Shit!"

"Yo, what the fuck?"

Dylan and Mason each stared in disbelief at the creature. Mason yelled, "Someone better be fucking filming this."

The monstrosity shifted, pulsing. Crackles of staticky white lightning popped as two massive wings unfurled from its midsection. They stretched outward as far as they could in the confines of the trap before curling back in.

The liquid collided with the salt; the powder absorbed it almost instantly. The carbonation caused a bubbling reaction as the powder clumped in a semi-solid state, breaking the outer circle.

Trevor pointed at the masses of salt and yelled, "That's not normal. What the hell is in there?"

"I told you not to drink them."

Trevor growled. "You're the one pushing them all the time."

"Yeah, but not to you. You're my friend."

"Can we please focus?" Dylan yelled. He took a step forward just as the creature stretched upward.

Eyes, incandescent and too many to count, surveyed the room the creature found itself in. Each pupil dilated with timeless knowledge. Wings unfolded from around the being's legs. Then from its face. Hundreds of luminous tendrils sprouted from its back. All six wings stretched up and outward as the energy drink began to eat at the inner salt circle.

Finally free, the Seraphim stood in all its glory, pausing before the trio for only the briefest of moments. Mason took two steps back, trying to get a better shot on his phone, only to realize the creature wasn't showing up on the display. "Oh, what the fuck?"

As Mason looked up, wings as sharp as diamond edges whipped forth in a lethal flourish. The bodies of his supposed friends thumped lifelessly to the floor; a fleeting spray of blood landed shortly after.

Mason stumbled back. His eyes watered as a primal scream lodged itself into his throat. He turned to go up the stairs but found himself face to face with Benuel Eberson, the bishop of the church. Mason did not know how, but he suddenly knew the man's name and position when they'd never spoken.

"What did ya do?"

Mason grabbed the man's suspenders, pleading, staring into the man's soul. "I'll pay you anything you want. Just get me the fuck out of here."

Benuel stared past Mason, his eyes locked on the divine being rising to its full height. The creature's lowest set of wings dragged across the floor, pushing the salt around and erasing the remnants of the magic circle that had once confined it. All six wings flapped at once, sending small electrical currents coursing through the dense, dust-filled air. The Seraphim pushed against the ceiling as the basement had grown too small to contain it.

Mason looked to Benuel Eberson, screaming, "Is that. . . is that a fucking demon?"

"Demon? Angel? One or t'other. Seraph or Shedim. It dunna

matter. If one exists, t'other exists. God exists. Lookin' upon it, ya know the truth."

Knowledge flooded Mason's mind. He suddenly understood things he'd never considered.

"That's how you baptize your community? That's how you get them to stay? You show them the truth?"

"When you've seen with your own eyes, it's near 'bout impossible to deny He's real."

"It killed my friends."

"It'll do fer all of us. The hour's upon us." Benuel retreated up the stairs.

Mason looked back at the monster. "What hour?"

An explosion of pure light illuminated every crevice, crack, and burrow. A wave of sudden self-awareness rolled through Mason as more knowledge drove itself into his brain. Every imperfection he had, every vulnerability, glowed in his mind as his ignorance turned into understanding, shame, and guilt.

The ceiling ripped with the creature's surge and shattered into a billion wooden splinters as it escaped, leaving Mason alone with the pain of his thoughts.

Mason reached the top of the stairs and ran out of the church just in time to see it happen. He'd dropped his phone along the way, but that no longer mattered to him.

A split second of vacuum-like silence preceded an ear-shattering blast, rupturing the calm and ripping apart the solid beams of the barn. The members of the community emerged from their homes, gathering on the rubble-strewn field of splinters and shards, lost in bewildered gasps and muted exclamations. They congregated in their night garments, unable to pull their gaze from the blazing body above.

The end came very quickly for most. The being lowered to the ground, leveling itself with the community, before spreading its great wings and slicing at the people directly in front of it. The devastating gale bore not death but a curious grace. One by one, each villager answered a silent call, drawn toward the radiant being as though lured by invisible threads. There was no pandemonium, no fear, only piety and acceptance as the angel touched every true believer. They departed this realm in soft tendrils of golden light; men, women, and children lifted from their positions in neat rows, like sheaves of grain harvested by an unseen scythe.

Elizabeth Graber stood next to Mason, but neither looked at the other as the angel took its place before them. Beneath Elizabeth's capped bonnet, strands of golden hair wrestled in the cool breeze as she continued to stare upon the heavenly apparition. Her cheeks burned rosy with anticipation and uncertainty as she clutched at the front of her homemade frock.

The Seraphim's multitude of luminescent eyes locked onto hers, radiating an omnipotent comprehension. Its lower wings folded delicately, obscuring its lower half. Another pair covered its face. Unyielding sadness surged through Elizabeth's veins as tears spilled over her smooth cheeks, not out of the devastation of being left behind, but out of the sheer overwhelming feeling of having borne witness to heavenly grace. Finally, the Seraphim unfolded its wings to reveal its towering majesty once more, and with one powerful stroke, it shot into the sky.

She turned to Mason and only said, "It was my pride what done it."

But he understood.

He saw everything now. How she'd put her own desires above the church, even when she'd seen the truth. Jace Sullivan had followed, begging her to leave with him. She begged for him to stay. When he couldn't, Elizabeth violated the church and took

Jace to the basement. She forced the truth upon him with no regard for the consequences, hoping it would make him stay. He'd used his phone to take pictures of the creature, inadvertently photographing the scroll instead. And then he ran and ran and never looked back for her.

She'd given up everything for him.

"I can only spend my life trying to repent. I'll never be forgiven, but it's all I can do."

Elizabeth pushed past Mason, leaving him out there alone as she entered the piece of the barn that still stood. She sat on a bench and began to pray. Mason could see it. He knew she'd never be forgiven.

Worse, he could see that whatever minuscule chance Elizabeth Graber had at redemption was exponentially more than he'd ever have. Nothing could save him. Not the private jet. Not the mansion. All the likes, shares, and comments in the world were meaningless, as was everything in his bank account. He surveyed the empty settlement and what was left of the people who had nothing and still couldn't take what they had with them. What hope was there for Mason Quinn?

What he wanted more than anything was the feeling that disappeared right as the angel did, the absence of which was absolute Hell. He needed it back. That feeling was the only thing that mattered. And even though he now saw that he would never get it back, he would try.

He was *Mason Fucking Quinn*. He could do anything if he tried hard enough.

Mason slid onto the makeshift pew next to Elizabeth and began to pray.

MOIRA

JAMIE FLANAGAN

I'm eight years old when my mother asks for the book.

My grandmother pulls the diary from a dusty shelf in the kitchen as my other grandmothers exchange a glance across their weaving. It does not seem odd to me that I have three grandmothers. Nor odd that the kitchen should be used to house so many books. The cottage is filled with them. Stack upon stack, shelf upon shelf.

My grandmother hands the diary to my mother, boasting of her handiwork as she stirs a pot of stew. "Coptic binding, hand stitched with mare's mane."

"Horven ink," says my other grandmother. "On parchment from Slieve Gullion wood."

"Bound in vellum from Milo's calf," says the third. "He grumbled about it, Milo, but came 'round in the end."

"Carried it here himself when he learned it was for our Moira."

"For old time's sake."

"What's old time?" I ask.

"Like now, but heavier," one answers.

"And a bit blurry," adds another, tying off a stitch.

My grandmothers have names, of course. Clio, Lochley, and Attie. Though I've never been able to tell them apart.

"I'd like Moira to have it," says my mother.

A silence hangs over the cottage like a cloud threatening to rain.

"For what purpose?"

"Moira," begins my mother, stifling a cough, "is afraid of the world."

Three pairs of rheumy eyes turn to me. My chest tightens as my throat closes, and my cheeks begin to burn. Without a word, I can guess their answer.

Dinner comes and goes. Then it's goodbye kisses and tight embraces. "Tell that man of yours we said hello," Gran tells my mother. My father never visits the cottage. It's not—I'm told—a place he belongs.

That night at home, as my mother tucks me in, she gives me a conspiratorial grin, then reaches into her bag and retrieves the diary.

"An early birthday gift," she says. "Just don't tell your grandmothers."

I take the book. It's thick and heavy, and its vellum is smooth and reassuring beneath my touch.

"When I was your age, I had a diary just like this one. Your grandmothers gave it to me. I read a little each day, and it made me feel safe, so long as I followed the rules."

"What rules?"

"Each day, you can read one entry. But only the entry for that same day. Don't bother with what happened yesterday or the day before. Life moves forward, and that's how it's meant to be read.

But—and this is very important—never skip ahead to tomorrow. Or after. Promise?"

"Promise."

"Good. Keep it close. Don't sell, lose, or give it away. There is one book for you in all the world, and no one—not even your grandmothers—can replace it."

She casts a serious gaze. I try my best to appear wise, responsible, and like someone who would never give, sell, or otherwise lose a book.

Once my mother's footsteps have receded down the hall, I huddle beneath the sheets, reading today's entry by flashlight. The diary makes no mention of monsters in closets or ghouls beneath beds. I lie down to sleep, and for the first time, I'm not afraid of the dark.

Sunlight spills through my bedroom window, warm against my cheek. It's the day before my ninth birthday. I can smell angel food cake baking and hear my father whistling from downstairs. In the afternoon, my mother and I fingerpaint flowers on my bedroom wall. She lets me paint a sunflower on her cheek, laughs, and—hands still wet with colors—holds me.

Before bed, I open the diary, longing to be reassured, and because I'm exactly the girl my grandmothers know me to be, break my promise and read about what presents I'll receive tomorrow.

Pages flutter beneath my touch

It's suddenly morning. I'm already dressed. I put down the book and head downstairs. My father greets me with a harried smile as he cleans up the remnants of what appears to have been a party.

"There she is," he says. "How about a little leftover cake for breakfast?"

I go to the fridge, and sure enough, there's my angel food cake, mostly eaten, with holes atop where candles should be. I'm confused. Then, memories surface. Details I somehow know. My friends arriving, the cake with lit candles, what songs we sang, and what presents I received. But they all feel like stories from the television. Like things I've seen that never happened to me at all. . .

That night, I visit my grandmothers. They lounge in their sitting room, playing a game that reminds me of Yahtzee but with a set of small bones instead of dice.

"Grans, I'm. . ."

"Confused," one finishes my sentence.

"Wants to know rules for a book she shouldn't have," says another, casting her handful of bones against the coffee table.

A pang of shame colors my cheeks.

"It's simple," says Gran.

"If a tad convoluted," adds the next. "For any 'today,' you can read all you like and still have those things to look forward to."

"If you read tomorrow or any further ahead, you'll find your-self wherever you leave off."

"Why?" I ask.

"Time's a fickle relative. Shy about the future, insufferably blunt about the present, and a disaster at record keeping. Tomorrow isn't meant for most eyes. You're half-kin, so you can have a few hours preview. Any more than that, you'll skip ahead with the pages."

They continue their game as though they've forgotten me entirely.

"Are you angry with me? Should I give it back?" I ask.

"No, dear. You were always going to have it, though we'd have never chosen to give it to you."

"Oh. Well then," I say, chuffed. "I should probably get home then. Thanks, Grans."

"You're welcome, poppet."

Then, as I turn to leave—

"Moira. . ."

I turn to face them. Three pairs of eyes, uncharacteristically sad, stare back.

"Enjoy tomorrow."

"Savor it," one tells me, handing me the bones.

"Know that you are loved."

"Before beginnings."

"Beyond ends."

Then, in unison, "Always. . ."

I limp my way through the playground at recess. It's been a few days since I visited my grans, and I've taken their advice to heart. I set my bag down—the book safely inside—as I take a seat on a seesaw. That's when the boy shows up.

"Can I play?" he asks.

I stand, holding the opposite seat at waist height. He accepts the invitation and joins me. Up and down we go. Back and forth. Slow and creaking, and after a very long time, he speaks.

"Why do you limp during recess but never during class?"

"What do you mean?"

"All week, you've limped during recess but never during class."

"Time," I answer.

"What about it?"

"My grans say Time's my relative or something. If I'm happy, it'll be happy and run fast. If I'm sad, it'll be sad too, and move much slower because it feels bad for me."

The seesaw creaks to a stop. His brow wrinkles in confusion.

"So why do you limp during recess but never during class?"

I step off the seesaw, careful not to let him plummet. I sit in the grass then remove one of my shoes.

"A trick my grans taught me. Hold out your hand," I tell him.

Tiny bones fall from my shoe to his palm. He sifts through them—a question perched on his lips—as I cradle my legs to my chest and rest my chin on my knees.

"I use them when I don't want something to end. Or when I'm enjoying something I wish would last longer."

"Do they hurt?"

"Yes."

"Then why do you wear them?"

"Because pain makes a moment seem longer."

"You're weird," he says, then drops the bones to the ground before rushing away.

A shrill whistle announces the end of recess. Other children rush past me in a blur. I finish tying my shoe then gather the bones.

That's when I realize my bag is gone, and—for a panicked moment which rivals eternity—my book, along with it. . .

During social studies, I sit stone still despite my dread while blindly circling answers on a multiple-choice quiz. I pass a note to the boy who'd shared the seesaw with me, asking if he has my bag. With a wince of distaste, he nudges it off his desk without reading.

Our social studies teacher, a severe woman with split bifocals, stops at my desk. "Class," she says, yanking the page from beneath the tip of my pencil. "Is this how we fold our paper?"

"No," a chorus of voices reply.

"How do we fold it. . . ?"

The class mumbles something else, but I can't hear it through the ringing in my ears as the muscles of my neck and face tense up. The last bulwark against a sob.

"Correct," she says, then stares down at me. "Down the center. Like a book." With that, she drops the piece of paper on my desk, and for a moment, the world is searing white. Then I'm in motion, on my feet, fleeing the classroom, searching for a safe place to cry.

When I arrive home from school, I hurry to my mother, then fall into her arms, as—

Pages flutter

In the dark, I stare across my bedroom at the novelty clock on the wall—the black cat with shifting eyes. My brow knots in confusion as the unlived memories of the last day and a half assert themselves. I remember crying. Remember my mother on the phone with other parents, trying to track down my diary, without luck. I somehow keep myself from panicking. I need to find whoever has the book and stop them from reading further than they already have.

I slip out of bed and run toward my parents' room. Ease the door open. Hesitantly call out for my mother.

She sits up in bed as my father turns on a lamp.

"Moira?"

I tell her that—

Pages flutter

Wearing a different set of pajamas, I stand at their bedroom door as a yesterday that never happened forces its way into my head. I sob, hands to my forehead, as I open the door.

"Bad dreams again, honey?" My mother asks through a coughing fit.

Pages flutter

I stand at the threshold of my parents' room. New pajamas. New night. I fall to one knee as an entire week rips through me. My mother sits up. Doubles over in a coughing fit. My father rushes to my side.

"It's okay, Moira, your mother's just feeling a little—"

Pages flutter

I open the door to their bedroom, where my mother—frail and thin, wearing a knit cap—sits on the edge of the bed, clutching a wastebasket. A missed month robs me of my ability to speak. To stand. My head cracks against the floorboards that break my fall.

Pages flutter

My father is asleep in bed. There's no sign of my mother. Before I can make sense of what I see—

Pages flutter

I'm sitting on the carpet of our living room on a sunny day as a cartoon plays on the television. My lips part, eyes hood over, as months of lost time etch themselves into me. Each thought like a sculptor striking stone.

On the mantle is an urn. Then I remember when my relatives gathered in their dark suits and dresses. How I was led by the hand toward a wooden box that both did and did not contain my mother and—in the living room—I am screaming.

My father, prone on the couch with his eyes closed and fingers resting gently against a liquor bottle, doesn't so much as twitch.

Pages flutter

My father leads me into an office of brown walls and leather couches. I wade through the quiet hum of central air conditioning and the smell of lemon-scented polish. It's a doctor for people who are soul-sick, I remember him telling me. I am ten years old, and I am screaming.

Pages flutter

Wearing a thin gown, I seem to float through a hallway lit by halogens. Paneled ceiling above. Checkered floor below. And many, many doors. Then I remember intake. My father's tears. Bimonthly visits. I'm twelve years old, and I'm still screaming.

Pages flutter

I stare up at the ceiling of my moonlit bedroom in Shady Pines Facility, quiet as a mouse. I'm awake. Can't move. Blame it on my meds. Or another one of my fits. I have a few different kinds. Manic. Depressive. Dissociative. This one, they'll call sleep paralysis. But it's the diary, inscribing the last three years into me. My arms itch from past cuts I've inflicted, trying to slow it all down. I just want it to slow down.

Pages flutter

I'm nineteen years old, and I refuse to panic. Not this time. I take stock of the immediate. The clothes on my back. The wooden stool beneath me. The easel in one hand, the paintbrush in the other. The canvas in front of me. Instead of fighting the deluge, I breathe and accept the last five years. I breathe, not worrying about time or order. I breathe and let my skipped life bloom. Develop in me, like a polaroid. Then I know where I am and where I've been. How I left the facility when my father—sober—finally came back to claim me. How I enrolled in community college. Older than my peers.

I gaze at a canvas awash with dark oil colors. A painted figure stares back. A black cat with clocks for eyes, old beyond counting and cruel beyond reason. I've looked for you. Called old classmates. Most didn't remember me. Others hung up.

Whoever you are, please stop reading.

Please.

Pages flutter

I fall to the twin bed of my dorm room then curl into a fetal position. Out of community college and into a state university. Art major. My chest vibrates as sobs breach my lips. Lottie, my roommate, lies down beside me. A soft parenthetical at my rigid back, whispering that everything will be all right.

It won't be.

I know it won't.

Pages flutter

I'm twenty-five, seated on a high-pile carpet in a studio apartment, a warm box of white rice in one hand and chopsticks in the other. Surrounded by moving boxes and a few lit candles. She hasn't been here long enough to call the power company, the acquaintance across from me, dimly lit by candlelight. A friend of a friend. I'd agreed to help her with the move. After eating a dumpling, she wipes a bit of sauce from her lip, then gazes at me in a way that makes me feel warm. Seen.

I make a fist with one hand. Dig my nails into my palm, hoping the pain will turn these seconds into minutes.

Just let me stay in this moment. Please let—

Pages flutter

I lie next to a man, early thirties, in a large bedroom in an expensive flat. A pristine, sterile space. Lifeless. He rises to dress. I stare at him—this person I abandoned my desire for to share in his safety. And I pray for someone to come along with my diary so I'll no longer feel beholden. So I can find peace on my own terms.

Pages flutter

The bed in the loft is disheveled. It's a bohemian studio of red bricks and dark metal accents. Looks small and cheap. Still costs more than we can afford. Holding down a job isn't easy, given my condition. In my free time, I paint. Art supplies and musical instruments are spread throughout the studio. The latter belong to her. At the nearby sink, a woman in her forties—the same age as me—applies dark eyeliner. She asks why I won't be attending her concert this evening. That's when I realize I can't get out of bed. That I haven't for a day or two, save for a trip or two to the bathroom. Like my last partner's wealth, her confidence has been carrying me. And I've had nothing to offer in return.

Her makeup does little to hide how much my silence hurts her. She crosses the room. Reaches for her dark overcoat on—

Pages flutter

The coatrack. Nothing hangs there except a scarf of mine. Most of my jackets are on the floor, tangled amongst the rest of my clothing. An alarm clock sounds as I roll over on that same bed in the same studio. I reach out, silencing it. Take stock of what I've missed. The musical instruments are gone. The paint supplies in disarray.

I am forty-five years old.

I'm alone.

Pages flutter

It is loud in the art gallery. Louder than I would like. The size of the crowd is encouraging. But I worry about the critics. My black evening gown scratches at the seams. I look over my collection, which at long last, I've managed to get on display. The portraits all share one thing in common. The subjects are dead.

I stare at a portrait of my mother. A wound four decades old (though somehow, only minutes) splits further open. I am forty-seven years old and still don't know how to mourn.

A man in his eighties, frail and much smaller than he'd been in my youth, approaches. Asks if the paintings are selling, and no, they aren't. He nods, then looks at the portrait of my mother. It's exceptional, he tells me. His voice cracks with age and regret.

He says he wishes he'd taken her more places. Seen more of the world with her. If only they'd had a little more time. Then, with a kindness I cling to like a life preserver, he stares at me and tells me he's proud. He is so, so, very proud of—

Pages flutter

I stare at a portrait of my father, which hangs in my collection.

I stand there, split in two. Half of me sinks as the other floats away.

I am fifty years old.

Pages flutter

I pass beneath the vaulted ceiling of a vast space. My footsteps echo as I pass Roman soldiers, pharaohs, cavemen, dinosaurs. Things lost to time.

I take a seat on a bench. Admire a painting that hangs on a wall. Grateful for the soothing din of passersby.

A girl, about eight years old (younger than me, and not), wearing a puffy blue coat and knit cap, wanders over. She adjusts the straps of her backpack as she stares at the painting. I greet her. Ask if she's here for school. She's shy. Shakes her head yes. Moments later, her teacher seeks her out. Relief washes over the woman's face. She'd thought she'd lost one.

The girl asks me what I do.

I offer to show them.

Later, in a backroom few can access, I invite the teacher and the girl to sit beside a worktable, upon which rests an aged canvas. I put on a pair of vinyl gloves. Remove the nails from the wood with a pair of pliers. Mix putty, apply it to the holes and cracks, then use a hot iron to affix strips of fabric. I flip the canvas over. Examine the painting with a black light. Find the places time has eaten away. I mix my paints to match their colors, then fill in what's been lost.

"A restoration artist," the teacher tells her student. "She restores them. See?"

"Good as new?" asks the girl.

"No," I tell her as I use a Q-tip and a bit of solvent to make a dull orange bright again. "It'll never be as it was. Or like it was supposed to be. There's damage, changes, even in repair. It won't keep forever—but it'll stay as long as there's someone around who believes it deserves to."

"Which things get to stay?" she asks.

"No telling. Most don't. Nor do the people that made them. That's what makes them beautiful. And a little sad. And that's okay. That's the way of things."

"Aside from fixing stuff—did you ever make anything? Anything that stayed?"

The question cuts deep, but I don't let on. A practiced smile that's long since become reflex crosses my face. A small, sad thing that answers her question without answering it.

Then the girl and the teacher have gone. I apply varnish to finish the piece. Hang up my smock and throw away the gloves, turning off the lights behind me as I go.

I return to the bench in the gallery and admire the painting which hangs there, restorations and all. I imagine my life in the same fashion. The fraction I've lived and the bulk I haven't.

I feel a pain in my arm. Then, in my chest.

The lights above dim. A subtle warning that it's nearly time to go.

I stay where I am.

I'm too old—and young—to follow such rules.

So I sit with the painting. And my regrets. I should never have waited so long for something to come along and save me. For someone else to make me feel safe.

Tomorrows are frightening until you start to run out of them.

And what's left of my book is thin.

I think back to the early parts, when scenes played out in their entirety, and the tone was the stuff of fairy tales. So it's no surprise when one of my grandmothers sits beside me, disguised as my shadow.

Though I couldn't name her as a child, I recognize her now. Gentle Atropos. The one who shelves the books.

I wish my grans had taught me better ways to stretch a moment. For all the pain, mine went by too fast.

I can't blame you for that. Though, for a while I did. All you did was find a diary. And pages are meant to be turned, so read on. There's comfort in endings. But before Attie returns me to the stacks, if it isn't too much to ask...

Turn back to the morning before my ninth birthday. To the sun on my skin, my mother's baking, and my father's whistling. Draw a sunflower in the margins so I'll feel held.

Before beginnings.

Beyond ends.

Always.

LONG, WHITE, AND WRIGGLING
KEL BYRON

It was only after coming home from the hospital that I started having dreams about worms.

Sometimes, it was in my chest. In the dream, I would be standing in the bathroom, naked and looking at a writhing mass beneath the skin just below the long, horizontal surgical scars. But it didn't stay there—it would start to move, crawling up to my collarbone and toward my neck, tangling through my ribs or winding around my lungs to suffocate me from the inside. Sometimes, it would move downward instead. I could feel the tickle of it traveling all the way down my thighs toward my feet. It made the skin bulge around it. Sometimes it hurt, and other times it just felt. . . wrong, grotesque, and alien.

But then, I dreamt about the drains again. I could smell them even in my sleep. One of the things I wasn't prepared for when I got my top surgery was that after they remove the breasts and put in a pair of drains to filter out the oozing liquid, sometimes little *pieces* come out with it. That sickly sweet smell of spoiled fatty tissue would forever remain in my nose, reminding me oddly of rancid seafood. The dreams were worse, though. Something else would come out of me, slithering through the tubes and into the drains. I was consumed with the need to open them up and pull out each long, dripping parasite or to slice open my skin just enough to grab them. I could feel them so vividly. That squeamish, queasy feeling of something wet being dragged through the muscle made my body hair stand on end, and my flesh crawl.

But still, I couldn't stop myself from doing it again and again: cutting open the skin, pulling out the parasites, and then going in for more until the bathroom sink was a squirming mass of pale, bloodied worms.

The bubbling in my gut was what woke me up. My eyes opened in the dark of my bedroom; vision speckled with little flickers of light from a pounding headache that made my ears beat with a pulse of their own. I tossed myself out of bed, my pajama pants tangled around my legs, and threw my mastectomy pillow to the side. Those six steps to the bathroom had never seemed so daunting before, but after clipping my elbow against the door and dropping to my knees, I felt the immense disgust and relief of everything leaving my stomach in an instant. I coughed, catching my breath, feeling the chill of cold porcelain beneath my hands and the hard tile under my legs.

The light made my eyes sting. I squinted, standing at the sink and brushing my teeth to get the bitter taste out of my mouth. Every time I looked down at the drain, all I could imagine was that final, extended vision from my dream: a basin full of worms, crawling over one another as if searching for a way out. Or, perhaps searching for a way back into me.

After rinsing my mouth, I caught my own pale face in the reflection. Something was. . . *different*. Thinner, perhaps. I traced the outline of my jaw and the narrow cheekbones beneath my eyes, the cold, clammy skin chilling my fingertips. But no, it wasn't about my face. There was something else.

Below my bare chest, beneath the bandages, I spotted something new at the bottom of my rib cage. It was a bump that wasn't there before. That skin-crawling sensation returned as I brushed a fingertip over it, finding it oddly soft. As I pushed against it, I had to bite down on my bottom lip, not because it hurt but because the nausea returned almost as soon as I gave it that experimental poke. It was squishy, malleable, like a pocket of water beneath the skin.

But then it moved.

When I felt that small bit of movement against the tip of my finger, paired with an eerie sharpness in the skin, I jumped back with a hoarse gasp. A full-body chill passed from the tip of my toes up to my neck. I felt fearful and defiled, as if something had made its home in this sanctuary that once was mine alone. Almost immediately, I lunged back toward the mirror and looked for the spot again—nothing was there. I patted my waist, slid my hands over the skin again and again, and even tried to reach around my back to find any sign of the soft, fleshy lump that had migrated from one body part to another, but it was gone. It had left.

The disgust, however, did not.

That unpleasant sensation followed me for hours and into the next day. It was like every time I thought about it or felt my own skin, I experienced a powerful chill that went all the way up my spine and tangled around my nerves. My body was already difficult to live in without the thought of something growing inside of me, unwanted and unfamiliar. It was sickening, but it wasn't real. I kept reminding myself of that.

"I was startin' to think you got lost," one of my coworkers, Charlie, snickered at me as soon as I stepped out of the employee bathroom. The convenience store was dead at this time of night, but it was just as well. My brain felt like it was moving at half-speed, struggling to keep up with my every thought. "You're pale today. Got a case of the stomach flu?"

"Something like that," I told him, my voice hoarse and scratchy from vomiting.

"You should'a asked for the day off." Charlie was using a boxcutter to open up a shipment of snack cakes to put on the shelf. "You know I like ya' just fine, buddy, but I don't want your germs."

"I don't think I'm contagious," I told him. My hands were still shaking as I cracked open a box and started putting little tree-shaped air fresheners on the end cap. My dexterity was all wrong, making me drop them more than once. This anxiety buzzed around in my brain like a panic attack that never ended.

"What, are you pregnant?" Charlie asked with a sharp laugh. It was a joke, of course, but the word made my guts flip and my skin crawl.

"Don't even say that." I sneered at him, feeling a heavy, rotten discomfort. My heart was racing. The thought alone made me want to scream. "That's the absolute *last* thing I ever want to think about—"

"Didn't mean nothin' by it," Charlie said, smiling in that awkward, amused way that said, *I mean well.* "Sorry, bud. It was a joke in bad taste."

My expression softened the tiniest bit, that ache still present but pushed down to a dark spot where I hoped to forget about it. "It's alright," I finally said. My hands were moving faster and less clumsily now, that anxiety replaced with anger and bitterness. "I know you didn't mean anything by it. It's just, I've been fighting for two years to get all that shit removed so I never have to worry about it. For some reason, insurance companies and surgeons alike seem to think my uterus is the goddamn Ark of the Covenant. A fuckin' treasure. It's like one day I'll suddenly change my mind and want it back." I paused, letting out an irritable sigh and trying to change the subject. The second subject I had in mind wasn't exactly better, though. "You, uh, ever know someone who's had a parasite?"

"Parasite?" Charlie chuckled. "No. Not personally. Had an old dog with heartworms once, though. Would *not* recommend looking that up."

"Real bad?"

"Nasty shit." He made a disgusted expression as he pushed one box away and started opening another, pushing it toward me so that I could restock the cigarette lighters. "Makes your skin crawl just lookin' at 'em. Fatal, too. All from a mosquito bite, can you believe that? They took the damn thing out, and it was straight-up *burstin'* with these wiggly little bastards. Looked like bean sprouts."

I grimaced, happy that I was looking in the opposite direction so that Charlie couldn't see the way my face visibly sank. *Great,* now I had something else to worry about. There were dangers out there that I couldn't avoid, ones almost microscopic and unstoppable. I was thinking about the way that bump on my skin migrated. If it could get to my chest, to my abdomen, to my neck, where else could it go? The image of my organs busting open with twisting, bloated colonies of thin, white worms filled my head and made me feel sick with dread all over again.

For days, I tried to get it out of my head. I couldn't. When I fell asleep, I dreamed about my insides bursting with parasites and maggots. When I opened my eyes, I checked every inch of my body for strange lumps, feeling even more suspicious when they weren't there. I held my breath whenever I went to see my doctor —the surgical spots were healing great, but they weren't ready to talk about removing the rest of those unwanted parts. *We'll talk about it in a year,* the surgeon said. He patted my shoulder apologetically when he saw the way my face sank. A lot can happen in a year.

I was thinking about it when I was vomiting in the bathroom at my apartment, holding my stomach and praying for it to be over while Charlie's words kept echoing in the front of my brain. I was thinking about it while I was standing in the aisle at the grocery store, staring at a pregnancy test but ultimately too afraid to put that long pink box in my cart. And still, I was thinking of it while slicing open packages at work and placing individually wrapped snack cakes on the shelf.

Those ideas blossomed into something else: a plan.

"Don't think that shelf can get any fuller," Charlie said. His voice was distant, as if submerged in water. "You alright?"

I soon realized what he meant. I had been stacking cakes up higher and higher until the shelf was overflowing. My breath came out shaky and labored, held deep within my lungs for too long. "Yeah," I whispered hoarsely. "Yeah, I'm fine."

Another slice of the box cutter easily gliding through thin tape. *I'm fine.* Another unpleasant flip in my lower stomach, another ache below my naval. *It's a case of the flu.* I set the box aside, grabbing another one. I extended the box cutter another inch, and it cut even deeper into the cardboard this time with a satisfying motion. *We'll talk about surgery in another year.*

I don't know how long I stood there, repeating the same actions. It seemed like seconds, but I knew it must have been much longer by the way the door chimed with each new customer who entered. There came a time when I was no longer in control of my own movements—it was how I ended up standing in the employee bathroom in the first place, listening to the drip of the rusty faucet and the clank of old pipes in the walls.

The box cutter was still in my hand. I used my thumb to slide it open and closed rhythmically, biding my time. I was filled with a deep, gut-churning anxiety but also a sense of purpose. I knew what had to be done. I knew that no one else would do it but me.

"I know you're in there somewhere," I whispered into the mirror, meeting my own eyes. I was searching every bit of exposed skin, checking my face and my neck for lumps or squirming masses. There was nothing, but that didn't mean it wasn't there. . . It just meant it was too deep beneath the skin for me to see now.

It was getting hard to breathe. Was it in my lungs? No, no, I was just nervous. I pushed against my chest under the scars, digging under the bandages. I felt the rough texture of my stitches and lumps of scar tissue, but nothing soft and malleable. It wasn't there anymore. My fingers pressed into my waist, my arms, my neck, and every thick, fleshy part of my body that I could find. When my fingertips pushed hard against the bone and muscle, it ached, but nothing moved or slithered beneath the skin.

That was when the pain came back. It was low and powerful, stirring in the pit of my stomach just below my naval. It moved in waves, crawling around as if doing backflips in my gut. It made a lot of sense now: that constant fear of something growing inside of me, the desperation to dig it out, the vomit-inducing disgust I felt in the wee hours of the morning.

I slid open the box cutter again. It felt light in my hand, almost like it belonged there. It would be so easy. I knew where to cut. I had obsessively watched videos about surgery, read countless

articles, talked to surgeons. All I had to do was follow the pain—
that creeping, crawling pain.

"I know where you are," I whispered, pulling up the edge of
my shirt. I could see it now. That bump on my stomach was
moving and squirming, a tremble passing over the spot as if
something was under the bloated area of flesh.

The bathroom door was locked. I knew Charlie would come
knocking if I took too long. I thought very briefly about waiting
until I got home, but by then, perhaps it would move again. I
couldn't miss this opportunity to get it out. As I stood next to the
drippy faucet, I let my eyes focus on a bit of creeping mold that
was spreading out from behind the cracked mirror. There was
dark grime that had been caked into the tiles since the late 80s,
and the smell of rusted water filled my mouth with a sour,
metallic taste. This was a sorry excuse for an operating room, but
it would have to do.

My shirt was rolled up, stuffed into my mouth like a makeshift
gag that tasted like sweat-soaked cotton. The first cut was the
hardest. I pressed the blade against my stomach, tracing the
pattern of a C-section scar without cutting the skin. A deep breath
cleared my head, but the sharp pain stopped me in my tracks. It
repeated like that for a while: a deep breath, a sharp pain, another
deep breath, another bitter sting that made me second-guess
everything. But then, the mass under my skin moved again. I had
no choice.

Tears streamed down my face when I made that initial cut.
First, I was scared, but one look into the cracked bathroom mirror
kept me going. *I could see them:* long, white, and wriggling, soaked
in bright red blood and tumbling over one another like a barrel
full of eels. My stomach was bursting with worms and maggots,
all of them trying to crawl back into the warm, wet cavity I had
just stolen from them. They slithered over my hands, tangling
between my fingers as I held the skin taut. That first slice wasn't

enough. It was jagged, uneven, and insufficient. I imagined their nesting spot in the swollen, bloated center of my uterus, where it wasn't enough to just slice the tissue and expect them to all come tumbling out. They would come back, these uninvited guests who tried to take my body as their own. I had to get rid of it all, like destroying the hive to keep new growth at bay.

Even when I became numb to the pain, the smell was strong, mixed with rust and cheap toilet cleaner. I scooped a handful of worms off my belly as they came tumbling out, slapping them into the sink with a wet sound. My fingers left bloody prints on the yellowing porcelain. The flickering light overhead made their movements even more erratic, those fleshy tendrils crawling over one another in a disorganized heap as more and more joined them, now falling onto the floor and getting stuck between the tiles.

I cut deeper. Further. A sickening wet sound followed, a bloated sac of flesh popping open to release a gush of dark fluid that dripped between my legs. I fought the urge to vomit as my fingers dug inside the newly sliced hole below my belly button, digging around until I found what I was looking for. My shaking, partially numbed fingers gripped a thick, fat worm and tugged it out inch by inch like a wet shoelace. It fell to the floor with a slap, twitching and curling around my feet. It wanted back inside; I knew it.

My eyes were glazing over, my head dizzy, my stomach sick. I tasted vomit in my mouth and my legs gave out with a surge of vertigo. I slid to the filthy, stained floor, my blood now mingling with years of mold between the piss-yellow tiles. My arms instinctively cradled the loose meat and intestines as I went. They moved. I didn't know intestines moved like that. They wiggled like one huge worm—the mother of all the rest. I jabbed at them too, hoping the blunt edge of the knife would stop the incessant squirming I felt between my fingers.

More maggots. More long, white worms. I couldn't get the uterus out in one clean cut. The box cutter was stuffed deep inside that wet, open cavity, carving out chunks one at a time while a pile of warm, red tissue grew on the floor next to me. It was like gutting an animal after a hunt, piling up the pieces while letting the blood drain. After a while, it didn't feel any different. I didn't recognize that flesh as mine anymore. My pulse pounded in both ears but, I could still make out the sound of Charlie's fist on the door and his voice calling out for me. I could hear him saying words, but they didn't make sense.

I watched with mixed horror and fascination as more living, squirming parasites crawled out of my stomach and up my chest, digging into the flesh between my stitches. I slapped them away, trying to pull them out before they could disappear, but they were quick. I was slow. My hands were growing numb and heavy as if I had fallen asleep on them.

They were trying to get back in, those bastards. With a whimper of pain and fear, I started to pull myself across the floor, watching my intestines and the ragged pieces of my reproductive system trail after me, cocooned in their own slick mucus that shimmered in the glow of the buzzing fluorescent light. The parasites climbed back in at every available opportunity. They pushed into my skin, tangled around my organs, and dipped into the open cavity until they blended with blood and tissue. Just when I had stolen a single breath of freedom, they crept back in and reminded me that they weren't done with me yet.

I reached for the box cutter. My fingers were too weak to curl around it. The sound of jingling keys was sharp in my ears, followed by heavy footsteps and voices I didn't recognize. Charlie was cussing loudly and calling out something that may have been my name, but it was alien to me now—he sounded far away, on another planet.

He crouched beside me, his face white and horrified. "What

the fuck have you done?!" I saw his mouth move to the words, but I couldn't hear them.

I tried to explain. *Parasites. It was parasites.* My hands reached for them, scooping up a pile of my own bloody, warm flesh between my fingers.

They weren't there anymore.

I think they moved again.

BY THIS PHANTOM HAND

ZACHARY ASHFORD

Focus. If Blue couldn't regain it, he was bound to lose again, but already, the sweat on his brow had dried up. The hope had dissipated. The result of the contest was pretty much a given. His mind was drifting. He should have been thinking about nothing but the memory of masturbation and the feeling of his long-gone, minced, and shredded hand working his cock backwards and forwards, but his mind was consumed with other thoughts. The incidental: the whirring of the fan, the buzzing of the fly against the window, the fact Finn was clearly close to spattering the biscuits first again. The constant: the tingling, throbbing pins and needles in an extremity that no longer existed. And the troubling: the disappearance of their support group's leader, Parker.

Parker had been missing for months, ever since the night his wife and daughter were murdered. Most people figured he was responsible. Not Blue, though. Parker might have once had issues that fundamentally changed his life, but he was a good bloke. The only reason Blue didn't feel completely adrift as he came to terms with his amputation and the loss of his mother was because of Parker's attention. Blue's old man had been distant, choosing to live like nothing had changed—while keeping intimacy with his son at arm's length—and at nineteen, most of the mates Blue had before the accident had left for universities and cities miles away from home. Parker, having been where Blue was, didn't let him disappear into depression.

It was no mystery why. Parker was a quadruple amputee. What most people in mainstream society didn't realize was xenomelia, amputee identity dysphoria, was a real thing, and Parker had it bad. At least, he used to. Trains were his chosen method, but that was in the past. The official reason he operated the support group was because he'd recovered from his issues, but when he had no limbs left, that was easy to say. The less official reason was he was "teaching" his young charges telekinesis. He claimed the ability was real, and with the correct mental training, it was the perfect way for young amputees who felt like they'd lost some of their agency to reclaim it. So far, it wasn't working out for Blue, but he had seen signs it wasn't only a distraction from his self-loathing and survivor's guilt. The phantom pains hurt more when he was trying to move things with his mind, and he was certain it hadn't been his imagination that had got him hard. On at least a few occasions, he'd felt the touch of non-existent hands working his shaft. Just. . . not on this night. . .

A loud moan from Finn, who was really getting into the night's contest, brought Blue back to the moment. Finn was breathing heavily, panting, piston-pumping his arm beside his erect cock—as if to jack it off—despite having no hand to hold it with. Blue's boner shriveled as he came to terms with losing again.

In the other chair, Jai thrust his hips maniacally, fucking the air with vigor. So far, this technique had never worked for him, but he was still going for it like a little jackrabbit. Today, it looked like the result would be close. Either way, there was only one person here who was going to be eating the biscuits. And Blue was bloody sick of it.

Finn let out a lower moan and dropped to his knees. He pumped his arm faster and faster. The stump of his wrist was a blur of motion. The fluorescent lights in the community hall ceiling flickered. Buzzed. Sparked.

Blue flipped his pants over his flaccid Johnson with the stump of his wrist and stared up at the light. Deep within the neon tube, a red glow was spreading. "Guys," he called. "Stop!"

Neither of his friends stopped. They were locked in a race they were both desperate to win.

"Fucking STOP!" he called, louder this time.

BANG!

The light above exploded.

Finn groaned. He splashed the biscuits with his seed and cheered.

BANG-BANG! BANG! Three other lights followed suit, plunging the room into darkness. Glass rained down on the three boys.

Finally, Finn and Jai stopped. Their hard-ons wobbled with their movements as they stared up at the light directly above them. A thin wisp of smoke, backlit by the dying glow of the tube, trailed away from it. The acrid scent of burned-out fuse wire filled the room, covering the chlorine smell of Finn's victory.

The emergency lights clicked on, bathing them in a soft orange glow.

"We should get the fuck out of here," Jai said.

"Grab the biscuits. We can't leave them," Finn added.

"Fuck you, you're the one who made the mess."

"That's why I don't have to grab them. You know the rules."

Blue looked at both boys carefully. They'd flopped their dicks into their pants, but Jai's stood rigid, bulging like a tent pole beneath cotton.

Blue's own penis was tucked away, sleeping as if never harassed. He'd done a fair bit of reading on telekinesis lately, and the lights blowing at that exact moment had him wondering about something. "Shut up, both of you. You don't think—"

"Ha! Blowing lights as I blow my load!" Finn called out, raising the stump of his hand in victory."

A loud electric buzz filled the room. The television on the wall began to glow.

An image of a familiar face faded onto the screen. It was impossible to tell if it was smiling or grimacing. Wires ran from the nostrils, the corners of the eyes, and the lips. The unwired parts of the face were scarred and discolored. Deep crevices and crow's feet scored the visage. Stubbled regrowth barely pushed through mottled skin.

The screen flickered, and the face disappeared, replaced by a caged rat. Voices could be heard, barking instructions. "Do it," one of them said. "Do it. Don't hold back."

The rat pulsed. It heaved as if coughing and then flopped to its side.

Nothing Blue had read in his studies made sense of this. Determined to prove to himself the phenomenon *was* real, and Parker hadn't been playing them for fools when he moved objects around the room, Blue had been reading about Uri Geller and James Hydrick. The disproving of their supposed acts of telekinesis had dented his faith in Parker's claims, but this here, the hijacking of the television screen, was some Max Headroom shit, and what it showed could only be real. It was too grainy, too impulsive, and too spontaneous to be an act.

"What the fuck is this?" Jai asked.

"Shut up," Blue said. He didn't know anyone who could be behind this level of fuckery, but he'd seen the face somewhere before. Well, maybe not the face. The eyes. Some movie, maybe? This had to be a special effect, a prank. . .

The rat pulsed. It swelled. Rolled over as if in extreme agony, and then with a final squeal, it exploded in a visceral spray of blood. Bits of fur and tail stuck to the cage. A chunk of its snout could be seen hanging from a hinge in the cage door. The men off-screen began to cheer and clap. The bizarre face reappeared on the screen, closer this time. A reflection could be seen in his eyes. One man with a video camera. Another without. Both looked to be in overalls or jumpsuits. The face winked.

Blue recognized the wink immediately. It was Parker.

"Guys!" Blue said.

Before either could respond, there was rapid movement as the camera spun. Panicked shouting followed. Blue tried to follow the disorienting commotion, but it wasn't until the camera settled, framing a tilted angle from somewhere higher up in the room, he saw the two men in grey overalls and the full picture of Parker. He sat on a high-tech chair. Electrical cables and tubes hung from the top of it, vines snaking into the sleeves of his shirt and the legs of his shorts. Blue didn't have time to point out the obvious. Those tubes no doubt penetrated the mutilated stumps at Parker's shoulders and below his hips. A long tube ran into his scalp. He was fixed into place, but he was laughing maniacally, even as one of the men in grey held a screwdriver to his throat and screamed at the other man, who was reaching for the camera. "Don't worry about that! Get the sedative, Jerry! Get the sedative!"

The other man, Jerry, gave up on the camera and ran to the bench. He frantically started fumbling with syringes and vials while Parker laughed harder and harder.

"Guys," Blue said again. "It's Parker!"

Jai gasped with recognition. "What happened to him?"

"Is this some sort of prank?" Finn asked. "Did you set this up with him, Blue?"

"No! What the hell?"

"You were always his favorite. Maybe you've been—"

"Shut up, Finn. Just watch," Jai said.

On the screen, Parker spoke. His voice was unmistakable. "You'd better hurry up and do it before I get nasty," he told the bloke with the screwdriver. And then he stopped laughing.

Blue had no idea who was controlling the camera, but it showed Parker clearly spinning his head to the cameraman as he approached with a syringe.

Parker's eyes flashed.

Grunting, the guy with the screwdriver pulled it away from Parker's throat. Rigid as a marionette, he straightened and turned to face Jerry. He roared with exertion and raised his arm, trembling, shaking, screaming in frustration, his face a picture of terror. He speared the tool through the cameraman's eye with a vicious thrust.

Jai swore.

Finn raised his stump to his mouth. "That looked too real."

Blue watched as the screwdriver was withdrawn and blood sprayed from the wound.

Onscreen, Parker laughed.

What the hell was this? It had to be a joke. Had to be.

Nevertheless, the camera rotated, guided by an invisible hand, and settled on a window, revealing the room where Parker was fixed to the mechanical apparatus. He was somewhere high, a laboratory with views of the city skyline. A crack appeared in the glass. Parker laughed and the window shattered into a million cubes of safety glass.

No. . . no, he couldn't be. . . Blue was frozen in place, unable to look away. Then, screwdriver man began stumbling towards the void beyond the broken window. He turned to face the camera. He jammed the screwdriver into his own eye and staggered. His feet scrambled on glass rubble, and then he was gone, falling out the window.

A heavy weight settled in Blue's guts. And then Parker's mutilated face reappeared on the screen. "Find me, Blue," he said. "Find me."

The screen went black.

"Holy shit," Jai said. "What the fuck was that?"

"How did you do it?" Finn asked.

Blue turned to Finn. "That was fucking real, man. Don't you dare act like I had anything to do with it. Don't you think that if I knew where he was, I'd have called the cops?"

Finn raised an eyebrow. "You're the one who said you don't think he did it, that it was a set-up."

Blue shook his head. He had said that; it was true. In fairness, though, that had been when he doubted Parker's abilities. Blue figured someone had framed him, that Parker might have been into drugs or something and gotten mixed up with the wrong people.

"Are you gonna try to find him?" Finn asked.

"No, dude, we watched him kill two people. There's no way I'm going anywhere near him. In fact, I'm gonna call the cops straight away."

"What are you going to tell them?" Jai asked. "Your old amputee support group leader called you out on television?"

"I think that message was for us," Blue said. "He knew where we'd be."

"Shit!" Finn said. "Do you think he knows we jack off in here?"

Blue stared at the congealing jizz on the soggy biscuits and shuddered. "Look, if it's real, someone's gonna find the bodies. One dude took a swan dive from what looks like a high floor."

"Either way," Blue said. "The cops will investigate, and I can't imagine Parker is going anywhere. That machinery he was hooked up to looked like it was fixed tight."

"So what does that tell us?" Finn was sliding his stump into his prosthetic. He had the look of a man ready to get the hell out of dodge.

BY THIS PHANTOM HAND   105

Blue checked the time. Their rides would be here to pick them up soon, and they needed to get the place cleaned up. "Nothing," he said. "But they'll investigate the building and find him. We don't have to do anything."

"What we don't know," Jai said, "is why he killed those guys."

"Dudes!" Finn said, picking the biscuits up. "What if he's in trouble? What if they're the ones who killed his family?"

Blue snapped his head to Finn. For once, he might be onto something.

"Anyway," Finn said, grinning. "You gonna eat these or what?"

Blue didn't sleep well. His old man had ticked the "ask what's wrong" box, but Blue couldn't exactly tell him he was sick to death of losing the game. His dad was a pretty cool guy, but he wouldn't understand soggy biscuit, let alone continuing to play despite losing every time. After all, Blue kissed his mother's funerary urn with these lips.

On top of that, he couldn't get the whole scene that played on the community center television clear of his mind. It hadn't made the news because the first thing his dad would have said was, "Hey son, we saw the support group guy who killed his wife on the news. Looks all fucked-up. Any idea what happened to him? Oh, also, he killed a couple of guys," and he hadn't said that, so apart from the three of them who'd seen the incident, no one else knew, not yet anyway.

The morning was different, though. Morning television's lead story was the death of two men in strange circumstances. One had plummeted from the top of an abandoned high-rise building downtown and been left a smear of brains, a puddle of blood, and a human-shaped outline of obliterated bones inside unbranded grey overalls. All except for one thing: a prosthetic leg, still wearing its boot. The other body was in the building's derelict foyer. It had been stabbed in the eye and had two prosthetic legs.

Blue pushed his Count Chocula around with his spoon, hoping the reporter would say where the building was located. He pictured Parker's face again. The mechanical apparatus he was connected to. How could the cops say the place was empty? They must have missed something. Parker couldn't have gotten out of there, not unless he had help. Before his wife was murdered, Parker had gotten around on a specially modified sip/puff wheelchair designed for paraplegics and quadruple amputees. So either he was in the building, he had an accomplice to help him escape, or Finn's idea about him being framed was bang on the money. For Blue, that meant one thing. He was going to take Parker up on his invitation and find out what exactly was going on. If Parker needed help, Blue had to offer it. He'd been there when Blue needed him, and it was possible he'd only killed those people because they'd kidnapped him. *What if they were the ones who'd killed Parker's wife and kid?* There were too many questions, and as dumb as tracking the man down might be, Blue was going to follow through with it.

He sent a message to Finn and took his bowl to the kitchen.

Dad was already in there scarfing his breakfast: Ritz with ham, cheese, and mayonnaise. "Want one?"

Blue eyed the concoction distastefully. "Nah, I'm good."

"Your loss," Dad said, dipping a finger into the mayonnaise. "It's the real stuff. Fresh!" He licked the finger clean and groaned with exaggerated pleasure.

Blue cringed. "Made lunch already. Cheers, though."

"Suit yourself. They're good." Dad bit into one. Mayonnaise dropped from the cracker onto his knuckles. He licked it up eagerly, winking at Blue. "Love this stuff! Anyway, I'm off. Be good."

Blue scrolled through the news on his cellphone. They'd found the body on Third Street.

Blue jumped on one of the inner-city buses. If he rode the length of Third Street, he'd eventually find somewhere taped off from passersby. Surely, the police would have a cordon set up. It wasn't like they could scoop Jerry's remains into a bag and then pressure wash the stain off the footpath. That'd be barbaric.

As the bus rattled and chugged its way downtown, Blue inspected his phone and messaged Finn to keep him posted about his movements.

Finn messaged back, telling him he was "out of his mind," but he'd vouch for Blue if anyone asked.

Blue didn't think Parker would get aggressive, but he had killed those two people last night. And possibly his own wife. And daughter. *Yeah*, Blue thought, *precautions were obviously going to be necessary.*

It was hard to reconcile that against the fact that Parker's support for Blue had gone beyond the public sphere. When the others weren't around, he'd always told Blue he had the most potential for power out of all the members of all the support groups Parker visited. Shit like that felt good.

Since he'd lost his mum in the crash that took his hand, Blue's dad had been kind, but he'd not exactly been a source of positivity and encouragement in Blue's life. Parker had filled that hole and lifted Blue, giving him somewhere to focus that dragged his mind away from the past and towards the future. So when Finn was winning telekinesis contest after telekinesis contest, Blue was able to know that in the future, his turn would come. If he could fulfill the promise Parker saw in him, maybe his survival instead of his mum's wouldn't be such a waste. She had been holding a family together while working nine to five. What had Blue ever done? He couldn't win a game of soggy biscuit to save his life, and if he couldn't do that, how could he make her proud? She would be seething in her urn, wondering why she had died while her loser adolescent son couldn't win a race to blow his load. What made it all worse was that he was so deep into the game he could never quit. If he did, the other lads would give him more shit than they already did.

The bus drove past a billboard advertising moisturizing cream and pulled into a stop nearby. From his window, Blue saw the building. Not only was it unmistakably the one from the news, but a guy with a pressure washer was blasting an area of cordoned-off pavement in front of it.

Blue hopped off the bus, fighting the urge to listen to his better judgment and go to college. He took a picture of the bus stop and the building then sent them to Finn. He slid a finger under the sleeve of his prosthetic and scratched the butt of his stump. The pins and needles in his non-existent hand had returned.

Before he could consider getting entry, the pressure washer cut out. The cleaner swore and inspected the tool. He clicked a few buttons, then, with a dismissive wave of his hand, made his way around the side of the building.

Once he was inside, Blue didn't waste any time. After inspecting the tenth floor and finding it empty and devoid of drama, he went to the eleventh. When the lift opened, Parker was in the lobby, resting comfortably on his wheelchair, a cracked grin spread across his ravaged features.

Beyond the smile, Parker was barely recognizable. The implants in his face and orifices made him look like a cybernetic monstrosity.

His eyes, once so bright and full of life, were beady and glassy. His skin was raw and swollen, bruised around the implants. His hair was gone. What looked like a needle jack adorned his scalp. He was thin. Barely human. "How you been, buddy?" he asked, as if nothing had ever changed.

Stupidly, Blue could only respond in the most natural way. "Good. You?"

Goddamn, he was dumb. He'd witnessed what was possibly a miracle last night. The bloke behind it had reportedly murdered his own family. Blue's response was woefully inaccurate. If he had two hands, he'd have facepalmed real hard.

Parker didn't dwell on it. "I'm glad you came," he said. "I thought you might be chicken."

Blue tightened the strap on his prosthetic and narrowed his eyes. "Why'd you kill them? Did they kill your family?"

"That's a story for another day. Just know they had it coming."

Blue swallowed. "Why'd you call me here? Out of everyone."

Parker chuckled. "I wasn't lying when I said you had amazing potential. You've got a brain like a sponge. It's your self-confidence that stops you from having the success—and the power—you want. Well, your self-confidence and one other thing, but we'll talk about that in a minute. Follow me."

Parker's wheelchair began to move, but Parker wasn't using the sip/puff controller.

Blue followed.

"Tell me again how you lost your hand," Parker said.

Blue held up his prosthetic. After a truck driver had barreled through a merge lane without slowing, running them off the road and killing his mum in the process, the vehicle they were travelling in had rolled. Instinctively, Blue had stuck his hand out to soften the blow of his head hitting the tarmac. His window had been open, and his hand—and wrist—had been forfeit to whatever gods patrolled the gutters and feasted on pressure washed blood and chunks of flesh.

"And how do you feel about it now?"

Man, Parker *had* gone weird. "I've gotta tell you, I preferred having a lower arm, a hand, fingers. . ."

"A fist?"

What? "Yeah, I guess so."

"So it wasn't something you wished for."

"Fuck no."

"And herein lies your problem, Blue. You'll never win your silly game when you keep looking at your mutilated arm like something lost, like something fundamentally less."

"How. . . how do you know about the game?"

Parker stopped at the door to room seventeen. When he turned and spoke, his eyes flared. "I'm going to show you another way of thinking," he said, grinning. "As you know, anyone can learn telekinesis, but if you're prepared to make meaningful sacrifices of flesh, blood, and value, it'll come to you much faster. Why do you think I gave up my limbs? The amputation doesn't mean you've lost something less. With the right training, it means you've exchanged something. When you understand, you'll wonder why you hadn't taken your own arm sooner; a power so all-encompassing you'll freely give another limb to drink more of its intoxicating draft when we're done here."

Blue cautiously followed Parker through the door. Inside the room, the mechanical apparatus Parker had been hooked up to sat ominously, a hideous mess of sprawling wires and tubes like the tentacles of a jellyfish.

"What does it do to you?" Blue asked.

"*To me?* Nothing. It's a tool. The fools who brought me here thought they could use me for their own desires, but they didn't know what they were doing. You could say plugging me into it was one of the all-time backfires."

Blue backed towards the door. He'd seen *Akira*. He knew how this ended.

"You're not going anywhere," Parker said gently. "I need someone I can trust to know that when I refused them, they took my wife and kids. That. . . *that* was a sacrifice far too costly for the power they offered."

Blue had seen *Austin Powers* too. He knew a supervillain monologue when he heard one. He stepped towards the door. It closed gently, seemingly of its own volition.

"Please," Parker said, "Listen to me."

When Blue turned to his old mentor, he saw tears running down the man's mutilated face. He swallowed, choking his tears. "What do you need me to do?"

"I need you to help me. Using this, I can find them and get revenge, but I'm not powerful enough. I need your mindpower too. Together, we'll be able to find them. Stop them from doing this to others."

"Who are they?"

"People like us. People with the power of telekinesis. People addicted to the power of it."

Blue wiped his face with his forearm. "Let me get you real help. Police help."

"I know you have no self-confidence in your abilities, but have you ever wondered why you haven't been able to unlock your potential? I can show you the trick."

A strange sensation probed Blue's mind.

"You'll never lose soggy biscuit again."

Visions of Finn's gloating smile. Of Jai's smirk. Blue inspected the implants and wires running from Parker's face, the tubes sliding inside his shirt sleeves. "Tell me," he said, "but no promises, and I can't let you do *that* to me."

Parker smiled. "The only person who'll do anything to you," he said softly, "is yourself. The power comes from sacrifice. Why do you think I have so much of it?"

Blue gasped. "I can't. I've lost enough."

"Just try it," Parker said. "A toenail, a sliver of skin. Please."

It couldn't be true. Finn and Jai hadn't self-harmed, not so far as Blue understood. They'd been caught in accidents too. Jai had fallen while doing the floss near a woodchipper. Finn had lost his arm while riding on a stolen motorcycle. He'd cut across lines of traffic, and when he spoke about it, he said it was his own fault.

Blue had to think. He had to go home and consider all of this. "I have to go."

Suddenly, Parker levitated. His eyes darkened. The wounded skin around his implants flushed red. "Not until you try it."

Blue started to cry. The sight of his old mentor, his old friend, hovering in the air above his useless wheelchair was too much. "You're scaring me!" He waved his prosthetic hook at Parker. "I hate being like this. I wish it never happened. I'd rather have hands than telekinesis any day. And I'm fucking shit at it anyway!"

"Go then! Get out of here, you pissant. Choke on your cum-coated crackers and enjoy being a weak little man, always lesser, always longing for more. Never making your mother proud."

Objects around the room levitated. Broken glass, tools, the wires and tubes of the machine. They swirled around Parker as he raged. If this was what he could do when he wasn't hooked to the machine, Blue could only wonder at the power it offered.

The door burst open.

Blue stepped towards it. Looked at Parker with bloodshot, teary eyes. "Just tell me how to find them. I'll tell the police. They'll help you clear your name."

Parker ignored him and levitated to the machine. He set himself onto the seat, and the wires and serpentine tubes moved towards him. One by one, they connected to his implants and the jack on the top of his head. "Go," he said. "I'll find someone else to help."

Blue couldn't get hold of Finn for hours after he left. For the whole ride home, he kept picturing Parker's angry face, the tubes and wires plugging into him with practiced ease, and his final words. *I'll find someone else. . .*

Blue didn't need to think too hard to know who that would be. Finn's failure to answer his phone practically confirmed it. Finn was a social media junkie. He was always on his phone, always. The fact he'd ignored all messages, calls, and emails meant he was deliberately avoiding Blue.

Deciding to change tact, he tried Jai's number.

"Yo!" Jai said after the call connected. "Finn says you went out to find Parker!"

"When did you hear from Finn?"

"He's here. Loudspeaker's on. Talk to him."

"Hey man, did Parker contact you?"

"What? No. Why would he?"

Blue's heartbeat dropped instantly. Thank God Finn hadn't gone out to the building. The thought of Parker teaching Finn more telekinesis would take Blue's own opportunity away. And then he pictured Finn smirking at him over a plate of baby-battered graham crackers. If Finn had that extra power, Blue would never be able to reconcile his losses, and he didn't know how else he could prove himself.

Blue scratched an itch on his stump, feeling the vague impression of a phantom pain. If he wanted to do that, he'd only have to make a small sacrifice. If he didn't, well, nothing would change, but if he did, his help would benefit him also. It could offer the chance to have one small success in life, something he could use as justification to not feel guilt over his mum's death.

Fuck it, he thought. *There was an easy way to test whether Parker was being truthful.*

"Blue! You there?"

"Yeah," he said. "You up for a game tonight?"

"Shit, dude," Finn said. "If you're hungry, you only have to say so. Same place as usual? Want me to drink some pineapple juice?"

Blue clenched his fist. "See you in an hour."

After he'd hung up, Blue went into the garage and plucked his old man's needle-nose pliers from the toolbox. Parker had said a toenail would prove the difference. It was time to see if it would.

He slid the blade in at the dead center of his big toe. Not wanting the nail to snap and make the job harder than necessary, he applied pressure, digging in deeper so he could get a better grip when he yanked it free. Pain flared.

He bit his bottom lip and applied more pressure. He felt his nail tear from the meat of his flesh and let out a low groan of pain. He pressed on. If he could survive his mother's death and the loss of his hand, he could lose a toenail without bitching about it.

A drop of sweat fell from his forehead. He levered the pliers. The nail moved. Around the edges, the skin stretched, not wanting to tear. He stepped to the skirting board, making sure the tool didn't come loose, and bit his lip again.

One. Two. Three.

He kicked the skirting board, driving the pliers deep. This time, the pain didn't flare, it exploded. Underneath the nail, blood darkened the translucent keratin. As he moved his foot, he felt the pliers wobble and the nail shift.

He reached down. Pictured Finn and Jai's spooge on the crackers. Never again.

He...

...yanked.

The nail tore free. Blue roared in pain and let it fall. He pressed tissue tight over the bleeding nailbed. The nail had come free in one complete piece. Tags of frayed skin stuck to its underside. He thought about inspecting it, and it rocked, a turtle on its back.

What. The. Hell?

He concentrated again.

The nail levitated.

Holy shit.

He thought about putting the nail in the bin, and it floated there of its own accord. Parker had been telling the truth. It had worked. A little sacrifice had already made Blue more powerful. *Imagine the possibilities.*

Before leaving, though, he had to make sure he could do one thing. He turned on his laptop and unbuckled his belt. Edging was against the rules, but Blue didn't care. For once, Finn was going to guzzle gravy, and Blue wanted there to be lots of it.

***

Finn and Jai were waiting for him when he limped into the community hall. They had brought a tub of real butter with them. "They fixed the lights," Jai said. "That was quick."

Blue gestured at the butter. "What's that?"

"It was only yesterday that I emptied my balls," Finn said. "Don't want your dinner to be too dry for you."

Blue waved his stump dismissively. The butter skidded across the room and crashed into the wall with a lot more force than he'd expected.

"Dude! What the fuck?" Jai said.

Blue hadn't expected it to move at all, let alone crash into anything and make a mess. He'd have to be careful. If a small wave of the hand could have so much power, he'd need to make sure he didn't rip his own dick off. He limped to the plate of biscuits on the floor. "You ready to lose?"

Finn laughed. "Angry wank. Nice!"

Jai looked scared.

Within seconds of them getting into it, the lights began to flicker. Blue ignored them. He concentrated on the job at hand and worked on his technique, using the tingling in his phantom hand as a sign he was on track. Finn was getting into the groove, and Jai was well and truly into his hip-thrusting routine, but Blue was feeling good about his chances for the first time in months. The pain in his toe *would* be worth it.

BANG!

The light above him exploded. Glass sprayed them.

BANG-BANG! The others went as well. Darkness swallowed them.

His concentration broken, Blue looked spasmodically around the room, wondering when the emergency lights would come on. And then Finn started groaning.

FUCK!

Blue returned his attention to his dick and tried to focus, but it was no good. Finn ejaculated all over the crackers and cheered louder than ever before.

Desperately, Blue tried to get his act together, tried to rebuild his rhythm, but his mind was gone. The previously welcome phantom pains escalated from pulsing and throbbing to aching. His toe stung. He had one eye on the black television and one on his shriveling schlong. He had to focus or else the sacrifice wouldn't matter.

Jai dropped to his knees and added the second layer of topping.

FUCKFUCKFUCK!

"Why don't you magic the butter over here?" Finn asked, laughing.

"Fuck you!" Blue screamed. He tried to will the plate into the air so he could slam it into Finn's smug face. It stayed where it was.

"Here, I'll help." Finn picked the plate up.

Blue's frustration boiled over. He'd been so close! He could almost taste the victory. He knew he'd need to make a bigger sacrifice, but he was sick of being humiliated. Sick of eating the fucking crackers. Sick of Finn. Sick of Jai. He smashed the plate out of Finn's hands. The contents clattered to the floor.

"Dude!" Finn said.

"It's all right," Jai said. "You don't have to eat 'em if it means so much."

"Yeah, he does," Finn said. "A deal's a deal."

Parker was waiting for him. This time, he hadn't bothered with his wheelchair. He levitated all the way. "You've learned a valuable lesson today," Parker said.

"How the fuck do you know?"

"Cameras in the community hall. If I didn't wipe them for you every night, you lot would be YouTube-famous by now."

The shock subdued Blue's rage. "You mean anyone could have seen us? Uploaded video of us?"

Parker laughed. He looked more mutilated than he had the day before. *What had he been doing to himself?*

Blue wondered if Parker was sicker than he let on. "I did what you said, and it gave me a boost, but it died off. Why?"

Parker sighed. "The sacrifices were too small. They'll give you a little boost, but you'll need to be focused and in tune with everything to feel it. You had it for a bit, but once you became distracted, it was game over."

"So, how do I make it last?"

"The sacrifice has got to be significant," Parker said. "A digit, an ear, a limb. If it's not something you can't hide, something you wouldn't want to explain to your mother, it's too small."

Blue shook his head. Inspected his prosthetic hook. He'd been losing the game for months, and he knew he could never walk away until he'd won at least one contest. From there, he could retire as champion. He could choose to never see the boys again. He could run away and join the circus. He couldn't, however, mutilate himself further.

"There's got to be another way," he said. "How did you get this power? You haven't always had it." Blue paused. "Have you?"

Parker watched him, not speaking. He floated to the mechanical apparatus. "I've been training my mind for a long time. Long before I sacrificed my limbs."

Blue paused. "So why did you never show us the actual power you had? Why didn't you train us in that?"

Parker laughed. "Because those of us who know about it are sworn to secrecy. Not that it matters anymore. I need you to know because I need your help, and I *know* you won't tell anyone. As I told you, it's not some ridiculous magic that comes when you lose an arm. It's a skill. We're practitioners." He lowered himself onto the mechanical apparatus. "And like any skill, you're always looking for ways to perfect it. To improve it. At some point, it became more than a hobby."

Blue's phantom pains were playing up something fierce. The hackles on his neck pointed to the sky. His gut was heavy. "What aren't you telling me?"

"Some of us found out about the relationship between power and sacrifice. It started small: a fingernail, a patch of skin, a toenail. And then a toe. And a finger. And before you knew it, I was laying on train tracks, hiding under a blanket so the driver wouldn't see me, wouldn't stop."

"You've told me this before. What's the part you're keeping secret?"

"More and more members of the group learned. Began to sacrifice digits and limbs."

"Is that who the two men you killed were? Group members. They had prosthetic legs."

"They were the last living group members. Apart from me."

Suddenly, Blue's concerns about soggy biscuit and getting one over Finn were insignificant. This whole story of Parker's was far bigger than he could ever have realized. "And they killed your family? Why? It doesn't make sense?"

Rage crawled across Parker's face. "Revenge."

"Revenge?"

The tubes hanging from the mechanical apparatus snaked upwards and began to wriggle as they wormed towards Parker. "Because power is addictive, Blue, and we found out self-sacrifice wasn't the only way to get more of it."

The revelation hit Parker hard. "Shit," he said, "shit." He looked for a seat. Finding none, he squatted to his haunches and supported his weight with his prosthetic hook. "Why did they want revenge on you in particular?"

The tubes and wires snapped into place. Parker's angry visage crawled with emotion. "Because we found out if you killed someone with the power, you got more of it than if you self-sacrificed. We found out the only way to get more and more powerful was to actively hunt down others and take it from them. You must understand it was years ago, but it was a bloodbath, and during that time, it was kill or be killed."

Blue puffed air out from between his cheeks. His legs were aching, and he had to stand up. He stretched to his full height. "Who did you kill?"

"Their brother, after they killed my best friend."

"And they killed your family in revenge?"

A tear ran down Parker's scarred face. "Knowing I would come after them. We were supposed to be at a truce, but they never let it drop. They were waiting for me. They trapped me here with sedatives, and. . ." He leveled his manic gaze on Blue. "I knew they would come for you. They tortured me for info on others like us. That's why I reached out to you."

"But that doesn't make sense. You killed them? Why tell me? Unless. . ."

Energy ran through the mechanical chair, and the door behind Blue slammed shut.

"Why did you close the door?" Blue rattled the door's handle.

Parker laughed.

"Parker, you're scaring me. Why did you close the door?"

"Because I want you to see first-hand how it works."

Blue twisted slowly, watching Parker. "What do you mean?"

The television mounted on the wall turned on, revealing the downstairs foyer area of the building. Finn and Jai wandered through it, heading to the elevator. "This machine is a weapon, Blue. It converts the ability to move things and focuses it into a tool of destruction. But even with the deaths of the other two, it's not enough. I need more! Now, choose which of your friends will be the first to die."

Blue spun. "Fuck you! No!"

Parker laughed. His eyes blazed. The tubes attached to his stumps, to the jack on top of his head, pumped. "How did you hear everything and not realize what was about to happen? Are you so stupid?"

Blue rattled the door handle. It turned, but the door wouldn't budge.

"Choose!"

From the corner of his eye, Blue saw something solid flying towards him. He dropped to the floor, narrowly avoiding it: a telephone! It must have been ancient. It had a cable running to the wall. When he looked at where it had come from, he saw broken glass hovering and swirling beyond Parker. "You can't kill them," he said. "Please!"

Parker laughed. His maniacal face contorted again. "I can easily kill them. Unless. . ."

Blue met Parker's eyes. "Unless. . . unless I do it, right?"

Parker nodded, grinning.

Blue wondered whether he could, if he wanted to, of course. Sure, he was mighty pissed with them, and he was sick to death of losing soggy biscuit, but they didn't deserve to die. And, if he was being honest, he couldn't expect to ever live up to his mum's expectations if he had killed people, so that made it an even bigger no-no. "Tell me," he said, "what's the endgame here? You kill them and then what? Everyone with even the most rudimentary amount of power is dead except you. What then? Where do you go?"

"You don't understand," Parker said.

Damn straight. Blue couldn't understand it at all.

Parker spun away from him and turned his attention to the screen. Finn and Jai were gone. The elevator must be on its way up.

Had Blue told them what floor Parker was on? He didn't think he had.

And then, the screen revealed the inside of the elevator. For fuck's sake! Was there anywhere without cameras these days? The two boys were checking each floor. Finn was holding the door while Jai disappeared off camera after exiting the lift. *At least they were working together,* Blue thought. Jai returned to the lift and the doors closed.

"Watch this," Parker said.

Jai fell to his knees, clutching his head. It pulsed, swelled like the rat had. Blood ran down his nose. He screamed.

Parker laughed.

Blue picked up the telephone, charged forward, and smashed it into Parker's head with as much power as he could muster. He didn't get much purchase, but it was enough to throw Parker's concentration. If only he had another weapon, or at least a better way of holding one. And then, as the phantom pains in his missing hand grew from a steady throb to a pulsating rage, he saw another projectile come flying towards him.

The toolbox thudded into his chest and sent him sprawling backwards. He skidded across the floor and crashed into the wall. His toe hurt, the tingling of his missing hand had evolved into burning, and now his chest and back were in agony as well.

A splintering sound of something tearing from the wall forced him to push the pain from his mind and look at Parker. A cabinet hurtled through the air.

Blue raised his hand to shield himself from the blow, expecting imminent impact. The cabinet froze where it was, hovering, trapped between two forces.

Parker screamed.

Blue roared.

The cabinet flew in the direction it came from and exploded against the wall.

Parker laughed. "Now you're getting it!"

Blue forced himself to his feet, wondering where the next attack was coming from.

"Come, let's kill your friends and fight afterwards! It'll be so much more fun!" Parker bellowed. Broken glass, bits of rubble, small tools, and pieces of debris swirled around him. "Come, watch," he said, turning to the screen.

Blue gathered himself. The horrible pain in his phantom hand had plateaued and become a constant hum. Finn and Jai might be assholes, but they were Blue's friends, and this goddamn psychopath was *not* going to kill them. Not if he could help it. He unbuckled the strap on his prosthetic hook, and with a scream, he pointed it at Parker. "Think fast, fuckwit!"

The hook ejaculated into the air, spinning like a ninja star. Parker turned as it collided with his face. The hook hit him fair in the eye. It punched through something soft, and a spurt of jelly burst outwards, looking remarkably like a load bound for a graham cracker. He screamed, but Blue didn't relent.

Screaming like a banshee, he gestured to the tubes, and they wound around Parker's throat. With a fast movement of his arm, Blue pulled it taut. Not wanting to take any chances, he ran for the cables and grabbed them, ratcheting them down, tightening their constrictive grip on Parker's throat. He dropped to his ass and pushed against the machine with his feet, choking the life out of Parker.

The other cables, wires, and tubes thrashed around, whipping the air, cracking against Blue's head and neck, but he held on, certain Parker had probably only trained him so he could harvest his power as his own. Blue withstood the onslaught, holding on until Parker's ragged breath stopped. For the first time, he wished he'd never met the bloke. He didn't know what to believe, but as far as facts went, only one set would matter. Parker had disappeared the night his family died, and he'd killed two blokes in this room. Whether anyone could prove what happened was another matter, but it was time for Blue to get out of there and check on his friends.

He took one last look at Parker's purple face. Blood ran from his eyes, ears, and nose. Blue shuddered and walked to the door, realizing he felt pretty charged with energy. The door opened effortlessly. He ran to the elevator. Jai was moving, clearly pained, but at least he was alive.

Wondering at how it had all clicked for him in those final moments, he thought of stories of people lifting cars and boulders trapping their children. *Had it been the sacrifices? Had it been desper-*

ation? Had it been the knowledge that he'd only make his mum proud if he did everything he could to save his mates? Either way, with the phantom pains now tingling mildly again, he knew when it had mattered, he had done something important. He had saved lives, and that was reason enough for him to be here.

Mum, he thought. *I hope you saw that.*

Back in the community center, Blue and Finn sat staring at the soggy biscuits.

"I'm not eating it," Finn said.

Blue smiled. He waggled his eyebrows, and the biscuits lifted off the floor. "A deal's a deal. You know that."

"Yeah, but without Jai, it's practice. It's not happening."

Blue laughed. "Look," he said, "I'll tell you what, if you follow through once Jai's on his feet, letting you skip out on this one. . . *that's a sacrifice I'm willing to make.*"

DEFACE THE MUSIC
ALVARO ZINOS-AMARO

Everyone has been seduced by their own song. Everyone is late, or dying. Linda, only Linda, answered my call. No, that's not right—she rang me? Either way, I was understandably nervous to make contact. We hadn't spoken since long before the first reports broke out, so I had to consider the timing of her reappearance in my life suspect.

She said she could meet me at the diner at midnight. She sounded sure of this, which might have been a step in the right direction, or the kind of glaring portent of doom that only someone with desperation-induced myopia would overlook. I showed up an hour early and kept myself busy waiting. I asked one of the servers if it was okay to close my eyes for a few moments before my friend joined me. The server said, "Sure. You deserve the rest."

What follows is that everything else.

My head is on the table, pancake-like, when Linda's voice rouses me.

I shake off the dregs of syrupy exhaustion and stretch my neck.

Linda sits down in front of me. Our booth can accommodate four, but four are not presently available.

To our left is a parallel row of unoccupied tables and chairs, splayed like spread fingers, and beyond that, the diner's galley, a long, thin cave of gleaming silver metals and dimly glowing cook-tops, bookended by built-in larders.

From the galley, we hear the radio being dialed to one of the new pretend pirate stations, whose conceit is bootlegging shanties from newfound seas.

"Reza," she says. "You're looking."

"Well," I reply, our old joke.

I can see Linda has something else besides a smile on her mind; perhaps back-taxes on the promises we broke, or an insurance claim against the policy of our shared experiences.

"You're wondering," she says, "if it's really me. If you can trust me."

Linda, with her large, voracious brown eyes and cheeks that always seem to settle a millimeter before dimpling, was once my closest companion. The smell of her hair, a heavenly mix of sandalwood and jasmine, saw me through a divorce and triple bypass surgery. It's amazing what a few well-placed, correctly-timed molecules can do.

"I suppose it's useless to fret," I say. "If it isn't you, that means it's already too late for me anyway, right? I'm grateful you're here."

She nods. "Same."

Our server brings water and writes down our order.

After taking a sip from an emaciated-looking straw, Linda says, "Who was the first in your circle to go?"

My jaw moves, shifting a girding pressure until it snaps into a place where it can be cradled indefinitely, like a child's car seat sliding around a bit before it clicks in. "In hindsight, I suppose it was my son, Ben," I say. "In the beginning, when he seemed overwhelmed and distracted, I thought it was standard teenage angst. I made a few attempts to break through, which at the time felt like significant efforts but which I'd presently characterize as half-hearted. Anyway, after he was ensorcelled away from me, I realized it had been the seduction all along."

"Poor Ben," Linda says. "I remember his laughter when he was a toddler."

"Do you think it's gone forever?" I ask.

"I think," she says, "that it was never meant to last."

Invisible hands in the galley kitchen change the radio station to folkloric tango-like tunes.

"How about you?" I inquire.

"Started with my mom," she says. "Like you, I misdiagnosed the issue. That's how they got away with it at the start, isn't it? Initially, I thought it was the early stages of dementia. How foolish. Mom's mind was perfectly whole—just not entirely her own anymore."

"I understand," I say. "It went quickly for me after Ben, but the grief fog was so thick I couldn't really see it unfolding. First my sister. Then, two of my friends at work. Afterwards, my parents. Several neighbors. My boss. Faster and faster." I squint. "Have you ever caught yourself wondering, 'Why not me?'"

"You always had that talent," Linda says, throwing her head back a little. She's referring to my gift for resentment. Eventually, it's hard to cope with not being chosen, even if you can't stomach who—or what—is doing the choosing. There's no cruelty, I decide, to Linda's implicit observation. I don't consider resentment a negative trait, but rather a useful measure of self-protection that sensitizes painful memories and activates them at critical times to prevent further injury.

"I don't want to be seduced," I say. "I just want to understand what sets us apart. I've been searching for criteria, you see, however absurd they might be. But the data topples every hypothesis. I always find cases that don't meet the parameters."

Linda lets out a soft chuckle. "Reza."

"What?"

"You haven't changed a bit."

"I'll take that as a compliment," I say. "It means I've staved off decay."

"What if seduction is selected for by unquantifiable factors?" she says. "Maybe for some people it's triggered by the intensity of the love they feel. Or their fear. Or the feelings produced by their dreams. To be so effective, the seductions must be custom-built."

"There are ways to approximately measure all those things, based on brain states," I counter. "Everything we experience subjectively has an objective correlative that will show up in a detailed enough neural scan."

"Maybe it's even more abstract," she says. "What if the binary conception of resistance vs. surrender is itself the trap? Maybe when our minds birthed the ideas of independence and assimilation, victory and defeat, we primed ourselves for conquest. Perhaps we lost before ever starting."

"But everyone believes in those concepts," I say.

"Do you, truly?" Linda inquires. She grins. "For that matter, do I?"

The truth is, I've always seen myself outside any given system. I haven't attached any value judgment to this position, simply accepted it. In any closed logical framework there is always an undecidable proposition; is it so far-fetched to think that in any social system there will likewise be undecidable individuals, entities whose worth cannot be ascertained by the network's criteria?

At this moment, the radio falls quiet. The diner's two servers and short-order cook gather at the edge of the galley, hunched forward.

In a powerful baritone, the cook says, "Weg-Re-Su."

He repeats the syllables three more times in a steady rhythm, and the servers join in.

They chant the sounds—giving the distinct impression that they comprise a name—in unison for about half a minute and fall silent.

Utter stillness.

Then, a soft tapping sound emanates from below the farthermost stove.

I frown. Linda seems mildly amused, though I've misread her before. We observe the scene as the small crowd inches closer to the stove. They clear a berth several feet wide in front of the storage compartment at the stove's base.

The tapping sound continues.

Our server steps forward, places her hand on the heated stove, and screams. After an instant during which I'd swear I can hear the micro-sizzle of her skin, she withdraws her wounded hand and takes a step back.

The fuzzy, dull thuds in the storage compartment become more regular and insistent.

The other server and then the cook do the same as our server, yelping and hollering briefly while the palms of their hands hiss against the stove's grate for a split second, then retreating.

After several more taps, the metallic door of the storage compartment slowly swings open.

I rise, my clammy hands urgently pressing down on the diner table's Cola-red Formica top. I feel the table holding my body, but nothing can counterbalance the congealing balloon of anxiety pressing upon me from the inside.

Linda, meanwhile, has edged back in her seat, settled into a sort of reverie.

The door of the storage unit beneath the stove is wide open now.

I peer into a deep, ancestral darkness.

Shaggy, thin, black limbs protrude, probing at first, then more secure as they venture onto the kitchen floor.

One leg, two legs, three legs, four legs. . . I keep count because arithmetic feels real, grounded somehow.

Five, six, seven.

Eight.

Eight legs.

The spider is over two feet long.

It pauses when it has completely emerged from the storage compartment.

Its black abdomen is covered by a black felt mottled with reflecting silvery strands, like stray beams of starlight trapped by adhesion. Somewhere in space, an enormous distance away, I imagine a distended void swallowing sunshine and digesting it into a gruel of misery.

The creature turns in our direction.

My eyes follow reluctantly upward from its abdomen to its bulging cephalothorax, which rather than culminating in a standard arachnid set of eyes tapers off into a rippling intumescence one might mistake for a neck.

Appended to this pulsing girth is the face of a rat.

"What the fuck. . ." I whisper.

Linda says nothing.

As I look on, I can't tell if the enormous arthropod has been a chimera since primordial time, or if the rat head somehow became conjoined with the arachnid body through some elemental force of necessity long after gestation.

The first server to sear her hand turns on the radio.

A woeful, dirge-like tune, played on solo oboe, pipes through the diner.

The rat-spider amalgamation begins to move in concert with the music. It lifts its limbs with visible effort and turns its head from side to side with an expression I can only think of as resignation.

The whiskers on the rat face droop and the eyes become half-closed.

And yet it pushes on.

"I haven't seen this dance before," Linda says.

At the repetition of an interval in the music, the creature supports itself on its four hindmost legs and two frontmost and raises its foreshortened pedipalps until they touch in mid-air.

The three onlookers jeer in exaltation.

"Is that...?"

"Yes," Linda says. "It clapped."

The funereal song plays on, and the rat-spider repeats its intricate, slow-motion pattern of movement, retracing its tired steps but this time counterclockwise.

As it spins widdershins, its spinneret exudes a thin stream of glittering silk.

The music ends.

The rat-spider lifts its head towards the three architects of its display in a protracted search for approbation that even at a distance reeks, to me, of self-loathing.

The small crowd breaks out into applause.

"Fantastic," says the cook.

"Marvelous," says our server.

"Best one yet," adds the second server.

The creature bows in what could be shame or simply the melancholy recognition that its purpose has been fulfilled.

Shambolic, head down, it plods back inside the storage compartment.

The silk left in its wake evaporates.

The cook resumes his post deep inside the galley. The unneeded server stares longingly at the storage compartment, sighs in satisfaction, and closes the compartment door.

Our server returns to our table and refills our water. She's positively glowing.

"Isn't that. . ." I begin, but no straightforward description of what we've experienced seems possible. "Isn't that some kind of, uh, health violation?"

Our server's eyes seem tickled by the suggestion. She waves it away. "Not at all," she says. "The cocoon is deep inside the earth. No transfer of materials."

She and Linda exchange a look.

"Anyway, I'm glad you got to see it," she says. "Not many do. Your food will be out shortly!"

She jaunts back towards the galley.

I study Linda. "Some kind of. . . mascot?"

"Everyone needs a pick-me-up," Linda replies. She says it in a chiding way, as though reminding a stubborn child of a lesson they keep refusing.

I look back at the spot in the kitchen where, minutes earlier, the beast, marionetted by a responsibility I shall never understand, performed its wearied dance.

"I don't think I can eat anymore," I say.

Linda's lips part and remain so for a few beats.

I gaze at her as though seeing her for the first time.

We've been through so much together.

The world has been through so much. . .

What will she say next?

———————

A few days later, I find myself standing motionless in the foyer of my apartment building, remembering what Saturdays used to feel like when I'd walk down to the local farmer's market and pick up fresh produce for the family, and I'm picturing the market stalls as they must be now, mostly abandoned, food decaying out in the open, when in the faraway recesses of my mind I hear the words, "Weg-Re-Su," faint in the beginning, then ever more crystalline, like a window into another place.

I blink.

If this is the foyer, why does it suddenly feel like a cocoon?

What is the distance that at any given moment separates outside from inside?

Everyone is late, I remember, or dying.

But what if late merely means being on time to a different destination? What if dying is a means of communication, essentializing the fluidity of nature?

Weg-Re-Su. The words cycle through a dozen times, and despite all the restless nights and the heaviness in my body, the seed of an ancient dance germinates inside me.

I step out into the blanching sunlight.

The music calls.

And now that you have read these words, I promise that one day the same will be true for you.

THE UNBURIED BOX
KEVIN DAVID ANDERSON

The box was unremarkable. New enough to still function but too old to retain the labels that could have identified its original purpose. Whatever it was made for, it surely wasn't created to house the ash, bits of bone, and one partial human molar. A decent undertaker would've made sure the cremated remains were nothing but fine gray powder. A decent undertaker might have provided the bereaved with a more dignified container. But even in death, coloreds didn't get the same level of service as whites. Not in 1985. Not in Thankful, Alabama.

Malcolm wasn't sure why he hadn't disposed of his daughter's ashes. Nothing in the box reminded him of the vibrant twenty-year-old heading out to the bus stop on her way to Los Angeles. All she ever talked about was getting out of Alabama and putting her toes in the Pacific Ocean. He never knew where his daughter's west coast obsession came from, but damn, he admired her for following that dream. No, this unburied box didn't remind him of her at all, but three years after her horrendous, violent death, it was all Malcolm had left.

He placed a hand on the box, sliding it a little closer, as a sheriff's car pulled onto his property. Sitting on the porch his grandfather had built, Malcolm poured another whiskey. If they were coming to arrest him, for what he couldn't imagine, he sure as hell didn't want to go sober.

Deputy Gail Cobb stepped from the car wearing street clothes. It was the first time Malcolm saw her out of uniform, but her choices in attire didn't surprise him: loose fitting blue jeans, a baggy T-shirt half tucked showing a robust thick leather belt with no design or pattern. The unmarried twenty-eight-year-old who had chosen a profession most imagined the domain of men had generated the kind of rumors discussed in hushed voices and small righteous circles.

She ran a hand over her slicked-back, dirty-blond hair and looked up at the porch. "Hey, Malcolm."

Using Malcolm's first name, like they were old friends, pissed him off. Disrespectful, but not uncommon in Thankful, Alabama, a town that never acknowledged losing the civil war.

"Afternoon, Deputy."

"I ain't no Deputy. Quit yesterday. I'm on my way to drop off this car, and then I'm movin' west."

"You drive all the way here to tell me your travel plans. We ain't said more than twenty words to one another."

"Yeah, that's part of why I need to. . ." She looked down at her sneakers as if the words she was looking for were hidden in her well-worn laces. Her eyes came back up. "It shouldn't be that way between us." She pointed with a thick folder she carried toward a chair. "Mind if I sit?"

He wanted to tell Gail to just state her business, but there was something odd about her manner. She didn't have that superior swagger all white folks with guns carry when moving about on this side of town. The deputy looked more like someone needing to talk, needing to confess.

If a preacher's what she's looking for, Malcolm thought, *I can pretend.*

Gail stepped onto the porch and sat; her head hung low like a ten-year-old heading into the principal's office. She looked at the box under Malcolm's hand. "That Breonna?"

Malcolm hoped to skip the chit-chat. "I've never seen you on this side of town. Not even in uniform. You obviously here for a reason. So, let's get on to it."

Gail ran her hand over her hair again. "Got nothing but respect for you and your family. You served this country in Korea and Vietnam. Took a bullet in each I heard. Hell, your daddy was a Tuskegee Airmen for God's sake." She closed her eyes, clearly picturing something upsetting. "It just wasn't right."

"What wasn't right?"

"What they did. . ." Gail looked at the box. ". . . to your Breonna."

Malcolm's eyes narrowed. "The man who hurt my little girl is in the ground. Shot dead by your boss his-self."

Gail shook her head. "Just a seasonal farmhand. A Mexican come up for work. He wasn't even in Thankful when your daughter. . ." Even though Gail sat in the shade, sweat bubbled on her brow. "Sheriff killed the Mexican when we found out who *really* killed your daughter."

Malcolm glowered. As long as he lived, he was never gonna be alright with how Breonna died. No parent could. The one glimmer of satisfaction he'd held onto for the past three years was that the man that had done it was worm food. Now this bitch was gonna take that away. He sat forward and took a deep breath. "Go on," he said.

"Know the station she tried to catch the Greyhound?"

"Yeah."

"There's an apartment complex across the street. Real shit-hole. We're out there twice a week, if not every day. The owner

installed video cameras, keeping an eye on his tenants and property. The tape from that night ain't around no more, but. . ." Gail
reached into the folder and pulled out three eight-by-tens. "I had
these stills made." She slid them across the table.

Malcolm saw shame on Gail's face but didn't give a damn. He
scanned the images. They were all different but told the same
story. Four men dragged Breonna into a pickup truck. The pictures
were black and white, but they didn't need to be in color to see
that none of them were Mexican. The Confederate flag bumper
sticker told Malcolm what kind of men they were.

"Told me to shred this." Gail brought up the folder and set it
on the table. "It's all there. Identities, witness statements, *the* real
autopsy report. I wouldn't read that. I really wouldn't."

Malcolm took the folder.

"After I found out who had done it, I was ordered to sit on it
for a day or two. Next day, they shot the Mexican. Case closed,"
Gail said. "You'll understand why after you read that."

Malcolm flipped through the pages.

"I planned to take that to the FBI a dozen times. Even chose a
secret meetin' spot like that Deepthroat guy. Never went through
wit'it. I'm good at planning but piss-poor at follow-through."

Malcolm felt sick. "Why you tellin' me this now?"

"Been wantin' to leave for a while now." Gail stood. "Thankful
ain't the kind of place. . ." She trailed off for a beat. "I don't want
to have any kind of family in a town that elects a Grand Wizard for
mayor." Gail looked at Malcolm expectantly. It seemed Gail
paused for him to acknowledge or maybe even congratulate her
for being a white person who didn't like that kind of thing. If true,
Gail would have a long wait. Whatever her reasons for leaving, be
it systemic racism or bigoted views of lifestyle choices, Malcolm
didn't give a damn.

"Now that you know," Gail stood and stepped from the porch,
"what're ya gonna do?"

Malcolm's hands trembled. He could feel his temples begin to throb. Good thing none of his guns were within reach. "You sit on this for three years, and on your way outta town, tail tucked, you gots the nerve to ask me, 'what I goin' do?' Fuck you, Gail."

"I deserve that." The former deputy took a breath and then headed to her car. She pulled open the door and turned back. "I have it on good authority they'll *all* be there tonight. Some punk-ass kraut-band comin' in. You know the place."

Malcolm nodded. Everybody knew the fucking place.

Gail drove away like someone who knew they'd just lit a fuse. Fast and not looking back. But before she did, she said, "Good luck to you, Malcolm."

Malcolm didn't need luck. All the luck that ever came his way always ran south. No, all Malcolm needed, all he wanted, was in a footlocker he'd brought back from Vietnam.

If ever the KKK had an unofficial clubhouse in Thankful County, it was Corky's. Outside of town, flanked by longleaf pines with its backend hanging over a gator-infested swamp, was a roadhouse that catered to all kinds of assholes, Klan, neo-Nazis, neo-Confederates, and a new group of youthful white-supremacist shit-stains calling themselves skinheads. Malcolm had no idea what a skinhead was, but the folder Gail dropped off said it was a busboy, a skinhead named Luke, who came forward to finger the men that took Breonna. The poorly-typed report Malcolm studied while sitting in his Nova, parked a quarter mile from Corky's, didn't say what caused the kid to come forward. Maybe a Sieg-Heil here and there was okay, but kidnapping, raping, and setting a young black woman ablaze was a bridge too far.

Gail was right though. Once Malcolm knew who *really* killed his daughter, he understood why they'd pinned it on a Mexican.

Poor S.O.B. Although, there was a bit of respect discernable in the gesture. Most black folks suffering a similar tragedy wouldn't get any answers or even an investigation into their loss. They at least respected—or feared—Malcolm enough to try and give him some kind of closure. Even though it was a lie.

Malcolm held the four rap sheets one last time, making sure their faces were seared into his memory. Rob Packer, oldest of the foursome, sported a ZZ Top-beard, was an avid Holocaust denier, and hosted the most popular right-wing AM radio show in all of Thankful County. Nick Ochs looked clean-cut in his mugshot, but the thirty-four-year-old son of Thankful's mayor was anything but. He'd beaten two rape charges and served as the local Klan's Nighthawk, a position often overseeing the enforcers or Wrecking Crew. Kevin Seefried, fifty, who owed the truck decaled with a Confederate flag, and Adam Johnson, thirty-six, both served time for assault, but neither had any known Klan association. But it's not like they advertise membership. There's a reason they wear hoods.

Malcom stepped from his Nova and realized he'd parked too close to the swamp. Driving in with his headlights off, he'd misjudged and put his back wheels in deep mud. He'd need a tow to get out, but that probably wouldn't matter anyway. The likelihood of him coming back was slim. He tossed the keys on the dash, grabbed Breonna's box and his gear, then headed to Corky's.

It was two a.m. when the band stopped playing. Its name, *Stoze Jungs*, was painted on their van in large Nazi propaganda-style lettering. From Malcolm's vantage point, he could see a small crowd inside, eight vehicles outside, counting the band's Nazi van parked around back. But only one vehicle concerned him. The one his daughter had taken her final ride in. Kevin Seefried's truck was there.

From a crouched position behind a stump, Malcolm eyed the band carrying their equipment out the back. That gave him an idea. It was more likely than not they'd leave the back entrance open. That's where he'd enter. Without any idea what the layout was, he thought it best to move quietly, stealthily, until it was time to make his presence known.

When the *Stolze Jungs* finally pulled out, Malcolm tucked the box by the stump and started his approach. It felt odd to leave the box. It was at that moment he realized he hadn't been more than a few yards from it in years. He couldn't explain why he felt the need to keep it close. He knew his daughter was not in the box. Not really. But another part of him, the part that still wept when her image moved through his mind, wanted to believe that some part remained, still wanting to dip her toes in the Pacific Ocean. Even if that part was just a product of his imagination, he didn't want it, or her, to see what he intended to do. The box would have to stay.

It'd been fifteen years since he'd worn his fatigues, and they were tight in all the wrong places along his six-foot-four frame. But the combat boots, the KA-BAR blade strapped to his belt, the Browning-High Power single-action handgun he'd won in a poker game from a drunk Australian officer, and the M16 he'd hunted Charlie with during two full rotations in Vietnam all seemed to feel just right.

He moved along a rickety dock connected to the building's rear, then stepped onto the stairs leading to the deck that hung over the swamp. He held his breath, moving up the steps. If anyone came out the back, they'd bump into him immediately, and the element of surprise would be lost.

As luck would have it, he arrived at the back door unnoticed. He could hear the jukebox in the main room, twangy, guitar blaring. The hinges on the door squealed like a pig, but no one could hear his entrance over the music. Malcolm moved into a hallway, bathrooms to the right, and what looked like an office door, closed, on the left. The main room was straight ahead. Judging by

THE UNBURIED BOX   141

the outside, it was probably a thousand square feet. Lots of places to move, lots of places to hide. He snuck down the hall until he caught sight of the pictures proudly mounted on the wall. Some black and white, some in color, but all telling the same horrific history. Holding rifles like they were big game hunters, Klansman posed in group photos over dead, mutilated black bodies. Just good ol' sportsmen of the south, lording over trophies of dark-skinned men, women, and children.

Malcolm's blood boiled. He'd always known certain white men considered Malcolm and his kin nothing more than animals. But he couldn't imagine them feeling free and safe enough to take pictures like these, frame 'em, and display'em on their fucking walls.

Pondering the grotesque art gallery caused Malcolm to momentarily take his eye off the ball. The office door behind him opened. Malcolm spun on a heel and found himself face-to-face with Rob Packer.

The man zipped up his fly as if he'd just taken a piss. His eyes tightened. "What'cha doin' here, boy?"

Malcolm didn't answer, just glowered.

Packer's eyes slowly widened, suddenly recognizing Malcolm, and perhaps remembering why the heavily decorated combat veteran might come looking for him one day. Packer took a step back, and that was all the confession Malcolm needed. Fast as lighting, he unsheathed the KA-BAR and without pause, thrust the well-used blade up. The knife entered Packer under the chin and then cut straight up, impaling the brain. With a practiced twist and arcing withdrawal, Malcolm retracted the blade, making sure it did far more damage on the way out than it did on the way in.

As the body crumbled, grey beard turning crimson, Malcolm pushed it back so it'd fall into the office. He stepped inside to the sound of a scream. A young orange-haired woman peered up at him with brown eyes. On her knees and naked from the waist up, she had her hands on the hips of a bare-chested man, a swastika tattoo across his chest. The man's pants were around his ankles; he didn't bother pulling them up before lunging at Malcolm. Stumbling, hands reaching out, he fell. As he did, Malcolm dragged the KA-BAR across his throat. Swastika-man fell to his knees, hands clutching his throat, attempting to stop the fountain of pulsing liquid exiting his neck.

The woman had seen enough. She bounded up and bolted. Malcolm kicked the door closed, and she ran headlong into it like a cartoon character. Malcolm grabbed a fistful of orange hair, pulling her close. He pressed the blood-soaked blade under her chin. "Your name, girl?"

"Stephanie," she managed, lips quivering, semen drizzled on her chin. "Stephanie Baez."

"Well, Ms. Baez, way I see it, you got two choices. On the other side of this here door, you can turn right, head on out there, and warn them yahoos what's comin'."

There was a sickening plop as swastika-man finally fell forward, dead on the floor.

"Or you could turn left, tiptoe out the backdoor. Maybe live long enough to think about some of your life choices." He lowered the knife, then opened the door slowly. When he let go of her hair, she turned slightly to look him in the eye. She was maybe twenty-five. About the same age Breonna would have been.

Her eyes darted around, unsure. Malcolm gestured with the knife toward the door. Stephanie backed into the hallway, keeping eyes on Malcolm. He had no idea what she'd do. Could go either way. But Malcolm never relished the feeling that lingered inside him after killing a woman. In-country, he'd done it one too many times and, although they'd tried to kill him, it never felt right.

Stephanie took a breath, then turned left.

Making better choices already, Malcolm thought, as the slap of the back door echoed in the hall.

In the corner of his eye, he saw someone stumble into the hallway. Malcolm stepped back and closed the office door, hoping it was someone heading to the can. The feet shuffled closer. Malcolm could tell by their irregular cadence that their owner was drunk. To his dismay, the shuffling did not disappear into the bathroom.

The man in the hall pounded on the office door. "Hey, Rob. You guys 'bout done. Ya'll need to leave some Stephanie for the rest of us, man."

Malcolm grabbed Packer by his ZZ Top beard and dragged his body on top of the other dead man. It would look confusing to anyone walking in, one white man on top of another, if only for a moment. But a moment is all Malcolm wanted.

The man pounded on the door again, and this time began to open it. Malcolm stepped behind the door. The man staggered inside, looking at the pile of limbs and white flesh on the floor. "What the fuck you homos doing?"

Malcolm closed the door. The sound of it caused the man to spin around, and Nick Ochs got his first and last look at Malcolm. With an enormous hand, he covered Ochs' mouth and pushed him back against a wall. Nose to nose Malcolm said, "You remember my daughter, Breonna?"

The man tried to scream, and that's when Malcolm sunk all eight inches of the KA-BAR into his crotch. "Yeah, you remember."

Slicing upward, the blade got hung up on the man's thick gator-skin-belt but, with some elbow grease, Malcolm powered through. Afterward, it was clear slicing all the way to the collar-bone. Ochs' eyes rolled back. He was already dead when Malcolm stepped away to avoid the splash of innards now free from their confinement.

He stood in the middle of the room, surveying his work.

Malcolm couldn't believe his luck. Although pleased with how things had gone so far, he was getting tired of this one-at-a-time shit. He cleaned the knife on the back of Ochs' shirt and put it away. He unslung the M16, peeked outside, then moved from the office. Plodding down the hall, he glanced at the gallery of nightmares on the wall. Horrific, but it fueled his rage.

Walking into the roadhouse like he owned it, Malcolm fired into the jukebox, silencing Lynyrd Skynyrd and grabbing everyone's attention. He scanned the faces of the six men in the room while aiming at the figure behind the bar, a fat man in suspenders, slowly reaching under the counter.

"You the owner of this establishment?" Malcolm barked.

Fatman's eyes beamed with pride. "Been in my family three generations." His hand clearly still reaching for a weapon.

Malcolm gestured toward the hallway. "So, you're responsible for the art gallery back there?"

Fatman grinned and shrugged like it was no big deal.

Malcolm fired three times. One bullet went through the neck, the other two through the chest, severing a suspender. The shotgun Fatman grabbed flew up above the bar briefly before disappearing along with its owner.

Malcolm eyed the five men huddled by a pool table. "Well, I'll be damned." Kevin Seefried and Adam Johnson stood amongst them.

One of the nameless others stepped forward with a pool cue in his hand. "You're one dead nig—"

Using the SS insignia on the man's T-shirt as a target, Malcolm released another burst. The man fell back onto a table, sending half-full beer steins crashing. He had thought to mow them all down right then and there, but before SS-man hit the floor, Malcolm knew his luck had run out.

Malcolm heard the familiar ping-clunk of the rifle failing to extract accompanied by a hot gas smell, gunpowder residue from a corroded chamber. A new M16 was pure shit. But one sitting in Malcolm's closet for fifteen years was a whole new level of FUBAR.

Shit.

The men rushed Malcolm, seizing weapons on their way, pool balls and cues; Seefried grabbed an American flag and pole, a black swastika emblazoned across the red, white, and blue.

He dropped the jammed rifle and went for his sidearm. It had just cleared the holster when three of them tackled Malcolm. They went down in a tangle of limbs, fists flying. Malcolm felt the barrel of the Browning touch crotch. He fired, sending a slug and a set of testicles to the floor.

Adam Johnson, now a eunuch, screamed and fell back, both hands clutching the pulpy mass between his legs. A fist clutching a nine-ball smashed into Malcolm's face. He felt hands grab for the Browning. Knowing he had only seconds before it was wrenched from his grasp, Malcolm flicked his thumb up, locking the slide by engaging the safety.

Two nameless men sat on Malcolm's chest. One, bald, with neck tattoos, had the Browning. He turned it around and placed the barrel on Malcolm's forehead. "Bye-bye, Spear-chucker!" He tried to pull the trigger. "Shit!"

He frantically turned the gun around in his hands like a teenager with a Rubik's Cube. Malcolm chuckled, knowing it was only a matter of time before the dumbass figured out the problem. "What's wrong, cracker?"

Baldy suddenly smiled as he found the safety. He turned the gun back on Malcolm. "So long. . ." Before he fired, his head jerked violently left to the sound of a gunshot. Baldy's noggin had a gaping hole in the side. He fell forward.

A voice behind them shouted. "Get off him!"

With his one free hand, Malcolm pushed Baldy to the side and looked over in astonishment. Gail stood between them and the front door, her revolver aimed at the other man still holding Malcolm to the floor. "I said, get the fuck off him!"

Malcolm met her eyes. He had never been so happy to see a white person in his life. "Gail?"

She stared back. Her expression was resolute, brow hardened, eyes focused. Nowhere near the woman full of regret that had stepped onto Malcolm's porch. There may have even been a glimmer of satisfaction in her eyes.

"Wh-What the hell are you doin' here," Malcolm said.

Before Gail could respond, her body spasmed. Something exploded from her chest. Seefried, who had chosen not to join the melee on the floor, snuck up behind the ex-deputy and impaled her with the flagpole, the red, white, and blue bursting through her breastbone.

The man on Malcolm grinned. He turned his attention away from Gail, who had dropped to her knees, hands at her chest. He drew a fist back but quickly changed his mind about throwing the punch. Malcolm, having freed the Browning from Baldy's dead grasp, pointed it at the man on top of him, and with no hesitation, shot him in the face. Malcolm sat up, meeting the agonized gaze of Johnson, curled into a ball, screaming about the state of his little Johnson. To shut the man up, Malcolm put two in his chest.

A blur of movement raced toward the door. Seefried, after impaling a woman in the back, had apparently had enough. Without aiming, Malcolm emptied everything the Browning had left. Seefried made it through the door, but Malcolm knew at least one shot found its mark.

Malcolm stepped over to Gail and knelt. He'd seen enough wounds to know she didn't have long. Her hand came up, and Malcolm took it. "You're the dumbest white lady I ever did know."

"High praise," Gail said.

"What about your plan? Going west, startin' a family?"

"I told you." Gail coughed blood. "I'm good at planning, just piss-poor at follow-through..."

Malcolm felt her hand go slack. He laid it down, then closed the dead woman's eyes. "Dammit, Gail."

A moan came from outside. Malcolm got up and moved to the front door. Seefried had at least two slugs in him, one in the left knee, the other in the hip. Malcolm looked around for something blunt to end the man's cryin', and something red caught his eye. A Confederate flag hung down off the roof like a banner. Malcolm ripped it down and spun it, making a hideous rat's tale. He rolled the crawling man over onto his back and then plopped down on his chest.

"Tell me something, Seefried." Malcolm wrapped the flag around his neck like a noose. "When you set my baby on fire, was she alive?"

Seefried stopped squirming for a second, eyes going wide. In his last moments, he seemed to find some courage. He nodded, grinning.

Malcolm then strangled Seefried slowly, never looking away from his dying gaze.

Before setting Corky's ablaze, he carried Gail's body outside. He wrote a quick letter to whoever might give a shit about her and stuck it in her shirt pocket. Folks, black and white, had a right to know what she'd done and what she'd given up to do it. At the very least, she deserved a proper burial, unlike the rest of them.

For two days Malcolm drove west, using the keys in Seefried's pocket. Keys to a pickup truck that in life had carried Breonna to the place she would die. Now, in death, that same truck was taking her to a place Malcolm hoped they would both find some peace. He stuck to back roads. It was only a matter of time before they'd come for him. He didn't sign the note left with Gail, but he'd let orange-haired Stephanie go, and even though she probably didn't know Malcolm's name, Thankful's sheriff would put it together. He just hoped he had time to do this last thing.

Exhausted, Malcolm parked the truck right on the pier in Santa Monica, California. He grabbed Breonna's box and got out. Moving down the pier, he didn't realize how much he staggered. He hadn't stopped to eat or sleep, didn't think it was worth the risk. People cleared a path, especially when they eyed his blood-splattered fatigues.

His vision got cloudy as he heard voices around him.

"My God. He's covered in blood."

"Think he's got a knife."

"Call a cop."

"Shit, I think he has a gun."

"Police!"

Not even halfway down the pier and feeling faint, he moved to the railing. Leaning against it, he tried to catch his breath while looking out at the waves breaking below. The West Coast sun felt amazing on his face, and he wished his daughter could feel it. He looked down at the wet sand. *This was as good a spot as any.* He held the box in both hands as two cops ran up behind him.

"Drop the gun!" one screamed.

Malcolm had no gun to drop. Just a box. He tried to turn around, show them what he held, and that's when the first bullet struck. It hit his back with a meaty thud, followed by a second, then a third. He fell against the railing. It wasn't the first time he'd been shot, but it was the most chicken-shit. Even the Viet Cong had the decency to shoot him in the front.

The box fell open as Malcolm hit the pier. The breeze blew ash out over the water. "You made it, Breonna. You made it." With his final breath, he reached out and pushed the box forward.

Unaware of the violence above her, eight-year-old Gabby Rodriguez walked out from under the pier where the water met the sand. The skirt of her dress was pulled up into a pouch cradling her day's catch of seashells. Eyeing what looked like a sand dollar, she stopped and reached down, just as something splashed behind her. Startled, she turned quickly, a few shells flying out from her dress. It was a box.

Standing under the edge of the pier, she gazed up. Someone up there must have dropped it. She didn't see anyone, so she returned her attention to the box. It was an odd shape, not unlike her abuelo's cigar boxes. Young Gabby had come to live with her West Coast grandparents after her father had been killed a few years ago. Abuelo had said not to pick up trash on the beach, but she knelt next to it, thinking it might make a great container for her shells. She was about to grab it when she saw a hand reach down and pick it up.

Gabby looked up at the woman who seemed to have appeared right next to her. They both stood slowly, the woman examining the box, Gabby taking in the woman. She was tall and thin, wearing a faded dress. Her skin was darker than Gabby's and it glinted in the sun like water over smooth beach stones.

"Is that yours?" Gabby said, gazing up into the woman's soft brown eyes.

The woman nodded, lifted the lid back, and turned it upside down. A handful of grey dust drifted down and into the Pacific Ocean at their feet. The woman seemed mesmerized by the dust mixing with the water, sunbeams bouncing off the surface.

"It would make a nice shell box," Gabby said, hoping that the grown-up would take the hint.

The woman smiled and gazed down at Gabby. "Well, I guess I don't have need for it no more." She held the box open and low enough for Gabby to dump her shells into it. Gabby emptied the dress, and shells spilled into the box. The woman shut the lid and handed it over.

Gabby took it in one hand, then gazed down to slap the sand off her dress. "Thank you," she said as she continued to brush the sand away. When there was no response from the woman, Gabby glanced back up. But there was no one there to return her gaze. Gabby quickly scanned for the woman down the beach, under the pier, and even in the water. Nothing.

Gabby shrugged. Grown-ups are so weird sometimes.

She gazed down at the water, marveling at how the ashes broke apart in the salty liquid and settled into the wet sand. Then without a care in the world, Gabby returned to her shell hunt carrying a brand-new box that could easily hold all she could collect on this beautiful day or any other.

BLUNT FORCE TRAUMA

S.A. BRADLEY

Leonard had no idea he wanted a cigarette until he saw the advertisement in the liquor store window. He also had no intention of walking through the door.

Cravings were like that.

As the door chimed, Leonard didn't expect the store owner behind the counter to yelp in surprise and drop the big wad of cash in his hands. And he certainly did not expect Winston Wilson Dupree, a six-foot wall of muscle and tattoos, to turn and drive a crowbar into his skull.

Luck was like that.

It was a low-tech liquor store robbery. Dupree threatened to beat the attendant to death unless he emptied the register. Instead, the doorbell chimed, and the steel fangs of the crowbar found a new target. They sunk into the top of Leonard's head, turning his skull into fragmented daggers that stabbed his brain. Leonard had time to see a pair of wide eyes full of terror and rage, followed by an impossibly strong flash of white light that popped and faded like antique flash bulbs. The door chime reverberated in his mind, mutating into a sound like two bricks grinding between his ears.

Leonard immediately fell to the dirty linoleum floor, face first, unable to move or close his eyes. They didn't even close when his blood pooled on the tile and filled them. The pain was an ice bath, a sharp bite to every nerve, which slowly turned into horrifying numbness. Nothingness.

He regained consciousness, possibly for the last time, in the employee's bathroom. The weeping shop owner cradled Leonard, prayed in Farsi, and swaddled his head with the linen roll in the ancient towel dispenser, stained grey from thousands of hands.

"It isn't fair. It isn't fucking fair at all," Leonard repeated to himself, unsure if he said the words aloud. This shit wasn't supposed to happen. Leonard was on his way to see someone, on his way to do something, but he couldn't remember what. It dawned on him that he couldn't remember anything except this. Leonard could feel it all slipping away.

There came a moment when the fear left him, and he found a bittersweet calm in realizing it was almost over. A sense of gratitude for everything in his life came over him. He gained acceptance for the universe and his place in it.

That didn't last long.

Survival was a violent, ruthless cunt that inflicted far more pain on Leonard than Dupree's single blow did. A depressed fracture of the skull from the blunt force trauma drove bone into the brain, and a subdural blood clot added dangerous pressure. Before the surgeons could piece together Leonard's head like Kinsugi masters, they'd need to drill a fresh hole to remove the clot. Surgeons reconstructed his skull, but there was a possibility that tiny bone fragments might still hide in the brain's lining, which could later form a granuloma. Even a decade later, nightmares of bone chips trapped in the folds of his cerebrum haunted Leonard as if they were maggot larvae burrowing deeper to spread rot in his grey matter.

However, after nearly ten years of physical and mental rehabilitation, Leonard was on the threshold of a full recovery. Tonight would be a turning point for his health. When the physical pain and crippling depression were too much to bear, the thought of this night helped him through. Tonight, Leonard would murder Winston Wilson Dupree.

This moment was more important than the first day he walked out of physical therapy under his own power. More important than when his psychiatrist cleared him to leave the trauma recovery center and return home. It was even more important than the day he bought the Ruger Blackhawk with the serial numbers filed off from a street entrepreneur.

All those moments, which others might call victories, were merely steps in service of tonight.

It was no small feat getting here. Leonard counted on the crime that nearly killed him being unexceptional in the eyes of the courts, and they would reduce the legal process afterward to a series of checkmarks and boxes. He knew the tragedy would fade from judicial and civic memory if he filled those boxes without deviation. And Leonard did everything he could to make himself and the incident forgettable.

He said all the right things at his Survivors of Violent Crime support group. He knew that every year, his counselor asked him leading questions around the anniversary of the incident to see if Leonard would be triggered and need more supervision. Leonard acted as if Dupree's imprisonment gave him closure. He even attended the support group voluntarily after being released to keep the illusion of his spiritual growth intact.

Leonard worked so hard to pass himself off as a grateful survivor willing to move on with his life that he almost convinced himself that he wasn't going to murder the man tonight and piss on his corpse. But he most certainly would. And it would please him to do it. Leonard imagined that little bone fragments severed his amygdala so he would feel no remorse.

Winston Wilson Dupree, inmate #145731, was easy to track. The online prisoner locator informed Leonard about Dupree's parole. After that, a careful search on social media sites and a catfishing expedition gave Leonard all he needed. The promise of soiled panties in the mail got him a location.

The convict lived in a tiny apartment in a neglected and invisible part of town. It only took a week of surveillance to realize that Dupree was a pathetic creature of habit. He worked in the warehouse of a charity group that hired ex-cons. After work, the man sat on a wooden chair outside his apartment, smoking and staring beyond the power lines. When it got dark, he walked a few blocks to a windowless bar, where people drank to keep from screaming. At closing time, Dupree staggered into an alley comprised of chop shops with rolling steel garage doors where he would piss and sometimes puke.

Leonard waited in the dark alley and surprised Dupree while the convict pissed on a garage door. Leonard pointed the loaded revolver at the man. Dupree shut off his stream like a spigot. Leonard thought his victim might raise his hands, maybe plead for his life. He didn't count on Dupree shouting and becoming a moving target, weaving erratically around the alley's width. Leonard also didn't count on the force of the weapon's recoil or how loud it would be in a narrow passage surrounded by brick and sheet metal.

Even though he aimed at Dupree's chest, the Blackhawk's mulelike kickback raised the bullet's trajectory. It tore into the man's left trapezius muscle and shattered his clavicle. The injury stopped Dupree in his tracks, but the explosive sound of the gunshot also momentarily stunned Leonard. The weapon's jolt twisted his wrist violently and made him look down in shock.

That frozen moment was enough time for Dupree to tackle him and try to knock the gun free. Leonard was on the ground in a flash, with Dupree straddling him and trying to grab the Ruger. Leonard kicked his legs to buck the man off him. He had forgotten how large Dupree was.

Dupree had his hand on the pistol and tried to push it down and away from his body, but Leonard pulled the trigger out of reflex. The bullet blew through Dupree's hand, tore through the man's scrotum and rectum, and came to rest deep in Leonard's left leg.

The impact of the bullet was so violent that it felt to Leonard like the small lead pellet dragged his body across the concrete like an attack dog would. Both men screamed and writhed in pain as they tried to grasp what just happened to their bodies. Dupree moaned in terror and misery, holding his defiled body, and Leonard pressed the palm of his free hand over the hole in his thigh. With the other shaky hand, he aimed the revolver at Dupree's head and pulled the trigger. The head disintegrated.

It ended with the intense smell of cordite and shit and blood and death. Three deafening shots. It took too long.

Leonard knew he had to leave that alley immediately and picked himself off the ground. The pain in the torn quadricep muscle in his leg was burning hot, but he stayed upright.

He and intense pain had danced before.

I need to run. Fuck the damage, I need to go now.

Leonard lurched forward, and the first step on his wounded leg made him involuntarily dry heave. He could feel strands of torn, striated muscle peeling away from his thigh.

He broke into a run anyway.

Adrenaline helped him limp the three blocks to where he parked his old car. Leonard rarely drove and had an expired license and bald tires, but his apartment was two miles away. He knew he had to risk a getaway car because public transportation was unreliable, and if Dupree's blood got on his clothes, he'd be a sitting duck. He could not be on a bus looking like he did right now.

Leonard spilled into the driver's seat just in time. He grabbed his thigh and groaned as sitting brought the pain back instantly. The fading cabin light illuminated his leg long enough to see the hole in his jeans and the absence of meat beneath it. Blood pooled out like a bubbling spring. There was no exit wound. He could feel the slug deep inside his leg. It felt like the bullet was molten, expanding, moving, and twisting like a worm in wet earth.

Leonard pulled his belt from around his waist, cinched it tightly above the wound, and reached for a gym bag on the passenger side floor. The bag held a change of clothes, but the t-shirt was now a makeshift gauze bandage. Leonard struggled to get the keys out of his pocket and into the ignition. His stomach sunk as he looked at the car's stick shift.

Fuck. Even the slight force of depressing the clutch would flex his quad. He took a deep breath, turned the key, and pushed down the clutch. Leonard felt the bullet shift inside him, the hot pain radiating down his leg.

He slowly let out the clutch, and as he did, the metallic lump squirmed down through his thigh muscle and into his knee. The slug caught in the pocket of ligaments and bones like a popcorn hull under the gumline. Leonard gasped and popped the clutch. The car stalled.

Leonard was afraid to move. Was his knee jammed and locked in place? Could this be happening? He worked up the courage to flex the joint. The blockage was not there, just a phantom sensation.

It's nerve damage and muscle pain, and it's spreading. It just felt like something was moving in there, Leonard told himself as he started the engine again. Every second he stayed in this neighborhood, he was one second closer to being caught. Leonard worked the clutch this time, and the car took off down the street. When he pushed down the clutch again, he swore he felt the hunk of lead bite into the back of his calf. A warm trickle of blood pooled into his sneaker. He'd need to repeat this action. Many times.

Two miles. It's only two miles.

It wasn't until his third try that Leonard realized his apartment key wasn't going in the lock because the blood on his hands made it difficult to grasp it.

If you panic, it's all over. Slow the fuck down.

Leonard held his breath, pressed his tongue against the back of his teeth, and focused on the narrow lock aperture. The key hit home, and the lock turned. He looked back down the hall of his apartment building.

He had just limped through a gauntlet of metal doors and peepholes. It was after three a.m.. Nothing moved. Leonard looked down at the cheap dark blue nylon carpet stretched down the length of the hallway. They designed carpets like this to hide stains, but he was leaving a substantial mark. A halo of dark crimson surrounded his blood-drenched left sneaker.

How obvious is the trail I left? The carpet? In the elevator? The foyer? The sidewalk? Millions of things to hide. Millions of things, all of which require an alibi.

But Leonard knew that nothing mattered as much as stopping himself from bleeding out. The T-shirt he held against the wound was already soaked and dripping. The belt around Leonard's upper thigh slowed the flow, but any clotting ripped away when he exited the car and walked inside his building. He pushed open his apartment door and slid inside.

Leonard fumbled for the wall switch in the dark. When the lights finally came on, he saw how much gore he had smeared on the wall from performing this simple act. Until that moment, Leonard managed his terror by rationalizing that the extent of his injury was only as bad as a drenched pant leg. Seeing the familiar confines of his home, choked with red and coated with his plasma, crushed any illusions he held—the apartment filled with the humid metallic smell of fresh blood.

The sweats hit him instantaneously. This apartment was the location of his last chance. There was no going to a hospital after what he did. The gravity of that thought made Leonard woozy.

Leonard turned on the bright light in his bathroom and grabbed the sink to steady himself. His left foot was numb, and he couldn't risk falling on the tile floor. He might never be able to get back up.

Don't look at your face in the bathroom mirror, he told himself. *You don't want to see how pale you are.*

He reached for the suture kit sitting on the toilet tank. He purchased the kit online to prove that he had thought of every- thing but never envisioned needing it. It sat on his sink in its absurd protective wrapper. Leonard lowered himself slowly onto the toilet seat and tried to open the shrink wrap, but his hands would never be dry enough. Instead, he chewed on the plastic seam until the wrapping finally tore. An instructional CD fell to the floor with a thin clang.

"This isn't fair. This isn't fucking fair at all," Leonard said to himself over and over again.

As Leonard opened the suture kit and saw the scalpel, skin hooks, and rat-toothed tissue forceps, he wondered if he dared to do what he needed. He nearly fainted when he initially looked at the hole in his leg in the harsh light of his apartment elevator. The torn flesh at the hole's edges swelled like lips, and the skin peeled away with hairs sticking out of it. But the worst was the gaping damage pouring out his lifeblood.

He had placed the T-shirt over the wound; that was the last time he looked at it. Now here he was, preparing to slice into his flesh, to pull it open and probe into the wrecked mass of nerves and meat to remove the bullet and save his life. His mind flashed to a video he watched where an EMT removed a massive spider from a person's ear canal, a nightmare secreted in someone's body, and he gagged.

Leonard's leg was numb, but he knew that wouldn't last. He needed to act fast, yet he couldn't bring himself to move the shirt and look at the wound.

You stupid fuck, this is it. Dupree doesn't get to end you today. The police don't get to end you today. Shit on them all. Do what needs doing, you useless fuck.

Leonard gave himself a standard three-count.

One. This isn't fair.

Two. Fuck you, Dupree.

Three. Fuck me.

Leonard pulled the shirt away, grabbed the scissors, and cut his pants at the entry hole. He pulled back the blood-soaked denim to allow room for surgery. What he saw made him forget to breathe.

The wound was gone.

Blood coated the skin, but he couldn't see the hole. *It's covered over with blood,* Leonard thought, and he grabbed the tiny bottle of isopropyl alcohol from the kit. He braced himself for an unholy sting, but there was none. The alcohol ate away the blood, and all that was left was his thigh's clean, unmarked flesh. Leonard grabbed his pants leg with both hands and tore it open.

Nothing. Leonard ran his hands around his leg, which was still numb, but he found no wound. He started to feel like he might scream.

I don't know what's happening, but it's still there. It's fucking in there.

Leonard brought the scalpel to rest on the bleached skin of his leg. It felt distant like he was watching another video. He slid the blade backward, and the flesh separated with a pink sigh. And then the blood started to pour out. He moved the blade perpendicular to the first cut and sliced himself open again.

When he plunged the forceps into the center of his incisions, Leonard swore he felt something tap off the metal, then tap again. His stomach turned as he moved the forceps tips across the raw dermis. Leonard felt the tap again and snapped the instrument in that area. He felt a small, hard mass trapped between the forceps blades.

He took a deep breath and used his other hand's thumb and forefinger to open the gash. Blood submerged the business end of the tool so that he couldn't see what he grabbed. As he pulled the forceps out, whatever was there wriggled free with enough force to vibrate the forceps, and the blades snapped together. My God, whatever was there fought to stay inside.

Just like that spider, Leonard thought.

Leonard suddenly felt a sharp, burning pain in the lower right-hand side of his back, a pain so intensely focused that it had a shape like a bean. And then he felt the fabric of his shirt there getting wet. Leonard reached his hand back and touched the wet spot. When he pulled his hand back, it was slick with fresh blood. It was a much darker shade of crimson than what flowed from his leg.

The pain in Leonard's back intensified. It came from deep inside him, and he swore he could feel something vital within him shut down, and his body was in shock. Leonard got up from the toilet and staggered towards the bathroom door. He swung the door to reveal a full-length mirror nailed to the other side. Leonard had to see his reflection.

Don't look at your face in the mirror, he told himself. *You don't want to see how pale you are.*

Blood covered the back of Leonard's shirt. He slowly raised the soaked fabric to expose his skin.

There it was.

The wound had moved.

Leonard heard himself moan in terror as he looked into that familiar hole, exposing the delicate meat under his dermis, oozing out blood as black as oil.

He staggered back to retrieve the scalpel and the forceps. Leonard knew the position and angle of the wound would make the extraction much more challenging, but he knew the bullet was still inside him and needed to get it out.

He returned to the mirror, turned around, and raised his shirt.

It was gone.

The skin above the location of his right kidney was bloody but unbroken. But he could feel the slug hidden behind his skin, an ice ball destroying every cell around it, killing his kidney and poisoning his blood.

He'd have to be extra careful with his cuts this time so he wouldn't cause any more damage to the organ than the bullet had already done. This time, there was no numbness to mask the flesh trauma. This time, he could feel the cold temperature of the blade as it entered him. The pain of the incision came shortly after as if it rose on the blood that started to pour from him.

Suddenly, he felt the familiar burning pain bloom on his right nipple. Crimson marked his chest. He didn't need to look. Leonard could feel the lead slug sink into his lung, incinerating bronchioles with its deathly presence. *I need to get ahead of this*, thought Leonard as he sliced his nipple in half, then quartered it with a second slash and sunk his fingers into the meat.

Those same fingers were dead now after the wound moved to his trapezius muscle, and Leonard severed the nerves and the muscles in his shoulder, rendering his arm a dangling corpse.

He could sense it before he felt it. The wound was once again on the move.

Millions of places for this wound to hide. Millions of places, all of which require a cut to reveal.

And suddenly, Leonard was seized with an unstoppable need to look at his face in the mirror. A compulsion to raise his chin and slowly fix his gaze to stare into his own eyes hit him. It was an action as inexplicable as the wave of gratitude he felt in that liquor store bathroom a decade ago and no less intense. He stared at his reflection.

Leonard's face was not pale white as he expected it to be. It was grey. His skin was the color of clay stretched tightly across his cheekbones. And that made the small pink hole, which slowly blossomed like a lotus between his eyes, all the more vivid.

WE ALL GO THROUGH CHANGES
JONATHAN MABERRY

1

"There's something wrong with me," I said.

It took courage to say it out loud, but it's been screaming inside my head for a long time. Months.

Nanny—that's what we call our grandmother—got out of her rocking chair and came and sat down next to me on the top porch step. She's about a zillion years old but doesn't look much older than Mom. That's kind of cool. Kind of weird, too. Her brown hair was threaded with a gray that was only a shade darker than her eyes, and there weren't a lot of lines on her face.

"What do you mean, Sam?" she asked. Unlike the rest of us, Nanny had a strong French-Canadian accent. She and Grand-pop moved to the States before my mom and her sisters were born. Nanny speaks French, German, and a bunch of other languages. I can barely make my way through English.

Now that I'd gone ahead and *said* something, there was no stepping back from it. Which, of course, glued my mouth shut.

But Nanny waited me out.

"It's weird," I said. "And. . . a little embarrassing."

She half-turned and studied me.

"Tell me anyway," she said.

After a while, I did.

2

I'll tell it to you the way it happened.

3

I had been sick for nearly two weeks. Some kind of flu, I think. Mom didn't take me to the doctor, though. The Hunter family tends to rely on home medicines, natural cures, and homeopathy. I never even had an aspirin until I was going through my first divorce. But that's not part of this story.

I was fourteen and sick as a dog.

I'd never been sick much as a kid. One or two colds, but that was about it. No chicken pox, no mumps, no measles. None of that stuff. So, the flu thing was new. And it knocked me out. Chills, body aches everywhere, and a fever that kept going up. Mostly at night. During the days, it would be down to maybe a degree or two above normal.

But at night, I caught fire. That's how it felt.

And it was a weird fever. What Mom called a 'dry fever,' meaning my temp was sky high but I wasn't sweating. Not at all. It was like being roasted in the desert or maybe a convection oven. I wasn't a fan.

The dreams were the worst part.

I know about fever dreams from books, movies, and the kids at school. We even had a creative writing exercise back in sixth grade after flu season had ripped through every class. The teacher asked if we'd had fever dreams, and enough hands went up that she made it an assignment to write a short story based on one of those dreams. I was one of only three kids who, until that point, had never had fever dreams.

"Well. . . then just make something up," she said. So we did.

I wouldn't want to turn in any story based on the dreams I had when I got the latest version of the flu. Or, what I thought was the flu.

The one I had the night before that conversation with Nanny was the worst.

It started weird. There was no build up to it. It just started in motion.

I was running through the woods.

It was around twilight, but the sun was still visible through the trees. A big, red blob of fire the color of blood. Like when Aunt Mercy kills one of the pigs. Oh, yeah. . . I grew up on a farm. Lots of chickens, turkeys, cows, pigs, and sheep. None of them are pets.

I was hunting in the dream.

That's not something we do. We kill what we raise for the table. We're not gun people. Nanny won't have one in the house. In rare times when we hunt, it's with a bow and arrows. Takes more skill and is very, very quiet.

In the dream I was definitely hunting, but without a bow or even a knife.

Running, running, running. Moving better than I do in real life. More athletic, a lot nimbler. Better balance and a hell of a lot more speed.

The forest was distorted by shadows and slanting beams of lurid light. It made it hard to see rabbit holes and draped vines. Or. . . it should have. Instead, as I ran, I seemed to be aware of everything. Leaping over dips in the ground, twisting to avoid tree limbs and vines, jumping onto boulders, and then jumping off with huge bounds.

It was absolutely exhilarating.

It was fun.

It was terrifying.

When I dream, there's always a part of me that's aware that I *am* dreaming. Like I'm a spectator. Like there's two of me—the one who watches and the one who does. And, get this, the watcher *knows* he can't do the stuff that the dreamer is doing.

The dreamer me is kind of a badass.

In the dream, I moved so fast. Like I'd been born an athlete and trained every day. The truth is that aside from gym class and Xbox, I did no activity worth mentioning. I was short, a little dumpy, and about as coordinated as a block of lead.

Not in the dreams.

Especially not in *that* dream. The one I told Nanny about.

The forest was *mine*, and I knew it. I could feel it.

Everything made sense to me. The trees and bushes, the weeds and flowers were all known to me. It was like I'd always lived there. Deep in the forest, where people don't usually go. Where the only sounds you hear are those made *by* the forest. No city noises. No chatty campers or hunters telling lies about animals they bagged. No airplanes or cars.

Only the breeze whispering as it moved through the trees and the ten thousand replies made by the leaves. Each tree, each kind of leaf, had its own dialect, and I could understand them all. Just as I knew what the bees were saying and the crickets and the birds and everything.

I ran with so much freedom. Nothing slowing me down—not doubt or the unknown or fatigue. Running with all the power of who and what I was.

And that's where the dream suddenly went from being weird-cool to weird-strange.

I was me in that it was my brain and personality, but it also wasn't me.

You see, I don't run on all fours.

And I'm not an animal.

Except in those dreams.

4

Not sure what I was.

I ran on all fours. I knew I was big. Bigger than a deer. Bigger than a coyote. Not as big as a bear. I'm 150 pounds and I knew somehow that the animal I dreamed was the same weight.

Only he was 150 pounds of solid muscle. No fat. No slack muscles.

He ran so fast that the watcher part of me was having a hard time keeping up with all the dreamer was seeing. The animal senses were ten thousand times sharper. And though I was *aware* of him processing everything, the human watcher was limited to the speed of human perception. It was like watching a video of yourself but sped up ten times.

Even that doesn't explain it right.

But... damn, it was a rush.

I ran for miles, up and down hills, into hollows, and over fallen logs. At first, I knew I was running for the sheer joy of it. The unencumbered thrill of it. The fun of being able to run, and doing so was its own reward. It was amazing.

Then, gradually, I felt a shift. Instead of just running, I was now searching.

There was that perceptual lag time before I realized that *searching* meant *hunting*.

And, yeah, I was hunting.

It was then that I realized how scary that was. Not because I was inside the mind of an animal, but because it gradually dawned on me that I was not hunting another animal. Not as such. I mean, sure, an animal in a way, but not how my watching mind defined it. Not then, and certainly not now—remembering all of this thirty years on.

I remember trying to explain to Nanny that I was hunting a person.

She stopped my narrative right there.

"Look at me," she said sternly. When I did, I saw how fierce her gray eyes could get. Piercing, ice cold, powerful.

"What. . .?" I asked.

"I want to ask you a question and I will know if you're telling me the truth," she said. "You *know* that I'll know."

She was right. We all knew not to lie to Nanny. No sir.

"I promise," I said.

Nanny said, "Do you remember what you were feeling when you realized you were hunting another person?"

"I. . . think so."

"Be precise," she snapped. "This is important."

I said. "Yes. I remember."

"Tell me what you were feeling."

Because I wanted to tell the exact truth, I thought about it for a few seconds. Then I hesitated because I didn't know if the truth was going to be the right thing to say. Those gray eyes, though. . . damn.

"I was hungry."

"No," she said. "That's need. I want to know what you *felt*."

I licked my lips, which had gone suddenly dry. In a very small voice, I croaked, "I wanted to catch him."

She studied me. "Go on."

"I. . . wanted to hurt him."

She said nothing.

"I wanted to kill him."

Nanny took my hands and held them in hers. She had oddly strong hands. Everyone joked about it. If there was a jar with a tight lid, they'd give it to her before one of the boys. Those lids always popped open.

Her skin was warm, too. Almost hot.

"Now tell me this, Samuel," she said quietly. "*Why* did you want to kill him?"

That question hit me with odd power. I sat back, still letting her hold my hands, and thought about it.

She said, "Before you answer that, tell me this. . . was it the *animal* mind who wanted to hurt him or *your* mind? Your *watching* mind. Which was it?"

"The animal."

"What did your watching mind want?"

I hesitated. "To hurt him."

"But not kill him?"

"No."

"Be sure, Sam."

"I am."

She squeezed my hands very tightly. Painfully. "One more thing," she said. "If the animal caught the man, could your watching mind have stopped the beast from killing him?"

It was such a complicated question that I had to think about it. And it was hard to do while she squeezed my hands harder and harder. I had to push my way past the pain. Or. . . through it. It wasn't easy. It was really freaking hard.

"Y- yes," I said.

But I heard the doubt in my own voice.

Her grip was close to breaking my fingers.

Then she abruptly let go and moved away from me on the step, leaning her straight back against the upright of the porch rail, studying me all the time without blinking even once.

"You'll have more dreams like that," she said.

"How do you know?" I gasped, trying not to rub my aching hands.

"I know," she said. I didn't think she was going to say anything else, but after a minute she said, "It's a family thing. We all hunt like that."

"You mean you have dreams like I did? Dreams about being an animal and hunting someone?"

Nanny stood up and looked down at me.

"I want you to tell me about your next dreams. Mind me now, Samuel. I want you to try to control the animal when you dream again. And then I want you to tell me about it, whether you succeed or fail. Do you understand?"

I didn't. Not really. But I said, "Yes, ma'am."

She went inside and did not speak of it again.

5

I dreamed again that night.

This time it was different.

When the dream started, I was *me* running through the woods. Human me. Running naked as a jaybird through the woods. The branches whipped at me. I tripped over roots and stepped in rabbit holes and fell down the slopes. It was clumsy and it hurt. And I was not watching it. I felt it from the inside. I was both watcher and dreamer.

I reached the top of a rise and stopped, crouching, sniffing the wind as if I could tell anything from that. I cocked my head and listened, knowing that I couldn't tell anything from the woods at night. I was no good in the forest.

Then...

I heard it.

The sound of someone else running.

No. Not some*one*. People.

The more I strained to hear, the more details I could pick out. There was someone running light and fast. Making sharp little yelps now and then. A woman, I thought, or maybe a kid. Really scared.

And what's scary about *that* is I swear I could smell the fear.

Maybe a hundred yards behind those sounds, I heard heavier steps. At first, I thought it was one man. But the harder I strained to hear, the more certain I became that it was at least two men. Big men. They smashed through the woods. Their feet vibrated through the ground. Don't ask me how, but I felt it.

I heard them yell, though I couldn't make out what they said.

I heard them curse. And I heard them laugh. The wrong kind of laugh.

They were all too far from where I crouched for me to see them, but my mind painted a picture. The person being chased was. . . I was almost positive. . . a woman. A young woman. And she was absolutely terrified.

The men chasing her wanted to catch her. This wasn't hide-and-seek. It wasn't a game. My senses told me that. My instinct screamed it.

I was a kid, too, but old enough to figure out what they wanted. What they were going to do when they caught her.

And then I was running, too.

There was no real memory of starting to run, no decision to do it. One second, I was hunkered down at the top of the slope, and the next, I was running.

Fast.

Really fast. But on two feet. For a while.

Then I fell.

I don't actually think I tripped. It was just that I plunged forward onto hands and feet, skidding through fallen leaves, scraping my skin.

For a moment, I just stayed there, panting, sweating, with sparks swirling in front of my eyes.

Then the pain.

Oh, God... the pain! Not from the scrapes or the fall. This pain came from inside of me. Deep, deep inside of me.

It was so sudden, so unexpected, so intense that it strangled the scream I wanted to let out. It was as if every nerve in my hand had exploded with fire, and as I watched with horrified eyes, the shape of my hand *changed.*

White-hot agony rippled up my arm, exploded through muscle and sinew. I began to cry, but when the tears rolled down to my mouth, they were hot and salty and so wrong. So very wrong. I was weeping tears of blood.

"What's happening?" I moaned. There was too much pain to scream.

The light in the forest changed. The early twilight sunshine flared to supernova brightness. It was like being stabbed in the eyes. I squeezed my eyes shut, but that didn't help. It made it worse. It felt like my eyes were too big to hide behind the lids.

And then it started.

I mean, I could feel *what* was happening.

I could feel my eyes *changing.*

Shifting. It was the most nauseating thing I had ever felt. And then it got worse. So much worse.

All of my senses suddenly exploded as sights and sounds and tastes flooded in impossibly fast. In the span of a single second, I saw grains of pollen—each as separate and distinct as planets orbiting the sun—floating on the breeze. A swarm of insects flashed into view, and I could smell the traces of vegetable matter and animal blood on each proboscis. I could count the minute hairs on their tiny legs, could discern each delicate lacy line of their gossamer wings. Water running in a brook became a torrent in my ears. My mind staggered under the sensory assault.

But it kept going. Kept getting worse. I could feel every separate bit of what was happening to me.

My skin felt hot, as if every cell in my body was a separate furnace. My breath quickened until I was panting like an animal. I'm telling you this now, filling in the blanks of what I did not and could not understand in that moment.

The landscape of my brain shifted as new glands formed and pumped chemicals in combinations no one—no human being—could endure. The normal human processes faded and simply died away.

I screamed, and knowing that I *could* scream, I kept on screaming as the changes kept happening faster and faster. I could feel my body changing as bones bent to horrific new shapes and muscles tore apart and merged together in unnatural ways. My mass shifted beneath my skin. Bones thickened to support new and heavier muscles. My skin burned and itched wildly as new hair follicles formed and began sending stiff black shoots through my flesh, tearing their way out.

My feet expanded, and black claws tore at the ground. My heels rose, and those claws dug into the dirt. Searing pain flared in my jaw as my molars shifted forward to allow the growth of strong new carnassial teeth, and the incisors and canines became sharper and more pronounced.

I screamed for Nanny, but an animal's roar was what shook the forest. There was no trace of my human voice in that roar. The sound was so loud that bark splintered from the nearby trees. Flowers withered, and the grass beneath me turned brown and brittle. The roar was as loud as all the pain and fury and despair in the world. It funneled out from deep inside my chest and tore at the night sky.

It was not the cry of a fourteen-year-old boy.

It was not a human sound at all.

Then it slowed. Slowed.

Stopped.

I stood up.

I thought after all that pain it would be hard, but I got up all at once. No effort, though my chest was still heaving. I looked down at my hands. If you could call them hands. Every inch of my skin was covered with thick brown hair.

No.

With fur.

My fingers were wrong, the knuckles thick and knobby, and each ended with a long, curved black claw. My whole body was no longer human. I was covered with fur, and the shape of my legs was weird, twisted.

The pain was fading, but in its place were three things. Terror. Absolute terror.

And hunger. God, I had never been so hungry in my whole life. It was bottomless, like there was no way I could ever eat enough to satisfy it. Never.

The other thing I felt was the worst, the strongest. It was like a dark tidal wave rising up inside of my chest and my mind.

Rage.

A red-hot fury mingled with a level of hate I had never before felt.

I wanted to kill something.

Someone.

I threw back my head, and a sound burst from deep in my lungs.

A howl.

The dreadful, terrible howl of a wolf.

6

I ran through the woods.

So fast.

And now I was watcher and animal all in one. Two minds forced into one brain.

But the body we shared was pure animal.

If animal was even the right word.

I—we—whatever the hell you want to call it—ran on two legs at first. I tore through the darkening woods with all the grace and speed and ease I had when I dreamed about being an animal. There was nothing that could trip us. No branches smacked us in the face. No vines choked us.

It was such a smooth acceleration, too. Like an eel in the water. My body leapt and dodged so gracefully.

I. . . I *loved* it.

For a while, I ran, and all the human part of me could do was revel in the power. I had never felt really powerful ever in my life. And now I was more powerful than anyone I knew.

Then, a sound cut through the shadows and changed everything.

It was a scream.

A woman's. Or maybe a girl's.

It rose up above the trees, scaring birds into flight. It ripped through the woods until it found me. The scream slapped and tore at me. It threw gasoline on the fire inside this twisted shape I wore. Heat and rage exploded, and I threw myself in that direction. Hateful. Hungry.

For a moment, I thought I'd tripped and fell. But it wasn't exactly that. I fell forward, yes, but as I did so, there was fresh pain in my arms and shoulders. In my chest and upper back. When I realized that I was now running on four legs, I screamed.

It came out as a snarl.

The pain vanished as I surged forward, running five times faster on four legs. Ten times faster. Impossibly fast. Even at that speed, I was aware of everything. The squirrels cowering in the trees. Lightning bugs that went dark as I passed. Coyotes that fled in terror.

On and on, I ran.

My human mind still fought to process the inrush of sensory data. By slow degrees, I was getting better at it. Aligning with it.

There were moments when my thoughts were not human thoughts at all. I felt a kind of darkness creep into my consciousness, and that sent a new flash of fear, but I realized what it was. And it made Nanny's questions make sense.

I was losing myself to the animal.

Its hate was becoming my hate. Its hunger was mine now.

It was soooo hard to fight to keep me *as* me. Not as the wolf. That's what Nanny meant. When I had told her that I could control the animal and she approved, this was what she meant. It was on me to be in charge. The animal—the wolf—could have my body. That was fine. But what it wanted to do with that body had to be my decision.

Or I would be lost. I knew that as clearly as if Nanny told me straight out.

That was how this worked, whatever *this* was. Me and the wolf. He was the hunter, the killer. I had to be the thought, the reason.

The girl screamed again.

Closer.

Louder.

More thoroughly poisoned with fear.

A split second later, I heard a man's voice. "There she is."

The other man's answer was a laugh. Very ugly, promising awful things.

As I ran, I could smell them. Even from that distance.

The girl was sweating. She was bleeding—there was the coppery stink of it that made my mind recoil and the wolf's stomach growl.

The men were sweating, too. But I could smell tobacco. Food stains on skin and clothes. Beer. Testosterone. There was some of her blood on them.

God damn, how I hated them.

Hated them worse than anyone I had ever actually met.

"Go 'round," cried one man. "Cut her off."

"I got her!" howled the other, and he punctuated it with a laugh that was immediately buried beneath the sound of another scream. Higher, pleading, but also filled with despair. With an acceptance of the sure knowledge that there was no escape. No way out.

I ran so fast.

I burst through a wall of shrubs and stopped.

It was all in front of me now. The girl was maybe a year older than me. Fifteen, maybe sixteen. She wore underpants, a T-shirt with the logo of the high school my cousin, Eileen, went to. Her clothes were filthy, torn, and spattered with blood. Some of it dry, most of it not. Then I saw her wrists and ankles. The skin was rubbed raw as if she'd been tied up and fought against the ropes. Her face was dirty and bruised. One eye was swollen shut and her lip was split. She had a lot of bruises, old and new. Whatever had happened to her had been going on for a while.

The two men wore jeans and sneakers. One had on a denim jacket over an AC-DC shirt; the other wore a pale green dress shirt buttoned to the collar and neck. They had bloodstains on them, too. The guy in the jacket had a huge welt across his face that was still swelling. The girl had gotten him with something. Maybe that's how she ran.

The guys had their arms out wide, creating the illusion of a cage, and the girl was trembling, unsure of what to do, her shoulders already beginning to slump in defeat. The men grinned with their own kind of hunger.

None of them saw me.

Yet.

Then I saw something that twisted the night into a different shape.

There was another wolf on the far side of the small clearing in which the three people stood. It was smaller than me, and instead of dark fur, its hide was pale gray. It looked past the people directly at me. Staring at me and into me with cold gray eyes that were a shade paler than its hair.

I felt the weight of that stare. It was like a punch. No. . . more like hands closing around me. Strangely, unusually strong hands. Holding me still.

It made no noise, and yet I could feel a communication on some level I'd never accessed before. It was scent and body language and those eyes. Telling me so much. Telling me everything I needed to understand.

And I did understand. It was like she was speaking to me. A conversation taking place right then, and another coming from deeper in my mind, moving like an echo.

Do you remember what you were feeling when you realized you were hunting another person?

That's what she had asked. And I said yes.

Tell me what you were feeling.

The wolf wanted to answer that it was hungry. But what I said was,

"I wanted to catch him." Him in that dream. *Them* now.

Go on.

"I. . . wanted to hurt him. I wanted to kill him."

Was it the animal mind who wanted to hurt him or your mind? Your watching mind. Which was it?

"The animal."

"What did your watching mind want?"

I hesitated. "To hurt him."

If the animal caught the man, could your watching mind have stopped the beast from killing him?

Though, in that moment, I heard her say *them*.

The conversation was as clear as if we were still sitting on the porch steps. But it was a different conversation than it had been. The words were almost the same, but the meaning had evolved. It had metamorphosed, as I had done.

I want to hurt them, I told her without speaking. *I want to kill them.*

Those gray eyes stabbed into me. *Why? For meat? For the joy of the kill?*

I recoiled from that. *No!*

Then why?

I raised my head toward the girl. *For her. For... this.*

The gray wolf watched me.

Is it wrong? Am I a monster? They were questions I so needed to have answered.

There was a strange light in those eyes.

Look at them. They are monsters. Are you like them?

I shook my head.

They have done monstrous things, she said. *They will never stop. They enjoy it. That is what evil is. There is nature. There is nurture. And there is choice. Goodness and evil are born from choice.*

I kept shaking my head.

You said not to kill.

Her eyes sharpened.

I never said that. What did *I say?*

It took me a few moments. Or maybe all of this was happening at the speed of wolf senses. The figures down there seemed not to move. Time had stalled.

You asked if I could stop the wolf from killing because it wanted to.
She waited.
This isn't what the wolf wants. It's what I want.
That was what I said.

I blinked and the wolf was gone. Instead, there was my grandmother. Tall and regal and powerful. She stood in deep shadows, so all I could see were those terrible, beautiful eyes.

We are not human beings, I felt her say. Or think. Or whatever. *We are not wolves.*

I wanted to cry. *What* are *we?*

She said we are Benandanti—the good-walkers. The hounds of God. We are older than mankind. We have hunted such as these since time's dawn. We are not slaves to hunger. But we are not merciful.

And then I understood. About her. About my family.

About me.

I looked at the two men as I took a step forward. Rising with those steps to stand on two legs. Smiling with a mouthful of death.

My grandmother came for the girl, turned her away, sheltered her. And they vanished.

The men screamed as I approached.

I did not feed my hunger. Not in that way. I don't eat spoiled meat.

Their screams rose into the night as the sun ducked behind the mountain and closed its eyes.

They screamed and screamed.

For as long as they could.

For as long as I let them.

In the shadows, I could feel eyes watching me. Mom, my aunts, my sister. Others of my kind.

Others of my pack.

ATMOSPHERES OF PRESSURE
ALEXIS DUBON

In spite of all her prayers and wishes, Madeline could not stop Thursday from coming. Tea with Lydia—something she never looks forward to. This would be a rough one, though.

She brought three thick pads, hoping that would be enough; Lydia's bound to get curious if she takes too many bathroom breaks. And tampons aren't allowed, so she can't double up on protection. But she's bleeding a lot. The doctor told her that's normal though, after yesterday's procedure, not to worry unless she sees a clot the size of a lemon. A lemon.

But Madeline can't cancel, even today. Last time she did that, it ended up being a bigger headache than if she'd just gone. She's never been a good liar. Lydia still checks whether she's up to date with her car servicing. It was a stupid excuse. Cars don't just break down one day and miraculously recover the next. Madeline knew it was a bad idea to drive to the supermarket after calling off their Thursday plans; she knew the run-in risk was too high. And, of course, Lydia was there—she always goes shopping on Fridays. Madeline should have just sucked it up and done laundry

Saturday instead. Detergent wasn't worth it. But Paul was out of socks.

Lying is out of the question, and Madeline can't bear to tell Lydia the truth. She'll have to keep it together during the inevitable "so when are you going to turn my brother into a daddy" conversation.

She arrives early, in case by some stroke of luck Lydia is there already and she can get this over with sooner. But, true to form, Lydia arrives fifteen minutes late, which clocks Madeline at thirty-five minutes seated in that pink and white upholstered chair. The last thing she'd ever want to bleed through onto.

Adding insult to injury, Lydia's not alone. Her cousin is beside her, grinning under an oversized straw hat.

"I hope it's okay if I invited Ysa too!"

"Lydia told me you two were coming here and you *know* how much I love this place, so I just had to tag along. And a garden table—how could I pass that up?"

"Oh, yes, of course. So good to see you again, Ysa," Madeline says, trying to sound sincere.

They say their hellos, and she excuses herself to the lavatory. One pad down and they've only just gotten started. She should have known Lydia would run late—she always runs late. She should have brought four and changed into a new one as soon as she came, knowing she'd be waiting. But *shoulds* can't change the situation that is.

When Madeline returns, Lydia and Ysa are absorbed in conversation, extolling the many virtues of the Nuna car seat— how much safer they feel now than with those monstrosities that were available for their first children.

"And how great we thought *those* were back then. It's amazing how quickly things improve," Ysa says.

"You'll see," Lydia says. "One day." Generously bringing her sister-in-law into the conversation. Madeline curses herself for marrying into Paul's family. She curses Lydia for inviting Ysa. Lydia's difficult enough on her own, but that cousin of hers brings out the worst.

The waiter comes to take their order—rose tea for Lydia, green for Ysa, and coffee for Madeline.

"Oh, and could you please wait until you bring mine to the table before you put the strainer into the pot?" asks Ysa. "Last time, it steeped for too long and was bitter when I poured it."

"That's a great idea. Me too," Lydia says.

"Would you like milk for your coffee?" he asks.

"Yes, please. Half and half."

"You know, Maddie, you really should switch to non-dairy milk, like oat or almond," Ysa says.

Lydia nods in agreement. "Or they even have macadamia milk now," she adds.

"But oat is still my favorite." An obvious command from the obvious captain of this crew.

The waiter looks to Madeline, who repeats that she'd like half and half. The other two exchange glances as if to say *we tried*, and he walks away.

They launch into recaps of their week, how each of their three children say just the funniest things, and are each so ahead of where they should be developmentally, and *how is Paul, and Madeline have you been staying on top of that car—regular mainte-nance is so important, you know.*

It feels like the waiter will never come back. Madeline needs those finger sandwiches and their drinks soon because she's not getting out of here until every pot is drained. Eventually, he returns, tray full of silver vessels embellished with floral patterns and sugar bowls and that unmistakably creamy half and half. Beside it is a second creamer, filled with dull, grey-beige liquid, the color of filthy sock.

Ysa is recounting a story about a new employee at Williams

Sonoma who was rude to her and ignores the arrival of her tea. Even in this heat, steam rises from the spouts in wet hot clouds.

The waiter comes again a short time later with a tiered tray of finger sandwiches, scones, cookies, clotted cream, butter, and a variety of jams and preserves. The sight of strawberry jam makes Madeline's throat go dry.

"Oh, this looks divine!" Lydia says.

"Absolutely indecent!" Ysa echoes.

Madeline reaches for a smoked salmon sandwich, drawing disapproving looks from the other side of the table, but what was all that food there for—to be admired and not consumed? Besides, the sooner they finish, the sooner she gets to leave. Ysa and Lydia watch Madeline chew in a brief moment of judgmental quiet.

Her insides cramp, and she asks Ysa about Garrett, her middle —and favorite—child, for a distraction.

Now on her second story, Ysa still hasn't put the strainer into her pot. It's just been sitting there next to the empty cup. Maybe it was a mistake to bring her son up. In an attempt to distract herself from her body, Madeline's distracted Ysa from her tea.

She, on the other hand, requests a second pot of coffee, having already finished the cup and a half provided by the first.

"And may I also have another creamer of half and half?"

"Why, Maddie? You have all that oat milk right in front of you. You won't even try it?" Lydia asks.

"Thank you, no, I do actually prefer half and half."

Madeline hates herself for ordering coffee. She wasn't expecting it to be so contentious, but she should know better by now. She should have gone with green or rose tea and muscled through it.

Her jaw aches from all the forced smiling over Garrett and his adventures in fine dining. How he refused to try steak tartare and would only eat duck fat fries.

"Excuse me," she says and stands up. She glides her fingers over the upholstery as inconspicuously as she can manage, checking for any signs that she seeped through. All clear, but she knows she pushed it with this one.

"Again?" More looks volley between Lydia and Ysa, and Madeline blames the coffee and heads to the bathroom. Under the microscope, as always.

Her body tenses. A gentle hum in her bloodstream, a barely perceptible vibration. Friction in her veins. Heat. Must be nerves, she tells herself.

She walks with stiff legs, too aware of her body. Tamping down humbling rebukes she'd only say aloud to her shampoo bottles later that night, the hacksaw tone she dreams of unleashing upon these women. Feral cries pound against the walls of her lungs, begging for release.

Cranberry clumps speckle her fully saturated savior. None lemon-sized, but chunky enough to make her head light. This gruesome composition produced by her uterus. So much blood in such varied textures. She studies the chaos of it for a moment, feeling herself drip into the toilet, hoping to alleviate some burden for the replacement pad, hoping to buy herself a bit more time before she has to leave for the table again. Maybe in her absence, some progress might be made on those canapés.

But she can't hide out too long. Add yet another improper behavior to the list.

When she returns, her coffee is waiting for her, thankfully with a creamer of half and half alongside it. Ysa stirs her tea strainer into her silver pot and clears her throat. Finally.

"An awful lot of bathroom breaks," Lydia says, and her and Ysa's mouths slowly unfurl in tandem, their smiles showcasing rows of too-straight, too-white veneers.

"I guess? I did just drink that whole pot of coffee." Unrelenting ache crawls from Madeline's jaw to the back of her head and throbs at every pulse of searing hot blood.

"Oh, Maddie. Shouldn't you be drinking decaf?"

"Why would I drink decaf?"

The cousins stare smugly for a moment before Ysa pours her tea.

"Maddie. We know," Lydia says.

There's no way they could know. What she's been through is something that would never occur to them, with their effortless conceptions and perfect pregnancies.

Ysa sips her tea and scowls at the cup before placing it back in the saucer and flagging down the waiter.

"Sir, I'm sorry. We come here all the time, and this is just not okay. Last time, my tea was over steeped and bitter. This time, it's tepid. Barely even warm. Lydia, how is your tea?"

"I thought it was fine, but I guess now that you mention it, it isn't as hot as it usually is."

"Ysa," Madeline says, "I think you maybe just waited too long to pour it. It's been sitting there for a while and if it got cold, that's not really the restaurant's fault."

"We'd both like a new pot, please. *Hot*, please." Ysa shoots Madeline a dirty look.

The waiter skitters off with the unacceptable beverages, his demeanor entirely changed from the cool and composed person who greeted them.

Something stirs inside of Madeline, but she won't give herself away. Keep a poker face. A pleasant face. Everything has to be nice and lovely, even with her combusting interior. Presentation is reality, isn't it?

She brings the cup to her mouth and drinks, looking down her nose at perfectly caramel-colored coffee that oat milk could never achieve, and tiny bubbles dance along her lips, a gentle simmer. Alarmed, she clatters it against the saucer a bit too dramatically, prompting more disapproving looks from Lydia and Ysa, who must have thought her abrupt gesture had something to do with them. After all, doesn't everything?

While waiting for new pots of tea, Madeline does her best to relax. She tries not to think about how this will prolong the afternoon. Deep breaths, calming practices they teach in yoga. Focus on the food, how beautiful it is, how lucky she is to be served such a spread—if she were allowed to actually eat it. Focus on all the good movies she'll get to watch later, under a heating pad, lying in bed with her dog. She looks up to the sky, attempting to re-center. The leaves of the tree overhead are already beginning to turn color; their edges bright, almost glowing, like freshly lit kindling not yet brought to flame. Early in the season, but it's been a dry one. An unusual transition from summer green to autumn red, the way it's creeping from the perimeter inwards, but maybe she hasn't paid as close attention before, and this is how it goes.

Nothing is working.

"So," Lydia says, leaning back in her upholstered chair, "back to what we were discussing before this disaster with our tea—you couldn't have thought we'd let you off so easily. Just tell us. We figured it out. You can admit it."

"Admit *what*?" Madeline buries rage down in her guts, knowing she can't let it out of her mouth—as much as she wants to. Pain shrieks through her skull. She grabs a macaron, which promptly deflates. Melts between her fingers, leaving sticky pink residue on her skin and a depression in the once light-as-air cookie, now thin and crispy. Embarrassed, she lets it fall to her floral-patterned porcelain plate.

"No need to manhandle the pastries, Maddie," Lydia says. "And it's really not a secret anymore, you can stop the charade."

"*Maddie*," Ysa cuts in. "This is always how it is. We all spend like eighty percent of our first trimester on the toilet. I must have peed a thousand times a day when I first got pregnant with Suzanna."

"You think I'm pregnant?"

"This constant back and forth to the bathroom? And you and Paul have been married now for what, three years? Yeah. You're pregnant."

The waiter returns with fresh pots, all steamy once again.

Ysa makes a big show of thanking him, exaggerating her gratitude like the good person she's sure she is. His face remains blank and distant, but she moves on without even a breath between subjects.

"You can't fool us. We *know*."

"Honestly. I swear I'm not pregnant."

"Okay, well clearly it must be pretty early on. Maybe you're not ready to tell us yet. It's bad luck to announce too soon. But when you do, we'll act surprised," Lydia says. Her eye contact is focused with the intensity of a safe cracker.

"You even said—I'd be drinking decaf if that were the case."

"Yeah, but you're you. You never do things the way they're supposed to be done. I wouldn't expect you to give up coffee; you'd probably think it was stupid. Even though it's not. Like how you think it's okay to consume all that dairy milk."

Madeline rubs her temples and shuts her eyes. The storm inside her head rumbles, thunderclouds pound her eardrums, lightning streaks behind her retinas. Heat radiates from her scalp. Her attention is inward, working to quiet the tempest, temper the ache, when something lands at her feet.

"What was that?" Lydia looks lazily to the ground.

On the slate-tiled floor, a sparrow lies dead.

"It's a bird." Madeline's never seen a bird just fall to its death like that, and it's too late for fledgling season. This is a fully grown bird, an adult.

Ysa, pouting at the disruption, raises her hand to summon

the waiter. "We have to get someone to come clean it up. I can't just drink my tea with that thing so close. It's probably diseased."

The waiter arrives and takes note of the bird, struggling to act calm so as not to startle other patrons. He apologizes and hurries to fetch a broom and dustpan. Shortly after he returns—*plunk*. Another bird drops from the sky, this one landing on the mostly-full display of treats at the center of the table.

"We were still eating that, and now it's ruined," she says, more annoyed than alarmed.

He looks at the women, mortified, as though he could have had anything to do with this odd interruption, apologizing to Ysa in particular, who rolls her eyes in disdain.

Madeline's hair twinges with electric charge, a sensation she hasn't felt since she used to chase her little sister down the carpeted hallway of their house, armed with shock-touch fingers, socked feet dragging against tufted floor. What she wouldn't give to swap Paul's sister for her own right now.

She examines the dead sparrow while the waiter retrieves a pair of gloves and a cloth napkin to dispose of it. Every feather on its wings is singed. Charred along the edges. The smell of burning chokes the cloying sweetness of the tiered silver tray.

Lydia and Ysa are having a side conversation about how it's always *something* when they come here. They seem less concerned with the implications of burnt birds falling from the sky than they do with their tea time being disrupted in general, and how last time it was that bachelorette party and how this place *used* to be a peaceful sanctuary from their daily lives.

"Again, I am so sorry about that," the waiter says. "Shall I bring another tray?"

"Yes, definitely. And we would like to be moved to a different table."

"Certainly. Please, take this one here," he says, indicating a table closer to the edge of the patio, where hydrangeas bloom pink in a late-summer garden bed.

His face is ghostly, bloodless, his gaze at once far away and intensely present. Madeline tries to sneak him a sympathetic look, which he's too preoccupied to catch. This is not the first time she's seen a waiter debased so brutally, and she wants him to know she sees the wrongness of it. Make him feel supported in this lion's den. That she recognizes he's going above and beyond and being punished for it. Scorched birds dropping from the sky couldn't be something he has to deal with regularly, but he moves with such a detached anxiety, he seems to barely absorb it at all, focused only on damage control. She wonders whether he's even had a chance to register how odd a thing a charred sparrow plummeting to their table actually is. It might not hit until later, when the adrenaline wears off.

"Oh," Ysa says to Lydia once they move, "this table is much better. Let's just hope we'll be spared from whatever bird plague seems to be happening over there." Then, to the waiter she says, "We'd like new drinks as well, please. Those may well be contaminated too."

"Certainly."

Madeline calculates the limit she can stretch this second pad to, hoping maybe on her next trip inside, she'll find someone who could spare one of theirs. Someone who doesn't use tampons or a menstrual cup. She only has one left, and at this rate, it won't be enough. She needs a miracle. She'd ask one of the waitstaff but it's only men working.

Among the pink summer blossoms, they resume their perfectly normal afternoon, leaving that strange occurrence behind. The birds are forgotten, but not Madeline's interrogation. Like the new table somehow restarted the entire event, except for that one thing.

"Well, if you're *not* pregnant, Maddie, or if you're just not ready to tell us yet, I will say this—nothing in this world is more fulfilling than motherhood," Lydia says. "To have someone who loves you, who *needs* you. To have created something that is a part of you. It's just incredible. It really gives your life meaning in ways you would otherwise never know."

Madeline grinds her teeth, willing herself not to say anything she'll never be able to take back. Family is important. Paul loves his sister. Every Christmas and Thanksgiving would be tarnished forever—an outburst is something she'd never live down. Not in that family.

They're already enough of a strain on her, these people she could never relate to. And somehow, the man she married is infinitely kind. So unlike the rest of his life. Madeline finds herself falling down that old familiar hole, wondering how someone like Paul even ended up with a person like her. How maybe if he'd married somebody else, someone more like his family, he might be a father by now. Another woman could have had a pregnancy that stuck. This last one was promising for three months until it ended with a D&C. Just over eleven weeks—the longest so far. She really believed this would be it.

"Oh, would you look at those hydrangeas?" Ysa—probably bored of Madeline being the center of attention—admires the flowers that are so dramatic and bright. So pink.

Except they aren't. As soon as Madeline turns to them, they wither, wisps of smoke tendriling from their color-leeched petals up to the sky canopied with gathering black clouds.

"I didn't realize before how wilted they are," says Madeline.

"They're really letting this restaurant go to ruin, aren't they? They used to be so on top of *every* detail. It's a shame," says Ysa. "These are supposed to be hearty plants. They ought to survive longer than a single tea service."

"Maddie, would you stop looking up there?" Lydia always keeps track of forecasts, which gives her the certainty to disregard the darkness brewing above. "They said no rain today. We're down *here*, don't be rude."

The waiter arrives with a whole new spread—tea, coffee, pastries, accouterments, all of it, even the unwanted oat milk.

Madeline reconfigures the cross of her legs in hopes that doing so might affect the distribution of blood soak on her pad, extending the life of it.

"Maybe we should finish this up quickly," she says. "I don't want to get stuck in a downpour."

"It's not going to rain." Lydia fills her cup and moves on to another topic of conversation, something about a new must-have toy. Ysa has yet to steep hers and Madeline envisions a fourth pot being brought and a fifth and a sixth, and her headache intensifies as she watches that woman's silver pot of hot water just sit there, dried green tea leaves forgotten next to an empty teacup, and the clouds that have swallowed the last remaining blue in the sky, and the hydrangeas are still smoking, turning black now.

"Oh my god!" Ysa jumps from her seat at the shock of her teapot rattling on the tabletop, rapping against cloth-covered wood with dainty silver feet. Steam spews from its spout and bubbles overflow from its closed lid. Thick white froth spills over like a pasta pot nightmare, dousing the tablecloth.

Four birds hit the ground in rapid succession, landing just feet from where they'd relocated. Worse than the first two. Their scorched bodies shatter on impact, leaving sprays of soot in halos around black carcasses. Chests cracked open, their exposed bones sparkle against crust and char. Glitter against the grim. Ribcages, perfectly intact, cast dancing shimmers of light from their burnt little corpses.

Then, like a deluge of raindrops falling all at once, the ground is pelted with dozens of tiny coal pellets, too small to be birds.

This seems like something that would send these two into an

incensed rage, but it doesn't even phase them. Something to actually be upset about, but they are unbothered.

"That's odd," Lydia says, "They look like the fried capers that
come on that kale Caesar salad from Osteria Bella."

"Oh, they do," Ysa agrees.

"They look like fried flies," Madeline says.

"We haven't been there in *forever*," Lydia says as if Madeline
hadn't spoken at all. "That salad is just to die for, too. I wonder
why we've let so much time go by since we've had it. That dressing? Amazing."

"We really do need to get back there one of these days," Ysa
says.

Madeline peers at the sky, saturated black with clouds, whispers of lava-orange light tracing their edges, the only thing differ-
entiating one from another, separating each from an otherwise
indistinguishable mass of gloom.

She wonders how long it takes these women to get through
that kale Caesar salad they're going on about. Or whether they
just let it sit uneaten between them, like this gigantic tower of tea
snacks. Her head throbs thunder.

"I think maybe we really should settle up and go," she says.

"Oh, please," Ysa says. "We're not going to let this ruin our tea
time. This is *our* time, Maddie. We pay for it whether this place
has gone to hell or not, so we might as well stay. We just know we
won't be coming back. They've lost themselves three customers.
And that waiter is trying real hard to lose his tip."

"I haven't even had a scone. Not one sandwich or cookie. We
can't leave with that entire tray untasted," Lydia says. "And we
finally have hot tea. Too hot by a mile, but I prefer that to a too-
cold pot."

"Something's going on." Madeline doesn't mention the electric current that's running through her hair or the shattering
headache that won't relent or the fact that she can't rest her arms

on the table because a moment ago, she burned through the tablecloth, melted the polyester fabric.

"Would you stop?" Lydia says. "Something's going on with the weather, yes, but it's not going to rain, so we're fine."

"Yeah, just birds falling from above, no big deal."

"Should we move inside? Would that be better?" Ysa suggests disingenuously. "Maddie, why do you always have to be so diffi-cult? And please stop wiggling around in your seat so much. It's really not great for my anxiety and I'm breastfeeding. That's going to affect my body chemistry and go straight to Bayleigh."

Madeline stifles the growing anger that bubbles in her chest and her hair emits an audible buzz. She apologizes, agreeing to stay put next to those clumps of cinder that not long ago were hydrangeas and pulls a petit fours from the tray, which crumbles to soot at her touch, a shadow of smoke lingering between her fingers. The tablecloth is dusted in black powder, and her hand reeks of forest fire. She's terrified at what Ysa and Lydia will say, the looks they'll give, but neither notices—they're discussing the failure of attention that must have caused such an unhealthy garden.

"What about the birds?" Madeline asks.

"They obviously got caught in that weather system. Must be an electrical storm or something. But don't worry, it's not going to get us down here. They're just birds, Maddie, it's not like you knew them. I'm more upset with those flowers. It never used to be like this here. Trashy."

Madeline stands from her chair. One pad left, and she needs it now.

"Excuse me," she says, and Ysa and Lydia roll their eyes at each other.

Alone in the bathroom she inhales deep. Surrounded by the too-pretty femininity of gleaming white tiles and pink floral wall-paper, she can no longer contain herself.

Her face does not belong in that beautiful gilded Rococo mirror over the sink. Hollowed and defeated. She's become a composite of repression—of secret mourning, of unvoiced and unrealized dreams, of resentment, of loneliness deep enough to drown in—all crammed into an emotional urn ready to burst. *Her sister's first question would have been if she were feeling okay.* But she's not here. Just Lydia and Ysa.

And Madeline screams.

It's a scream that could shake the stars. An ugly sound. All that pressure, all that heat, compacted inside her for so long—she can no longer contain the eruption. She doesn't even care who hears. It echoes and booms, reverberates off spotless tiles and pink-painted metal stalls; immaculate sterility reflects her voice, too impenetrably pristine to do anything but volley it back away from itself.

A cleansing serenity overwhelms any embarrassment or shame she feared she'd feel. She's exorcized a million poison emotions silently stored since her first miscarriage, since she first realized she'd married into a family of terrible women with flawless reproductive systems and would never know the feeling of gestation herself. All Paul's relatives who prodded and hounded her about when and why not yet and everything she's missing out on. That vice tightening around her, compressing her for years. A million suns scalding her from within that would be improper to acknowledge out loud.

Madeline runs her fingers through her hair, no longer charged and buzzing. She splashes cold water over her face and goes into a stall to break out her last pad, bracing herself to return to tea. If they're not done soon, she'll have to come up with an excuse. That feels like something she can do now.

On her way back, she passes the waiter, hunched in the barista station, sobbing. She'd like to comfort him, but, same as her, he still has to interact with those two. They'll both know comfort once her companions are gone.

Madeline steps outside, ready to get this over with.

It's quiet out here. No chatter. No sounds of pouring tea. No clink of porcelain.

The table is there, tray full of mostly-untouched pastries and such, teapots and coffee just as they were when she left.

It's Lydia and Ysa who stop her in her tracks.

Everyone else is gone. Abandoned half-drunk rooibos teas and cucumber cream cheese finger sandwiches short a single bite litter empty tables. Empty chairs are scattered disorderly from rushed departures.

Two broiled bodies still sit upright in burnt pink and white upholstery, little more than black crust, charred beyond recognition. She's seen similar sights in museums, casts of corpses unearthed in Pompeii. But this is different. This is something else.

Hesitantly, Madeline approaches the remains of her sister-in-law and Ysa. The storm has lifted and sun shines bright on their crisped carcasses from a cloudless blue sky. Beneath the cracked and cratered coal, bones glitter in the daylight, refracting prismatic rainbows onto white cloths that cover neighboring tables.

She studies the pair as they have so often studied her. Picks at the delicate plating of charred flesh that crumbles at her touch, examines their armorless interiors. Madeline knows tragedy; she understands loss, but she feels none of that at this moment. She just basks in the beautiful quiet. No sounds in the garden but the rustling of leaves and birdsong.

Long, exposed femurs and curved cages of rib reflect disco ball glitz all around. Like a showcase at Tiffany's, brilliant and silent and full of luster. Sparkling, just like those bird bones. Not bone anymore—diamond.

BURLESQUE!

ALBANQUA PROUDLY PRESENTS PARSIPPANY PHOENIX AND THE DANCE OF THE SEVEN VEILS (SPONSORED BY FRANK CROWN BUICK)

BRIDGET D. BRAVE

The lights dimmed, and a hush fell over the crowd of the Albanqua Civic Center and Event Venue. This was the Albanqua Burlesque-A-Fest, brought to you by Burlesque! Albanqua (Sponsored by Frank Crown Buick). Now considered a tradition after five annual events, it had become *the* event to end the winter blahs. The only available cocktails were cutesy concoctions named after some of the Burlesque! Albanqua regulars. They were also fourteen dollars, which was outrageous. Luckily, they tasted like candy, and they were poured generously (the James Bondage and the Harlot Bronte were especially strong). As a result, the energy in the venue was positively *electric*. The prior performers had left the audience in a rowdy revelry and the stage a mess of sequins, fallen feathers, and glitter. Now came the culmination of this event: hailing from deep in the Mohave desert, Parsippany Phoenix.

The curtain parted and a single light shone on a figure wrapped in translucent, iridescent veils. As a slow, steady drumbeat hit, she raised her arms above her head. Parsippany Phoenix began to wriggle while the veils swished lightly around her. A woman's voice, low and whiskey-and-cigarette raspy, poured from the speakers.

"It is believed that the dance of the seven veils was first performed to commemorate the death of John the Baptist. This may or may not be true. This is a dance to be performed by a singular dancer. This is a dance about what is and is not real." The dancer began to undulate, her arms weaving back and forth like twining snakes. "Tonight, we invite you to participate in the great unveiling. Remove the fabric that obscures your vision and embrace truth."

A few titters rose from the audience over the sound of tinkling glass. Someone near the back tried to suppress a cough. The drumbeat sped up, and Parsippany Phoenix took a step forward.

In front of the stage, eight tables were arranged in a crescent with groupings of two or three people seated. These were the "VIP" seats that came with either a hefty price tag or a paid sponsorship. The center tables were reserved for the event's sponsor, Frank Crown (of Frank Crown Buick), and the attendees who had paid extra for the honor, the brothers behind School of Hard Knox Construction, Consulting, Contracting, and Capital.

Parsippany stopped in front of the first table and shifted her hip toward the seated couple, gyrating as she wriggled her fingers at the veil resting there.

"Remove the veil," the recorded voice intoned. "Unveil your truth."

A man in a button-down shirt, open at the collar, laughed nervously and made an exaggerated thumb point toward the woman next to him.

"Remove the veil. Unveil your truth."

With a sheepish look toward his wife, Ralph Lewis, orthodontist and slightly above-average golfer, shrugged. His wife, the much younger Amy Lewis, slapped one of his hands in mock irritation and reached out to tug on the veil at Parsippany's hip. It slid over the jeweled belt she wore low around her waist and drifted onto the table, revealing a smooth expanse of creamy pale leg.

The drumbeat stopped. Parsippany froze in place.

The voice sounded over the speakers. "Your first love was your last."

Ralph sputtered out a noisy laugh and threw his hands up in the air. A few others in the VIP roared with laughter. He leaned over and clapped his hand on his wife's shoulder. "I'm sorry, baby. Guess it's me forever."

The drumbeat picked back up, and Parsippany twirled toward the second table, the six remaining scarves swirling around her. A similar scene played out at the next stop, with the veiled girl shifting her stance to display the other hip. Three girls in their early thirties started squealing with excitement, pushing one another's hands away to reach for the veil. The victor was Melanie Moyer-Brown, a rising associate attorney at the prestigious Brown, Brown, Brown & Clydesdale law firm. Melanie eagerly snapped the scarf off Parsippany and let it drift into her lap.

The music stopped. Parsippany paused her undulations.

"You will not become your mother. You are already far, far worse."

The other two girls screamed cackles and poked at their lawyer friend as she gave them each distracted smiles, her eyes wide with panic. When Melanie finally reached for her sugar-rimmed martini glass of Lucha VaVaVoom (just a tequila sunrise, she had noted with exasperation), her hand was noticeably shaking. "What the fuck?" she whispered to herself.

If Parsippany Phoenix had heard the question, she showed no sign. Her attention turned to the third table. Seated there, Benjamin Farruci IV, local real estate magnate and known philanderer, had one arm draped over the scowling blonde at his side. Parsippany turned her back to the table and did an impressive backbend as she shimmied from side to side, presenting her torso to the seated couple. Big Ben wrapped his fingers around the scarf that protruded from her glittering bikini top, pulling it toward himself.

"You are not capable of true happiness."

This got some scattered laughs, one muttered "wow," and a handful of cringes. Everyone in town knew Big Ben had left his wife of twenty-seven years for the girl next to him and was now being sued for half his amassed wealth.

Big Ben's ears had gone bright red, and he was making a fist with his right hand. His new girlfriend noticed and put her hands on his arm, making soothing noises as she snuggled against him.

Parsippany took no notice of this display, instead kicking a leg high and spinning on to the next table. The Venture Capital firm of School of Hard Knox had purchased this table, and the attendees were the two founding partners, Davis and Chandler Knox. Both graduates from Albanqua High School, they returned to their hometown to "invest" in the community with a little help from Daddy Knox's accounts.

So far, that investment had only resulted in half a finished condo building and a multitude of violation notices from the city.

Parsippany turned her back to this table and dropped forward dramatically at the waist. After mugging the crowd for a moment, the taller of the two lifted the veil that covered the dancer's g-stringed backside. Davis Knox flourished it like a bullfighter and laid it over the head of his little brother.

"You left your laptop unlocked."

The crowd again roared with laughter, the two young men joining in. As Parsippany Phoenix began to skip-hop away, Davis stopped laughing. An odd look had come over his face, and he began to pat down his pockets.

Three veils remained. Four tables remained. The nearly-naked dancer lifted to her toes and spun past the fifth table in the crescent, heading for the two men seated sixth in line. Parsippany rolled her shoulders backward gracefully, presenting her right shoulder to the man on the left.

Meanwhile, Davis Knox had located his phone. The screen read "27 MISSED CALLS." He opened his texts and began to scroll.

Just as Davis felt his heart plummet to his bowels, there was a commotion at table one. Ralph had his wife by the arm. "Let me go," she hissed at him as she roughly yanked her arm away. He and several others watched her storm off toward the back of the theater.

"Who the fuck is Christine?" he called after her, his mouth hanging open in confusion. "The girl in college? Amy!" Ralph gathered up his jacket and scarf to chase after her. At a table near the center, one that had been blissfully skipped in this unveiling of the truth, Amber Mae Crown stood up. The school psychologist, who believed herself "good in a crisis," patted her husband gently on the wrist and left to check on Dr. Lewis and his wife.

The table that held Parsippany's attention was frozen, watching this happen. Just beside them, Davis was hurriedly yanking on his coat as his brother mouthed, "What's wrong?" Davis had his phone at his ear. Someone was sobbing loudly on the other end, only able to articulate partial sentences, which were audible to those he pushed past on his way to the exit. "It was just there. . . kicked in the door. . . took the computers. . . what the fuck did you do, Davis? . . . looking for you. . . warrant."

Will Beryl's mouth had gone dry. He shifted back in his seat. Parsippany leaned further, nearly brushing his nose with her veiled shoulder. Now, up close, Will smelled something like crushed dried flowers, old leaves, the stale stink of a festering cavity in a decaying tooth.

The music stopped. "It's too late."

Will nodded as his face fell into a frown. His hand found the spot right below the ribs, "upper left quadrant," according to the radiology orders.

The blonde at table three burst into noisy sobs. Big Ben threw his hands in the air and rolled his eyes heavenward. "For fuck's sake, I'm fucking happy. What the fuck do you want from me, Stacey?"

Melanie Moyer-Brown was on her fifth Lucha VaVaVoom, her friends watching with concerned expressions. One had tried to take away the last drink, and Melanie had pinched her arm in response. The girl rubbed the sore spot as she sat, still in disbelief that her friend had actually *twisted* as she pinched like a playground bully.

Parsippany glided back to the central table, where Frank Crown of Frank Crown Buick (proud sponsors of Burlesque! Albanqua) now sat alone. He wore a grim, pursed-lip frown as he watched the dancer weave toward him, pausing to lightly shake her right shoulder in his direction. Frank snapped the veil away and dropped it, crossing his arms across his chest.

"Your fears will never come to fruition. You will be dead before anyone finds out what you did, Frank."

Frank slumped forward, his palms resting on the table before him. His head hung low, as if something fascinating was happening in his lap. Parsippany spun back toward the stage, and an uneasy murmur started in the balcony seats. She was now clad only in a rhinestone-encrusted string bikini, the remaining veil covering her head. The light suddenly seemed a little too harsh, and beneath it, the dancer's skin no longer gleamed like milky porcelain. Now they could see that the tone was more a blanched grey, mottled with blue swollen veins and lumpy deposits under the surface. It was the bloated, strained flesh of a waterlogged corpse in this new light.

Someone in the second row gasped. Melanie Moyer-Brown vomited onto her table, her friends grabbing their purses and scrambling back to avoid the splatter. Will Beryl began to cry, his shoulders shaking visibly. Stacey had abandoned Big Ben, who was now consoling himself with a purple pint glass of something named Cher Noble.

The dancer spun wildly and rushed left, away from the stage. She stopped near one of the doors with an illuminated "Exit" sign above it and beckoned the security guard to come closer. The guard, an off-duty cop who took these gigs on weekends to supplement a burgeoning cocaine habit, approached her warily.

With her back to the audience, Parsippany lifted her final veil.

All of the color drained from the cop's face. Tears began to well up and run down his cheeks as he stared at the girl before him in absolute frozen terror. Then Parsippany leaned toward him and whispered in his ear.

The drumbeats increased to a crazy crescendo as Parsippany raised her arms above her head once more and stood on her tiptoes. She began to slowly turn.

Those who saw her face had a difficult time describing it. Words like "skeletal" and "death" got thrown around, but you could tell that the words felt insufficient for what lay beneath that final veil. Despite the sold-out crowd at the Albanqua Civic Auditorium, only a handful of people were still watching Parsippany's performance.

The rest watched that coked-out cop shoot Frank Crown right in the fucking face.

BENCHMAN FINANCIAL'S DEBT RELIEF PROGRAM

VINCENT V. CAVA

Mathew Stern knew the circumstances surrounding his morning meeting sounded too good to be true, but it wasn't like he had a lot of options. Why Benchman Financial, a company that dealt in the buying and selling of corporate assets, had contacted him out of the blue and offered to erase every last penny of his medical debt was beyond him, but he figured he should at least come down to their office and hear them out.

Of course, he'd done his research first, and, as far as he could tell, the company was the real deal. He didn't watch Fox Business or MSNBC and he didn't own a subscription to *The Wall Street Journal*, but a quick web search of the company's name brought up thousands of hits from reputable news outlets all over the net. From commercial real estate to big tech, they seemed to have their tendrils in everything, although he couldn't help but notice they didn't have much of a presence when it came to nonprofit or charity work. There was, however, one exception—a program started by the company's founder that awarded grants to hand-selected people who met certain, unspecified criteria.

One fluff piece Mathew found online ran a story about a

southern California woman who'd been the recipient of their most recent endowment. He skimmed the article, read the woman's testimony (which had only glowing things to say), then accepted Benchman Financial's request to meet. Now he was sitting in the lobby of a swanky office on the top floor of a west Los Angeles skyscraper, fiddling with the sleeve of his one good blazer, and wondering if all the people who worked there could tell he was poor.

"Sir?"

Mathew glanced up to see that the gorgeous, young blonde who worked the front desk was now hovering over him. In her designer dress and stylish pumps, she looked more like a fashion model than a secretary, and just being within her immediate proximity made him uncomfortably aware of his own mediocrity. For a moment, he was sure she was about to accuse him of wandering in off the street like a stray dog and have him escorted from the premises, but when she parted her perfect, plump lips to speak, the tone he was met with was nothing but polite and courteous.

"Mr. Wilcox is ready to see you now."

He followed her from the lobby, watching her hips swoosh back and forth as they passed endless rows of glass boxes, each occupied by a professionally dressed, perfectly coiffed suited-drone, either on the phone or pecking away at their computer, until they reached a large door on the other side of the office. She knocked, and the two waited quietly for a few awkward moments until a muffled voice from inside acknowledged their presence and granted Mathew permission to enter.

It wasn't until the secretary had closed the door behind him that Mathew was able to grasp just how massive the office really was. Against one wall was a full bar stocked with pricey, top-shelf liquor. Against the other was a television, so large it could have accommodated IMAX movie screenings. In the center of the room, directly in front of the floor-to-ceiling windows looking out on Beverly Hills was an oversized desk, more expensive than Mathew's car, and sitting behind it was the man he had come to meet.

"Mathew Stern!" said the man. He flashed Mathew a set of impossibly white, impossibly straight teeth. A small figurine twirled between his fingers. The man set the statue down in front of him when Mathew approached, then extended a hand outward. "I'm Brad Wilcox, Vice President of Philanthropy here at Benchman Financial."

Mathew accepted the handshake and took a seat in a chair so low to the ground he could barely see over the edge of Wilcox's magnificent desk.

"I understand you recently accrued some serious medical debt?" said Wilcox.

Mathew nodded.

"Six months ago, I had a stroke, and my insurance denied coverage on my hospital bill."

"Scoundrels," Wilcox grumbled while shuffling through paperwork on his desk. "And thank God you found us."

Mathew stared at the small statue Wilcox had been playing with earlier. It was an interesting little totem carved of polished stone, a creature with the body of a man but with three distinct goat heads, all looking out in different directions. He wondered where it came from. Was it a souvenir brought back from travels abroad? If so, what sort of culture would craft such a thing? He realized he'd let his mind drift when he glanced back up and noticed Wilcox was waiting for him to respond.

He cleared his throat.

"About that. I never applied to your program. I'm not even sure if I qualify."

Wilcox threw his head back and let out a laugh.

"Oh, you qualify. No need to worry. Benchman Financial has already reviewed your case, and we're prepared to cover your entire bill. All. . ." His eyes scanned the open file on his desk. "$114,678.32 of it."

Mathew nearly swallowed his tongue. For once it looked like something was going his way. He didn't know how or why Benchman Financial had come to him, but he wasn't about to look a gift horse in the mouth. Erasing his debt would mean he could finally get his life back on track. Maybe he could even start looking at wedding rings for his girlfriend. He leaned forward in his chair.

"What do we have to do to get the process going?"

"It's all pretty simple. When we're done here, my secretary, Mimi, will provide you with forms to fill out. We'll need some info, of course—proof of residency, social security, the usual stuff. Then, on the next blood moon, you'll need to perform a human sacrifice."

"Excuse me?" said Mathew.

"Mimi. She's the pretty blonde that led you to my office. She's got some forms—"

"No. After that."

"You'll need to perform a human sacrifice."

Mathew shot to his feet. He could feel his face getting hot.

"What kind of sicko plays a practical joke on someone in need?"

His rage quickly turned to self-pity. Even though he'd been trying to stay guarded, some part of him had hoped this meeting would be the answer to his problems.

"Hang on!" said Wilcox. He rushed around his desk, palms out in a show of peace. "I know it might be hard to believe, but we aren't playing a prank. This really is our offer. Benchman Financial will pay off your entire hospital bill on the condition you perform a human sacrifice on the next blood moon."

Mathew shook his head and laughed.

"Human sacrifice? You're talking about murder?"

"I wouldn't put it that way. Murder is violent. This is more of a spiritual practice, you know? And don't worry about the cops. We've been running this program for fifty-two years. If there was any chance you could be caught, trust me, you would have heard about it by now."

"So is this like some cult stuff?" asked Mathew. The meeting might have been a bust, but he figured he could at least amuse himself by seeing where the conversation went.

"It isn't like some cult stuff. *It is some cult stuff!*" Wilcox plopped down on the edge of his desk, loosened his tie like a cool substitute teacher, then leaned over and pressed the button on his intercom. "Mimi, can you bring in the demo?" He took off his jacket and began to roll up his sleeves. "It's hard work keeping a business like this in the black. I'm not ashamed to say we need a little outside help and I'm not talking about Congress. We already have a few of those idiots in our pockets, but let's be honest, who doesn't?" Wilcox snagged a picture frame off his desk then spun it around, revealing to Mathew a portrait of a scowling old man that looked like it should be hanging on the wall of some haunted plantation house. "That's why our company's founder, Jarvis Benchman, made a pact with an ancient god. The deal was simple. We satisfy our quarterly quota for human sacrifices, and our deity will ensure that our profits continue to meet shareholders' expectations."

Mathew was hearing what Wilcox was saying but was struggling to take him seriously. He wasn't sure if he should be mad at the man for wasting his time or laugh at the sheer insanity of what was being suggested. That debate would be put on hold the second Mimi returned to the room. Nothing about the conversation continued to be humorous after that. Especially when he saw the gurney she was wheeling and the naked man strapped to the top of it.

The man looked homeless. This, Mathew deduced from his

long, patchy beard, matted hair, and dirt-caked hands and feet. In his mouth was a ball gag. Leather bands were fastened tight across his arms, waist, legs, even his neck, restricting his mobility. He'd been struggling against his restraints. Dried blood formed in crusty red rings where his skin met the unforgiving leather straps.

"What the hell is this?!" Mathew shouted. He was hoping the practical joke angle was still on the table, but deep down, he was starting to panic. Mimi produced a satin pillow and kneeled in front of her boss. Sitting atop it was an ornamental dagger, its hilt topped with the head of a three-faced goat.

"I figured you'd be skeptical," said Wilcox as he took the dagger in his hand, "so I arranged for a demonstration." Wilcox approached the man, dragging the point of the dagger's blade over his chest. "You'll aim for the heart. That gets the best results."

He lifted the dagger over his head, and Mathew could see the ruby-red eyes of the three-faced goat sparkle in the sunlight coming through the window. Then, so quick he barely had time to blink, Wilcox drove the dagger down, burying the blade all the way to the hilt inside the man's chest. The homeless man's eyes shot open. He let out a scream so loud that—even with the gag in his mouth—Mathew was certain the entire office could hear him. His body spasmed. His muscles tensed. While this was going on, Mimi flattened a plastic tarp across the floor, then wheeled the gurney on top of it. She shot Mathew a smile on her way out of the room.

"Oh my God!" screamed Mathew.

"Not your God," laughed Wilcox. "Hang on. It's going to get messy."

He placed his free hand against the man's ribs, then yanked the knife out. The homeless man let out another howl, this one more awful than the last, as blood erupted from the gaping hole in his chest. It sprayed like a broken sprinkler, nearly splashing the ceiling before settling into a low, steady gurgle. Wilcox walked over to his desk and retrieved the goat-faced totem he'd been playing with earlier. When he returned to the man on the gurney, he jabbed the stone figurine inside his wound and began to spin it maliciously.

"Drink, my Lord," he said.

Mathew's stomach churned.

"Th-this is insane."

"Does that matter?" snapped Wilcox, still spinning the totem in the man's chest. "It could be positively batshit. Who cares so long as you get paid?"

Mathew glanced at the homeless man. His breathing was becoming more shallow, and his face had gone pale. He'd lost a lot of blood, and it was clear he didn't have much time left.

"Why?" Mathew blurted out. "Why do you need me for this?"

"Now that is a good question!" Wilcox pulled the totem from the man's chest cavity and sat back down on the edge of his desk. "Our god is picky. It's not just about sacrificing someone in his name. It's about who is doing the sacrificing. Believe me, if we could satisfy him ourselves without involving outside people, we would, but this little demonstration you just watched me perform wouldn't pop our stock for an afternoon in a bull market."

"So you killed a man just to prove to me that you're serious?"

Wilcox shrugged.

"It worked, didn't it?"

Mathew's head was swimming.

"I don't understand."

Wilcox sighed.

"Look at it like this. My bank account is eight figures. I own three exotic cars you probably couldn't pronounce the names of. And if my kid wants to go backstage at the Taylor Swift concert, all I need to do is make one call, and *boom*, she's there. I'm rich as hell, so it's no big deal if the death comes by my hand. The wealthy sacrificing peasants is kind of par for the course, you know? Our god couldn't care less about that. But you, a regular Joe? That's the stuff that gets his juices flowing. It needs to come from a place of desperation. Poor, worthless, pathetic losers spilling human blood for the kind of money a guy like me wouldn't even roll out of bed for."

Mathew gawked at the man, who was now very clearly a corpse. His body was still leaking blood, although it was more of a trickle than a gush at this point. These people were nuts, but he didn't want to end up like the man on the gurney if he said no.

"I need some time to think about it."

"Of course!" smiled Wilcox. "You have until tomorrow night to make up your mind. That's the blood moon. If you're not here to perform the sacrifice, we'll need to go with our backup, and you'll be left to deal with your medical bills on your own. Please understand there is someone on the waitlist behind you, and you won't be offered this opportunity again."

Mathew nodded and started towards the door but only managed to take a few steps before Wilcox spoke up again.

"Oh, and Mathew?"

He stopped in his tracks. Mathew didn't want to turn around, but he forced himself to. Once he had, he wished his eyes were anywhere else than on Wilcox. The man was still sitting on the edge of his desk, only now he had popped the blood-coated totem in his mouth and was spinning it between his lips like a lollipop. He stared at Mathew as he ran his tongue over the small figurine, slurping and sucking on it, then pulled it out and grinned. The blood smeared against his too-white teeth looked as if Wilcox was smiling at him with a mouth full of peppermint candies.

"When you stop by Mimi's desk on the way out, remember to get your parking validated."

Mathew spent the rest of the morning at home on the couch, trying to process what he'd just witnessed. Wilcox, Mimi, and quite possibly the entire West LA branch of Benchman Financial were utterly insane. That much was clear. What he was unsure about was how much danger he was now in. He was dealing with people who believed murdering another human being would somehow magically improve their company's bottom line. It was safe to say they weren't playing with a full deck of cards, but would they come after him if he turned their offer down? They hadn't threatened him directly, but that wasn't enough to make Mathew feel safe.

He considered calling the police but remembered when Wilcox had suggested the company had connections with the cops. Was it possible the LAPD was in Benchman Financials' pocket? He wouldn't be surprised. They were the LAPD, after all. Plus, even if that wasn't the case, who would believe him if he waltzed into the police station and reported what he'd seen? Pulling a stunt like that would just cause him more headaches. A part of him wanted to pretend the whole thing never happened and move on, but he couldn't shake the image from his mind of Wilcox driving that dagger into the homeless man's chest.

His thoughts wandered to the woman from the article he had read who had also been part of Benchman Financial's debt relief program. It only took a bit of searching before he had it pulled up on his phone again. According to the article, her name was Leticia Jackson. Nothing about her smiling face in the picture gave him the vibe she was capable of committing murder, but the fact that she had accepted a grant from the company just one year prior meant she had killed someone in much the same way Wilcox had.

He needed to talk to her. If anyone would know what he was dealing with, it would be her. A bit of internet sleuthing brought him to her social media profile. He gave considerable thought about what to write her. This was his one chance to get inside information on the company. The last thing he wanted to do was scare her off. Once he was ready, he typed out a message.

You don't know me, but my name is Mathew Stern. I've been contacted by Benchman Financial to take part in the same program you were involved in. I was hoping we could talk.

He punched in his phone number then pressed send.

The door of his apartment flung open, and for a second, he thought it would be Wilcox, grinning his blood-smeared grin, eyes ablaze with fire, and goat horns sprouting from his forehead. Mathew threw himself back in his seat ready to scream, but when his eyes fell upon the door, his pulse began to slow. Standing at the entrance was Nina, his girlfriend, who had been shopping with friends all day at the mall.

"Hey!" she said.

Nina skipped toward him, shopping bags in hand, then dropped them at his feet and took a seat beside him on the couch. She started chatting him up about her day but stopped mid-sentence and cocked her head.

"What's wrong?" she asked.

"Nothing," Mathew lied.

He glanced at the bags, taking a mental estimate of how much money she'd spent. Nina didn't know about his medical debt. He hadn't told her his insurance refused to cover his bill. He'd been afraid to. Before his stroke, she'd made it clear just how important financial security was to her. Sure, she had expensive tastes, but up until recently, it hadn't been a problem. The occasional weekend getaway or moderately priced handbag had never been something they couldn't afford. Lately, however, he noticed her spending habits had increased, and with his debt looming over him, Mathew found himself wondering how they could maintain their lifestyle and still keep the lights on.

She raised an eyebrow.

"You're not about to nag me again, are you?"

Money had been a point of contention between them as of late. Not just because she'd been spending more but because he'd been on edge about it. He thought that in her eyes, he'd become a cheapskate—someone who'd rather horde all his money than go out on a nice date with her. They'd had more than a couple fights over it, and every time, it left him feeling guilty. But he feared if he told her the truth, she'd run for greener pastures. Who would want to sacrifice their happiness because of their partner's screw-ups?

"Why would I nag you?" he replied.

"Good," she gave him a peck on the cheek.

His phone rang. He checked the screen and saw it was an unknown number.

"Who's that?" she asked.

"Probably a telemarketer." Mathew set the phone on the coffee table and leaned back in his seat. "Why don't you show me what you picked up at the mall?"

Her eyes lit up. She pulled out a dress and resumed the conversation about her day. He watched her talk, and as she did, he was reminded how much simpler life was before his finances went to hell. He wanted to tuck himself away in that feeling, but no matter how hard he tried to forget about it, that debt was always there, bearing down on him like a hydraulic press. For so long, he had thought his massive medical bill had been an accident. He was insured, after all. There was no way he could be saddled with such ridiculous debt, but after countless phone calls with his insurance company, reality started to sink in. He'd been played. Through some loophole, he'd been paying into a limited coverage plan, despite believing otherwise.

She held the dress up to her body.

"How 'bout I try it on?"

Mathew caught a glimpse of the tag. He knew the brand. Nothing they made was cheap.

"I'd love that."

She leaned in and pressed her lips to his, letting them linger for a long moment before breaking their kiss, then grabbed her bags and headed for the bedroom.

"Wait till you see it on me."

He didn't think he deserved her. Before the stroke, he'd been working up the courage to pop the question. When he was laid up in the hospital, Nina had stayed by his side all day, every day, leaving only to sneak him candy from the vending machine, and that just made him love her even more. When he got the bill and saw how much he owed the hospital, he realized marriage was further away than ever. He couldn't afford a ring with that kind of debt looming over him, and the lavish wedding he knew she dreamed of was out of the question.

Tying the knot meant entangling their finances. He wasn't sure how she'd react if it meant she had to take on that kind of burden. He wanted to do right by her, but at the moment, it seemed as if the only option he had was to take this Wilcox lunatic up on his offer.

He grabbed his phone and checked his voicemail, eager to see if the call had been Leticia. It had not. The message was from the hospital's billing department, notifying him that he'd missed another payment. Mathew let out a frustrated groan and deleted it. He'd been getting a lot of calls from random numbers lately, every single one hitting him up for money he didn't have. There was no reprieve. Email, phone, even post, they came at him from all angles. The thought of opening his mailbox and finding yet another bill scared him just as much as the dagger-wielding psychopath he'd met earlier that day.

His phone rang again. Once more, the caller ID showed a number he didn't recognize. He felt a rage boil over inside him. These leeches made him want to scream. Mathew needed to unload on someone. He didn't care who, but for once, he needed to feel like he was in control.

He answered the call.

"I don't have your money, you blood-sucking parasites!"

"Hello?" said the voice on the other line. "This is Leticia Jackson. I assume I'm speaking with Mathew Stern?"

———

Her eyes scanned the neighborhood behind him when she greeted Mathew at the door the following morning. Leticia appeared on edge, nervous, perhaps even a little afraid to speak with him, but their face-to-face meeting had been at her insistence once she learned about his offer. Gone was the smiling woman from the picture he had seen online. This one was thinner, more stern, and she looked like she'd aged years since that photo had been taken. A gray streak ran through her hair, and wrinkles creased her face around her eyes and mouth.

Once inside her home, Mathew was able to see a different side of her. He'd been anxious before walking through her front door, but the kids' toys scattered across the floor helped to ease his nerves. Aside from that, the rest of the home was neat and orderly. Pictures of children and grandparents hung on the wall. Knick-knacks lined the shelves—porcelain cats and overpriced candles. This was not the home of the cold-blooded murderer Mathew had expected to meet. No, this was a woman with a family.

She disappeared into the kitchen and re-emerged moments later with two cups of coffee. She'd even gone to the trouble of breaking out the fine china. Mathew accepted the drink and sat across from her on the living room's couch.

"It was a wildfire for me." There was a pained smile on her face. "You remember them from a year ago? Four hundred acres went up in flames. A lot of homes too. Mine was one of them.

Well, part of it anyway." She nodded to the kitchen. Mathew thought it looked newly renovated when he first sat down, but now he could tell it had been completely rebuilt. He remembered the fires she was talking about. Just north of Los Angeles, they were all over the news. The air quality was bad enough to turn the sun beet-red even where he lived.

"Of course, the insurance company didn't cover it. Act of God, they said. Appraisers told me I was looking at more than two-hundred thousand dollars to repair the damage."

Mathew took a sip of his coffee.

"And that's when Benchman Financial reached out to you?"

"Yeah." Her eyes fell to the floor. "You have to understand, I got kids. At the time, I had three boys living under my roof and no daddy to help with the bills. We didn't have anywhere else to live."

Mathew nodded.

"And you went through with it? You performed the sacrifice?"

All this time, he'd been judging Leticia for taking the deal, but now he was starting to understand how she was swayed. It wasn't easy being a single parent. Adding the threat of homelessness to that equation sounded like a nightmare.

"Do you know what it is?" asked Leticia, her voice a whisper. "Their god. The Three-Faced Goat. The Dark Prince of the Great Beyond. You ever hear about Goetia?"

Mathew shook his head.

"Demons. That's what they're worshiping over at Benchman Financial. One in particular named Nyzarleth. There's a book. It's called the *Lesser Key of Solomon*. Lot of people know about that. It ain't no secret. But there's a *Lost Key*. One that should've stayed lost. That's how they found out about this one."

He could see something stirring behind her eyes. It wasn't paranoia or even fear. No, this was trauma. He almost felt it was cruel to press on, but he had to know more.

"So you sacrificed a homeless person to a demon? Then what? What happened next?"

Leticia drew back.

"Homeless person?"

His phone began to ring. She stopped abruptly as he pulled it from his pocket.

"Who is it?" she asked.

Mathew glanced at the screen, expecting it to be yet another unknown number, but felt his heart nearly stop when he saw what it said. He raised the phone and showed her the caller ID that read Benchman Financial. Leticia recoiled and covered her mouth with her hands.

"Don't answer it!" she hissed.

He didn't listen. This was getting weird, but he needed to see things through. He pressed the answer button and raised the phone to his ear.

"Mathew!" It was Wilcox. "How you doing, bud? Could you be a pal and put your phone on speaker so Leticia could hear me too?"

Why on Earth was this psycho calling him now? More importantly, how did he know he was with Leticia? His heart was pounding. He didn't just want to hang up the phone. He wanted to chuck it through the window, but something compelled him to follow Wilcox's instructions.

"You've been very naughty, Leticia," sighed Wilcox.

"Please!" the woman shouted. There was a frantic look in her eyes. "I didn't tell him nothing! He just showed up here!"

"Oh, come on now." droned the voice out of Mathew's phone. "Don't lie to me, girl. And Mathew, I can't believe you'd throw away a golden opportunity like this. You just signed an NDA yesterday!"

"No, I didn't," said Mathew. "I was filling out the paperwork after our meeting, but when Mimi tried to print the NDA, there was a paper jam. She said I could sign it when I come back."

The voice went silent for a moment, and Mathew could hear the rustling of papers on the other end of the line.

"Son of a gun, I guess you're right," laughed Wilcox. "Mimi is the granddaughter of one of our board members, and between you and me, she's not the sharpest knife in the drawer. We definitely need that NDA signed A-S-A-P though. I'm going to have her email it to you. If you can go ahead and sign it electronically at your earliest convenience, it would be very much appreciated."

"Will do," said Mathew.

"And once that's done, there will be no blabbing about any of this. Do you understand?"

"I do," he replied.

"As for Leticia," said Wilcox playfully. "Girl, you did sign an NDA. I just pulled your file to double-check and it's right here, so you know what that means."

"It was all his fault!" Leticia had broken down into tears.

"You played a part in it," said Wilcox. He was speaking to her the way a kindergarten teacher might scold a child who refused to share their toys. "Mathew might not have signed anything, but you have, so I'm afraid we'll have to remove your grant."

"NO! Don't do that!" she screamed. "My boys! The bank will take the house from us!"

"Cut the shit, you selfish cunt," snapped Wilcox. "We both know you don't give a fuck about your kids. You can take me off speaker now, Mathew."

Mathew felt like an automaton, unable to do anything other than what he was commanded.

"No, no, no, no! You can't take my money away!" shouted Leticia. "That would mean it was all for nothing!" She lunged at Mathew, trying to grab the phone, but he shook her off and she fell to the couch. He stood up, still holding the phone to his ear.

Leticia rose to her feet too, but instead of leaping toward him again, she rushed out of the room.

"What's going to happen to her?" asked Mathew.

"You need to stop worrying about other people and do what's right for you," said Wilcox. "The blood moon is tonight. You're running out of time. Remember, we have a candidate dying to take your spot."

Mathew turned to the door.

"I understand that, but. . ."

He was about to make a plea on Leticia's behalf when he got the sudden feeling that he was no longer alone in the room. Slowly, he turned around and found Leticia had returned. His mouth went dry. She was holding a gun, and he was staring down the barrel of it.

"Is he still on the phone?" she asked.

Mathew nodded. Cautiously, he handed her the phone and stepped against the wall.

"Please, Mr. Wilcox. Ronnie and Devin. They're all I got left. We'll be on the streets in a month."

Mathew couldn't hear Wilcox on the other line, but whatever he said had caused her to drop to her knees. She crumpled into a heap, gun in one hand, his phone in the other and began sobbing. Mathew watched until he felt it was safe to creep up and take his phone back. She didn't even notice when he pulled it from her grasp.

"Are you okay?" he asked.

When she didn't respond, he took it as his cue to leave. He wasn't going to stick around any longer to console her. He walked out onto the front step, closed the door behind him, then lifted the phone to his ear once more.

"Mr. Wilcox? You there?"

The line was dead. Wilcox had hung up.

It sounded like a clap of thunder. A *BANG* so loud Mathew's ears started ringing. Leticia's gun had gone off. A sick feeling crept into Mathew's stomach, but it wasn't because he thought the bullet had been intended for him. In fact, he was sure it wasn't. He cracked the door again and poked his head inside Leticia's home. The first thing he noticed was her kids' toys strewn across the floor. The next thing he noticed was her brains scattered amongst them.

He threw up when he got back to the apartment. Before yesterday, he'd never witnessed a person die before. Now, he had seen it happen twice. Luckily, Nina was out. She had gone to some fancy restaurant in Santa Monica with friends. That was perfect as far as he was concerned. He needed to be alone right now anyway. He considered coming clean about his debt when she got home. If she loved him, she wouldn't dump him over money. But what if she did? He couldn't blame her for not wanting any part of his financial nightmare. She deserved fancy restaurants and new clothes that made her feel pretty. Choosing a life with him would be throwing away all of those things.

Mathew wiped his mouth, slogged back to the living room, then plopped himself down on the couch. There was some mail on the table. Nina must have taken it in before going to dinner. He picked up an envelope, opened it, then started to grind his teeth when he read the letter that was inside. It was from the hospital. He'd been sent a price correction on his bill. An extra four thousand dollars had now been tacked on for a physical therapy session.

"Are you kidding?!" Mathew cried.

He'd been up and moving just minutes after coming into the ER. His stroke had not been a major one, and he'd retained all mobility in his limbs. When would he have even gone to physical therapy?

Then he remembered. Just before leaving the hospital, he was approached in his room by a woman who introduced herself as his physical therapist. Her job had been to assess him and make sure he was capable of leaving. Together, they walked a lap around the hospital wing, then she asked him a couple of questions about how he was feeling before signing off on him. The whole interaction had been less than twenty minutes. Now, the hospital was charging him four thousand dollars for it.

None of this was fair. All he'd done was survive a horrible medical emergency, and now he was being punished for it. That debt was getting heavier. It weighed down on him so much he was struggling to breathe. It felt like the entire fucked-up US healthcare industry was sitting on his chest and that they wouldn't get off until they squeezed every last cent out of him.

All his life, he'd been careful, and now because of some scam artist insurance company, he was screwed. People like Wilcox took what they wanted, and it didn't seem like there were ever any repercussions from it. Morality was a myth. Fortune favored those who didn't run decisions through ethical filters. He didn't need eight figures in his bank account. All he needed was Nina, and he would do whatever he could to keep her in his life. Maybe it was time to get his for a change.

Saying no to Benchman Financial wouldn't save a life anyway. Wilcox had said it himself. If he didn't take them up on the deal, someone else would. Why miss out on a once in a lifetime opportunity? So he could say he didn't take the easy way out?

It's not like the homeless man he'd seen killed was living such a great life anyway. He didn't like the fact that anyone had to die, but the chances were high that the guy Wilcox stabbed wouldn't live to be much older on his own. Statistics showed that most people living on the street in Los Angeles suffered from debilitating drug addictions. Had there been track marks in his arms? Now that he thought about it, he could have sworn he noticed them. Junkies already didn't have high life expectancies. At least this time, something positive could come from one's death.

He pulled out his phone and dialed the number that Wilcox had called him from.

"Hello, Mr. Wilcox?" said Mathew. "I'm ready to accept your offer. Tell me what I need to do."

He'd been instructed to arrive after hours. It was quiet by then. Aside from the DoorDash guy he shared an elevator with and the few drones still pulling late shifts, the office was empty.

Like before, he followed Mimi from the lobby, but this time, instead of leading him to Wilcox's office, she brought him to a set of double doors labeled *Board Room*. She knocked, and a second later, the two were greeted by Wilcox.

"Mathew!" he smiled, his pearly white veneers on full display. "Come on in!"

There were no windows. Opposite the entrance was a private elevator, its glistening gold doors standing in stark contrast against the room's drab, green walls. Around the perimeter hung portraits of the sullen, white-haired executives of the company's past. And in the center of the room, sitting around the conference table were the sullen, white-haired executives of the company's present.

"Let me introduce you to the board. They'll be joining us for our sacrifice today," said Wilcox. He turned to address the group. "Everyone, this is Mathew Stern."

Mathew shuffled up to the table. He hadn't anticipated there would be anyone else watching.

"Who was your provider?" said one board member. He had removed his oxygen mask to ask the question.

"Sorry?" Mathew cupped his ear.

"Your insurance provider? The one that skipped out on your hospital bill?"

"Intercontinental Health."

"Ha!" snorted a geezer in a wheelchair. "I own a stake in that company."

Wilcox handed a clipboard to Mathew.

"We've got one more form for you," he said. "It's just a waiver. You'll be signing over your sacrificial benefits to Benchman Financial in exchange for the monetary compensation we discussed."

"Oh? Okay, I guess," said Mathew. His mind felt foggy. "Do you have a pen or someth—"

Wilcox snagged Mathew's hand and pricked his finger with a pin.

"OUCH!"

A bead of blood formed at the tip of his finger. Wilcox pressed it to the line on the paper where Mathew had been planning to sign.

"All set!" he said. "Let's begin!"

The board erupted in cheers, followed by wet coughs and wheezing. Everyone stood from their seat (except, of course, the geezer in the wheelchair), then began to strip.

"What's going on?" said Mathew.

"This part of the ritual is always a little weird," said Wilcox, peeling the socks from his feet. "Just go with the flow."

The board members approached Mathew and started to undress him. He tried taking Wilcox's advice, but he was already feeling vulnerable, and the naked old men and women pawing at his body certainly weren't helping. He fought a little, but they paid him no mind. They tore away his shirt and yanked at his belt buckle. Just as his pants were coming down around his ankles, Mimi returned to the room.

She was carrying a headdress topped with the skulls of three goats. A long, red cape flowed from the back of it. She lifted it high and placed it on Mathew's head. He knew he looked stupid but wrapped himself in the soft velvet cloak, thankful for the bit of modesty it provided.

Once she was finished dressing him, Mimi wheeled in a cart with a punch bowl and began pouring the board members drinks. It wasn't until the bitter, coppery scent filled Mathew's nose that he realized what it was she'd been ladling into the crystal chalices she was passing out. The board gulped the blood greedily, letting it run down their sagging breasts, bloated bellies, and shriveled testicles. They drained their glasses, splashed what was left of it onto their faces, then kissed it into each other's mouths.

As they rubbed their liver-spotted bodies against each other, their naked figures began to warp into something terrible. Spines gnarled, limbs twisted, tendons ripped and popped. Bat wings burst from their backs, and horns emerged from their brows, jutting into the air then corkscrewing into tight spirals at the sides of their heads. Their faces took on a feral look. All around the room, yellowing eyes rolled in ecstasy as vile moans poured from forked tongues.

They groped each other, tying themselves into a repulsive knot of loose skin and varicose veins. Mathew stood still, afraid to even move as the smacking of blood-soaked lips and the sickening scent of gore-coated genitals assaulted his senses. His body shivered. The undulating mass of flabby flesh was pushing him closer to the brink. He wasn't sure how long he was forced to witness the perverse performance, but as soon as Wilcox raised his hand, the madness ceased.

Mathew stared at him, perplexed. Unlike the others, Wilcox was still human in appearance. He may not have grown wings or horns, but his nude form now revealed a strange secret he'd been hiding. Mathew would have never guessed that beneath Wilcox's custom suits and Brooks Brothers shirts, the body of the man who recruited him into the program was covered entirely in sigils. They'd been tattooed in bold, black ink along his upper arms, legs, back, stomach, and chest. One was now even painted in blood on his forehead.

"It's time to head to the temple," he said.

They came to the elevators. Wilcox scanned a key card, and the gold doors slid open. Once everyone filed inside, he pressed the elevator's up button.

"I thought we were on the top floor," said Mathew. "Is the temple up on the roof?"

A chorus of snickering swelled around him.

"Up? It isn't up at all," replied one of the board members, an impish smirk on their face.

"It isn't down," chuckled another.

"It isn't left or right," cackled a third.

"It doesn't exist in three-dimensional space," crowed a fourth.

They grinned at him like a school of piranhas. If the elevator ride was longer, Mathew might have asked them to elaborate on their Mad Hatter-esque rant, but that no longer mattered the second the doors opened. Any questions he might have had were gone after that. They had tumbled down the rabbit hole along with what was left of his grip on reality.

He most certainly wasn't on the roof of the building, or any other building for that matter. The elevator doors had opened into what looked like an endless black void. A bizarre swirl of ever-changing colors, some of which Mathew knew, some he couldn't describe, floated over their heads like an enormous iridescent jellyfish, almost as long as a football field. It twisted into mind-bending mandalas before collapsing in on itself, then blossomed again into unimaginable geometric figures. A guttural echo, a thousand times louder than any foghorn, resonated from all directions, and, at times, Mathew thought it was even coming from inside his head. Extending out from the elevator was a stone bridge held up by seemingly nothing that snaked and zigged-zagged its way into impossible directions. Like something out of the mind of M.C. Escher, it switched back and forth, in and out, often doubling back and looping into insane lemniscates that somehow progressed towards a circular stone platform just a couple hundred yards off.

"Right this way," Wilcox said. Blood was once again smeared across his smile.

Mathew shook his head, unable to even utter the words no. He wished he could scream, but at this point, his mind was struggling to comprehend how to. Old hands pressed gently against his shoulders, nudging him from the elevator and onto the bridge.

They marched, the board members singing and chanting in a language he had never heard, their words strangely in sync with the horrible sounds blaring inside his skull. There were times when he thought he caught a hint of the word *Nyzarleth* and times when he thought their bizarre noises even disclosed disturbing secrets to him, but regardless of what he could or could not understand, every syllable invoked a horror inside him, and it took nearly all his strength not to fling himself from the bridge and into the abyss.

When they reached the platform, the group lined up into a semi-circle around Mathew, then started to grind on each other again. Wilcox gave Mathew a wink. He tilted his head into the air.

"Oh, Dark Prince of the Great Beyond! On this most sacred of nights, we bring you yet another offering. We shall shed the blood of the weak so that you may feed upon their hopelessness, their desire, their need."

He waved his hand, and the ground opened. From a trap door arose a pedestal. On top of it was a naked woman, bound and gagged. Mathew sucked in a sharp breath of air. He recognized her instantly.

"Nina?!" He turned to Wilcox. "I thought I was supposed to sacrifice a homeless person?"

Wilcox laughed.

"Didn't you read the contract? Paragraph four, Section C, Clause two: *The desperation of the party being sacrificed must be equal to or less than the desperation of the party performing the sacrifice.* The ritual doesn't work if you're punching down."

One of the board members held the dagger out to Mathew. He took it reluctantly as he looked into Nina's terrified face.

"But I love her."

Wilcox shook his head.

"Love, empathy, peace. It's all a bunch of lies designed to hold you back, and do you know who pushes that propaganda? Politicians taking bribes, clergymen abusing children, corporations destroying communities to increase their profit margin. The truth is, life is a zero-sum game! You've got to do what you've got to do to get ahead and damn everyone who stands in your way! You have no obligation to be loyal to anyone other than yourself. Not your country, not your friends, and certainly not your lover. The only real thing that matters in this world is money."

He wasn't wrong. Now that Mathew thought about it, Nina had just been a convenient excuse. If he really cared about her, then he would have consulted with her, given her a chance to talk him out of the offer, but maybe that wasn't what he wanted. Maybe all this time, he'd been looking for a reason to say *yes* to Benchman Financial. He'd had so many opportunities to reject Wilcox's offer and hadn't. Instead, he'd been fighting his conscience, jumping through hoops just to give himself the opportunity to be standing right here, dagger in hand.

He glanced down at Nina again. Did he really love her, or did she just make him feel good about himself when things were easier? Was that why they'd been arguing? Because, for the first time in his relationship, he doubted his worth as a person?

But no.

He couldn't do that. Sure, the money would be nice, but despite his anger, despite his desperation to relieve himself of his debt, there had always been doubt in his mind. Something deep inside him that he couldn't ignore, screaming that this was wrong.

"I can't," he said.

The group stopped their orgy. A dozen sets of yellow eyes stared at him from behind their bifocals. Wilcox pulled the penis from his mouth and stood back up.

"Mathew, am I to understand that you are backing out of our agreement?"

He ran his hand through Nina's hair.

"It isn't worth it. I'd rather live with the debt than hurt her or anyone else for that matter."

All he wanted to do was get Nina untied and get the hell out of there. It would be an awkward car ride home, but at least now the door was open to a conversation about his debt.

"So be it," sighed Wilcox. He turned to the rest of the orgy. "We're going with the backup, people."

The group broke from their embrace and went to work. They clawed at Mathew, tearing the ceremonial headdress off of him, leaving his ass exposed once more. Next, they untied Nina and removed her gag.

"Nina!" said Mathew. "I'm so sorry!"

But he wouldn't get the chance to say anything else because at that moment, the board members swarmed him. Wings fluttered in his face, and nails raked at his skin. He threw some punches and kicks, but the demonic, old bastards overpowered him easily. Even the wheelchair guy got some licks in. When they were done, he was tied up on the pedestal just as Nina had been. Mathew glanced over to see his girlfriend now wearing the headdress and holding the dagger. That horrible echo reverberated again so loud that it shook Mathew's skull.

"Oh, Dark Prince of the Great Beyond!" chanted Wilcox. "On this most sacred of nights, we bring you yet another offering. . ."

Up above, it seemed as if the kaleidoscope of colors was gazing down at him. As it moved in and out of itself, he thought he could make out three distinct goat-like faces amongst the ever-changing gelatinous mass. Mathew stared at Nina. She was horrified, but there was something else behind her eyes that sent his heart racing. It was a look of determination.

"Nina?" he said. "What's going on?!"

"I'm sorry, Mathew! The truth is, my spending has been out of control, and now I'm deep in credit card debt! I didn't think I'd ever get the chance to pay it off. I should have told you!"

"It's okay," said Mathew. "I should have told you about my medical debt."

She raised the dagger over her head.

"Do it now!" shouted Wilcox.

Mathew closed his eyes.

"At least one of us will get out from under these damn creditors," he said.

"Now!" shouted Wilcox again.

The board members began to moan, their sexual exhalations almost musical.

Nina gritted her teeth.

Wilcox's body trembled with anticipation.

"Stab him in the fucking heart!"

"I'm ready," said Mathew.

Nina swung the dagger.

"Fuck!" Wilcox cried. He looked down to see the dagger's blade sticking out of his own stomach. "You stabbed me, you bitch! You just blew your chance!"

She pulled the blade free, and Wilcox dropped to one knee. The board members stopped their gyrations and stared at her.

"The contract states the ritual doesn't work if we punch down," said Nina. "That I can't sacrifice someone more desperate than me. It doesn't say I can't sacrifice someone better off."

Blood began to trickle from Wilcox's mouth.

"I'm the Vice President of Fucking Philanthropy! You can't sacrifice me, you idiot!"

"Actually, Wilcox," said one of the board members. "Technically, she can."

"And we still need a sacrifice," said another, checking the face of his Audemars Piguet. "It looks like you're the only option we have left."

"B-but, why would you let these pissants kill me?! Haven't I done a good job?" He groaned and doubled over in pain.

The board members all glanced at each other and nodded.

"To be honest, Wilcox," said one of them as he pushed his glasses up what was left of his nose. "The board has been feeling like your quarterly projections have been too safe. We've already been thinking about bringing in someone who will take the company in a more aggressive direction."

"Too safe?!"

The group split off, half of them untying Mathew, the other half grabbing Wilcox. When they were finished, the two of them had switched places. Mathew was now standing beside Nina, and Wilcox was strapped tight to the pedestal.

Mathew turned to his girlfriend.

"I'm so sorry about everything," he said.

"Me too," Nina replied. "No matter what, we'll tackle this debt together."

Mathew looked down at Wilcox trying unsuccessfully to wriggle out of his restraints.

"And it looks like we're off to a good start. Here's our chance to cut it in half."

One of the board members cleared his throat.

"Oh, Dark Prince of the Great Beyond! On this most sacred of nights, we bring you yet another offering. . ."

"You can't do this!" shouted Wilcox. "Under my watch, the company's seen record profits!"

The board members laughed, coughed, and wheezed.

"That's what the last guy said," chuckled the geezer in the wheelchair.

That guttural echo sounded once more, vibrating its horrible secrets through everyone's bones.

Nina raised the dagger over her head again.

Wilcox screamed.

Benchman Financial was going to have a good quarter.

IN EVERY DREAM HOME A HEARTACHE

TIM MCGREGOR

The last ghost hunter ran from the house in a hot panic, clutching his electromagnetic reader in a white-knuckled fist. Not a ghost hunter. Ghost detective, he insisted. He wore a fedora and a trench coat of black pleather.

He assured me that he could solve my problem, swaggering into the foyer like some cartoon gunslinger. Clutching the EMF reader, he claimed he hadn't met a ghost he couldn't uproot. He lasted a whole hour before he ran off.

They all run off, of course. But there are always more where they come from. Ghost trackers, paranormal investigators, psychics. I've even had a few exorcists. They come to the notoriously haunted house on Trewsbury Lane, determined to unlock the mystery behind all the thumping and bumping in the night. A few square-jawed heroes have even tried to rescue the princess trapped in the castle.

It doesn't come cheap, mind you. I'm not running a charity here. You didn't think I'd let these people traipse through my house without paying first, did you? Price of admission. And a steep one, at that. It's how I've been surviving the last two years, charging people for the privilege of hunting the ghosts in my home.

The TV shows pay the best. They have real budgets. A camera operator and a sound guy following around the show's host as they stalk through the house, shouting loudly at empty rooms.

"Is anyone with us?" they bark. I don't know why these people act so aggressively when speaking to ghosts. Tough guys out to prove something, I suppose. They're obnoxious, but their cash is as green as everyone else's. "Show us that you're here. Tap a wall or make a noise." They hold their breath and listen for a sound. A door will slam on a different floor, or a window sash will thump. The crew trades glances before racing off to investigate.

They all leave frustrated or defeated. If they've upset the ghost, sometimes they leave terrified. One ended up in hospital, suffering a heart attack at the age of thirty-five. I had zero sympathy for that one. He had strutted in with his dick-swinging bravado, challenging the spirit to face him. I guess the ghost took him up on his offer. I tried not to smirk when the ambulance took him away, but then I realized he hadn't paid yet. I made sure everyone paid upfront after that.

The house is always angry after these visits, clanging its pipes or creaking the timbers. Cupboards refuse to open no matter how hard I pull. The bathroom faucet runs red with rust. Sometimes swarms of flies appear out of nowhere to buzz angrily against a window. The house doesn't like these intruders with their noisy spirit boxes, but I can't afford to turn them away. It's an ironic cycle—the haunted reputation brings in the ghost hunters and each visit only makes the house angrier, amplifying its paranormal reputation. But this strange cycle is the only thing paying the electrical bill. We're both stuck with it now, so when another ghost-chaser shows up asking to investigate, I let him in.

"Cash upfront," I say, ushering the latest visitor into the foyer.

The wind blows dead leaves across the threshold before I close the door again.

He reaches into a pocket. "Yes, of course. Five hundred a night, right?"

"That's the going rate." I thumb the bills in the envelope before stuffing it into my back pocket.

He's young. Mid to late twenties, maybe. I don't know. The older I get, the more young people look like children to me. He's slight, too. Underfed, like any college student.

"Where's all your gear?"

They usually come with armloads of equipment and odd-looking devices. The TV crews have lighting rigs and boom mics and endless loops of cables. This young man is empty-handed.

"Got everything I need," he says, dropping the small backpack from his shoulder. He reaches out a hand in greeting. "I'm Kurt. Nice to meet you."

"Molly."

"I know. I've done my homework."

They all say that. There's an embarrassment of articles and websites about this house and its ghosts. Most of it is nonsense, but some get the details right. I stopped reading them a long time ago. Some claim that the house is a portal to the other side or another dimension. An elevator shaft to Hell or a doorway to the realms of Cthulhu. Some of the websites refer to me as the *Red Woman*. It's the hair. How original.

I show him to the parlor. "Where do you want to start?"

"Here on the first floor. Then I'll make my way upstairs if that's okay."

The attic is where he wants to go. That is where the most activity occurs, according to the various articles. But he's being polite. He'll sweep the house and make his way up there for the big finale. They're all so predictable, these ghost hunters.

"Knock yourself out."

He peeks out into the hallway. "Is the kitchen back here?"

"This way."

Down the hall to the back of the house. It's gloomy back here. It's an old house, so the kitchen is tucked at the back like something shameful. Some of the lights don't work anymore, which is fine because it hides how decrepit the house has become. I used to be embarrassed by the state of it. Now, I just don't care. It looks how one expects a haunted house to look, I suppose.

I fill the kettle at the sink. "I was about to make a cup of tea. Would you like one?"

I don't normally offer tea. I usually retreat to the old sewing room across the hall while these people clomp around with their noisy toys. I can't stand loud or brash people, but Kurt is neither. He's soft-spoken and polite.

"No, thank you." He unzips his backpack. I expect to see more of these silly devices with the flashing lights and dials clatter out onto the kitchen table. What I don't expect to see is a simple coil of heavy gauge copper wire. He unfurls a length of it, maybe three feet, before trimming it with wire cutters.

"Are you making a magnet?"

"Sort of," he says, bending the wire into a V-shape with the clipped ends turned down. "It's a dowsing rod."

I've never heard of it. I guess it shows.

"My grandmother was a water witch," Kurt explains. "Someone needed a new well dug, she'd get her dowsing rod and find the best place to dig. But she also used to dowse for spirits. She taught me."

This I have to see. "Show me."

Holding the curled ends in each hand, he moves the pointed end of the copper over the room. It holds steady until it crosses the center of the scuffed floor. Then it dips.

"Here," he says. "Something happened right here. Something traumatic."

The linoleum tiles are dull with age, the floral pattern faded. If there was ever blood on the floor, it dried up and flaked away long ago. There isn't a stain or anything. Other people have paused over this patch of kitchen floor, psychics and physical mediums. I've watched them flatten a palm to the floor only to snatch it away again as if stung.

"Do you know what happened here?"

I shrug. "No."

The look on his face says he doesn't believe me. "You must know something."

"I've heard lots of different stories about what happened. But that's the problem, isn't it? They're just stories."

He still doesn't look convinced. "This was your grandmother's house, yes?"

He really has done his homework. I inherited it, a broken-down house with bad memories. Asbestos in the pipe linings and decrepit knob-and-tube wiring hidden in the walls. A nightmare to insure, but a house nonetheless. In a city where the real estate market has skyrocketed, pushing home ownership out of the reach of all but the very wealthy. What happens to a city if young people can't afford to live there? It rots.

"Why don't you just leave?" he asks. Like I've never thought of this.

"Why should I leave? I never asked the ghost to take up residence here."

He grins. He looks nicer when he smiles. His eyes are brown, lighting up with flashes of sympathy. No, not sympathy. Empathy. I hope it's empathy.

He's on the move, crossing into the dining room with his copper dowsing rod. I follow him.

"There's a lot of conflicting stories about what happened in this house," he says. "I guess you've heard them all."

I'm sick of them all. I watch him work his way into the next room. He looks a bit silly with his wire contraption held out before him. "Which one do you believe?"

"Not sure I believe any of them, to tell you the truth." He stops briefly in the hallway, then he's on the move again. Up the stairwell. "But I have a few favorites."

"Such as?"

The steps are so creaky he has to speak up. "The one where the father murders his whole family with an axe on Christmas Eve."

"Right. After taking the family to church for midnight mass?"

"Yes. They come home, have an early breakfast. Then he butchers them all. It has a real true-crime appeal."

On the second floor, he waves the rod past the bedrooms. Some of these doors haven't been opened in years.

"But you don't believe it?"

"It sounds too much like a ghost story. How, every Christmas Eve, you can hear the screams of the children and all that."

"I suppose," I tell him. "It adds pathos, don't you think? Screaming children at midnight. Tell me some others."

The copper rod sways a little. He stops to study it, but the rod becomes still again. "I've heard one about how, during the Depression, this was a rooming house run by a widow and her daughter. One of the guests molests the girl, but when she tells her mother, her mother doesn't believe her. So the girl bakes arsenic into a gooseberry pie and kills everyone in the house. Including her own mom."

I trail his steps, watching him work the rod. He's slender and his clothes seem to hang off of him. I don't know if he just needs a good meal or if this is the fashion these days.

"I'm a sucker for a good revenge story," I say. "There are gooseberry bushes all around the yard."

"I've never had gooseberry pie."

"It's not for everyone," I say. "Bit tart."

He goes through every room. My bedroom is the only one not coated in dust. Not once does his wire contraption dip or nod.

"Shall we try the cellar?"

"Don't you want to see the attic?"

A pull cord dangles from the ceiling. One tug and the retractable steps unfold from the trap door. *Everyone* wants to see the attic.

"No," he says. "I want to see the basement."

"Are you sure? There's nothing down there, really."

"Indulge me?"

A wave of my hand. "Very well."

Back on the first floor, he looks at me. "Do you know the one about the hippies?"

"Remind me." The basement door is tucked under the stairwell. I open it. The light flickers, then steadies. Uneven, raw steps trail off into the darkness. "It's like a Manson family thing, isn't it?"

He follows me down. "Sort of. A bunch of hippies squatting here in the seventies in a free love commune or whatever. One of them trips on some bad acid and thinks he's surrounded by demons. So, he unloads a shotgun into all his brothers and sisters."

"Groovy," I say. He laughs.

The cellar is, without a doubt, creepy. The brick walls are damp with moisture, the ceiling is exposed joists, wreathed in cobwebs. The floor is packed earth, like a root cellar. Broken furniture stacked up in one corner, cardboard boxes wilting with black mold.

Raising the copper wire, Kurt pivots slowly as he rolls the dowsing rod over the four points of the compass. No dip or tug from the copper. It remains steady as stone.

I take a seat on the step to watch this young man dowse for ghosts. "So, which story do you believe?"

"None of them," he replies, eyes on the copper end.

"None?"

"Stories are funny things," he says. "They swirl around certain places, get retold, mutate. They get drawn to places like this house. Haunted houses are like magnets for other stories."

I scrutinize my visitor. "So, if none of those stories are true, what do you think happened here?"

"Not sure," he says with a shrug. "Maybe nothing. Maybe it's not even haunted."

That's a new one. I inch closer, curious about who this person is. What was it he just said about magnets? He's like a magnet. He's not bad looking. Just skinny. Nothing a few home-cooked meals can't fix.

"If the house isn't haunted, what does that make me? Crazy?"

His smile is half-hearted. "I don't think you're crazy." The dowsing rod lowers, the ghost-hunting session coming to an end. "Lonely, maybe. But not crazy."

The house above us ticks and creaks the way old houses do. It fills the suddenly unpleasant silence.

"I've done my homework," he says. "You can really dig into the history of the house if you track down all the tax records and deed changes. Insurance claims and whatnot." He takes a breath and then spills it out. "There's no record of any untimely death here. No axe murders or poisoning. No hippie covens."

I watch the dowsing rod droop to the floor.

"I think you're stuck in a tough situation," he says. "You're saddled with this old house, so you squeezed some lemonade from it. Or rather, the folktales surrounding this house." He shrugs like he gets it. Like he understands me better than I understand myself. "People want to come hunt ghosts and poke around, why not charge them for it? I'd do the same thing."

I scratch at the polish on one fingernail. A bad home job. Who can afford manicures these days? "So, I'm a fraud?"

"No, not at all," he says. He's being empathetic again. "You did what anyone would do in a bad situation. You improvised."

This makes me angry. "Then why come here if it's not haunted?"

"Same as everyone else, I suppose. I was curious."

The copper wire in his hand dips upwards, like a dog finding a scent.

"Your dowsing rod," I say. "It's moving."

The wire rises, the sharp end pulling to the far corner. The surprise on his face is genuine.

"What the hell?"

Classic dialogue from every horror movie I've ever seen. Usually uttered moments before something terrible happens.

"You're doing that," I say. "You're making it point."

"I'm not. I swear."

His eyes widen as the dowsing rod tugs him forward. The copper draws aim at a riot of chairs and crates lined up against the north wall. He lets the rod pull him along.

"It's really strong. Jesus. What's back here?"

"Just junk."

The rod jerks harder, making him stumble. The business end zeroes in on an old sea chest fuzzy with dust. It's old and moldy and big. Big enough.

"What's in this?"

"I wouldn't open that if I were you."

Like that would dissuade him. He sets the wire down and flips the corroded latches. Pulls the lip open.

Hidden inside is exactly what you'd expect to find. It's folded up in the fetal position, knees tucked into the chest. Just bones now, fuzzy with dust. There is a surprising amount of hair clinging to the desiccated scalp. All of it a gingery red.

His face is almost comical as his eyes dart from the crate to me and then back to the thing inside the box.

All I can do is shrug. The jig is up.

To his credit, he doesn't run screaming from the house like all the others. It takes a moment to process, then he grins like someone who appreciates a clever magic trick.

He looks back at the parched remains curled up in the cedar chest. "I don't get it. If you're the ghost, why let all the ghost hunters in?"

"Because they pay. And the bills don't stop just because you're dead."

"That doesn't make sense."

"It's my house," I tell him. "And I want to keep it that way. I don't want to sell; I don't want to be uprooted. Where would I go? Out there, wandering around like all the other homeless? Screw that."

The furrow in his brow eases. I believe he's coming around.

"You see my problem? I still have to pay. Death doesn't protect you. Not anymore. The electricity, the water, property tax. It still has to be paid."

The copper wire falls and bounces on the floor, but Kurt doesn't seem to notice.

"And the insurance. God, don't even get me started on the insurance."

"That's insane," he says.

"I agree."

He looks at the floor and shakes his head. "I can't think of anything worse than being dead but still having bills to pay."

"That's late-stage capitalism for you," I say. "The afterlife is not immune to market forces. Even the dead are exploited for growth."

Kurt turns to the chest and gently closes the lid. He fastens the latches.

"You know, most ghost hunters run screaming when they

uncover the truth," I tell him. "But not you. I think I like you, Kurt."

"Thanks," he says sheepishly. "How about that cup of tea?"

My new friend is full of surprises. We turn to head up, but I point at the dowsing rod on the dirt floor.

"Don't forget the rod. Price of copper these days, you know."

We go back up to the kitchen. The kettle is cold, so I turn it on again. I open the cupboard, but there isn't much here. A mouse hiding behind a leaking carton of salt. Nothing else.

"I'm sorry, I don't have any cookies or anything to go with the tea."

"That's all right," he says.

Kurt sits at the kitchen table, looking through the mail stacked there.

"All bills?" he asks.

"That's all I get these days. I miss getting real mail. A personal letter or a card. But most of my friends are gone. No pen pals left."

I set the cups down. Steam rises between us.

"My aunt still sends me a card on my birthday," Kurt says. "She's never missed a year. It's nice."

That strikes me as divine. "Does she still put money in the card?"

"Five dollars."

We both laugh at that.

We chitchat for a bit, about the house, the neighborhood. He's astonished to learn that I've somehow dodged being part of the local HOA nonsense. The conversation dwindles down, and then he stands, says he has to go. I hide my disappointment. I've enjoyed his visit.

At the door, he stops.

"I'd like to know what happened," he says. "How you ended up in that chest down there."

"Oh, that's a whole other story," I say. "A long one, I'm afraid."

He looks out at the street. It's quiet. Not a lot of traffic here on Trewsbury Lane.

"I could come back for another visit. Say, same time next week?"

"I think I'd like that very much, Kurt."

He smiles and goes down the pathway. At the gate, he waves and marches into the night.

I lock the door. I suppose I'll have to buy some cookies for next time. Maybe a cake? More expenses. Oh well.

BOX FULL OF STRANGE
EVELYN FREELING

You haven't changed a bit since I died.

You're still so eager and dumb with greed, that when I show up on your doorstep in an unmarked box—cardboard freshly pressed, taped deliciously shut—you bring me inside. Apparently, your dad was so busy warning you about crazy women like me who'll say anything to get a little attention, that he forgot to tell you to beware of strange boxes.

Seconds pass and already the tape is shredding apart, the tip of a knife slides centimeters from my cold body, and there's the same yellow lamplight, sun dampened by thin green tapestries, pot smoke swirling perpetually in their glow.

Your eyes are still inflamed that crimson color which now reminds me of my blood mixing with bath water. You haven't gotten your hair trimmed in the month since you broke up with me because you "don't have the capacity to help someone with such extreme needs." But "no hard feelings, right?"

Are the circles under your eyes darker? Have you laid awake at night wondering if, maybe, I was telling the truth? I can't tell because as soon as you set eyes on my taut rubber d-cups and permanent blowjob lips, your eyes crinkle with a smile and you whip out your phone.

"Dad, you're a pervert, you know that? I thought you were kidding about the sex doll. What am I supposed to do with this? Don't answer that. Call me back, okay?"

You can't look away. The stupid, lopsided grin plastered on your face is the closest a grown man's mouth can get to a boy getting his first bike on Christmas morning. No thoughts of the dangers lurking behind such a shiny present—wheeling into traffic, crashing into a tree, bone breaking flesh, the blood. Oh! The blood! There is only pure, uninhibited glee.

You reach for me, but hesitate, fingers straining midair. Are you really going to do this, you seem to ask yourself. Of course you are. Don't be stupid. You're your father's son, from your stupid sand-colored hair to the corrupt bones giving your body form.

You set me on your leather couch, sticky with beer and resin, and pose me as you see fit, laughing. Wrists crossed in my lap, legs spread eagle. You bend and examine my plastic vulva, then slowly, with a nervous crook to your mouth, stick a finger inside.

Again, you laugh. "This is awkward," you say as you remove your finger and tussle the ends of my strawberry blonde hair. "I'm supposed to be celibate for the next year. I promised myself no more girls, see? I got a problem with picking them. My ex. . ."

You run a hand over your face, tilt your head.

"You kind of look like her, you know?"

Sitting on the chair across from me, as though the distance will help you resist, you chief from a blown glass bong. But your eyes never leave my exposed tits and after you finish coughing and choking on a lungful of sativa, your dick is in your hand, already hard.

Breath bated, you approach with tentative steps. What will this say about you, I imagine you asking yourself, that you would fuck the sex doll your dad bought you? Except he didn't. If he could tell you, you'd know that.

You grab me by the back of my head and push yourself into my mouth as far as you can. You pump and pump your unwashed dick, drawing shallow gasps with every thrust. They accelerate. Faster, faster still. I feel you at the precipice, ready to spill, but instead you scream. "What the fuck?"

Copper fills my mouth, dribbles down my perfect lips, into the peaks of my unrising cleavage, and still you scream. What would your father say, if he were me? *Calm down, it's not a big deal, it's just a cut. My teeth slipped; it wasn't my fault.*

Teeth, you might wonder, when did they start putting teeth in sex dolls? Doesn't that defeat the purpose? Aren't sex dolls supposed to be idealized women, made perfect for fucking? Where do teeth calculate into that?

Your hand shakes as you wrap your limp dick in paper towels. The phone trembles against your jaw. "Dad, something is wrong with the sex doll you got me. The manufacturer must've put glass in it on accident. Or something. Call me back."

Or something.

Someone knocks at your door the next morning. You grumble and pause the PlayStation game you've been glued to all night. When you return, a pair of cops follow behind. We're in Seattle, so your pot stash is legal, but even if it wasn't, your daddy knows the DA. One of them spots me, nudges her partner. They exchange a look, then tell you that you should probably sit.

You chuckle. "Shouldn't I be the one offering you a seat?"

Their silence crumples you to your chair. They tell you what I already know: Daddy is dead. Murdered. Castrated and cannibalized. Of course, they leave that part out. You blink at them like maybe you think they're joking, and only when they tell you they're sorry do you react.

"There's been a mistake. My dad can't be dead. He's got security guards, video cameras."

"Someone's looking into the security footage, but there were no eyes on his bedroom. It looks like it may have been a girlfriend. Was he seeing anyone?"

"I dunno. He liked to play the field, you know?"

"Is there anyone you know of who would want to hurt him?"

You rise and pace, rubbing your hand over your face. "My ex maybe. But she killed herself a month ago."

The officers exchange another look. "I'm so sorry," one says.

You flap your hands. We intended to spend eternity together, but a month has passed and your grief for me is reduced to a flap of your hands.

When they leave, you don't fall to your knees. You grab your PlayStation controller and hurl it at the television. You rip your floor lamp and shatter it against the wall. Overturn your coffee table. Glass rains, fists punch through plaster, mirrors crack and splinter on your knuckles. Everything is uprooted, thrown, broken, until the apartment Daddy paid for is destroyed, and there's nothing left for you to hurt.

Then, you spy me, sitting here.

I prepare myself for the onslaught as you march towards me. Whatever you do, it won't be worse than what your dad did. Oh, you know. You can tell yourself I lied all you want, that I was another crazy girl, a slip in judgment, but deep down, you know.

You surprise me, though. You wrap your arms around me, smother your face in my chest, and sob. Your tears trail down my naked body and pool in the crevice where my thighs kiss. You sniff, wipe your nose, and excuse yourself for a shower. When you emerge dripping wet with a towel wrapped around your waist, you don't notice that I've moved, that I'm now sitting in your chair. You collapse on the couch and stare at the ceiling.

"It feels like I should do something, but I dunno what. Nobody prepares you for this, you know? It seems like maybe they should, I think. Like, do I call my dad's lawyer? Does he already know? Do I wait for him. . ."

Finally, your voice trails off as you find the seat next to you, empty, then your chair now occupied. If I could grin, I would, but the doe-eyed, *o*-mouthed expression is the only one I have. It matches the look on your face perfectly.

After a full minute, you shake your head, load a bowl, inhale another lungful. You lumber from the couch and begin picking the pieces of your grief from the floor. Somewhere your phone rings. You take it onto your balcony. When you come inside again, you stop.

Music is playing on your record player. It takes a beat, but then your eyes go wide as you realize that it's our song. The one we shared our first kiss to and agreed had to be our first dance at our wedding after you proposed to me. You nearly fall as you race to the record player and push the needle off. Watch the album spin silently.

Slowly, trembling, you turn.

Your breath hitches at the sight of me on the couch. There's a glorious second which stretches taut into eternity, where everything registers and your terror is so thick I can almost taste it in the air, as metallic as your blood. You don't move, you don't dare.

That's the thing about fear: When you're standing before a drawn shower curtain or your boss's office door, the dread of pulling it open, of the possibility that something terrible lies in wait, is usually the apex. The shower curtain is pulled away. The bathtub is empty. You breathe a sigh of relief, shake your head, chuckle at how stupid you are.

Sometimes, though, everything you were terrified would transpire, does.

(Your boss and soon to be father-in-law is drunk. He pounces. Nobody believes you. Or they do, but they won't admit it. He fires you. His son ends your engagement. In a span of a few days, he ruins your life because you had the audacity to say something.)

You toss me back into my box and throw me outside. The heavy thud of the deadbolt turning punctures the sound of distant traffic, a chain lock grates into place. One by one, you secure your door. It's almost cute that you think they'll make a difference now.

A door clicking open awakens you.

"Hello?" you call from your bedroom.

The door whines, torturously.

"Hello?" you call again.

Your apartment isn't dark. You went to bed with all the lights on, as if they might somehow protect you. Your bed creaks, your feet patter, but you stop in the doorframe of your bedroom, spotting me across the open concept kitchen on your couch, the box resting tidily beneath my feet. You edge towards the kitchen and grab a knife, then creep back and slam your door. Something grinds over the floor, muffled but audible enough.

I imagine you stacking furniture in front of your door, then sitting in bed, blade clutched to your chest, eyes peeled open through the night, afraid to let them close.

I was right. In the morning, as you pack me into the box again, I can tell you haven't slept. Your eyes are red as ever, the circles beneath them ash gray. We drive in your Dodge Charger, which should have been my first red flag, let's be honest. Every minute you check your rearview mirror at me sitting in the back seat, making sure I haven't moved.

We stop at the precinct. You march me up the steps past the same officers who refused to take my report and promised me if they did, the DA would bury it. An officer leads you into a room with a one-way window. You sit me in a chair next to you, don't notice his double take at me, then plant your palms flat on the table in front of us.

"I think I know who killed my dad," you say.

The officer sits, leans on his elbows, all ears.

You nod towards me.

His brow knits. "I'm sorry, is this a joke to you?"

"This thing showed up yesterday. I thought she was from my dad. I told him I was going to stop dating, go celibate for a while. I have an issue with attracting crazy chicks, see? So he joked, said he would give me a sex doll. I didn't put it together until last night. If my dad was killed, he couldn't have gotten her for me. There was no postage on the package. Okay, so that's weird, right?"

"Uh-huh."

"And then—" Your voice gets louder, but you stop and force yourself to lower it again. That's good, I imagine you telling yourself, appear calm. If you stay calm, maybe someone will believe you. "Weird stuff started happening. She started moving around all by herself, playing music, opening doors."

"Playing music," the officer echoes.

"It was our song, my ex and mine's. She's the only one I can think of who would want my dad dead and I think—" You draw a breath and blow it out. "I think she's somehow possessed the sex doll, killed my dad, and now she's going to kill me."

The officer is quiet. He doesn't laugh like you did at me,

doesn't call you crazy. He sips his coffee, takes a minute to force the slight curl of his lips away, and clears his throat. "Look, losing a parent can be tough. I've got the number of a great grief counselor. Let me hook you up with her, okay?"

"You don't believe me?"

"I mean, come on, man. A possessed sex doll?" The officer smiles, but he still doesn't laugh. "Trust me, grief can really mess with your head."

You charge out and throw me in the dumpster behind the precinct before you drive away. I traversed the planes of the living and the dead to find you again, but okay.

Exhaustion and grief take their toll. Your lights are all on, but you are fast asleep, snoring. You don't stir as your wrists and ankles are bound. Not until your cock is in my mouth again. You moan then. That stupid lopsided grin curls your lips.

"Mmmm, Dinae."

So it's still me you dream of. If I was merely a sex doll, plastic hollowed out for your pleasure, maybe that'd satisfy me, but I'm not. Revenge fills this vessel.

You scream as I bite down and your cock is torn cleanly away. The blood puddles quickly, seeping into your top sheets. When you crane your head and peer down the valley of your body, you find me, blowjob lips dripping, eyes wide, as if to ask, "Who me?"

You toss your head back and thrash against your restraints, screaming in pain or maybe in outrage. No apologies or begging, no regret or remorse. Even as you lay dying, you're still incapable of change.

Already you're paling from the blood loss, but you yelp as your femoral artery is slashed open. When you look again, here I am, face the picture of innocence. Except, of course, for your blood and cock in my mouth and the kitchen knife you slept with in my hand.

You thrash against your restraints. "I knew it," you yell.

And you did. But nobody listened.

Isn't that a bitch?

LAS ENVIES
JOHN PALISANO

Angelique frolicked across the green hills, marveling at the expansive patches of woods below so reminiscent of slumbering giants. Far beyond the curving horizon, the snow-covered, sharply angled Midi-Pyrénées mountains loomed like the walls of a supernatural fortress.

Just below her, nestled within a large clearing, she spotted her home, Las Envies. The half-timbered home acted as a beacon, drawing travelers distant and near. Soon it'd be time to dine, and she never missed a meal with those who gathered. If she ventured too far from eyesight, Gabriel would tell on her and report her offense to Aleister.

Peering up at the crow, Angelique marveled at how he looked like he hovered in place as he flapped against the wind. "I wish I were free like you," she said. How many of her thirteen years had she been living under the spell at Las Envies? She wasn't quite sure.

His obsidian gaze met hers; his beak opened for a second as though he might caw but shut just as fast. *What foul things it ate*, she thought. "No wonder you're quiet. You're just as trapped as me, aren't you?"

Instead of answering, Gabriel peeled off and flew toward the house. She ran after, laughing for a few moments.

A shriek from the woods. Far enough away but close enough to freeze her in her tracks. Angelique couldn't help but look. Branches and leaves rustled, high and low.

One of the Lost had caught someone.

She told herself not to look and absolutely not to stick around. In the woods she'd stumbled upon an old guillotine, its wood still stained dark. She didn't dare ask if it was still in use. It'd only been a generation since France's revolution and its reign of terror had ended, and it stood as a grim reminder of the brutality.

The house wasn't far away. She saw Aleister on the landing, his arm outstretched, his sleeve waiting for Gabriel to land.

As Angelique hurried, the crow landed. She came upon them both just as Frederique raised a metal cup with his opposite hand. A small dribble of blood had run over and across his fingers. Could it be her blood?

She looked down at her arm and spied the newest hole, punctured by Mister Buies, the physician, just before she ran into the fields to play.

Gabriel drank. He must have sensed her watching because he stopped for a moment, looked up, and regarded her. Maybe he made the connection that what he drank was of her. After all, didn't animals have much greater senses of smell?

Angelique buried the thought, and Gabriel dipped his beak down once more into the metal cup.

"How was your play time?" Aleister asked.

"Wonderful," she said. "But I'm immensely tired now." She didn't tell him about the sounds in the woods.

"You can go to bed right after dinner service," he said. "I'll grant you that, little one."

She bowed her head and said, "Yes, sir," catching the shiny, green glint in his eye. His skin reminded her of the fancy dogs she once saw in La Merce long ago, before she arrived: light, copper colored, tight in most places, but with hard wrinkles in bunches around the neck and elbows. It was a trait most of the Lost Ones shared. Some were grayer, like elephants, while others might be quite dark. None of their shades were quite the same as she'd seen with people.

"Quite good of you," he said. "We all appreciate what you give us."

"Yes. Thank you. You're quite welcome." She said the words but wanted to scream and flee. Was he talking about the blood they siphoned from her?

She bowed her head and made her way past. Her heart raced being near him. It doubled its speed as she passed. Angelique turned her back to him. If he wished, he could lash out in an instant and end her. She'd witnessed it several times before when one of the purveyors they kept lost favor.

Put it out of your mind.

It took considerable strength to hold back and not run inside as fast as she could. Angelique knew that even if she did, Las Envies was not a sanctuary. The Lost Ones were inside, and it would only be a fleeting moment until they'd be upon her.

As long as my blood is young, they will want me. And I'll be young for quite a while yet.

Inside, Angelique came upon three sitting at the main dining table, their long limbs draped about the high-backed chairs. A pair laughed so loud it hurt her ears. They looked more like animals that belonged beside a river rather than people. She was sure each wore a wig as their hair looked much younger than it should have, considering their faces.

In the provincial home, the Lost Ones stayed as guests of Chef Aleister. Some learned to prep. But mostly, they were there because they wished for an existence free of cruelty.

"Angelique," cried Raphael from beyond the table and behind the large kitchen table. "Come quickly. We've much work to do." He was second to Aleister.

She sauntered toward him. As she passed the dining room table, the Lost Ones watched her, ready to strike, she was sure. Their instinct restrained only enough to secure their place in the house and enough not to claim one of Frederique's providers without being offered. She caught the same greenish glint in one's eye—was his name Grayson?—which reminded her of a lizard. Even so? They kept talking. Their speech was so fast, the pitch so strange, she couldn't make out much. Grayson spoke to Claude, who she felt had the cruelest tongue of all.

Once she made it to the kitchen, she noticed the large cookbook resting on its wooden stand, opened to a page, with Raphael staring it down. On its cover, emblazoned in gold lettering, she read Las Envies. The cravings. A priceless treasure of handwritten recipes gathered over two centuries, she'd been told, all prepared and safe to eat for their kind.

Angelique eyed the dastardly beings at the table, alternately gaunt or obese.

The Lost Ones desired a more upscale experience, like the kind they'd grown accustomed to before they'd been turned and before Napoleon's never-ending war. "They're like people who don't want to see how animals suffer before reaching their plates," Raphael once told her.

"What are we making today?" Angelique asked.

Raphael's expression brightened. "Sanguine posset," he said in his highest tone of speech. "Blood posset. Made from a once forbidden fruit."

She knew what that was for. It was the same main ingredient they always used. Blood. Or as Raphael referred to it—the fruit. "First, we shall infuse the sheep's cream with it. I've already set the cream to boil slowly. We'll add sugar and zest until it's reduced. The lush, buttery flavor will be firm and hold its shape on a spoon. It has a bright, citrus-like flavor but satisfies the base of what a vampire needs."

Angelique was fascinated by the preparation and the joy Raphael showed. She liked his dark hair and brows, as the features were reminiscent of her long-forgotten father. "I'm surprised as I thought the Lost Ones weren't able to consume anything other than fresh blood."

"You'll find that's not quite true as our makings didn't so much change everything, but rather, intensified our palettes and senses," Raphael explained. "Boiling will denature the cream and the blood. It will increase the acidic taste, bringing a nuanced, complex flavor. Our preparations make it possetable."

"Delightful," she said, waiting for instructions.

"We're using the new Mesures usuelles system, so we will have to translate the measurements as we go," he said. "Let us read the recipe in full."

BLOOD POSSET WITH CANDIED BITTERS

The dish requires several serving cups. Reducing the cream mixture to precisely 2 quarts will create the desired consistency. Transfer to a boil-proof measuring cup during cooking to ensure the correct amount.

Citric Acid Solution
20 grams citric acid
30 grams water

Posset
1 spoon of grated, dried artery zest
6 spoons of sanguine blood
2 quarts of heavy cream

⅔ quart (2 seizièmes) sugar

Candied Bitters
½ quart of toasted bitters (these are clots)
2 spoons sugar
2 spoons water
¼ spoon salt

"Where do we begin?" she asked, intrigued. She'd been asked to help in the kitchen and was delighted. A welcome break from routine. There were no other children at Las Envies she could play with, so the cooking was her best and only outlet.

"We've got the base already going, so now we must prepare the other ingredients," he said. "First? Please find and set out several of the small wooden bowls. You're familiar."

"I am." She turned and set about going to the cabinets and procuring them.

"This is the heart of what we do," he explained while she put them on the countertop. "Providing these meals is an extraordinary gift for the Lost Ones. It's why they come and stay. A respite from traveling alone and the constant worry of where the next meal will come. Also? We assuage their fear of being found and brought to the guillotine."

He slid a bowl across and under him. There were containers already on the counter. Taking a lid off one, she saw the glistening red inside.

"The candied bitters," he said. "Made of clots. Rolled in sugar." Using a spoon, he took out a dozen and put them in a bowl. "Those go on last, but we want them to breathe."

"Breathe?"

"Not like you and I, but a similar concept. Breathing allows the true flavor to bloom," he said.

"Wonderful," Angelique replied. She wanted to tell him she

wished it wasn't all made of blood. . . her blood and the blood of the others. . . and that it was just normal food. Of course, she had to keep it to herself. If they had any idea she wasn't completely loyal, they'd end her.

Claude called from the dining table. "My friends, that smells divine." She looked up to see him licking his lips with his pointed tongue; this one reminded her more of a slinky, hairless cat. Chills sprouted throughout her. He'd just as soon eat her, she sensed. Maybe preferable to the posset.

"Y-yes," she stammered. "It should be ready soon."

"I'm famished," Claude said, his voice clear and angry.

"Oh, won't you stop it," Ananda interrupted. "Have some more essence while you wait. Don't be so unrefined. Remember, you are at Las Envies and not on some dank street corner in Paris stalking some late-night drunk."

Ananda slid Claude a goblet filled with essence. More blood, Angelique knew. They always had room for more to drink, even when they claimed to be full. And Paris? That's why he looked like a hairless cat, she was sure. The Lost Ones all looked of their territories. She was reminded of Oscar the Russian. He was large and brutish and ate and ate. She was relieved when he finally chose to move on from their house and go off into the mist one cold morning. His hands were rough with her, almost as rough as his words.

"Pay attention, young lady," Raphael admonished. "The cream will burn."

Rushing to the pan, she lifted it off the burner and put it on the warming plate in the middle. "I'm sorry," she said.

For the next several minutes, she did exactly as she was told, following each instruction until it was time to plate the recipe. Las Envies smelled of sugar and crème. Despite knowing its ingredients, Angelique couldn't help but yearn for a taste, although she'd never partake.

She put her mind off it and gathered the small serving bowls.

"We will fill nearly to the top of each and let them cool for a moment," Raphael said. "Then we will garnish them with the bitters to compliment the sweetness."

"I never had enough sweetness," Aleister said, his voice booming behind her. "This is irresistible." He pointed at the bowls. "Well done, you two."

Angelique forced a grin. Aleister leaned down. "You will have a use well past your prime, don't worry."

As much as she tried, she couldn't stop her eyes from going wide from fear.

He backed away and said, "Don't be afraid."

———————————

Angelique watched them eat, some with the posset dripping off their faces and hands. How could they make such a mess with such a small amount of food? Others are delicately savoring each spoon. They didn't need, nor could tolerate, the same portions as people. A small amount equal to a side dish would do. It made sense to her when she thought it through. How much blood could they drink and subsist on when taking the essence in person? They likely didn't get more than a mouthful before the heart stopped beating and the blood would grow cold.

Once he finished, Claude lifted his bowl and ate out of it directly. He peered over its rim, unblinking, and watched Angelique.

He's going to try something, she realized. Something to hurt her. The predator had marked her.

She looked away but felt his stare remain. Putting a few things in order, she tried to ignore his intimidation.

"Angelique?" he said in his most seductive voice. "Can you please take this from me?"

She took in a deep breath, not wanting to. Looking to Raphael for reassurance, she found none. He just looked away and went back to tending to the cleanup.

Stepping out of the kitchen, Angelique felt vulnerable without the counter between her and Claude. Tracking every step, he locked in on her.

Was anyone looking out for her? Was no one worried or seeing what he was doing? Not even Aleister seemed to pay attention. Ananda had left for her room.

She reached for the plate. Claude held it out.

As she fetched it, he grabbed her wrist. Pulled her close. Lowered his voice. "I will taste you," he said. "Maybe not tonight. Or tomorrow. But one day I shall."

His lips flickered into a smile, and he let her go.

A chair screeched as Aleister stood. "How dare you intimidate and threaten her." His was a voice of gods' and shook the entire room. "This is unacceptable."

In a blink, Aleister was upon Claude, his long fingers around his throat, his thin, dark nails digging into the flesh. His face? A snarling, rabid dog who'd caught a rabbit.

Claude cowered. "No. No. Please. Forgive my transgression. I... I... forgot where I was. The beast still comes out unexpectedly." He looked at Angelique. "Please, little one. I would never harm you."

At that moment, he seemed entirely convincing, but Angelique knew better than to trust Claude. She backed away, his bowl in her hands. She felt something warm run off her thumb and through her fingers. Had he missed some? When she looked, she saw a dribble of blood coming from a small cut to the fat of her thumb. She pushed it out, aghast. How had she cut herself? Her mind raced. He must have done it in the split second when she took his bowl, using one of his nails. So sharp she hadn't felt it.

Breaking Aleister's grip, Claude charged her and was on his knees. His mouth clamped around her thumb and sucked.

She cried out. It hurt.

His metallic green cat-like eyes sparkled.

The offense lasted only a moment before Claude was ripped away and lifted high in the air. The others gasped.

"You will sleep outside with the cattle tonight, and you will be gone tomorrow," Aleister said. "How dare you break our sanctity after we've given you so much."

Claude said nothing, but his grin stretched across his face.

Angelique hurried to the sink and put the bowl in. She didn't want to soil any of the kitchen towels with her blood, so she put her hand into the pocket at the front of her dress.

She looked to Raphael, who had the recipe book under his arm and was nearing the door to the rooms. "I'm sorry, Angelique," he said. She glimpsed his eyes in the shadow, shining like the others, before he disappeared with the precious book with its 180 years of recipes and secrets. It was more important than anyone or anything, she realized.

A loud boom nearly floored Angelique. Aleister used Claude's body to bang open the front door. She watched him throw the offender out into the dark night. "You are no longer welcome here." He shut the door.

Once he made it to Angelique, Aleister put a hand on her shoulder. "I'm so sorry you had to endure that. That hasn't happened in a long time." He winked. "You must be very special for him to want to drink from you. There's a strength to you."

"I don't feel strong at all," she said.

"But you are. Much more than you realize."

As she tried to fall asleep, Angelique squeezed her bitten thumb with her good hand. It stung still. So rattled from the confrontation, she hadn't even eaten her potato soup. Her stomach rumbled.

Will I turn?

No. She knew better. Claude hadn't bitten her. He was very clever. He cut and drank but did not sink his fangs into her. He knew if he had, he'd have risked turning her. That would have definitely led to a much worse consequence than being thrown into the night. His head might have ended up on a stake.

Still, it haunted her. He was still close. Had he wished, he could have done much worse to her than to cut her thumb and drink her blood.

The other purveyors slept around her. All eight beds full; she inventoried them. Antione. Clarence. Sissy. Chanda. Roberto. Francois. Jean. The providers, all slaves to the Lost Ones. They were lost people who didn't want to be found. They wished for meaning, which they gave through their blood, so they claimed. Harvested by the physician vampire who does it painlessly with a thin needle and tubing, he keeps them relatively healthy.

And yet, how many had volunteered? Any? Were they all stolen from their lives to serve like cattle? Did they know they were all destined for the gallows? There'd be no escape. No redemption. No bringing them into the fold. They'd be dispatched the moment they weren't useful or wanted. They never spoke. They couldn't. They'd be heard. Even whispers. Sometimes, Angelique was sure they could even hear her thoughts.

Almost.

She had her thoughts to think, to plan, and to prepare.

Even with Aleister's promise, she didn't trust him. Everything they said could be washed away on a whim. Who did they have to answer to, after all?

If only I had their power...

The sounds of the large wooden door being locked woke her. The moon was high, she observed through the window. More noises of the night filled the room. The Lost Ones laughed as they made their way to their rooms. Somehow, they didn't lock her door. Were they drunk? Maybe it was the fight with Claude that made them forget. She didn't feel safe.

Maybe they'd done so on purpose, and it'd all been a show. She pictured Claude sneaking in, crawling on all limbs like a spider, slinking on top of her, wrapping her in his embrace before taking her deep into the woods and having his way with her. Feeding from her slowly. Gorging himself. Draining her until she'd die.

Those sounds she heard in the woods. . . were those others on the fringe too afraid to go inside and make themselves known? Or were they of the banished, like Claude.

Such ideas circled so much she couldn't sleep.

Her heart raced.

Sensing someone staring at her, Angelique looked up and saw Gabriel perched on a branch. Had he done this every night? She wondered if he could truly see her through the glass. He must, she believed. She hoped one day she would be free, too, able to choose where to go and not be enslaved. The crow was a slave, too, she knew, in its way. It'd likely grown dependent on the blood. Maybe Gabriel was like them, too. . . like the Lost Ones. . . needing it.

Angelique's stomach tightened as her anxiety crept back inside her belly.

One day, they would take her, regardless. Even if she ran away, they'd find her. There'd be no peace. Her life was spoken for.

But. . .

If. . .

The night air filled her chest. She would not be fooled into thinking staying at Las Envies would be anything other than a slow walk toward her demise. Afraid she'd run into Claude, she ran as fast as she could. She had a plan for him.

With the big recipe under her arm, Angelique felt she had the keys to the universe. The book was Las Envies, after all. Without it? They'd be forced to recreate the recipes from memory. It'd be a near-impossible task. Along with the recipes, the book acted as an informal history of Las Envies. Its discovery could undo them.

Above, Gabriel flew. He wasn't tracking her to tell on her, she believed, but was hoping she'd found an escape route for them both.

Footsteps behind her in the grass. She felt her senses align.

Claude.

She knew it was him. Come to claim the meal he'd only been teased with. Would he make it long and drawn out? Torture her to prove his dominance? Angelique was sure he'd try.

Across the grass field, she ran on the same one she'd played on nearly every day. Only she would not head back to Las Envies after an hour—she'd be heading into the woods. The prospect scared her to her core. The sounds she heard. The fluttering of the leaves. No good things happened in the woods.

Well, maybe one good thing might, she assured herself.

Crossing over into the first line of trees, she hoped she'd remember where the guillotine stood. There, she had a plan.

Within only a minute or so, she saw its silhouette. How could she have been so fortunate? Was fate driving her to the device, she wondered? It must be.

The footsteps stopped.

Her own made crunchy sounds with every step as leaves and sticks blanketed the forest floor. There was no escaping them.

She stood still. Clutched the recipe book tight as if it would somehow help shield her.

Angelique didn't hear any sounds of something approaching, so she stepped diligently toward the guillotine. Once there, she sat on the pillory and looked up at the angled blade. Would it still work?

She took the recipe book and placed it on the opposite side, where there was a trough to catch a severed head. She opened it to a middle page. Then she lay on the pillory, put her neck upon the gallows, and looked facedown. To her right, she spotted the release handle. Its rope appeared rather new and strong.

Waiting for a few moments, she sensed someone had approached from behind.

"You've come for me, Claude," she said. "And now's your chance to take me, but you must be quick before the blade drops. I won't give you the satisfaction."

There was no answer. However, she felt the unmistakable sensation of someone lingering.

"Claude?" she called.

A familiar voice. "You fool. It is not Claude. It is Raphael. What have you done? You've taken the book and stole into the night with it to what? Trap Claude? Do you really think. . . ?"

His voice was interrupted, and she heard a ruffling. There were two. She raised from her prone position and looked up in time to see Claude holding Raphael by his throat, raised in the air. "You pompous creep," he snarled. "Getting so close to a little girl."

Raphael struggled and fought, but it was to no avail.

"Leave him be!" Angelique cried. "He's done nothing to you."

Turning his gaze to her, Claude sneered and huffed. "You care for him as what? A father? A brother? A lover?"

"No. . ." she cried. "Please." She was up and off the guillotine, rushing toward them. Raphael's eyes darted to her and then the forest's edge from where she came. Silhouettes approached. Those from Las Envies, to be sure.

"Of course, they would come," Claude said. "They can all come as witnesses and experience horror instead of inflicting it on others." His motions faster than any animal or thing she'd ever seen, Claude rushed Raphael to the guillotine, slamming his body face down on the pillory. A crying sound escaped him before Claude shut the top of the stock and clamped it. Without hesitation, he pulled the release handle from its perch. The line went slack, then taught.

He let it go.

The angled blade fell.

"No!" Angelique screamed.

She heard the horrible clunking sound as the blade fell and severed Raphael's head. Another as it fell into the trough, on top of the recipe book.

The silhouettes hurried toward them. She had only seconds to choose what to do.

Claude turned and looked at her, his green eyes shining in the dark like blacksmith's ore. "And here we are, alone at last." His grin reminded her of that of a wild coyote.

She hurried to the trough.

Something huge came at her. . . a shadow. . . and she ducked. As she did, she reached into the trough and felt Raphael's hair. She grabbed and pulled out his head.

In the dark, she saw his eyes. They blinked, each on its own rhythm. "I can help ease the pain," she whispered. "One bite is all it will take, my friend."

She offered her wrist and placed it near his mouth.

How could he still be alive? She'd heard the severed heads could be conscious for a minute or more. Maybe much longer for the blood drinkers.

Angelique cried out, his fangs entering her. The bites burned like fire as he sucked. So strong. Was the blood pouring out of his neck his. . . or was it hers, having nowhere else to go?

Striking her, the shadow knocked her several strides from Raphael and the horrible device. She landed on her back, legs and arms spread wide. Her head spun.

She heard her name. The silhouettes arrived.

Claude then towered over her, his leering eyes and mouth drooling. He lunged down and Angelique made to block him.

Before she could, a loud noise rang out.

What could it be?

It sounded like a canon, only smaller. She looked up to see Aleister holding a firearm, smoke-like fog coming from its front barrel.

To her left, Claude grasped his chest, his fingers unable to fully cover the hole. He looked down, shocked and frightened. Turning his head to her, his eyes darkened for a moment before brightening more than ever before. He made a series of short guttural sounds that she thought could be words, but she'd never heard anything remotely like them.

Then, with two more utters. . . a curse. . . Claude backed up past the edge where he was visible. Leaves and branches rumbled, the same sound she heard so often when playing.

Liquid fire spread from her wrist to her elbow, to her brain and body. Her eyes were sore, and she shut them.

Sitting on the ground and gathering herself, Angelique stretched her neck and heard it crack. After a moment, she felt better. She knew they'd come—the near entirety of Las Envies. Even the purveyors.

"What have you done?" Ananda asked, eyeing Raphael's head, now still. "You've caused great pain to him. How will we sever his ties?"

"We have a way," Frederique said. "Gather him." He approached Angelique.

She stood to meet him. "Your words were right."

"Which words?" he asked.

"I am stronger than I thought, and my time at Las Envies will not be short," she said. Everything looked brighter. She felt better than she'd ever sensed, like she could jump into the air and fly if she wanted.

"And why is that?" he asked, but she sensed he knew because he looked right into her eyes and must have seen what she'd become.

"I've made myself like you," she said. "His fangs bit into me. It wasn't my original plan, but it became the only way. Claude would have ripped me limb by limb."

"He may still return," Ananda said. "I fear we haven't seen the last of him."

"Then let him come," Angelique said, "for I am ready as I now have the cravings."

Above, Gabriel flew with them, a shadow against the sky.

I am one like you now, crow.

Soon, she knew, it'd be time to dine, and she never missed a meal with those who gathered.

That night, she walked back carrying the recipe book to Las Envies not as a child but as one of them.

In time, it will be my turn to rise and repay them with the same mercy they've shown. I'll be the breaker of their hold and their locks.

And she thought . . .

As long as my blood is young, they will want me.

And I'll be young for quite a while yet.

UNNECESSARY NECROMANCY
J.A.W. MCCARTHY

A lock of his hair.

His saliva.

A toe- or fingernail.

His breath from the last room he was in.

Soil from the place where he died.

The last item is from a book I found in the library a few years ago. But that doesn't matter. None of these things matter. All that matters is that Cinda believes this. I need to keep her busy. Distracted. She needs to think that her love is enough to raise the dead.

The first one is the easiest. There are still strands of Jeff's dark curly hair twined in the teeth of his comb. Even though Cinda sees that comb every day, resting where he left it on the shelf above the toilet, her breath still catches when she picks it up for the first time after his death. Her fingers linger before pulling free the silky strands, and she briefly presses the small nest to her lips and

inhales. I want her to put it in her mouth and taste the bitterness
—realize this is a terrible idea and she needs to move on with her
life—but I don't say anything. She carefully slides the hair into a
plastic baggie and swipes her finger along the edge of the sink
basin, gathering the remnants of his last shave under her nail.

"I thought I'd be excited—you know, *happy*—doing this, but I
don't know," Cinda says, her pale eyes scanning the small room
for where I might be. Her gaze settles on the bathtub, where I
used to perch to hold back her long brown hair as she vomited
into the toilet. "Jesus, Mariel. I miss him so much and I know I
shouldn't, but I just need him, you know? I can't live like this. I
can't be alone."

She never could. That was why, when we were fifteen, I raised
her beloved beagle from the dead. I gave her a list much like the
one I made for Jeff, and the new sense of purpose got her through
those days of indifferent parents and an absent boyfriend. When
Ralphie appeared in her backyard, dusted with grave dirt but
otherwise unharmed, she made sure I wasn't the class freak
anymore. I became her best friend.

You can do this, I say.

She nods, her lower lip then chin quivering toward collapse. I
shift behind her so I don't have to witness the tears.

"I know I can do this," she says, her words wet, choked. "It's
just hard."

Then why did she choose him?

The toenails, though harder to find than the hair, are also easy.
Cinda takes out the vacuum cleaner and dumps its dusty contents
onto the living room floor. The detritus of her life with Jeff—
sandy dirt, shed brown and black hair, flecks of dry skin, all
married into tumbleweeds that once gathered in unreachable

corners, standing firm as the last record of their coupling—disperse across the hardwoods with her every breath, but she's undeterred. On her hands and knees, she picks through the grey dust until she finds a dull white crescent from Jeff's big toe. This does not make her cry.

It's the saliva, though, that makes us both cry.

His toothbrush is dry, any saliva long evaporated with the minty enamel gleam that is now turning dull in a box in the ground. Cinda pulls dirty dishes out of the dishwasher, then sends them crashing into the sink when she can't determine which glasses and forks he used. She wonders out loud if she can use all the forks and spoons for the ritual—"It'll still work if some of them aren't his, right?"—but I've told her that necromancy requires precision.

She's supposed to give up now. She's supposed to take this time, this frustration-thick, inertia-swollen moment, to realize the list I gave her—the very thought that bringing someone back from the dead—is as ill-advised as it is dangerous. *Is it worth it?* I want to ask her. Every time Jeff called her pathetic and needy when she asked where he'd been all night, his curdled whiskey breath smothering the air between them. The way he turned his cheating into something she somehow caused. Every fight made her smaller and smaller. "He works so hard. He's under too much pressure," she would tell me, wiping the tears away with a fluttering hand and a nervous laugh. "I'm being a big baby."

The vomiting came when she finally admitted she deserved better. "If you leave me, I'll kill myself," Jeff had sworn on more than one occasion. I assured her of what we both knew: his tears and apologies and threats were meaningless, each one a hollow tool to sharpen his control. I held the door open, and she packed her bags and walked through.

It was supposed to end there.

Cinda grabs a pumice stone from the shelf and, standing in

front of the bathroom mirror, saws it roughly against her lips until she draws blood.

What the hell, Cinda? Stop. Stop!

It's too late. Blood runs in rivulets from the dark smears around her mouth, loose pumice glittering on her torn lips. Her hands shake as she rubs the bloodied stone along the inside of the plastic baggie, mingling dead skin and fresh flesh and pink-tinged saliva with Jeff's hair and toenails.

"When I was walking out the door, I expected him to start screaming at me again, but he was so quiet and sad. It was strange. He said he loved me, and he kissed me," she says, swiping a bloody fingertip under her tear-swollen eye. "I mean, I knew he was manipulating me, but there was something different about that time, you know? And I should've known. I should've known." A small smile twitches on her lips, enough to release another tear. "I didn't eat and I barely drank anything all that day, then they called me and told me he was. . . And it was like I could still feel him, you know? I could feel his lips on mine, and I realized I was still carrying a piece of him on my mouth, and it was the last of him, and I knew I had to keep it safe. I've been so careful when I brush my teeth, when I eat and drink, making sure I don't wash away any of that, any of him."

It's not your fault, I say for the hundredth time.

"Okay, I know it's not my fault, but. . . He told me he would, and he did." Cinda's gaze swings around the bathroom again before settling on the edge of the tub. Is this how she'll always remember me, holding her hair back while anxiety and doubt twisted her gut until she retched up bile into the toilet? Will she ever remember me in a way that doesn't include him?

"I'm so sorry he did that to you, Mariel," she says, and the tears let loose all at once. This is the first time her tears are solely for me.

I start crying too.

The breath is a guess. Cinda can't be sure which room was the last one Jeff was in before he died. If he went out the back or front door. She holds a glass jar up above her head—at his height—and pushes it through the air as if she's wielding a butterfly net in front of both doors. She spends a little extra time trapping the air at the back door because she hasn't opened that one since his death.

Before screwing on the lid, she dips her nose into the jar and inhales just a sip, not enough to take it all into her lungs. I know it doesn't smell of the whiskey that fermented along the sides of his tongue or the poisonous words collected like plaque in the crags of his molars.

"I don't know. . . Is this him?" she asks, holding out the jar. I'm hovering over the kitchen island, another place I used to sit, glass in hand in happier times. "It just smells like my house."

Coconut body lotion, powdery musk, the tang of her scalp like overripe bananas on the edge of decay. I remember that from the car, thinking it was funny that being alone with Jeff in such a tight space—even without Cinda—and still he smelled of her. Even as he was threatening me, I was thinking of her.

He smelled like you.

"I'm afraid I forgot how he smells," she says, though her voice is more bemused than sad. She swoops the jar through the air again before screwing on the lid and placing it on the island. We both stare at it.

It's empty. It's nothing.

Jeff died intact in his sedan, his last breath smothered by the airbag, his chest crushed by the steering column, the light pole that stopped his car bobbing over the wreckage like an angler-fish's lure.

I died on impact.

An oak tree caught my body, the windshield glass and bark embedded in my face and neck, slicing me into unrecognizable pieces as I hit the ground.

The state trooper told Cinda it was a suicide; the lack of skid marks and acceleration of the vehicle made that likely. No one said the words "murder-suicide" to her, as if I too was responsible. No one knows that Jeff—as I was screaming, begging him to slow down—calmly reached over me and undid my seatbelt.

Cinda sits cross-legged in the dirt on this sidewalk-less stretch of road, thin fingers raking through sun-bleached, dry soil mere inches from where my head left skid marks. There are still spots where the soil is dark, and she gently scoops those up, cupping a palmful as she wonders if my blood lingers here, bonded with the dirt, making it nearly black and smelling unbearably rich and mineral-y like organ meat. She knows Jeff's blood never left the car.

It doesn't matter, I assure her. *He died here. We both died here.*

She slides the handful of soil into the baggie. It mingles with Jeff's hair and toenails and the bloody flakes of her own lips, all three of us becoming one, encapsulated in a disposable bit of plastic meant to house sandwiches and loose change.

"This is so much harder than I thought it would be," Cinda says, inhaling sharply.

Her eyes are red, swollen from crying in the car on the way here; she'll never be dry, something she's lamented a dozen times in the last two weeks. She inhales again, slow and measured, but it's not enough. The gradual collapse carves lines in her forehead, drags down her cheeks, her mouth, makes her jaw shudder on its hinges. One squeeze at the corners of her eyes and it's over—this is the same breath-smothering, gut-heaving sobbing I witnessed when she got the news.

I knew this would be the hardest one for Cinda.

I wasn't going to include soil on the list—I don't need it any more than the other things I instructed her to collect—but when she said it was Jeff she wanted to bring back. . . when she never once mentioned me. . .

I guess I did it to hurt her.

———

"You're drunk, and you call *me*?" Jeff had said, shaking his head, as I climbed into his car outside the Ruby Room. I was surprised he'd answered my call, even more surprised that he'd agreed to pick me up. "I don't know why the fuck I'm here."

"Cinda can't know," I told him.

"That you drank yourself stupid because you're in love with someone who doesn't want you?"

His words were a blazing dart in the center of my chest, acid branching up into my throat. I could almost believe it was the alcohol. "You don't know what you're talking about, Jeff—you never do."

I could've called an Uber, but four bourbons had convinced me it was time I finally experienced Jeff's gravitational pull myself. What thrall did he have over Cinda and all those other women he was cheating with? I leaned across the console, folded my hands atop his shoulder, then rested my chin on top. Everything was slippery, blurry, but he was solid, steady—was that what Cinda loved about him? The round, creamy scent of coconut thickened his powdery musk, a heady confection I could almost taste when I opened my mouth. Was this what intoxicated Cinda when he kissed her? What was so special about this man, his hands, the way he looked at her and all those other women?

Jeff leaned forward to start the engine, but I didn't let go. Instead, I grabbed his face with both hands and kissed him.

"Jesus, Mariel!" he spat, shoving me back into my seat. "What the fuck is wrong with you?"

My tongue felt fat and dry in my mouth. I didn't taste coconut or the comfort of familiarity, or even the bourbon I'd been drinking all night. I tasted nothing.

Jeff rubbed the back of his hand roughly over his mouth while shifting into drive with the other. "You're the third wheel. You know that, right? There is no *you* in this relationship. Cinda chose me, not you."

"And now she's chosen to leave you," I reminded him, unable to keep the smirk from my lips.

"You're pathetic, you know that? You don't know what she wants. You don't know her at all."

I twisted in my seat, pressed myself against the door as if I could get away from him even though we were in a moving car. "*I* don't know her? I've been Cinda's best friend since high school. You've known her for, what, eighteen months?"

"You have no idea what our relationship is like. We were working on things, but you ruined it. Always around, poking at the cracks, waiting for your chance to strike." He sped up, blew a stop sign at the empty intersection. "You've always been so jealous, so possessive of her. She only keeps you around because you're a necromancer. That's the only reason anyone tolerates you, because of what you can do for them in the future."

I'd heard those words before, even wondered them myself. The way kids started inviting me to parties and offering favors after I brought back Cinda's dog. . . I learned to keep my powers secret as I grew older, but even close friends treated me differently once they found out. Cinda was the only person I could trust, the only one who never asked for anything.

"What about you?" The words bloomed hot and crackling in

my chest, building with the speed of the car. I should've been scared of Jeff's carelessness, the way his anger was influencing his driving, but I was too angry myself, too drunk. "Manipulating her, threatening to kill yourself. Wielding guilt and her kind heart as weapons against her for what—so you can own her like a possession, this precious thing you can't even treat well? You're the one who's jealous."

He laughed loudly, mockingly. "God, listen to yourself. *You* treat her like she's helpless, like a precious little thing for *you* to protect and control. You know how I know that? She told me so."

"Fuck you, Jeff. She may have loved you once, but she doesn't anymore."

We were rounding a curve, the car hugging the edge of the road, throwing up loose pebbles and dirt fast enough to ping the windows and windshield. I screamed for him to slow down, but all he did was grin as his foot slammed onto the gas pedal. The road ahead was empty, but we were veering towards a dot of light off the road, the beacon that was supposed to guide us through the black night. Sobriety fell on me heavy as the realization of what Jeff was doing. His silence. His vacant yet focused stare despite my pleading, my own realization that his threat was never as empty as I had thought. The light ahead got bigger and bigger, as close and clear as Jeff's hand reaching across my lap—swerving the car, tipping me directly into his grip—then the click of my seatbelt coming undone as the light passed overhead and out of view.

As instructed, Cinda empties the baggie of ritual items onto Jeff's favorite spot in the backyard. His hair, saliva, toenails, soil—she carefully spreads them over the patch of grass where he used to drag a lawn chair and read, as if he had been her pet dog or cat with a favorite sunbathing spot. She releases his breath here as well, coconut and musk lost to the nothing of suburban air before she can screw the lid back on the jar.

This is all made up too. Something from that same library book I found years ago, the one I laughed over because none of this is how necromancy works. What Cinda doesn't know is that I don't need pieces of Jeff's body, or words in an ancient language spoken in a specific order, or my hands and mind concentrated over a grave. She never watched me work when I was alive, and I wouldn't have been able to explain it anyway. My power is as simple as a focused desire in a vessel born to do this one thing.

As I intended, Cinda busies herself with these distractions. Over the next few days, she settles back into the house she shared with Jeff, reclaiming her space, and slowly seeping into the cracks and corners he had touched. Her eyes linger on the sacred spot she's made in the backyard every time she does the dishes or pours herself a cup of coffee. She checks a couple of times a day to make sure birds haven't stolen the hair for a nest or the toenails haven't blown away in the breeze. If she still holds any hope, it's not evident on her face. Eventually, she sleeps through the night and goes back to her office and enjoys dinner with a good book.

I didn't give her a timeline, and she hasn't once asked when it will happen. To my surprise, she doesn't have a blanket waiting or any other comforts to ease the shock of Jeff's sudden return to the living. She asks me for no further preparations, no support. Even though I'm hovering here, everywhere she is, same as Jeff is hovering somewhere I can't see or hear. Waiting, hoping, wondering what happens next, same as me.

All I have to do is want air to fill Jeff's lungs and electricity to shock his heart back to life. I don't want it, but there was a time when I would've wanted it for her.

Cinda, it'll happen soon, okay? I finally tell her after two weeks. Her silence is not the resignation I wanted from her, but it's not cold. It's not the emptiness I expected, and that leadens the guilt creeping into my dead heart.

It doesn't take long before she grabs a large box from the basement and starts filling it with Jeff's clothes. She allows herself one long inhale against the peach-fuzz soft flannel of his favorite shirt before taking the box out to her car. Not once does she say a word to me or him.

I long for her to ask if I can bring myself back instead. Just once, for her to ask about my possible resurrection. Someone has to want it.

She stops checking Jeff's special spot in the backyard. Instead, when she's standing at the sink, she gazes out on the horizon and watches the sun set.

Then, one night a month later, Cinda walks out into the backyard with a shovel in hand. Her eyes are red, swollen with fresh tears, but there's a lightness I haven't seen in a long time, a lift in her chin, resolve stopping the slow collapse I've witnessed all too often since she met Jeff. Time is never kind, but today I see how she's crystalized lonely minutes into something new and entirely for herself.

"Mariel?"

I don't answer. I didn't expect to hear my name.

"Okay, Mariel. I know what you're thinking," she says, gaze crawling over the yard. Somehow, she settles on exactly where I stand, watching her from the back porch. "I know it's not my fault. But I can't help feeling that way," she continues. "I know I did the right thing, that he was manipulating me—I've always known that, okay? I'm not stupid." She laughs, dry and scraping in her throat, then swipes a knuckle roughly under her eye. "You always treated me like I couldn't be trusted to make my own decisions, like you had to take care of me. No one asked me what *I* wanted. You don't know how hard it is to pick up and leave and change your whole life. You made it sound so easy, but you've never been through that. And now. . . I know what he did, I *know* it was his choice, but he took you too. How can I not feel guilty about that? What the fuck were you doing with him, Mariel?"

I know I should answer, release the guilt I feel too, take some of the burden off her. But I can't admit it. Death didn't absolve any of my shame.

Cinda smiles, nods. "It doesn't matter. I wanted him back so I could ask him and tell him everything I didn't get to, then just be done with him, you know? Maybe I'd kill him myself for what he did to you. How we ended, though—it should've been my choice, too. I wanted it on my own terms, not his."

She stabs the shovel into the ground, unsettling a sparse wreath of Jeff's dark curly hair. She uses the shovel to scoop it back into place, then stabs the ground again, bringing up a heap of dry soil dusted with the rich, wet earth from the place where he and I died. I want to remember how that earth felt against my cheek—I can imagine it, soft and cool as cake crumbs, clinging to my lips, my eyelashes, coating my nose in that organ richness that was there before it met my blood—but I was already dead before my body hit the ground.

After a few minutes of digging, Cinda reveals a shallow hole a foot wide and a foot deep. She stops for a moment and inhales deeply. I watch her release the exhale, such a simple, overlooked function under her shirt that's too thin for the evening chill creeping in. I think of my body filling like a helium balloon in its grave, withered limbs rising until they meet the unyielding wood that encases them. Her breath giving life, just like my will used to.

"I'm sorry, but I have let you both go," she says.

She gently scoops up Jeff's hair and toenails and the soil soaked with my blood and tips them into the hole she's dug. Her blood is there too, coating the flakes of her lips, a last kiss she tried to save. She even scoops up the air low to the ground, what we both pretend to be Jeff's breath. All of it goes carefully, lovingly, into this little grave. A heap of dry, insignificant backyard earth goes on top, patted down and smoothed, so we—what's left of us—are nothing more than a bald spot in the grass.

I watch from the porch as she goes inside and pours a glass of wine and stares out at the setting sun.

THE TASTE OF OTHER PEOPLE'S TEETH

REBECCA CUTHBERT

Sherman wouldn't have even *looked* in the room where they stored dead people's abandoned belongings if his dentures hadn't been lost after that month's Taco Tuesday at Bronze Acres Senior Living Community, where he'd lived for the past eight months.

Forget trying to get another pair out of his insurance company —those bastards wouldn't give him a free fart from a willing donor's asshole.

Calling his son to ask for the money would only be a waste of his pre-paid cellular minutes. Robbie's Facebook profile said he was an "independent men's fashion consultant," but Sherman knew that was just a fancy way of saying he'd been fired again, this time from a Men's Warehouse.

And after being bled dry by this old folks' "resort-style" community, who could blame him for sneaking out of his room in the middle of the night to check what staff not-so-secretly called "Dead Man's Dump?" No one. *That's* who. Because Wednesday and Thursday had come and gone and he was already sick of eating liquid meals like the mumbling, piss-pants raisins slumped in their wheelchairs on the first floor.

THE TASTE OF OTHER PEOPLE'S TEETH   285

Sherman would off himself before becoming one of them, but he figured he had a year or three left in his relatively capable body and he planned to live them with chompers in his mouth.

If they had to be someone *else's* chompers, so be it.

Dead Man's Dump was in the basement. It couldn't be that hard to find; he'd just have to sneak past the night nurse first. Easy-peasy-booby-squeezy; she was usually napping. He'd get in, get some teeth, then get out. And next month, he'd be careful not to wrap the new-to-him dentures in a napkin after getting refried bean paste stuck beneath them, then accidentally throw them out.

It was a good plan, more or less, and he'd brought along his pen/screwdriver/flashlight all-in-one that Robbie got him, probably on clearance, for Father's Day. Its thin light was enough to guide him along the darkened first-floor utility hall, down a set of metal steps, and around stacks of odds-and-ends furniture without more than a barked shin and a bruised hip.

Dead Man's Dump wasn't locked; he slipped inside and stopped to catch his breath. Then he ran his little pen light over the walls near the door until he found a light switch and flicked it on. Overhead, three fluorescent lights zapped and flickered; two went out, one stayed lit.

Good enough.

Metal shelves lined each side of the narrow room. They were covered top to bottom with cardboard boxes, last names and dates written on their sides with black marker.

He ripped the tape off a few boxes close to the door: *McDaniels, Berger, Smith,* all from several years ago. He found framed pictures, pilled sweaters, and a couple little homemade animal statuettes—art projects from the grandkids, probably. Most looked like baked turds, but there was one he liked—a goat or a bull, maybe, standing on its hind legs, all shiny black glaze with tiny jeweled eyes—and that one Sherman put in his pocket. It would look good on his dresser.

Next, he explored other boxes, farther in, still old: *Jones* and *Rakesh* and *Seneca*. Nothing exciting—Rakesh had left behind dentures, but they were flimsy, plastic things; Jones and Seneca must have died with their natural ivories or been buried in their falsies. He did find an old Casio watch, though, and slipped it onto his wrist. Its hands were frozen still; he'd have to get a new battery.

He passed several shelves and came upon more recent dates and a few names he recognized: *Grantley, Montgomery, Siebert. Kuczynski*. These folks had all died in the last several months; he'd known them. "Grantley" was Bethany Grantley; she'd been sort of attractive in a Mrs. Potato Head way. Sherman almost asked her out to Bingo night in the cafeteria once or twice, but she seemed to have a thing for Ed Montgomery, though Ed told Sherman, with a wink, that he was a lifelong bachelor. Smart of him, Sherman thought. Who needed women anyway? Snazzy dresser, that Ed, and always friendly in the men's physical therapy steam room.

Ron Siebert had been an ass—always bragging about how his son was a doctor without boundaries. Some crap like that; Sherman never really listened.

Jack Kuczynski he'd steered clear of, though he couldn't put his finger on why. Jack seemed normal enough—even a bit boring, in wrinkled slacks and dark polo shirts—but he had a funny way of looking at people. Like he was measuring them for something. And he barely spoke. It gave Sherman the willies.

Not that any of them mattered. Sherman mostly kept to himself.

His wife had left him long ago—she claimed it was his drinking—and he got used to his solitude. Besides, what was he supposed to do? Go around the senior living complex, asking if anyone wanted to be his friend? Offer to share his dessert in the dining room? Good grief. He wasn't *desperate*. He wasn't even that lonely, most of the time.

The only working light fixture in the storage room flickered like a signal to hurry. Sherman pushed his thoughts away, tore the tape off Bethany's box of crap, and fished around in it.

Finally some good luck! His hand came out holding dentures that, at least in the room's shadowy dimness, didn't seem too cheap or too yellowed. Sherman wondered if they'd been cleaned after Bethany bought the farm, but beggars couldn't be choosers. Anyway, it was kind of hot, right? Having another person's dirty teeth in his mouth.

Sherman tried to laugh, but it came out as a cough.

Too much dust.

He backtracked through the storage room and out the door, remembering to flip the light switch off as he went. He expected to step into pitch darkness in the basement's main room, but he could just about see—moonglow filtered through the basement's leaded glass windows, creating little islands of light. Sherman crept close to one to examine his booty: he held up his new statue —black glaze, sparkling red eyes; took off his watch to inspect it —steel with a fake-gold face; admired his replacement teeth— only one small chip in a back left molar.

He felt like a skilled pirate and grinned; but his gums ground together, so he frowned, which was more comfortable.

Then he heard the basement door open.

"Anyone down there?" shrilled a voice. It was the night nurse.

Sherman froze, there in the pool of moonlight. He heard her put a foot on the top step. Then another.

"Hellllloooooo. . ."

Balls!

He couldn't get caught. They weren't supposed to, but some-times the staff withheld dessert or TV time from who they called "the troublemakers." And life here was dull enough without being grounded like a kid by snot-nosed orderlies still on their first sets of pubes.

The thought spurred him into action. He slid the watch back onto his wrist and shoved the teeth in his mouth, arranging them with his tongue. *Mmm.* They tasted like peppermint. *Nice, Bethany.* Not a perfect fit, though—a bit too small. Adhesive paste would help. He clutched the statue, feeling its smooth surface warm in his sweaty, nervous palm.

Sherman was an atheist, but a little prayer formed on his dry lips: "Please," he mouthed to no deity in particular, "don't let me get caught." Even those silent words made his new teeth shift out of place, so he added: "And make these damned teeth *fit.*"

Three things happened so quickly Sherman wondered if he'd doubled up on his blood pressure meds again and was hallucinating.

One, the night nurse backed up the steps and shut the basement door. Two, the moonbeam Sherman stood in glowed brighter. And three, dead Bethany's tasty left-behind dentures settled onto his gums so comfortably they almost felt like real teeth.

Sherman stood, amazed and blinking, running his tongue around his mouth.

But the moment's strangeness wasn't done—the statue in his hand went from warm to hot, stopping just short of a first-degree burn. It hit Sherman that, had he been younger, he'd have filled his trousers with liquid, terrified shit. At his age, though, all he felt was a daring curiosity and a few gas bubbles.

So, he decided to roll whatever dice the universe had given him one more time.

"And fix this damn watch!"

He held his breath, which was difficult to do after last April's bout of pneumonia.

Then he heard it.

The watch's tiny second-counting hand tick-tick-ticked around its face, followed eventually by the tock of its minute hand.

The moonbeam faded.

Left in the dark, thrill turned to a creeping sense of unease. He hadn't intended to pray to anyone—to anything. But that didn't mean nothing *heard* him. Whatever it was, did it still listen, there in the dark? Could it hear Sherman breathing? He shoved the cooling figurine into his dressing gown pocket and, hands out like a zombie to feel for obstacles, hurried up the basement steps, eased the door open, and closed it softly behind him.

Taking the steps, not the elevator, back to his second-floor efficiency apartment made Sherman wheeze and sweat. Once back there, he set his new belongings on his dresser and climbed into bed. He felt safer in the extra layer of his terrycloth robe, so he left it on.

And Bethany's teeth tasted so good in his mouth that he left those, too.

He'd brush them in the morning.

He gazed across the room, into the red eyes of his new knick-knack. Were the jewels real? Garnets or rubies? They seemed to glow in the dark, like they had their own light source. The longer Sherman looked, the brighter they shone, accentuating the lumpy curves of the statue's muscles. He still wasn't sure if it was a goat or a bull. Its hands looked human.

Well, whatever, Sherman thought. Art's weird and artists are weirder.

Then he shut off his bedside light and, faster than he thought he would after the night's spooky adventure, fell asleep.

---

290 OF REBECCA CUTHBERT

Sherman was the first person to get to the dining room for breakfast, feeling. . . different. Kind of chipper? As soon as a few other residents filed in, he waved them over to his table—an eight-person round instead of his usual two-seater that he never shared.

"Sit!" he said to the group. "Carl, right? Carl? Yes, and don't tell me. . . Doug. Carl and Doug and Michelle, is it?"

"It's Rochelle," the woman said. She patted her blueish curls.

"Of course! The lovely Rochelle!" Sherman said, surprised to mean it. Her hair was pretty fab. "Now sit, all of you!"

They did, exchanging looks with one another.

"So, how are things in your wing?" Sherman asked. He moved his elbows and said a quick thank you to the orderlies who brought over a coffee carafe and plastic trays full of eggs and mushy canned fruit. "What's new?"

"Pardon?" said Rochelle.

"The gossip, girl!" said Sherman. "Dish it!" He giggled. He must have picked up those phrases from a television show. They were so fun to say! And gosh, when was the last time he giggled? *That* was fun, too!

One of the men cleared his throat.

"Sherman?" said Doug. "You alright?" He doused his eggs in salt and shoved a spoonful into his mouth.

"Never better!" said Sherman. And he meant that, too. "Must have gotten a good night's sleep. I feel great! Might even walk down to the drugstore on the corner today. *Lord*, my elbows are dry as a desert noon! Gotta get me some lotion. Anyone need anything? Doug? Carl? Snacks? Baby aspirin? Rochelle? Maybe a new lippie? Something in an autumn shade?"

"Um. . ." said Carl. "No."

"Yeah. . . No thanks," said Doug.

Sherman turned to Rochelle.

She stared at him for a moment, then shrugged. "Sure. You

know, can I come with you? New lipstick would be lovely, but I really need to try a new brand of talc. My daughter brought me the cheap stuff." She rolled her eyes.

"Oh. My. *God*," said Sherman. "I totally know what you mean. The stuff my son brings. It's like, wow, Robbie, did you spend a whole five dollars? Jeez. But of course! It'll be so much fun. Ooh. Wanna take the community shuttle?"

"Love to!" said Rochelle.

"Woo-hoo!" sang Sherman. "Shopping trip!"

He held out his coffee cup and Rochelle clinked hers against it. Why did he do that? Another thing he'd seen on TV? But Sherman ignored his self-consciousness. For once, he felt something other than hatred for his life and everyone in it.

Rochelle was laughing. "I like this side of you!"

"Well! In that case, you're in luck. I've got sides upon sides!" said Sherman, leaning into his mood and laughing with her. "Including this *back*side of mine that won't stop growing! Ha. But who cares, right? A girl's gotta eat! I'm gonna get me some more of that yummy fruit cocktail!"

He wiggled in his seat and waved to a dining room attendant.

Rochelle laughed louder.

Carl coughed.

Doug ate his eggs.

That night, Sherman sat in the TV room, surrounded by a rapt audience. Doug and Carl were notably absent, but that was fine because Rochelle had brought down her friends Gina and Tilly and Millie and Kate. They were having a little party. Tilly had brought crackers, and Sherman and Rochelle shared the snacks they'd picked up earlier from the store: ding-dongs and corn chips and cheese sauce in a can.

Everything was great; Sherman was in the middle of sharing a particularly juicy bit of gossip—about how he'd noticed a few days ago that Nurse Brenda had a dark purple hickey on her neck and wasn't wearing her usual wedding ring—when a corn chip stuck in his throat. He'd opened wide to laugh; it felt so good to laugh! To really let loose and guffaw with the girls! And the sharp-edged chip lodged just south of his tonsils.

He hacked; blood rushed to his face. His eyes bulged painfully.

Kate came to his rescue. She was a big gal, strong arms, stocky frame, and Sherman felt himself picked up from behind in an aggressive, thrusting Heimlich maneuver. Kate's fists found the hollow space below his rib cage and hoisted him once, twice, three times, until *AACK!* The corn chip, along with Sherman's newly filched teeth, flew from his mouth.

The corn chip, soggy with saliva, landed on the faux-cherry-wood coffee table.

The dentures, being heavier, sailed a shorter distance, crashing to the tiles at Sherman's feet. The bottom denture broke clean in half, right between the front teeth. A perfect 50-50 split.

Kate dropped him into a wingback armchair, where he sat for a moment, heart racing.

Perfumed and permed women surrounded him, fussing. One was asking if he was okay, another trying to shove a glass of water into his hand. One of them—had he gone shopping with her? Why?—called him "Shermy."

"Get off!" he yelled, then coughed again. "Harpies! What do you want?" He scowled at the woman closest to him. She had an orange smear on her powdered chin.

They backed away. "Sherm?" said Cheese Chin.

No, not Cheese Chin. Tilly. They'd all been hanging out together, but what for? His memories of the day were in and out. He felt the way he used to before he quit drinking—not quite sure what was real. The withering muscles in his stomach hurt. Had he laughed that much?

Then he saw the teeth on the floor and felt, with his tongue, his bare gums, useless now for chewing anything.

"Goddammit," he said and tried to stand.

Two of the women pushed him back. He sighed. And he was thirsty, and his throat hurt, so he accepted the glass of water and let one of the bejeweled hands pet his head.

Then, when he felt a little better, he stood, getting clear of the women and their fussing. Muttering about his teeth, ignoring the hurt expressions on the wrinkled faces watching him go, he stomped back to his apartment, wondering, again, if he'd screwed up his medications, or if, even worse, his memory was going the way of his original teeth.

Back in his little efficiency suite, he knew what he had to do: return to Dead Man's Dump and pick up a new pair of pearly whites. Also, tackle more crossword puzzles to preserve whichever brain cells weren't already sleeping on the job.

———

This time, he fished in Ed Montgomery's box of leavings, coming up with a gorgeous set of dentures that must have cost a pretty penny. They were so realistic, even the subtle points of the canine teeth looked natural.

Sherman remembered the way Ed was always smiling— showing those teeth off to anyone who cared to look, charming the nurses, winking as he passed. Tall and fit up to the day he died. And always so well dressed. Only the best for Ed.

And now, Ed's best was Sherman's best.

Finders keepers, dead man's weepers, he thought. He grinned. His naked gums ground together. He lifted Ed's beautiful teeth and popped them into his mouth. Sheesh. *Salty*. Not a perfect fit—a bit too big. But nothing adhesive paste wouldn't fix.

He shut off the light and left the storage room, a little disappointed not to find any magical moonbeams shining through the windows. Then he felt embarrassed by his disappointment. Of *course* there were no magical moonbeams! Of *course* it had just been a medication side effect: the night before, the strange happenings. That or he'd stayed up too late. Or, hell. For all he knew, there was a gas leak in the basement. It would explain his lapses earlier in the day too—all the laughing and fun he half-remembered.

Just loopiness.

He shuffled up the stairs and went back to his apartment.

When he got there, he hung his dressing gown on the hook in his bathroom, swished and spat some mouthwash, then smiled at himself in the mirror. Ed's teeth looked great. They glinted in the light. Sherman held up his wrist so his watch would be part of the debonair reflection. He tried to wink, but the result looked more like a tic. He'd work on it.

"Lookin' good, Sherm," he told himself. "Lookin' *sharp*."

He took a piss and then went to his bed, sitting on the edge. He was ready to kick off his slippers and call it a night. He yawned; Ed's dentures flapped in his mouth.

"*Balls!*" he whisper-yelled. "Wish these damn things *fit*."

He was about to take them out, set them on a tissue next to his alarm clock.

His hand stopped halfway to his face.

His new statuette had moved.

The little bull. Or goat? Hoofs and human hands. He'd left it on his dresser, but now it stood on his bedside table. Maybe the cleaners had been in? The statue's red eyes were so shiny against the black glaze of its face. It really *was* a classy little piece of art, he thought—not like the grandma crap Hallmark sold.

He picked up the statue and carried it back to his dresser, shaking his head at the strangeness of the day.

The movement jogged Ed's dentures into place; they clamped down tighter than a deer tick on a dog.

"Well, I'll be damned," Sherman said. Then, looking at the statue, at its strange physiology, he knocked slowly on the wooden veneer of his dresser.

He was still an atheist, he assured himself. A little superstition didn't change that. And weird coincidences didn't mean a higher power—or a *lower* power—*or* a lower power's demonic minion— was present and listening.

Didn't mean one *was*. Didn't mean one *wasn't*.

Sherman turned out the light and lay down.

It took a long time for him to fall asleep.

In the morning, Sherman dressed in his navy blue chinos and a white button-down shirt, leaving it open at the collar to flash a bit of chest hair. He put a little Vaseline on his cracked leather loafers to spiff them up, ran a wet comb through his hair, then hit the dining room, shooting finger-guns and expert winks to the other residents he passed. They only frowned back at him.

Sourpusses.

He just felt *good*, he told himself. Like, *really* good. When had he felt this good in his body? It must have been the dress clothes —they gave him confidence. Why did he usually wear so much threadbare beige, anyway?

He spotted four other men who were similarly dressed; they'd appreciate his new look. He sat down at their table, saying, "Is this seat taken? Or can anyone join you handsome devils?"

Now, where did he come up with that? He sounded so *suave!*

Suave and witty. The men laughed and welcomed him. One of them, who introduced himself as Scotty, even blushed a little.

An orderly saw him and brought over the usual plastic tray of eggs and fruit, plus a fresh carafe of coffee. Sherman thanked him, spread a cloth napkin across his lap, and kept his elbows off the table while he ate, asking the men polite questions about their hobbies between bites. Twice, he made subtle but racy jokes about racquetball partners and ceiling shots.

The men ate it up.

"So where have you been hiding yourself?" asked Scotty when their trays had been removed. "I'm surprised we haven't met."

"Well," said Sherman. "Who doesn't love a surprise?"

"I love surprises!" said one of the other men.

"I love them more," said Scotty.

By the time they'd finished their coffee, Sherman had been invited to the men's physical therapy steam room that evening for what his new friends playfully called "Boys' Night."

Sherman showed up fashionably late, at about 8:10 p.m. He wore only a pair of shower shoes, a towel, and Ed's gleaming teeth. His new friends were all there, sweat already beading on their chests and running down to disappear into fluffy white terrycloth and the promise of gray pubic hair.

"So glad you could come!" said Scotty. "Sit here, next to me."

"Thanks for inviting me," said Sherman, sitting down. "I've had a weird few days. I could really use some stress relief."

"What do you mean?" said Scotty, scooting closer.

"Just like. . ." Sherman thought about it—how he felt like a new man that day, fresh and comfortable, but had trouble remembering the day before. How his mind was both clear and foggy—the *now* so real and sharp, the *then* muffled and blurred. Scotty was still listening. "Like, who even am I, you know?"

"Yeah, I do," said Scotty, and Sherman believed him. He was so earnest—it was an attractive quality. "But you don't have to figure it all out in one day. You can take time to get to know yourself. Experiment with. . . things."

Sherman closed his eyes and inhaled the piney scent of Scotty's aftershave. He felt peaceful; he was relaxed around these men. Like he knew them. Like he belonged.

"Here," he heard Scotty say. "Let me. . ." and he felt Scotty's hands on his shoulders, turning him away so that Scotty could massage his neck and back. He leaned into the other man's touch, and any remaining tension left his body.

A dim alarm went off in the back of his mind, trying to tell him he was doing something wrong. But what could be wrong about this? It felt wonderful. He moaned, drowning out the noise in his head.

Scotty's hands moved down Sherman's back, his sides, around to his front. Someone kicked up the steam; Sherman opened his eyes but couldn't see. The world had turned to white mist, hot and wet. Scotty murmured in his ear and pulled away Sherman's towel. Sherman reached behind him; Scotty's towel was gone, too. Skin pressed to skin. Hands found things to hold.

Time passed; Sherman got lost in physical sensations that felt both strange and familiar. Exciting. Eventually, the steam cleared and he found himself seated in front of a kneeling Scotty, and like everything else that day, it felt *right*. The other men—Charles and Ron—had gone. Sherman reached out a hand to hold Scotty by the hair; not to be rough, not to make him go faster or deeper, but because he wanted another point of contact with this man who made his body sizzle like a Denny's ham skillet.

Scotty must have felt the same; his strong fingers found Sherman's jaw; squeezed, forced open his lips and teeth. He stuck his fingers inside, and Sherman knew to lick and suck; it was a reflex; had he done this before? The younger man growled and shoved his fingers farther into Sherman's mouth, fish-hooking his jaw.

Sherman was so close; he felt his climax rising within him, when *POP!* Scotty dislodged his lower denture, sending it skittering to the floor. Sherman stopped. What was happening? His dick. His dick was—

Partial awareness dawned. Slowly, and again, like unwelcome sobriety. Hazy memories—dressing snazzy that day. Breakfast with the boys. Boys' Night. Ed's teeth. Ed dressed snazzy. Ed's teeth in his mouth—half his teeth still in Sherman's mouth.

His dick still hard.

He looked down at Scotty's head. Scotty, ten years younger. Scotty, who he suddenly knew, was his sometimes lover. No. *Ed's* sometimes lover. How did he know that?

Sherman wasn't Ed. But he wasn't quite Sherman. . .

He squeezed his eyes shut. W*as* he Ed? Had he been Bethany the day before? The basement. The statue. What had been listening? But that wasn't right—he didn't believe in that shit. People were just sacks of meat that eventually rotted. That was it. There was nothing out there. Except *was* there? Because. . .

Because of the dentures. His dentures. No—*their* dentures. He'd wished for them to fit.

And they did. They fit to him—or was that wrong, too? More like. . . *he* fit to *them*. But that couldn't be. Because the afterlife, demons, possession—that was all fantasy.

And yet.

Had he been *possessed*? He'd seen that crap in movies. *This* wasn't like that. Sherman remembered some of that day. Some of the day before. It was more like he'd been. . . overshadowed by Bethany and Ed. Him under them, them layered on top of him.

Which meant. . .

Which meant he'd kinda *liked* spending the day gossiping with girlfriends. That wasn't all Bethany. And. . .

He opened his eyes. He was *Sherman*, dammit, or Sherman enough to have pulled his cock out of Scotty's warm, wet mouth. So why *hadn't* he?

The dentures. The top one was still in place. That was why. All Sherman had to do was spit it out, along with Scotty's fingers, grab his towel, and make a run for it.

He could do that, but damn. His boner was a doozie. And shoot—when was the last time his Bingo marker had daubed a damn thing? His dick had been gathering dust for the better part of a decade.

So he left Ed's remaining teeth in, finished, and even managed a quick "see you around" before he grabbed his towel and ran, throwing the top denture in a nearby trashcan on his way out.

Sherman slipped into his apartment and slammed the door behind him, leaning against it. His heart stuttered dangerously in his chest. Sweat trickled down his back. Had anyone seen him? Did anyone *know*?

Know what? That he was a gay? But *he* wasn't one of them —*Ed* was. But it hadn't been Ed's cock in another man's mouth. . . Maybe Sherman was a *little* gay? At least gay enough to do gay stuff in exchange for a functioning hard-on.

Balls!

What a damn mess. He was his old crusty self plus a gossipy woman and also a snazzy gay man, except that Bethany was the woman and Ed was the snazzy one, which made Sherman what? A crusty, gossipy, not-snazzy, slightly gay man?

Despite blowing his wad for the first time in ages, which felt better than a prune-day shit, Sherman wished he'd never gone down to the basement. That he never found the creepy statue or put other people's teeth in his mouth.

He looked over at the little goat-man statue on his dresser. It seemed to look back.

"You did this," he said.

Of course the statue didn't answer, because it was only a statue. Nothing more. And even if it *was*—more than a statue, something with strange power, something *doing* all this—was it so bad? What had it really done, after all? Only given Sherman what he wanted. What he wanted but wouldn't admit, even to himself.

Being Bethany had been so easy—making friends, sharing laughs. Being Ed had felt good. Flashy and suave. Being himself, though—being himself was like stepping in fresh dogshit, day after day.

And here he was again. Same old Sherman. And still with no teeth.

He thought of Dead Man's Dump. Was it worth it? One more trip?

He could be careful. Pick someone super normal. Boring, a little. Like himself.

Third time was always the charm, right?

And it would be the last time, he promised himself.

He looked at his statue. At its red eyes.

"*Last. Time*," he told it.

It stared back and said nothing.

Sherman made the trip to the basement, feeling like a video, rewound and played for the third time.

He went straight to Dead Man's Dump, confident of the way even in the darkness. His pen light ran along the boxes on the shelves, skittering over Bethany's scrawled name, then Ed's, and landing on Jack's.

Jack. He didn't gossip and squawk to a gaggle of girlfriends. He didn't dress flashy and chase the good-looking younger men. Jack had been quiet and boring enough to be almost invisible. Maybe that's why he'd given Sherman the creeps—he was like a piece of furniture or a potted plant. But with dark, watchful eyes.

Now that he thought about it, that didn't sound terrible. Blending into the wallpaper. Just existing. After the last two days of shenanigans, Sherman was embarrassed—he didn't want anyone to notice him. Maybe being Jack—or partly Jack, *some* of Jack? Sherman couldn't quite figure it out—would be just about damn perfect.

He rummaged in the box. His hand closed around a set of dentures that he somehow sensed would be there. He didn't bother to inspect them for quality. He just put them in his dressing gown pocket and went back to his room, closing the door quietly behind him.

He sat on the edge of his bed. He felt so tired. He looked at the little statue and sighed.

"Last time," he said. "Do your stuff."

He wasn't sure if he was talking to the statue or the teeth or the whole baffling universe. Maybe all three. But who gave a shit?

"Not me," he said out loud. He remembered an old drinking chant from his alky years and gave it a new spin: "Through the lips and *on* the gums, grab your assholes, here *Jack* comes." In the old days, he would have followed that with a shot of cheap whiskey, but now, he popped the teeth in his mouth and clenched his jaw, waiting for what he knew would come.

Jack's teeth tasted like cigarette ash. Sherman should have soaked them in mouthwash. Too late now—he already felt them suctioning onto his gums, tighter than Scotty's mouth on his pecker. His dick gave a little twinge at the memory.

He clenched his bedspread in his gnarled fingers. No more of that—no more gossip sessions, no more skillful blow jobs in the men's steam room. He'd be boring old Sherman mixed with a little boring old Jack, and life would go on as it always had until it stopped.

Sherman lay down, not even bothering to kick off his slippers. He closed his eyes and, feeling sad in a way that he could not name, he fell asleep.

Sherman spent the next day slinking into corners and sitting near, but not with, the other residents. He wore khaki pants and an off-white polo shirt and orthopedic sneakers that made no sound on carpet or linoleum.

He listened to conversations, and he watched people. He breathed so shallowly that his chest barely rose and fell. He felt himself tuning into certain voices, paying attention like he was waiting for something. He wasn't sure what, but he knew it was something important. Like he had a job—some kind of responsibility.

As the day progressed, that sense grew stronger. A tension came with it. He was a bowstring strung taught. He felt powerful. Purposeful.

He sat at a table with his back to a group of residents eating dinner, listening to their conversation. They didn't notice him. No one did.

"Stop it, Doug," a woman was saying. "You're being unfair."

"Unfair my ass," said the man. Doug. "He's goddamn weird is what he is. Dementia, maybe. And that's not all. I heard a rumor about him playing pass-the-pickle with some of the other fancy boys here."

"Since when does dementia make a person gay?" said the

woman. "What are you even talking about? Maybe you're getting a little addled, yourself."

"Now why am I not surprised, Rochelle? Always sympathetic toward the freaks. Now it's Sherman. Before him, it was Monte. Before him, it was Jack, that *creepy* friggin'—"

"Stop it!"

"No. I was glad when that stroke took him out. It was. . ."

Sherman didn't hear the rest of their conversation. He'd gotten up, quietly, so quietly, and left the dining room, walking back to his room, thinking, thinking, memories coming to him, his and others, like puzzle pieces forming a bigger picture.

He smiled, closed the door behind him, and lay down for a nap.

He'd need it.

Late that night, Sherman crept from his room, his defunct American Express card snug in his dressing gown pocket.

He felt a warmth in his chest and stomach. It was kind of like being horny, but not quite. A sort of delicious anticipation. He liked it. He hadn't felt it in so long. Not since. . .

Well, not since Ed. Hot damn, had that been a good time.

Now here he was, on the second floor, in front of Doug's room. Doug, who'd called him a creep. Doug, who wouldn't get the chance to apologize.

Sherman used his old credit card to jimmy the door open. No security in this place, not really. The locks were child's play, purposely basic so that a master key could open them all.

Not that he needed it.

Plus, those few seconds of fiddling with the lock heightened his anticipation. Withholding what he wanted from himself for just a moment.

He opened Doug's door and closed it behind him, the latch clicking into place. He could hear Doug snoring, make out the placement of furniture from a dim nightlight in the adjoining bathroom.

For a long time—a half hour? More?—Sherman stood over Doug, watching him sleep. It was sweet—the way he tucked his hands under his cheek like a little child.

A naughty little child. Spreading rumors wasn't nice. Insulting him wasn't nice.

Sherman eased the pillow out from under Doug's head, moving so slowly, so gently, that Doug didn't even stir. Then, giving him one last, long look, Sherman put the pillow over Doug's face and pressed.

There was the usual awakening, muffled groan, and flailing limbs. Doug's hands slapped harmlessly against Sherman's arms, padded as they were in pajamas and a dressing gown. Doug stopped fighting, but still Sherman pressed, reliving fond memories of similar nights: Curtis, who had swiped Jack's fruit cup not once, but twice, when he thought Jack wasn't looking, fighting for breath until he gave up. Bethany, who had made fun of Jack's rumpled clothing to one of her girlfriends, struggling beneath her *Live, Laugh, Love* embroidered pillow. Ed, who had recoiled from Jack's advances in the steam room one night, getting a few good hits in before he, too, became just another corpse. He'd like Ed more for that—for days, he ran his hands over the bruises, pressing down, feeling the pain ease as they faded from purple to green to yellow.

He'd have one more beautiful memory now, thought Sherman —no, Jack. He was Jack. More Jack than Sherman, anyway, and maybe soon, not Sherman at all.

He left as silently as he'd come, reminding himself not to whistle as he stole back to his room. He flicked on his bedside lamp and, passing the statue on his dresser without a second look, opened his window. He took the cigarettes and lighter he'd bought earlier at the corner store from his dressing gown pocket and lit up, inhaling deeply, holding the smoke in his lungs until it burned.

Then he blew it out into the night, watching as it swirled in the darkness and then disappeared. He picked a fleck of tobacco from his lip, cleared his throat, and ran his tongue over his teeth.

He smiled and took another drag.

WHEN THEY COME FOR YOU
DOUGLAS FORD

It began with a stupid argument. One that Rick didn't even provoke for a change. He knew he had things to work on, like a temper that sometimes made him do and say things he later regretted. If Dr. Kline pressed enough, he would admit to that, but he felt less willing to concede that he ever talked down to his wife, Amber. No, she just tended to get worked up, especially by things neither one of them could control.

Hence, how the argument started that evening, the two of them enjoying cocktails by the pool. Amber barely touched her Mai Tai, instead turning to him with an expression that told him she had something serious on her mind.

"You can see it, can't you? Things are getting bad," she said, "*Really* bad."

Rick didn't know what the fuck she could possibly mean. Things were wonderful. Sure, prices kept rising, but he worked in a profession where that was actually a good thing. It paid for the pool that they could enjoy in the evenings, and besides, his buddies assured him that the political headwinds pointed toward a return to law and order that would make everything else great again. Plus, neither he nor Amber worked for minimum wage, after all. Good luck to those people. They were fucked, but not people like Rick and Amber. Not the people who counted.

He explained all these things to his wife. She waited for him to finish talking before she started shaking her head.

"I don't think you understand what I'm talking about. Just please, listen to me. I mean other stuff. The rulings from the court. The legislation. All this talk about restricting travel between the states. People wanting to make menstrual cycles part of public record. I'm worried."

"It doesn't affect us," said Rick, momentarily forgetting Dr. Kline's instructions not to interrupt or dismiss what Amber had to say. Before Amber could remind him, he said, "Okay, tell me why you think it affects us."

"It affects *us* because it affects *me*. I have a freaking uterus."

He shrugged. "We're careful. We use contraceptives." He could have added that neither of them wanted kids just yet. At least he didn't. Maybe later. Enjoy life first.

She shook her head. "It's more complicated than that. It's like a war they're waging, don't you see? It may not feel like one, but it is. I've been thinking: if things get really terrible, and they finally come for us, I need to know you're with me. Where should we go?"

Where should they go? He had no idea what she fucking meant.

The confusion must have shown on his face because she continued: "Meredith, Angela, and I were talking. Angela mentioned Canada as an option, but Meredith said we all ought to consider Scandinavia."

"Why," asked Rick, hardly believing his ears, "would you be talking about those places?"

She closed her eyes. "We're scared. Everything is changing fast. Look, we need a plan, and I need to know if you're with me or not. A time will come when we'll need to get out of here. Think of Einstein in Germany."

Rick laughed. "Einstein was Jewish. We're not Jewish. Honey, honey, you can't be serious. And it's ridiculous that Meredith would be part of it. What is she, seventy?"

"Sixty. Look, none of us feel safe anymore. I hate having this conversation. I know you love it here. I know you love this house. But a reckoning is coming. We can sell it while the market is good."

Once more, he laughed and then said something terrible. Later, he would wish he hadn't. Later, he would think of his response as what led to everything else. "You're crazy," he said. "All three of you."

She waited for him to stop laughing, then said, "It's more than three of us. A lot more. We talk. We've been afraid of this day coming. Some of us have made plans." She took a deep breath before taking his Mai Tai away and setting it on a table out of his reach. She took his hand in hers. The sun had begun to set, the sky smeared with purples and reds. Birds flew overhead, everything so peaceful and beautiful. He had large hands, hers so small in comparison, but she gripped his fingers with a strength that surprised him. "I'm sorry for doing this, but I need you to tell me tonight. Right now. Would you leave with me if it ever came to it?"

He almost laughed again but managed to stop himself. "Amber," he said, using a tone that Dr. Kline would no doubt approve of, "I will promise this: things will *never* come to that."

———

A week later, Amber disappeared.

At first, Rick assumed that she'd gone off to do something fun with her friends and simply forgot to tell him. Or maybe she did tell him, and he forgot. He didn't bother texting. He would pretend he knew about whatever plans she had to stay out all day and into the early evening. Dr. Kline would approve of that, wouldn't she? To act surprised and irritated might suggest he hadn't listened to something she told him. Besides, if he acted irritated, it would make him seem controlling. Rick knew he wasn't controlling at all.

The minutes continued to tick away. Before long, he found himself drinking Mai Tais by himself.

He barely remembered the conversation they'd had a week ago.

When the hour grew late, he started to worry. He reached for his phone just as Barry called. Quite a coincidence since he planned to phone Barry himself.

"Is Amber there?" asked Barry, not sounding like his usual jovial self.

"No. I thought she was doing something with Angela."

"Angela's not here. Not answering her phone either. And look, the weird thing is that a bunch of her clothes are gone."

"Gone? Come on, no. They're not gone. Maybe they're in the laundry."

"I checked, and they're not. Do me a favor: go check Amber's closet. Something tells me hers are gone, too."

"Give me a break," Rick said, but an unsettling feeling began to form in the pit of his stomach, and he hoisted himself from his lounge chair, the phone in one hand, his Mai Tai in the other. He went through the house toward the closet that Amber used for her personal items and peered inside.

"No, her clothes are here," he said into the phone.

"You sure?"

Rick tried to remember all the things Amber liked to wear lately. He began sliding coat hangers down the metal rod, noticing that many held no apparel at all. No, he wasn't sure. "I *think* they're all here. But this is dumb. Our women wouldn't just go off like that."

"Well, check this out." Barry went on to describe a conversation he had with Angela that sounded very much like the one Rick had with Amber. He responded the same way Rick did: things were great if you didn't count a little economic downturn, nothing that the next election couldn't fix. Like Amber and Rick, they lived a comfortable life without any kids to worry about yet, so they could travel, do practically whatever they wanted. Why would they want to move?

"What did she say when you asked her that?"

Barry sighed. "She said there was a war going on. I thought she meant overseas. Like, maybe she wanted to go on a mission trip to help refugees, but she said, 'No, a war here.'"

"A war here? What the hell was she talking about? Was she talking about illegals coming over the border?" Rick listened to radio talk shows where they talked about that kind of war a lot.

"She said a war on women. Can you believe that? I said she was nuts. Then she said something weird. 'We're taking that war to the next level.' What does that even mean?"

"I don't have a fucking clue," said Rick. Then he remembered how Meredith seemed to have a part in this drama. He told Barry that they ought to call on her. "I'll bet they're both over at her house. This is a practical joke."

"Do I know Meredith?"

"She's old. Look, it makes sense that she's the gang leader on this. She was burning her bra in the 70s. All that women's lib shit. Amber would tell me stories about that woman's experiences, and I'd say it was a good thing that nobody's doing that kind of stuff nowadays."

"She's putting ideas into their heads. A bad influence if there ever was one."

"A *really* bad influence." In a kitchen drawer, Rick found a business card with Meredith's address. She ran what looked like a legitimate consulting firm, not a shop selling healing crystals, which he expected from an aging feminist radical. He read the address to Barry, and they agreed to meet there within the hour.

As he drove, Rick thought about the question that Amber asked him about where they could move. Maybe he should have said the Bahamas sounded nice. Sun and surf all day, Mai Tais whenever they wanted. People down there worked cheap, didn't they? They could have a household staff. But something crawled at the back of his mind, little comments that Amber dropped now and then that he never thought about much before. Words like *exploitation*. Only a few years ago, she never talked about such things. Now, she seemed to watch the news with a worried expression, even though, as he told her over and over, things were really good, if you didn't count this or that.

During the drive, he tried to call Dr. Kline, thinking he should schedule a session for the two of them. The voicemail picked up, so he left his name and number, along with a request to call him back.

When he arrived at Meredith's address, he found Barry waiting for him. A jungle of trees and foliage covered the front lawn of a modest-looking house. Now, that looked more in tune with his mental profile of Meredith. She probably grew her own herbs. "Did you knock?" he asked Barry.

"Waiting for you. I don't like this. Everything feels too quiet."

"It's your imagination," said Rick. He led the way to the front entrance, where they didn't have to knock at all.

The door hung open.

"Hello?" Rick called out.

They both peered into the darkness, waiting for a reply.

When none came, they stepped inside.

Even in the faint light, it still looked like a battle had taken place inside: furniture toppled, papers everywhere, lamps broken.

Then they found the body slumped backwards over an over-turned sofa.

"Oh, my god, oh god," said Barry. "Is that Angela?"

At that moment, it dawned on Rick that Barry loved his wife more than Rick loved his. It hadn't occurred to him to worry that he'd just stumbled upon Amber's body. Even when the possibility presented itself, he just felt numb. Fortunately, the body looked too masculine to belong to Amber. An aging feminist, maybe, but not his wife.

The two of them circled the sofa until the man's downturned face came into view. Rick used the light of his phone to illuminate it.

An older, balding man gazed up at them, his face pale and bloodless with eyes wide open as if he'd died in a state of surprise. A gaping wound across his neck. Made with a hunting knife, Rick surmised. Blood covered the carpet under their feet.

"Who is this?" asked Barry in a whisper.

Rick shook his head. "Meredith's husband, maybe? I don't know. I assumed she was a lesbian."

"We need to call the cops," said Barry. He didn't need to say it, though. Rick had already started dialing.

Only once in his life had he ever had to dial in an emergency, back when he found his mother on her kitchen floor, dead from a stroke. Even though nobody could save his mother at that point, he remembered how someone picked up right away and how the ambulance arrived in no time at all. Now, standing there in a stranger's house, looking upon the aftermath of a homicide, the phone just rang and rang. Finally, he hung up and searched another number. "I'm calling the cops directly," he said.

Barry stared at him as once more, the phone just rang and rang. Eventually, a flustered voice answered. "Police department." Rick couldn't swear to it, but he thought he heard that as a question. Nevertheless, he launched into an explanation of what they'd found, and before he could get to the part about their wives missing, the cop cut him off.

"There's stuff like that going on everywhere. It's like there's a gang of psychos on the loose."

"Psychos?" said Rick.

"Or serial killers. Jesus, who knows, but we're short-staffed. Half the force didn't show up for work. You're going to have to wait."

"Wait here?"

Hearing those words, Barry began shaking his head. "No," Barry said, "no the fuck way."

"Look," said Rick, "we don't know if the perpetrator is nearby. We don't even know the victim. We—"

"Then don't wait," the cop said. "Tell me the address, and we'll dispatch someone if and when we can. Like I said, we're short-staffed. Most of the women on the force are unaccounted for. It's like they all—"

This time, Rick cut him off. "Left."

"Yeah, like they all just went away."

After giving the cop the address, Rick hung up and looked at Barry. "We ought to get out of here."

Barry looked like he wanted to vomit. "You can see all the way inside his neck."

Rick didn't want to examine the man too closely, but Barry's remark caused him to recollect something from long ago. "You remember when O.J. killed his wife?"

"And the waiter? Goldman was his name. Can't remember the wife's name. What about it?"

"He practically cut off her head. That's what this looks like."

Barry started shifting his weight from leg to leg like he needed to pee. "So?"

"So, a witness for the prosecution said a cut like that indicated a crime of passion. It was evidence that whoever did the crime knew the victim. They were intimate."

Barry's movements became more frantic. He looked like he'd start crying any second.

Maybe I need to slug him, thought Rick, like guys did to emotional women in all those old movies.

"I don't get it," said Barry.

"This guy was probably murdered by Meredith. He was likely her husband."

"Oh, God, has she gone psycho? Has she killed my Angela? My sweet, sweet Angela?"

A stronger possibility occurred to Rick. This idea of a war on women they kept talking about. A ridiculous notion, sure. Everyone knew there was no war, just some new laws, and nothing major. Nothing which affected people like them. Another recollection came to mind. In his first year of college, Rick dated a girl before he met Amber. They got a little careless, and she got pregnant. Rick freaked out because he didn't know what to do, especially when the girl—he couldn't remember her name—wanted to go to a clinic and have it aborted. She wanted him to help pay for the procedure. That night, he called his mother, blubbering and crying, and his mother told him that not only would he pay for it, but that he should go with the girl and make certain that she got to the clinic safely.

Safely? he asked, aghast that anyone would expect him to do such a thing. *Why does she need me to help get her there safely?*

Because, his mother said, *there will be picket lines. People will harass her, try to stop her, hurt her even, and you need to be there to stand by her. Make sure she's not alone.*

Rick told his mother he would do that. In fact, he promised her. She, in turn, promised to send him some money to help cover the cost, even though she lived paycheck to paycheck after his dad left. And even though he gave what's-her-name all the money, he chickened out on going with her to the clinic. He just couldn't bring himself to go through that embarrassment. Even worse, when his mother asked if he'd done it, he lied and said yes.

Did you see many protestors? She asked. He told her that he saw a few but not many. *That's what women have to fight against,* she said. *I'm so proud of you for being her ally.*

Barry couldn't stop shaking, so it didn't look like he could drive himself home, so they decided to leave his car there and pick it up the next day. They spoke little during the car ride. Fine by Rick. He didn't want to hear any more of his friend's moaning. They needed to focus and look out for each other.

Finally, Barry asked the question on both of their minds.

"Are they part of this? Angela and Amber? Are they the ones doing this? Did we do something wrong and end up on the wrong side?"

"Partner, that's crazy. I do wonder if they're in danger. Like, hostages maybe. Yeah. I'm thinking that Meredith is some kind of terrorist and she's taken our women hostage." Then, as if to help convince himself, he added, "Our women would never do something like this. They're—what's the word?"

"Compliant?"

"Yeah," said Rick, despite his doubts, "Compliant."

"I'm going to try calling Angela again." The conversation paused so Barry could dial and wait for an answer. "Baby?" At first, Rick's hopes lifted, thinking that Barry had reached Angela. Then he realized that Barry was leaving a voicemail. "Baby, I'm so sorry. I should have listened to you. I'm coming home. Rick is driving me. Please be there. Don't—" He looked at Rick before finishing his sentence in a softer voice, as if his friend couldn't hear him inside the confines of the car. "*—don't kill me, please. Don't kill me like you killed Meredith's husband.*"

"Jesus!" Rick grabbed the phone out of Barry's hand. Before his friend could react, he threw the phone out the window.

"The fuck, man!" Even though the phone had already flown out of the window, he pulled at Rick, scratching his eyes with his nails and grabbing the wheel.

Rick tried to keep steering while fending off Barry. "Cut it out!" he said. "Get hold of yourself." But Barry continued to claw at him, only becoming more desperate. "For fuck's sake! If this is a war, remember who has the guns!"

Even as he said this, a thought occurred to him. Did he lock the case where he kept his prized firearm? He pampered it like a lover, even juicing it up with a homemade bump fire stock so he could feel like Rambo holding down the trigger. If he did remember to lock it, did Amber know where he kept the key? He couldn't remember.

Hearing these words seemed to calm Barry—briefly. Then he said, "Oh, God, she knows I'm with you."

He started grabbing the wheel again, and this time, Rick lost control.

Before he could let off the gas, the car flew off the road and into a construction area, the crew having gone home for the night. They slammed into a rack of metal rebar, several of which sliced through the windshield, sailing like missiles past Rick's head, just before he felt the impact of the steering wheel against his forehead. The airbags didn't deploy.

If conscious, Rick would have cursed American engineering.

When he came to, he struggled to bring his surroundings into focus. By the flickering light of the dashboard, he could see his friend's arms and legs still next to him, covered in blood.

From the shoulders up, nothing remained, his head pulverized by the rebar that slammed into his face.

A quick survey of his own body confirmed that he made it through the accident in one piece, not counting a bleeding forehead and a headache. Blood covered everything, most of it from Barry. Outside the car, he heard distant sounds of gunshots and sirens.

He decided not to wait. Stumbling out of the car, he began walking toward home. A police car with flashing lights came up behind him at a high speed. He tried to wave it down, but it swerved around him and kept going, apparently rushing toward something more important. Rick picked up a rock and threw it at the vehicle, but it still didn't stop.

A red glow marked the horizon. Not a sunset, he realized, but a fire burning.

It all seemed so absurd to think that Amber was part of this. Surely, someone *had* taken her hostage. He thought again of his mother and that word she used when he lied to her about going to the clinic. *Ally.* That was a word people used in war.

The strangest feeling came across him. Had he unwittingly chosen a side all those years ago?

He needed to ask Dr. Kline.

Once more, he tried her number despite knowing that she had strict rules about patients calling her during off-hours.

He expected to reach her voicemail, but surprisingly, she answered.

"What is it, Rick?"

She sounded cold, irritated. Nevertheless, Rick launched into an explanation of everything he'd seen and experienced. "She's lost her mind, I think," he said, referring to Amber. "If you know where she is, you need to talk sense into her. This won't end well. Once the authorities get things under control, she'll lose a lot more than a few rights. I'll bet there'll be executions. Military-style executions."

Only silence from the other end. As he walked with the phone against his ear, his house came into view. So dark. Hadn't he left a few lights on? Maybe the power had gone off.

Finally, he heard a sigh. "Where are you, Rick?"

"I'm almost home. I saw my best friend killed just a little while ago. Murdered. They killed him."

"No, they didn't."

Dr. Kline always had an uncanny ability to sniff out his lies. How did she do that?

"Indirectly," said Rick. "They murdered him indirectly."

"No," Dr. Kline said, "you did. Always avoiding responsibility. Are you home yet?"

Reaching the door, Rick said, "Just now." Then it occurred to him that perhaps he shouldn't have answered.

"Someone will meet you there." Then she hung up.

Rick stared at his phone momentarily before hurrying in. He needed to get to his gun.

None of the lights worked, confirming that the power had gone off. No, he told himself, *they* cut the power. He stumbled around, using his phone to find the way to his den, where he kept his gun case.

There, he saw the door to the case hanging open.

"Hello, Rick."

The voice came from the other side of the room.

He followed the sound in time to see Amber emerge from the shadows. She held the gun aimed in his direction.

He tried telling himself that she didn't know how to use that weapon. Any weapon.

"You're going to get hurt, baby," he said. "Put that down. I don't know who's in this with you, but they're done for. It's not too late for you to—"

He left the sentence unfinished. It seemed crazy, but he suddenly remembered that girl's name, the one he got pregnant. Kimberly.

"To what?" asked Amber. "Come over to your side?"

"Yeah," he said. He wished he went with Kimberly to the

clinic. He wondered what became of her. Somewhere, perhaps, she stood in a darkened room like this one, holding a gun on her husband or boyfriend. Maybe these things wouldn't be happening if he just did something that day. If he made himself an ally; chose a different side.

But he couldn't admit such a thing now. Cooler heads needed to prevail. "Yeah," he said. "Come over to our side. It's a good life we have here. Everything we could ever want."

She looked sad and about to cry. His spirits lifted. Maybe he got through to her.

"Not everything," she said. "When you can't have something as basic as control of your own body, you don't have everything. You don't have anything."

Then she pulled the trigger.

And held it down, stepping closer.

As the bullets tore him apart, Rick's consciousness managed one last confused thought.

Not about how on earth she knew the right way to hold that weapon, even positioning it correctly in order to avoid recoil. Nothing at all about his beloved firearm.

Instead, the thought that flashed briefly through his quickly fading consciousness focused on how he hardly knew this woman. Didn't know her at all, in fact. In his last, fleeting moments of sight, as his intestines spilled from his rupturing abdomen, she even started to look like different people. Most of them faces he'd long forgotten, but for an instant, he saw what's-her-name, the one he gave the money to. Then his mother. Why, he thought in a fading flicker of synapse, would his mother ever want to shoot him into pieces? Then other women he'd known, some of them aggrieved, some not, but all of them there, blurring together into one face, each one helping to hold that trigger down.

A HOUSE OF ONE'S OWN
AI JIANG

They placed me in a doll house far too small for my body and even smaller for my mind. But it was better than my previous home, I guess, behind plastic encasings with false advertising labels and promotional text: *A perfect girl!*—until my limbs get lost around the house, severed accidentally or on purpose; *She speaks too!*—if I were *actually* allowed to speak, not the voice recorded nonsense they manufactured me with: *"Hello, I'm Joy!"*, they probably wouldn't allow me to speak anymore; and then the small fine print the parents glossed over, and the children didn't care about: *Accessories not included* and *Batteries not included*; but there were always a few parents who tried to return me when they finally realized I came with only *one* spare outfit rather than a wardrobe of bedazzled dresses or hair clips way too big and brushes with bristles spaced the width of my head, clawing more so at my ears than untangling any actual hair.

They covered the doll house in yellow and white striped wrapping paper after grumbling about my crumpled body shoved in the doll house's kitchen, back rammed against the sink, the ceiling threatening to snap off my neck, feet pushed against the windows, bent unnaturally upwards. If I had bones, my knees would already be fractured, joints unhinged, shattered bones splintering out from the flesh. But I was rubber, so I remained uncomfortably intact, bearing the pain they thought I couldn't feel. And I couldn't—for the most part.

I had only one wish, but it seemed even that was too much to ask: I hoped to have a house of my own, one I could choose, one that would fit, one that was loving.

My eyes couldn't shut, but my mind drifted to the thousands who looked and sounded like me. Still, I knew on the inside they were far from the same, even if we were pushed out in a factory line, evenly spaced on the conveyer belt, features all the same. Before we were boxed, I had imagined my sister's head turning, swaying aside her brunette locks as her dull green eyes bore into mine. But of course, she couldn't. And I had imagined myself turning to look at the replica of me only centimeters behind. But of course, I didn't.

What were their wishes?

The sound of wrapping paper tearing rustled my attention, and light glared from a single shredded hole from outside the windowpane by my feet, my shoes—pinching, rubber pink ballet flats—on the verge of sliding off; and they did, as soon as the young boy, perhaps thirteen years of age, split the house down the center, opening the chasm for both the fall of my shoes and my body. My mind pitched downwards with everything else.

But at least, for a moment, I was free, even if I was plummeting.

I was returned once, a few months back, by a young girl who was gifted me by her friend. She didn't like me. She didn't want to look like me. And so, she took the gift receipt that came with my box straight back to the superstore, where I then sat collecting dust with my other returned friends and the snobby new stock. The new girls always whispered their dreams about being treated lavishly once they were picked up, about becoming the idols of their children, about being pampered with the newest clothing for their perfect bodies. Us returned stock, spoke about the families we were briefly with, the people we had encountered: some lovely, some terrible—none like the ones the new stock imagined.

One sister had landed in the hands of a pretty angel of a child, but she was envious of the doll's perfections, the exaggerated portions the child couldn't have herself, and ended up forcing her parents to return my sister. Another sister was purchased by the parents who kept her for themselves yet neglected her until the return policy had almost expired before shuttling her back to the store, seal unbroken.

Sometimes remaining in the store was the better deal.

The mother picked me up from the dining room table with a frown, as though questioning why I was inadequate, what was so heinous about me it made her son cringe at the sight of me. After all, I had no defects, or else they wouldn't allow me to leave the factory. I'd be tossed in a bin with the rest of those who had eyes with faded ink, hair unevenly attached. It was not a crime for humans to be flawed, even if those around them made their silent judgements as vicious thoughts within their minds.

But for us, flaw meant death.

"You know I don't play with dolls anymore," the child said, a scowl on their face.

"But Lebena, you used to love them!" their parents exclaimed, their mother flailing me around, her tanned hand a blur, my hair whipping across my unblinking eyes. "She's *perfect*. Look! She even *speaks*!"

The mother had already installed my batteries, and she pressed the button on my lower back a bit too forcefully.

"Hello, I'm Joy!"

"Perfectly boring," Lebena said, cringing at the sound of "my" voice. Then, their attention flitted elsewhere. "If you're going to get me another one, at least get the latest version. *Those* at least say something other than. . ." the child artificially perked up, rounding and stretching their eyes, lips tugged up in an unnaturally bright smile. "'Hello, I'm Joy!'" they mimicked in a high-pitched voice that sounded oddly similar to what my robotic voice released.

Lebena took me from their mother's hands and chucked me back into the doll house. This time, I spilled from the undersized bathtub, the ill-fitting house creaking with my presence as if asking me to leave.

The doll house wasn't meant for me; it was meant for the tea house girls down the aisle.

That night, Lebena told me his name was Leben.

––––––––––

It was a month after Leben's fourteenth birthday, and his parents had gifted him a new set of dresses for me, and the same dresses for him, which he threw immediately into the trash except for one. He sewed the middle of the green dress's bloom, so it became flared pants instead. A one-piece jumper that resembled the same one sitting in his closet that he often stared at but never wore, hidden between his leather jacket and low-rise jeans and all the skirts and floral tops his parents bought for him. I was wearing the green one-piece now.

From where I lay in the house, the tub, by the corner of Leben's bed, I could hear muffled shouting downstairs.

His parents wanted him to pick up the violin, an elegant choice for his slender fingers, almost skeletal. But he didn't want that; he wanted to play a different stringed instrument—a guitar, an electric one at that. To perform under strobe lights and sweaty, cheering crowds, not in suits and tight ties, dress shoes with gelled hair, sitting erect in a chair with his back groaning for release. He muttered angrily about wanting to leave and whispered under his breath the elaborate plans he made to try to do so: tying his curtains to use as rope to grapple down the side of the house, which friend he would stay with, who was the least likely to snitch, what he would bring with him—

"Lebena!"

There was stomping up the stairs, the ripping open of the bedroom door, the slamming shut of the same, and the flick of the lock. This was the first time he had ever locked his bedroom door. Pounding came from the outside.

"Lebena!"

His mother.

"Open the door!"

"No!"

In his hand was a marred guitar, one he purchased in secret only a week ago. Its shiny embossed body with blue flames and contrasting gentle curls of orange was scratched up, the strings sliced, limp and free, a crack ran down the side of its neck. Leben's face stung red on the side I could see. I wondered how it felt— skin against skin rather than rubber against plastic. Leben's father owned a small pocketknife with a wooden handle he used to cut the wrapping paper when they first purchased me. I wondered if Leben's guitar had felt its blade, if *he* himself had felt it.

Surely, Leben did not believe this was a house of his own.

Leben's gaze fell onto the doll house with my face pushed against the bedroom window. He had only taken me out once in the past few months, and it was only to crop my hair short like his own and to toss out my useless brush before shoving me back into the house; this time it was onto the bed, with my legs pressed up against the ceiling, face turned and smashed against the window, arms hanging stiff off the inexistent sprayed on sheets and pillow. I wanted to say something, anything, but all I could manage was shifting just enough to jab my back into the corner of the plastic bed.

"Hello, I'm Joy."

Startled, Leben looked away, thrusting a pinky finger in his ear and blinking rapidly. He never looked over at me again—at least not that day.

But the next day, he ripped off my arms. I couldn't feel pain, but the extra space it gave me in the doll house felt too unfamiliar, even though it should've made me more comfortable. Leben placed the two severed limbs with the broken guitar he shoved under his bed.

Leben put me on the windowsill next to his desk. His fifteenth birthday had just passed, and his parents no longer bought him anything meant for me. They never did replace his guitar—neither did Leben himself. Instead, in his closet, a box sat filled with things he had stolen from friends, stores, even his parents: watches, jewelry, lottery scratch cards. There were also the drugs he purchased cheap off a friend and pills he swiped from the same friend when they had passed out drunk while the two hung out. His friend phoned, recalling the hangout and asked about the missing pills.

"Nah, I think you're tripping, man," Leben said, chuckling as easily as breathing, calm as still water.

There was an uneasy shift on the other side of the line over the speaker. When Leben hung up, his breathing became more erratic. Perhaps the lie did affect him a greater deal than I thought.

That day, he ripped off my head while he had a joint clutched between cracked lips and placed me above his webcam. My eyes followed his every move.

"Lebena! What is that smell? Were you just on a call? Didn't I tell you to stop talking to that Noahai kid?" Leben ignored his mother, as he had done for the past two years.

Though I couldn't move, I wondered when Leben might rip off my legs. I stared at my body with the feet jutting out from the half-opened doll house as though he wanted to taunt me with my headless body. If he did, he would only be taunting himself.

At sixteen, Leben had an abnormal growth spurt, shooting taller than both his mother and father. He had to duck to get out of his bathroom, his legs dangled off the end of his bed, and his head, propped up against the pillow sitting parallel to his headboard made his lolling head at night seem as though it might snap and roll away. Like mine. But of course, it didn't.

I eyed the university acceptance letter on his desk and knew he would take the first chance at escaping if he could and wished he would take me, though I knew he wouldn't.

When his parents told him they saved no money for him to get a bachelor's degree in music and much less for him to move into a dormitory halfway across the country, he argued, saying he would work part-time, full-time even, while he studied. They denied him, saying it was better for him to go to a local university, to go into tech, medicine, something "useful," and to live at home. Then they ripped up his acceptance letter.

That night, he tore off my legs.

———

The thing about dolls is that we never grow. We are packed away, cramped in unfitting houses, shoved into clothing we don't like, made to say words we don't want in a voice that doesn't belong to us. But for Leben, he continued to grow, and as though self-conscious of his height and features that looked far older than his seventeen years of age, the boy stooped forth and grew out his hair to cover his face, and dressed in a way that made him look like a reaper, his skin taking on the tone of a moon-cast shadow.

And then he moved out.

Of course, he didn't bring me.

———

Leben's mother found me when she cleared out his room five years later. With a horrified expression, she pieced me back together, unstitched the threads in the bloom of my dress. There was nothing she could do about my hair, however, though she did run a small pair of scissors through the strands to even out the choppy ends.

I was placed in a display case in the living room with a new dress next to a portrait of Leben as a child.

On TV played a band with a lead guitarist who looked strangely like Leben, but he was introduced as "Rage". When the song finished, a commercial came on, offering a discount on a doll that looked just like each member of the band. Rage's had wild, grown-out hair, the same ashy face as Leben from his youth, and a wicked smirk—the closest to a smile I had ever seen on his face.

Neon words flashed around the dolls: *Get your own mini member of the band! The best deal you'll get this year! Don't miss out on your chance to own Rage! He even comes with a small guitar!*

It seemed Leben finally found a new house, but was it his own?

The sound of broken glass coming from the kitchen stirred in me the desire to turn. A dark figure darted in all-black attire. Two large bottles in their hands. They poured its contents all over the hardwood floor where the carpets didn't cover, then on the carpets themselves, drenching the stains Leben's father left from his own drinking spills when the bottles sloshed liquid from the lip of the glass in his unsteady hands, darkening the material like the bruises on Leben's face when he was younger.

The intruder lit a match and dropped it onto the floor; a trail of fire blazed immediately. I couldn't feel the heat, but I knew my rubber would melt within seconds of contact. The stranger opened the glass door of the display and pulled me out.

Leben.

For a second, I thought he would take me with him, but he pressed the button on my back, for old time's sake, I suppose, and tossed me into the flame. I would never be able to return to my sisters now, but I guess I also didn't want to. And I was glad.

My mind wandered to the doll created to look like him, and I wondered if that was who he truly wanted to be. His expression of relief was the last thing I saw before the fire ate my eyes, melted my limbs, until I was unrecognizable. But in my own voice, I sputtered my last words: "*Hello, I'm Free.*"

And I suppose, even if I didn't have a choice, even if the house was suffocating, damaged, and not at all loving, I could still truly call these uncontrollable, free-spirited flames a house of my own.

AFTERWORD
JAMES SABATA

The *Shadows in The Stacks* anthology is directly tied to Spirited Giving, a horror-themed fundraiser, which serves as The Official StokerCon Pre-Party. This year, Spirited Giving's fundraising recipient of choice is the Library Foundation SD.

The Library Foundation SD is a catalyst for creating stronger communities through investment in the San Diego Public Library System—where access to resources supporting literacy, work readiness, and lifelong learning ensures equal opportunities for success.

Despite the endless benefits that learning with freedom offers, there's an increasingly influential and coordinated effort to challenge and ban books in public and school libraries across the United States. This effort disproportionately targets books that offer diverse perspectives, such as those from people of color and the LGBTQ+ community. According to the American Library Association, these efforts breed ignorance, misunderstanding, and hate and are associated with violence and threats against libraries and librarians.

Additionally, these book bans are a slippery slope to censorship and the stifling of diverse views in our cultural, community, and educational spaces. Intellectual freedom and representation of diverse perspectives are strengths that we should be celebrating, not stamping out.

In response to increasingly aggressive threats to intellectual freedom, the San Diego Public Library system joined the Books Unbanned Initiative, a library program that issues library cards nationwide to give electronic access to the library's digital and audio collections to teens and young adults living in locations where books are being challenged. The initiative was started by Brooklyn Public Library and joined by other libraries such as Seattle Public Library, LA County Library, and San Diego Public Library.

The initiative aims to support the rights of teens and young adults to read what they like, discover themselves, and form their own opinions, without being restricted by censorship or political pressure. Many of the books that are banned or challenged are by or about Black, Indigenous, People of Color (BIPOC), or LGBTQ+ people and explore their experiences, stories, histories, and movements. Reading these books can help teens and young adults understand themselves and connect to others, as well as develop critical thinking and intellectual freedom. This campaign resists book bans, promotes intellectual freedom among young readers, and helps cement libraries as a place where everyone belongs.

The money raised from ticket sales for Spirited Giving, along with the proceeds from this book, will allow the San Diego Library to continue to invest in books that are being banned/targeted, allowing and providing access to these materials not only in the San Diego area, but across the nation.

Thank you to the authors who contributed stories to this anthology. Thank you to Vincent and Jared, who did the lion's share of edits. Thank you to Shortwave Publishing for jumping right in to help this cause and ensuring we could make it happen.

And thank you for your purchase of this book and your ongoing commitment to ensuring continued access to these materials for everyone.

James Sabata
Founder/Director of Spirited Giving
February 11, 2024

ABOUT THE AUTHORS

Kevin David Anderson's debut novel, the geeky cult zombie romp, Night of the Living Trekkies, is a funny, offbeat novel exploring the pop-culture carnage that ensues when the undead crash a Star Trek convention. Publishers Weekly gave Night of the Living Trekkies a starred review and the Washington Post listed it as one of the top five Zombie novels of 2010. Night of the Living Trekkies and Anderson's follow-up, Night of the ZomBEEs were required reading in college courses, most notably, How to Survive Your Freshman Year by Studying the Zombie Apocalypse, at Mansfield University in Pennsylvania.

Anderson's short stories have appeared more than a hundred times in numerous award-worthy publications like the British Fantasy award-winning quarterly Murky Depths, and the Bram Stoker nominated anthology The Beauty of Death. Anderson's stories have been produced in audio productions and his latest book Night Sound: From Podcast to Print published by Grinning Skull Press is a collection of short horror stories that first appeared in audio on popular Parsec Award-winning podcasts like Pseudopod, The Drabblecast, The Horror Hill and the popular No Sleep Podcast.

Anderson also writes joke books under the pen name Giggles A. Lott and Nee Slapper with popular titles like STAR WARS: The Jokes Awaken, and Jurassic Jokes: A Joke Book 65 Million Years in the Making.

Zachary Ashford is the Aurealis-nominated author of When the Cicadas Stop Singing, The Morass, the Sole Survivor books, and his debut novel, Polyphemus, which was released through Darklit in 2023. He is an educator, occasional speaker, and cat-lover. His books usually feature literary themes, Australian characters, tonnes of page-turning conflict and more than a few dick jokes. He writes in a room surrounded by action figures, books, and heavy metal memorabilia. He wants you to know that he's never played soggy biscuit. You can buy his books in the usual places and find him on most of the modern social media hellscapes.

S.A. Bradley hosts the 5-time Rondo Award-nominated podcast, "Hellbent for Horror," which explores all things horror across books, film, comics, and music. Director Guillermo Del Toro described the podcast as "well researched, articulate and entirely absorbing."

Bradley is the author of the Rondo-nominated book "Screaming for Pleasure: How Horror Makes You Happy and Healthy." He is currently working on a follow-up book. Bradley's short stories are published in the anthologies "Shattered and Splintered" and "Medium Chill." He is also working on a collection of short horror stories.

Bradley contributes articles in Medium Chill, EvilSpeak, Horrorhound magazines, and multiple online outlets. He's lectured at Webster University, the University of the Pacific, and

The College of Idaho and performed his live show, "My Horror Manifesto," in NYC and at various horror conventions across the USA. Bradley's convention guest appearances as a panelist/moderator/lecturer include San Francisco Fan-X, StokerCon, Salt Lake Fan-X, Mile-Hi Con, Confluence, TusCon, BayCon, and others.

Bridget D. Brave is an author and reluctant lawyer who is really lousy at writing bios. She can be found nearly everywhere online under beedeebrave.

Kel Byron is a Michigan-born author and illustrator who loves to weave gruesome, spine-tingling tales about queer identity, grief, and human connection. Best known for her "Lonely Broadcast" series, she also works as an animal rescuer and won't shut up about alien abductions.

Vincent V. Cava is an author that specializes in the field of horror. His work has been published by Simon & Schuster, PS Publishing, Adams Media, and more. He is the co-writer, co-producer of the Creepypasta film (2023). He's written two graphic novels and his stories have been used to promote film and television for Fox, Starz, and Crypt TV. His work is available wherever books are sold.

Clay McLeod Chapman writes books, comic books, children's books, and for film/TV. His most recent novels include *What Kind of Mother* and *Ghost Eaters*.

Rebecca Cuthbert is a dark fiction and poetry writer living in Western New York. She loves ghost stories, folklore, witchy women, and anything that involves nature getting revenge. She is the author of *In Memory of Exoskeletons*, a dark poetry collection

(Alien Buddha Press), and *Creep This Way: How to Become a Horror Writer with 24 Tips to Get You Ghouling* (Seamus & Nunzio Productions). Rebecca is the Editor-in-Chief of PsychoToxin PINK, a feminist horror imprint.

Alexis DuBon is a work of fiction. Any resemblance to actual persons, living or dead, is purely coincidental. She is the author of It's *Going to Be Fine* (Off Limits Press, 2025) as well as co-editor of *No Trouble at All* (Cursed Morsels Press, 2023). You can also find her in publications from Cemetery Gates Media, The Wicked Library, and Southwest Review or on twitter at @dubonicplague.

Jamie Flanagan is a Bram Stoker Award© winning writer and actor. Writing credits include Netflix's *The Haunting of Bly Manor, Midnight Mass, The Midnight Club, The Fall of the House of Usher,* and AMC Shudder's *Creepshow*. Member: HWA, SAG-AFTRA, and WGA East.

Douglas Ford's short fiction has appeared in a variety of anthologies, magazines, and podcasts, as well as two collections, *Ape in the Ring* and *Other Tales of the Macabre and Uncanny* and *The Infection Party and Other Stories of Dis-Ease.* His longer works include *The Beasts of Vissaria County, The Reattachment,* and *The Trick,* his newest from Madness Heart Press. His novella, *Little Lugosi (A Love Story)* won the Literary Nastie award for best long fiction in 2022. He lives on the west coast of Florida.

By day, **Evelyn Freeling** is an author and editor of the dark, gruesome, and horny. Her short fiction has been published by Flame Tree Press, *CHM, The Arcanist, NoSleep Podcast, Dark Void Magazine,* Ghost Orchid Press, and more. She is also an Co-Editor-in-Chief of Hedone Books and the editor of the erotic horror anthology, LES PETITES MORTS. Stalk her on Twitter @Evelyn_Freeling.

Ai Jiang is a Chinese-Canadian writer, Ignyte Award winner, Hugo-, Nebula-, Locus-, Bram Stoker-, and BFSA Award finalist, and an immigrant from Fujian currently residing in Toronto, Ontario. She is a member of HWA and SFWA. Her work can be found in F&SF, The Dark, Uncanny, among others. She is the recipient of Odyssey Workshop's 2022 Fresh Voices Scholarship and the author of *Linghun* and *I AM AI*. The first book of her novella duology, *A Palace Near the Wind,* is forthcoming 2025 with Titan Books. Find her on X (@AiJiang_), Insta (@ai.jian.g), and online (http://aijiang.ca).

Lucy Leitner is the author of five novels and a short story collection. Her fiction has appeared in four anthologies. She lives in Pittsburgh, PA.

Jonathan Maberry is a New York Times bestselling author, 5-time Bram Stoker Award-winner, 4-time Scribe Award winner, Inkpot Award winner, anthology editor, writing teacher, and comic book writer. His vampire apocalypse book series, V-WARS, was a Netflix original series starring Ian Somerhalder.

He writes in multiple genres including suspense, thriller, horror, science fiction, epic fantasy, and action; and he writes for adults, teens and middle grade. His works include the Joe Ledger thrillers, Kagen the Damned, Ink, Glimpse, the Rot & Ruin series, the Dead of Night series, The Wolfman, X-Files Origins: Devil's Advocate, The Sleepers War (with Weston Ochse), NectroTek, Mars One, and many others. Several of his works are in development for film and TV.

He is the editor of high-profile anthologies including The X-Files, Aliens: Bug Hunt, Out of Tune, Don't Turn out the Lights: A

Tribute to Scary Stories to Tell in the Dark, Baker Street Irregulars, Nights of the Living Dead, and others. His comics include Black Panther: DoomWar, The Punisher: Naked Kills and Bad Blood. His Rot & Ruin young adult novel was adapted into the #1 horror comic on Webtoon and is being developed for film by Alcon Entertainment.

He the president of the International Association of Media Tie-in Writers, and the editor of Weird Tales Magazine. He lives in San Diego, California.

J.A.W. McCarthy is the Bram Stoker Award and Shirley Jackson Award nominated author of *Sometimes We're Cruel and Other Stories* (Cemetery Gates Media, 2021) and *Sleep Alone* (Off Limits Press, 2023). Her short fiction has appeared in numerous publications, including *Vastarien, PseudoPod, Split Scream Vol. 3, Apparition Lit, Tales to Terrify*, and *The Best Horror of the Year Vol 13* (ed. Ellen Datlow). She is Thai American and lives with her spouse and assistant cats in the Pacific Northwest. You can call her Jen on Twitter @JAWMcCarthy.

Tim McGregor is the author of *Wasps in the Ice Cream*, the Shirley Jackson Award nominated *Lure, Taboo in Four Colors, Hearts Strange and Dreadful*, and the *Spookshow* series. A former screenwriter and active HWA member, Tim lives in Toronto with his wife and kids.

John Palisano's novels include *Dust of the Dead, Ghost Heart, Nerves*, and *Night of 1,000 Beasts*. His novellas include *Placerita, Glass House* and *Starlight Drive: Four Halloween Tales*. His first short fiction collection *All that Withers* celebrates over a decade of short story highlights.

He's won the Bram Stoker Award© in short fiction for "Happy Joe's Rest Stop" and Colorado's Yog Soggoth award. His short stories have appeared in Weird Tales, Cemetery Dance, PS Publishing, Independent Legions, Space & Time, Dim Shores, Kelp Journal, Monstrous Books, DarkFuse, Crystal Lake, Terror Tales, Lovecraft eZine, Horror Library, Bizarro Pulp, Written Backwards, Dark Continents, Big Time Books, McFarland Press, Darkscribe, Dark House, Vincere Press and many more.

Non-fiction pieces have appeared in Blumhouse Online, Fangoria, and Dark Discoveries magazines and he's been quoted in Vanity Fair, The Writer and the Los Angeles Times.

James Sabata is a horror author, screenwriter, editor, and co-host of TheNecronomi.Com; a weekly podcast with over one million downloads, analyzing horror films as social commentary. James is the founder and director of SPIRITED GIVING, a pop-up horror-themed fundraiser helping local communities. He lives in Phoenix, AZ with his wife, daughter, two cats, a tarantula, and the ghost of an older gentleman with a hilarious sense of humor.

William Sterling is an independent author, screenwriter, and the host of the Killer Mediums podcast. His stories tend to play in the realms of "popcorn flick horror" with high body counts, absurd set pieces, and soft spots for unexpected endings. His latest novels include STRING THEM UP, which is a small town murder puppets novel, and the upcoming DEAD MENS CHESTS, which will be part of Dark Lit Press's pirate horror novel series.

Alvaro Zinos-Amaro is a Hugo- and Locus-award finalist who has published over fifty stories and one hundred essays, reviews, and interviews in professional markets. These include *Analog, Lightspeed, Beneath Ceaseless Skies, Galaxy's Edge, Nature, Vastarien, The Los Angeles Review of Books, Locus, Tor.com, Strange Horizons, Clarkesworld, The Year's Best Science Fiction & Fantasy, Blood Business, The Big Book of Cyberpunk, Nox Pareidolia, Multiverses: An*

Anthology of Alternate Realities, Looming Low: Volume 2, and many others. *Traveler of Worlds: Conversations with Robert Silverberg* was published in 2016 to critical acclaim. *Being Michael Swanwick*, released in 2023, is Alvaro's second book of interviews. His debut novel, *Equimedian*, is forthcoming in 2024.

A NOTE FROM SHORTWAVE PUBLISHING

Thank you for reading *Shadows in the Stacks*! If you enjoyed it, please consider writing a review or telling a friend! Word-of-mouth helps readers find more titles they may enjoy and that, in turn, helps us continue to publish more titles like this.

OUR WEBSITE
shortwavepublishing.com

SOCIAL MEDIA
@ShortwaveBooks

EMAIL US
contact@shortwavepublishing.com

Donald R. Guillory
Author, Historian, Educator

Merging History and Horror

www.DonaldRGuillory.com
https://linktr.ee/donaldrguillory